THE WET DREAMS OF DEAD GODS

A LOVECRAFTIAN OMNIBUS

EDWARD LEE

Madness Heart Press
2006 Idlewilde Run Dr.
Austin, Texas 78744

ISBN: 978-1-955745-86-4

Cover Art by Simone Tammetta

Interior Layout by Lori Michelle
www.TheAuthorsAlley.com

Edited by Lisa Lee Tone

For more information, address:
john@madnessheart.press

www.madnessheart.press

THE DUNWICH ROMANCE

AUTHOR'S NOTE

Though a portion of H.P. Lovecraft enthusiasts are sure to curse me into the deepest pits of the Shoggoths for daring to 1) append one of the greatest horror stories ever written, and 2) for doing so in such an indelicate, microscopically sexual, and scatological manner, I suspect that a good many readers may indeed enjoy this bit of work. Moreover, I'm very grateful to those of you who are fans of my material and have continued to support these intermittent excursions into the venue of the Lovecraftian. Thank you! As a further note, for non-Lovecraftian readers, it would be much better to first read the original masterpiece, Lovecraft's *The Dunwich Horror*; and for those of you who have read it in the past—I hope you are many—treat yourself to something special and read it again. It's the type of story—like so many of the Master's—that becomes more brilliant each time you read it. It can easily be found for free at Dagonbytes and other such wonderful websites. My effort here is merely a wee, insignificant ornamentation to the ingenious original. Long live Lovecraft!

E.L.

March 15, 2011

(I)

THE END OF the Dunwich affair left it granted that the entirety of Wilbur Whateley's hand-written records had been directed into the possession of the renown Dr. Henry T. Armitage (A.M. Miskatonic, Ph.D. Princeton, Litt.D. Johns Hopkins, Dr.Ing. Erlangen-Nürnberg) of Miskatonic University. Dr. Armitage is due considerable credit for having broken a complex acrostic/substitution code into which these records were enciphered, and the nature of the information gleaned makes it more than reasonable that said data was never publicly released. Instead, a counterfeit explanation devised by authorities spuriously stated that the records were but gobbledygook, an account much more easily digested by all who might be interested.

To reiterate: the existence of these records is granted. What is *not* granted, however, is this: not quite all of Wilbur Whateley's records found their way to Dr. Armitage.

$$(II)$$

SARY SLADDER WAS being molested, quite creatively, behind a briar-bordered stone fence which paralleled some unwholesome pasturage on the westerly outskirts of Dunwich, when her dismal and quite mediocre life changed forever. Though attractive in body by most local judgment, the unkempt twenty-three-year-old had long-since resigned to an existence of questionable nutrition (of which semen played a depressingly large part) and poverty so absolute it was better left undetailed. Any world-view or personal doctrine that her grey matter may have engendered will remain equally undetailed; however, it might be relevant to delegate a few words to her physical aspect: very long, tar-hued hair; curvesome in contour to a voluptuous degree while yet hardily lean; adequately bosomed and tumescently nippled; with skin that was, as goes the cliche, alabaster-white. Lips—if anything, *overly* full—adorned a mouth bereft of front teeth, thanks to a father whose explosive psychological climate was all too commonplace amongst Dunwich men; yet this misfortune reversed, as Sary soon identified the act of prostitution as her only feasible mode of income-production (more than half of her engagements in this sad yet aeonian trade consisted of "oral succor," and the aforesaid missing incisors to quite a degree magnified the effectiveness of the service). All of her physical enticements, however, ended with the remainder of her visage: a mastiff attack when very young had left her minus one ear and scarred on both cheeks; she had a hopelessly collapsed nose (thanks, also, to her toper of a father), and an absolutely unvarying facial dermatological outbreak. (Less kind Dunwichers referred to her as "Stew Face.") But another disability that (like the knocked-out teeth) took a turn for the better was a grievous sinus infection during infancy which completely obliterated her sense of smell; hence, without ever even knowing it, Sary's destitute existence was brightened, as the groins of Dunwichers were not known for their olfactory immaculateness.

Sary, at this moment, found herself on the less-advantageous end of an awry business proposition. Ten cents was all she charged, yet the target of her commerce today, the burly, harelipped Rufus Hutchins, son of an alcoholic well-digger named Elam, made an alternative offer:

"Wal, I got ten cents, Sary, but I also got ten suthin' else."

"Ten . . . *what?*" Sary asked, not in reception of his meaning.

Whack! came the meaty sound of both fists slamming into her face. "Ten *knuckles,* ya dutty whore!" Rufus replied, pronouncing "whore" as "hoo-ah" in his mushy backwater dialect. He laughed and watched Sary topple to the grassy verge next to the fence.

Her senses skewed, she saw proverbial stars as big sandpaper hands hauled her flannel dress up and roved her nude body. Fingertips pliered her nipples; a fist clenched her pubic thatch and *yanked,* and she yelped. "Gonna bust this hoo-ah pussy *up* with my dick, ee-yuh," assured Rufus, as the organ to which his vernacular referred had already been extracted. It dangled half-limp but when—*whack!*— he struck her once more in the head, the organ erected with an instantaneousness so thorough one would've taken it to be spring-loaded. Sary's vision smeared; she managed vocal incoherencies through the fist-induced stupor, and when she attempted to strike Rufus's contorted face, her arm only flopped about.

"My pa fucked yew onct," Rufus reminded her. "Said yer cum-hole smelt wuss than a moose-gut pile ben in the woods a month," and then pushed her face to one side, exposed the unattractive aperture where her ear had been bitten off, and, for some reason knowable only to one as deranged as Rufus, expectorated liberally into that aperture.

These few moments of outrage sufficed to revive some of Sary's vitality; she whipped her head back and forth as if to jettison the sputum from her ear-hole, and shrieked, "Yew're right, your daddy fucked me, but his dick was so little, I didn't even *feel* it! And I also heerd yew suck *dog dick!*" Sary, in truth, had heard no such thing, but felt the invention appropriate.

Rufus tensed. "Oh, so's I suck dog dick, yew say?" and then the well-digger's son brought two index fingers to his mouth, whistled quite piercingly, and called out, "Heer, Brooter! Heer, boy!" after which Sary's guts shriveled as she recalled a bit too latently that the Hutchinses owned a collie named *Brooter,* and a *vicious* collie at that.

Over the fence bounded the mangy, yellow-fanged collie, its insane eyes keen with interest. Rufus snapped his fingers, commanded, "Roll over, boy!" whereupon the animal (curiously, as if *used* to this command) circumducted itself upon the ground and spread its hind legs. Testicles large as a human's lolled in their fleshy sac, and a glistening pink tip of flesh had already begun to extrude from the penile sheath. Sary did not require notice as to what she would next be required to do.

"Thet's a *good* dutty hoo-ah, thet's a *good* Stew Face. Jess yew go on'n suck Brooter's dick . . . " her captor approved as Sary performed the unmentionable onus, yet with Rufus's hands about her throat, alternate options did not present themselves.

In no extended time, however, the girl's skills proved sufficient to summon the bestial emission. Her first reaction was surprise—at the sheer *volume* of fluid that suddenly materialized in her oral cavity—then the *horror* kicked in, for the taste, texture, and temperature of this aberrant discharge all combined at once, proving itself in all likelihood the most revolting substance to ever occupy space in her mouth. Her innate reflex, of course, was to expel it all as abruptly as it had appeared, yet at the same instant she would do just that, Rufus's hands tightened about her throat, and he gave every guarantee: "Yew dun't swalluh? Wal, then I'll jess have ta crush yew're head with one'a these fence-stones, then *fuck yew dead.*"

When Sary swallowed, she was impacted by the feeling of one having just been dropped into a mile-deep abysm, and as the revolting taste began to trail down to her stomach, Rufus had already pushed her on her back. "Naow we'll git'cha some cum in yew're baby-maker." He paused on a reflection, then blurted excitedly, "Ee-yuh! We'll make ya a *Rufus* baby! Then, in nine months, when it come out? I'll cut'cher tits off so's it'll starve ta death!" and as Rufus prepared to rape Sary, she unwisely pointed to the aggressor's erection, laughed, and offered, "Why, *dang*, fat-boy! Yew're dick's even littler than yer daddy's!" This, by the way, was true, and also a verisimilitude Rufus did not appreciate being reminded of.

Rufus's face went blank. "Aw, naow, Stew Face, shouldn't arter've said that," and then his face bucked forward with a grimace, and he snorted fiercely, launching dual plumes of mucus out of his nostrils and into Sary's face. Sary froze in mortification, and more so when Rufus was kind enough to spread the mucus around with his big hand. Already, he'd pinned her immobile to the ground via the placement of his knees into her elbows. He grabbed her head and forced it to one side, then whistled again for his mascot. "Heer, Brooter! Heer, boy!" The sated animal jumped up to tend to its master, as its master had brushed aside Sary's hair in order to divulge her remaining ear.

"Sic, boy! Sic!" Rufus snarled. "Bite that ear *clean off!*"

Sary screamed as the unhinged canine surged forward

with snapping jaws, and when said jaws had just begun to close over her ear, Sary screamed all the louder.

"*Eat* that ear, boy! *Goooooooooood* dawg!"

Against the ear, the jaws pulled; Sary could feel the beginnings of connective tissue tearing, even over her outraged screams. What had she done to warrant so brutal a molestation? *Gawd DANG, Gawd!* came her protestation. *I'se sorry fer bein' a whore but, holy bull-flop! What choice I got things bein' the way they is?* I.e., in spite of her horror, Sary was indignant. *Yew think mebbe Yew could have Jesus help me?*

Another few seconds were all that would be necessary for the canine to detach Sary's ear from her head, but in slightly *less* time than that . . .

An oddly angled shadow darkened the scene—and Brooter . . . released Sary's ear, yelped, and drew away, hunched down as if threatened by some awesome adversary.

"Brooter? What's wrong with yew, huh, boy?" Rufus complained. "Durn't ya wanna eat on this dutty fuck-pot's ear?" But then Rufus turned and looked up into the direction to which his animal's attention had been so abruptly diverted. At once came an eardrum-quaking—

BAM!

—so loud the sequent concussion caused the surrounding air to *thump*. The foam-mouthed canine yelped again and flipped completely around in mid-air. The unbidden somersault dropped the dog flat and dead, and half of its cranial matter had expeditiously launched from its skull.

"Why, ya done kilt my—" Rufus began to rage, but then all objections ceased when his vision acknowledged to his brain, first, an obvious firearm—a large revolver, a Webley .455, to be precise—and second, the source of the awkward shadow.

It was a man—or some horrific *exaggeration* of a man—cumbersomely jointed as if afflicted by some disorder of the bones, the crown of whose head ran amok with dark crinkly hair, and who stood over seven feet tall. This intruder—if that he really be—wore huge, hand-sewn boots, trousers of tent-canvas, and, oddly, an overlarge long-sleeved shirt buttoned tightly at the collar and cuffs in spite of the day's warmth.

Rufus's eyes slowly opened wide enough as to be lidless, and he choked out this fear-imbued acknowledgment: "Yuh-yuh-yuh-yuh . . . *yew* . . . "

The colossan responded, "'T'would only be a man with a soul made'a pig shit ta dew suthin' to a gull like what *ye're* doin' ta that 'un," yet the vociferation sounded unrepresentative of any human voice to ever register in Rufus's ears. The words issued resonant yet shallow, tenuous yet at the same time deep as a basso choirist; and, ever more odd, *mumbly* as though the heavily lipped mouth were attempting to speak around solid obstacles, or as if the vocal organs themselves suffered from some manner of maladaptation.

In truth, however, the voice could be better described, to those more imaginative, as otherworldly.

Rufus, even in spite of his urine-releasing fear, found himself able to challenge, "Yew're thet warlock's grandkid, and thet retart witch Lavinny's son!"

The titan intruder stared, his face obscured by half-shadows.

"An'-an'-an'-they'se ben some *kids* missin' thet them daown at Osborn's say *yew* snatched–fer warlockin'n' *spells!*"

"Dun't talk of what ye know nuthin' abaout," responded the peculiar voice.

"An'-an'-an' . . . yew kilt my *dog!*"

"Yer dog all savage and askew in its head from bad raisin'—like ye. *Lotta* dogs like that raound heer—so's I kill 'em. Whether a man or a dog, if it's ugly in its head, it dun't desarve ta be a-livin'. Kilt a Hutchins' dog, wal, ten yeer ago, too, 'cos it were jess as crazy as this 'un. Made me happy, it did, to feed that animal's carcass ta the hogs. T'would make me jess as happy ta do likewise with ye."

Rufus began to crawl backward, absorbing the monstrosity's implication. "Daon't yew do nuthin' ta me! My pa'll come awf-tuh yew!"

Some perverted facsimile of a chuckle escaped the giant's lips. "Yer pa say the same thing way back when, and he in a wheelchar naow. But dun't worry—I en't gonna kill ye"—then, with a remarkable agility, the tall shape reached down with speed like a mouse trap, snapped a hand to Rufus's bare groin—"but it weren't good to see what yew were a-doin' ta that gull, so's I figger it best ta crunch these up, on accaount the likes'a ye dun't need ta be reproducin' none"—and then, amid a grisly and most noisome sound, crushed Rufus's testicles within the scrotal sack.

Rufus's vocal reaction was less like a man's scream and more like the outright caterwaul of some beast of Mastodonic proportions. He bucked against the ground, his plentiful body fat jiggling. The colossan felt the ruffian's testes begrudgingly divide and sub-divide into cohered chunks, then said chunks were fractionated as well until only an oatmeal-like slush remained extant within the malodorous scrotum.

The desired effect was hence achieved; the giant figure's actions left Rufus transformed into *pain incarnate.* He flopped ludicrously on the ground as his caterwaul sputtered down; then, with a face ballooned and reddened, he began a haphazard crawl over the fence, his trousers still down and one hand to the ill-treated scrotum. Agony hoarsened his words: "I'se a-tellin' my pa'n my Uncle Will tew!"

"Jess ye dew that," the titan replied in a clipped garble, "an' I'll kill 'em, an' ye're mama as well. She ought be 'shamed of herself for birthin' a boy like ye."

Rufus crawled away, sobbing.

It was then that the towering, oddly proportioned figure, who'd effectively saved Sary from sure peril, turned.

"Hi," he said.

Sary shivered, naked but no longer terrified in spite of her rescuer's physical and—in particular—facial aspect, for that aspect would be found by most to be extraordinarily terrifying: chinless, elongated as if vised, sporting a rowdy beard, skin of forehead and cheeks large-pored and yellow, quite like fresh-plucked chicken skin.

Sary wasn't sure how to cogitate this situation; what she felt with the most immediacy, however, was gratitude. She dragged herself up to a sitting position and offered, "Hi. And thank yew much fer sendin' that Hutchins boy away—"

"Never like that boy," came the sonorous voice. "All evil in his head, he is, like his whole family. Warn't good ta see him doin' such things ta ye . . . " The voice drifted as the giant's eyes seemed to quell an inner rage. "Folks is jess . . . so bad raound these parts it seems."

Sary replied cheerily, "Oh, they sure is—some'a the wust folks ever."

"Heer," and then the giant's hand, timidly as if conscious of a desire not to alarm her, lowered, a clean handkerchief in it. "Why'n't you let me wipe that ugly boy's snot off'a ye."

Sary stiffened, then sighed a relieving sigh as the gesture cleaned the mucous from her face.

"Thuh-thank yew." She sat up, unabashed at her near nudity. The titan man seemed to take downcast glances at her body. Sary knew her face was hideous but knew also that men *liked* her body, and since this man had in all probability saved her life, it only seemed fair that she allow him to engage in coitus at no charge. She spread her legs and ran a hand through the profusion of coal-black private hair. "Can't think'a no other way ta shew my proper gratitude 'sept ta let'cha fuck me, so go on ahead, if yew've a mind tew."

Her colossal rescuer stood awkwardly in a long pause as the lowering sun beamed behind his head, eclipsing him. Sary could not compute a reason, though she felt with certainty that the man was suddenly uncomfortable. "Naw, wouldn't be right nor decent considerin' what'cha jess been through."

"Huh?"

His strange yet interesting half-garble lowered. "Wouldn't feel good in my heart doin' suthin' ta ye that ye didn't likewise have a want for. I calc'late yew're aout'a sorts by what that fat boy'n his dog was puttin' ta ye."

Sary could not conceive of such words coming from local rustics; indeed, if anything, the local men at large seemed exclusively to exhibit a flagrant if not *innate* bankruptcy of all moral ethos. Instead, she sat inclined, breasts healthily plumpened, and she stared with puzzlement at the sun-halo'd black cut-out head. She could surmise no response to his explication.

"But naow, if ye'd like, ye can come back whar I live'n have a rest, and-and I see that black-hearted boy done tore yer gown, so's I can stitch it back for ye on accaount my mother larnt me haow ta sew."

Sary felt beside herself. Any other denizen of Dunwich, she knew, would be on top of her already, but here instead was this strange fellow offering her a place to rest and to mend her gown. *Can't believe what I'm heerin',* she thought.

The man went on in some indefinable excitement: "Oh, ee-yuh, and I'se also got a bunch'a white-tail rabbit in the smoker which I hand-rubbed fust with seasonin' like from my grandmother's recipe. It's quite fine, it 'tis, in the event that yew're hungry."

And now the endowment of a free meal! Aside from some raspberries filched from Frye's fields, and a luckily stumbled-upon radish that had most likely fallen off a motor-truck, Sary had consumed no solid food for over a day; and, hence—not taking into account the ejaculations of several oral suitors—no other sustenance. She nearly lost her breath over the giant's charitability. "Oh, I would jess *love* that!" she wailed, hauling her ravaged gown back down.

It was sensed more than espied a desperate smile come to her rescuer's face. "Heer, lemme help ya up," and then the hand at the end of the very long arm clasped her own. "Theer yew go—"

But when Sary was left to stand upon her feet, she teetered in place, cried, "Aw, buggers!" and would've fallen over had not the colossan caught her in a misproportioned arm.

"Yew all right?"

"My, I—I got all a-wobbly in my knees," she replied in his embrace. "I guess what that boy were doin' left me more shook up'n I thought—"

"'Tis understantable, but dun't worry. I'll carry ye."

Sary felt levitating as the giant cradled her up in his arms and, as though her weight were no more a burden than an empty potato satchel, stepped over the low stone fence and loped toward the distant easterly tree line. Sary made a pleasant moan in her throat; for once, she felt safe. She lolled in the cradle of her carrier's arms, rocking gently with each loping step.

As he conducted her across the field, her eyes scanned her surroundings. A more beautiful day could not have been wished for, she mused, but then when her gaze stopped upon the sheer face of the distant Round Mountain, her appreciation of natural beauty retarded a gobbet; closer in the distance, she spied the several odd round hills, most of whose tops were barren of trees and displayed instead peculiar arrangements of stone columns that she'd heard went back to Indian days. She'd also heard that the loftiest of these hills—*Sentinel* Hill—boasted an altar of some sort, which had existed there "Sinct afore the time white folk come ta this land from acrost the Big Water," her mother had said, "for a amaount'a time longer'n ye're head can understant." But when Sary made inquiry as to the precise *nature* of this altar, her mother had gone silent. There were several times, too, when Sary had attempted to hike all the way to the summit, to bear witness to the altar for herself, but she always fled back in the direction she'd come, for the emanation of the strangest sounds, sounds that urged her to think that words were actually being uttered *beneath the ground* . . .

It was in a place well behind her that she put the unsettling thoughts, to enjoy this moment of comfort. The rent in her gown betrayed a breast, and when she glanced errantly up, she captured the giant's big, dark, and somehow sensitive eyes seeming to marvel upon its shape, but then they flicked away. It was an ordinary thing for men to look approvingly at Sary's body, a gesture which she, in secret, loathed, for such glances reminded her of her father; now, however?

The notion of this unusual man's appraisal . . . charmed her.

From the first, a shyness, a *tongue-tiedness,* was intimated—a *gentleness,* even, in spite of the potential terror that his unnaturally overgrown physique commanded. Yet, the query whirred at the most rearward portion of her cognizance: what might the day's *remainder* bring?

"Haow silly'a me!" she chirped. "Hope ya dun't think me rude. Yew gone ta all'a that trouble helpin' me and heer I am not even tellin' ya my name! It's Sary!"

His eyes seemed to float all about her. "Ee-yuh, I know it."

"Yew dew?"

"Wal, sure. I seen ye heer'n thar."

"Whar?"

The man shrugged, now maintaining a forward gaze. "See ye strollin' past Sawyer's cow field on occasion, and Ten Acre Meadows, and comin' out the old covered bridge a number'a times when I be up in the hills, the bridge that branch off the Aylesbury Pike." He loped on, the large boots crunching down knee-high grass. "Maybe just a week past, I seen Doc Houghton droppin' ye off at Dean's Corners after givin' yew a ride in his fancy motor."

"Oh, yeah, Doc Houghton. He gimme a ride ever so often," Sary acknowledged, and to refer to his motor-car as "fancy" was no magnification of the truth; a *Duesenberg,* he'd called it. It was Sary's understanding that Dr. Houghton enjoyed some success in his trade, more so than one would expect of a simple country physician. Still, rumors circulated that the good doctor supplemented his income handsomely by, one, foreshortening the lives of the elderly at the financial behest of relatives in wait of inheritance and, two, the drastically illegal termination of pregnancies. And while she did acknowledge that the doctor had given her much-needed rides in his exorbitant motor, she did *not* acknowledge that, with some frequency—and for a princely two dollars, no less—he bid her to his home in Aylesbury for the expressed purpose of masturbating as he half-stood on his head, while Sary slid a disturbingly stout mattock handle in and out of his anus and smacked his testicles with her opened palm. The sought-after climax involved the redeposition of his semen from his penis to his mouth.

No. Sary did not acknowledge *that.*

"I've knowed him for a spell," was all she said in augmentation.

"So I figgered," said her carrier next, "and since I knowed him myself, on account 'twas him who come to the haouse when my grandsire was a-dyin', I didn't see no harm in my askin' him what it 'tis you're called, so's he tolt me. He tolt me 'Sary.' Oh, and I seen ye onct, tew, last yeer, when I was comin' daown off'a Sentinel Hill. You were swimmin' in the lily pond 'tween the Corey's'n the ole mill ruins."

"Yeah. I warsh there when I can, when it en't tew cold . . ."

"But it weren't on purpose, mind ye," the man seemed to add with some haste. "I can't have ye thinkin' I were watchin' yew with any bad intentfulness. Jess happened ta see ye when I was comin' daown."

The implication made her smile, and she actually touched his hand. "That's okay. Lotta fellas seen me with nothin' on. But I can tell, yew wouldn't watch me on purpose, not all sneaky like."

The man, oddly, seemed to gulp. "Hard not tew, I'll—I'll admit ta ye, though, 'cos I can't lie to good folks. Naow, bad folks, wal, I reckon it en't no transgression ta lie ta *them* . . ."

Sary peered at the words. "What'cha mean by *that?*"

"Wal, bad folks, see, they lie ta me withaout thinkin', so's it's only fittin'—"

"No, no," came her interruption. "I lie tew bad folks ever chance I get. But what'cha mean by haow it's hard not tew? Hard not tew *what?*"

Several more sturdy lopes of contemplative silence. Was it the heat of the day that broke beads of perspiration out on his forehead? "Hard *not* ta look at a gull naked when she be beautiful as ye."

Sary lay numb in her hammock of strong forearms. Scarcely in her entire life had she been complimented, save for infrequent endorsements of "customers" with regard to the skillfulness and even ingeniousness she demonstrated via certain of her carnal modus. One time, Elmer Frye retailed to her: "Stew Face, yew could coax a nut aout a dead man's dick, yew could;" once, also, "En't nevuh cum so fine in all'a my life as I jess did naow, gull. If yew're face warn't so Gawd-damn *awful* on the eye, why, I'd wring my flop-tit wife's fat neck'n marry *yew!*" So much for the compliments directed toward "Stew Face." This man seemed much nicer, however, which he'd made evident thus far, not to mention some subjective component about his tenue that she ascertained via her intuitions. Finally came her reply: "Oh, yeah, I know fellas find it pleasin' to look at my body withaout no clothes on. Jess not my face."

The man halted as if bidden by an inner quandary; he looked at her with directness, in her face. "En't jess ye're body I'm talkin' abaount, no. Ye're face tew. *All*'a ye."

Sary felt a tempest in her head. What benefit could there be in his making false statements to her? What strategy could exist through inauthentic compliments to potentially make her compliant for sex when that she'd already offered? *This fella could'a fucked the tar aout'a me whethers I fancied it or not,* she reminded herself. What he'd just communicated comprised, indeed, the kindest words ever spoken to her.

"Ee-yuh." Again, he redirected his gaze ahead. He whispered, "Ye're jess . . . so . . . beautiful . . . ," and then recommenced in his steady, long-strided lope across the field.

A mile must've passed behind them in which she rode in silence, antsy, confused. Sary, in fact, felt as though she understood nothing at this moment, save for one verity. Being in his arms, feeling shielded from all harm, furnished to her an emotion that scarcely visited her bleak existence: happiness.

A second mile must've lapsed when she thought to ask, "Hey! I'se forgot! What's *yew're* name?"

"Wilbur," the deep, warbling voice informed her. "Wilbur Whateley."

(III)

July 28, 1928

MY FEAR NOW *iz it will get too big to keep contained by time Equinox comes round. Sinse I fail at Miskatonic, I had no choice but to make the trip to Cambridge and ast to copy their version of p. 751 of the Latin. But they treat me the same, and I calculate it was Armitage who told em to do just that. May Yog-Sothoth blast that man and throw his body evurlasting into the Basin of the Shoggoths. What difference it make to Armitage? Just another fool like the others, cant understand bout someone who look and think different. But now I keep hearin my grandsire's words—what he last say to me that night just before the Whippoorwills try and get him, "More space, Willy!" he say a-gaspin, "more space soon! Yew grow—an' THAT grows faster." Well, I done what he told me . . . but that One inside just keep growing. Got to keep it qwelled, keep its size down so it dont bust quarters afore the time. Have been feeding it smaller varmints, no more of Sawyer's Alderney cows.*

Getting nervous. I maye have thougt out things improper. If only Grandfather hadnt up and die.

It all be in the house now, whole house, like Grandfather want. Was easy tearing out the ceiling and planking, all the windows and doors. I got the old tore out wood in a big pile in back, but I know the town folk are talkin bout it. Some of them creep up at night, they do, lookin, snoopin. I live in the sheds now, so Im sure they see that. It can only be the most stalwurt of em, though, for the thing's drippings have gotten more volumous, raising more and more a its smell. Sometimes when I see these folks and their snoopin, I'll read one of the Alko Hexes that putts on em the burdin of nawwzeeating dreams, or give em blood in their pee and cum.

I pray ta Yog-Sothoth on High fer His wisdom. I hope He help me do it all right at the right time.

Best thing that happen today was I finally meet her, Sary. Was the fattest a the Hutchins boys trine to hurt her and fuck her aginst her will. Made her take his dog's dick inner mouth, an it made me so mad. Wanted to kill that boy butt thouht it best to bust up his nuts and give him pain like he never know. Kilt the dog, shot it. Remind me when I kilt the Hutchins colly Jack back in 1916. Elam Hutchins promise ta kill me fer it, but a while laytur I see him rimmin one of his wells, so I walk up till I'm standin over 10 cubits off and he starts a-railin at me and shakin his fist, so I jest smyle and recite one of the Ambulation Spells from p. 124 of Remigius Secret Chapter, and I red it in the Eltdown Langwidge, so it work extra good, just like Grandfather say. Elam fall right into that wellhole, he did. He still alive today but lives in one of them chairs with wheels. I no he wont do nuthing bout me nooterin his boy, for feer of what I'd do ta his hole family.

But Sary. She sleepin on my cot jess behind me, wearin my Mother's black dress. I sit heer writing an keep lookin back at her laying so beautiful like that. Erlier while she be asleep, I went out an bring back the dog carcass n feed it to that One inside. But before I come back in the tool-house ta write this, I got thinkin about Sary and got all hot till I cudn't stand it any mor so I had to make my seed come out with my hand. Doin that a lot since that first time I see her at the pond. Cant help it.

Sary's so beautiful. She all low feeling bout how her face look, but I cant calclate what she meens. It's ALL uv her that's beautiful, even her voyce, even her name. She *make all that's round her beautiful jest by standing theer. Way I feel about her is sumpthin I never felt before, ever.*

So far nothin bad happen. Thoght she wudn't want to come back hear cuzza me, but that didnt happen, then I think shee'd wanna leave right off on account of the powerful smell of that One's drippings. I mention it—the smell, nott that One insyde—but—praise the name of Him Who Is Not To Be Named—Sary tell that becuz of a ailmint when she was a tot, she got no sense a smell at all! I know that Yog-Sothoth is blessin me.

Leest for today, I guess. Must stay humble an keep wurthy. What I want more then anything is ta open the Gate proper for Yog-Sothoth, but the onlee thing I want below that is for Sary ta have good feelings about me. I'd give anything for her to feel about me what I feel thinkin bout her. I could do it with one of the spells in the Von Prinn, but that wouldn't bee honest. She a good person in a whole range of bad folks. Would be false for me to MAKE her have a fancy for me cuzza a spell.

But when we'd got bak, I fed her, fixt her tore gown, then we talkt some, which was nice. Got distrakted, though, bein' so close ta her after pinin so long. She's so nice, so wunderfull.

She's still now. I jess look at her and smile.

Got that hot sence agin tingling below. I'll hafta go out and beat off myself again. When I do it while thinkin about her, it feel so mutch better, and all I can ponder is what it ud feel like if SHE made it come out. Hard too even reckon it.

But thatll not happen. Got to be reelistik. Got past the smell part but theres still ME. I know I don't look like NUTHIN like men hereabouts under my garments. If Sary ever wan ta do it with me, what ud she think lookin at my body with no clothes on? She'd likely run out skreemin.

In the name uv the Shining Trapezohedron! Everything bout Sary, not just her bodee but all of her, when I think of it, I get this stranje, warm, confoundin feelin in the place where I gess my hart is.

Pleese, Yog-Sothoth. Hear my prayer.

(IV)

NEVER BEFORE HAD Sary laid eyes upon this particular house, which was reasonable inasmuch as the manner in which it seemed to hide furtively behind the hill. Betraying not even an inkling of fatigue, Wilbur had transported her in his arms a considerable distance until he'd turned into the wooded fringe that half-circumscribed the Whateley property. The house had quite oddly been built right into the weedy, rock-knobbed hill itself, nearly as though the hill were attempting to consume it. Ramshackle barns, most with concaved roofs, sat greyly and decrepitly farther out, while closer stood several aged but sturdy sheds, one of which released a plume of sooty smoke—Sary estimated this to be the previously remarked upon smokehouse.

"Heer it 'tis," said her tireless bearer. "Property been in the family for couple'a centuries. See, thar be lots'a Whateleys raound heer, but the fust, comin' direct from Salem, built *this* haouse."

"Waow. Two centuries, yew say?"

"Ee-yuh. That'n more."

So complacent was Sary just then that she'd heretofore remained insensible of the dwelling's most irregular feature: "Why—Wilbur. Why's all the winders of yew're haouse boarded up?"

Slowing his pace, the giant deliberated amid a pause, then adduced, "Wal, see, I dun't live in the big haouse no more"—and upon this curious statement, his steps veered away from the edifice to approach the most substantial of the sheds. "Haven't for a spell. 'Tis this tool-haouse I live in. It be plenty sizable."

But Sary eyed the house proper as she was carried past it.

"And I'se boarded up them winders and doors on accaount'a I dun't want no thievin' folks a-breakin' in. Lots'a them raound heer—*reprobate scum,* my grandsire called 'em. Ever naow'n then I see one mopin' abaout. So the haouse jess be used for storage naow—"

At the moment of this verbal revelation, the looming house seemed to emit a series of hefty creaks, a *thunk!* and then—

Sary flinched in Wilbur's arms.

—a sound that could best be detailed as a phlegmatic *snuffle,* akin to that of swine, only of incredible sonic proportions, something almost elephantine.

"Wilbur, yew say ya use yer haouse for *storage?*" Sary felt predisposed to ask. "Is it animals yew're storin' in thar?"

"Uh, ee-yuh . . . " He kept his gaze straight ahead. "Of a kind."

Due to his extraordinary height, Wilbur had to bend over in order to enter the tool-shed. Sary found the structure commodious indeed, yet strangely lacking in the implements of its namesake. Bookshelves, instead, hung where one would surely expect tool boards to be evidenced. Only the most diminutive windows emitted the light of day, while candles sat perched abundantly about. A woodstove, cold now due to the season, sat bulkily erected in one dim corner, and another corner was occupied by a vast, intricately carved writing desk full of letter slots and tiny drawers. The desk stood nearly as tall as the man who attested to live here.

Wilbur gently put Sary down on her feet. "Knees still a-wobblin'?"

"Naw, I feel much better naow—thanks! My, 'tis a big place, as yew said," Sary remarked, reveling in a mental luxury of having an abode similarly sized and equipped to sleep in. "En't never seed a woodstove so big neither. But . . . what's 'hind that cartin theer?"

The wood floor creaked as Wilbur stepped toward the indicated curtain, which he withdrew. "Warshin' cove, see?"

"Waow!" exclaimed Sary, for she'd never seen an apparatus so extensive, which consisted of a wide tin tub to stand in, surrounded by an oak frame of some craft. A length of sisal rope, serving in the function of a cable, rose from a wooden lever to a watering can on an axle mounted between two studs of the frame. Another lever, lower, sprouted from a hand-pump, servicing a narrow rubber hose which conveyed water from a large barrel all the way up to the watering can.

"A *shower's* what it's called," Wilbur reported, then stooped to demonstrate. "Fust ye work this pump till the can up top sturt a-tricklin' doawn. 'Tis a real spring barrel we gots, so dun't worry none 'baout usin' water—in the winter, we'se jess heat the water up fust. Then when ye're ready"—his hand indicated the higher lever—"jess pull this so's the water'll come daown on ye."

"I en't never got to warsh so fancified!" Sary celebrated. "Jess ponds or warsh tubs."

"Ee-yuh. 'T'were my grandsire built it, fer me mainly, on accaount I'se got ta warsh three times daily."

"Three times!"

"Ee-yuh. See . . . wal, suthin' 'baout me that give me a smell stronger'n most folks. Grandfather say I'se"—the giant paused to deliberate upon a word—"he say I best be . . . *inconspicuous,* which mean I shouldn't be obvious ta folks hereabouts. The smell's even wuss abaout the house— I'se surprised ye didn't make no mention of it. Hope it en't botherin' ye."

"What? Smell?" replied Sary inattentively, for she remained rapt upon the elaborate washing instrument. "I *carn't* smell. Don't really even know what smell is 'cept what my ma 'splain to me. 'Tis like tastin' and hearin' and seein' only through yew're nose. But I en't got it 'cos of a 'fection when I was little."

Wilbur peered down. "Got ye no sense of smell, you say?"

"Naw, none."

Was the tall man shivering in place, his stout lower lip trembling? Near as Sary could ascertain, the paltry information regarding her lack of an olfactory sense had left Wilbur shocked in the best of ways. Eventually he recovered from his silent jubilation. Now his hand offered a grayish lump. "Oh, and heer's some soap—"

"Soap!" she squealed.

"Ee-yuh. My grandsire larn't me haow tew make it—simple, really. Jess boil animal fat with ashes from burnt leaves, then ye cook it daown till this is left. It work fine."

Sary perceived the bizarre washing erection as an object of enthrallment, and the soap a delicacy.

"Hot day like this I figger ye might have a hanker for a shower." Wilbur's unusual eyes seemed to sense the young woman's intrigue. His large, long-fingered hand pulled back the curtain. "Go on, step on in, then close the cartin for yer privacery, and ye can get yourself aout'a that dress so's I can sew it fer ye."

Sary's molested face turned up with a smile of excitement; she stepped right in the tub, holding the piece of soap as if it were an exotic bauble. It had slipped her mind to close the curtain as per Wilbur's suggestion; instead, she pulled the torn gown up over her head and off, then turned, obliviously naked, and handed it to him.

The giant man seemed to flinch—did he even close his eyes? She placed the gown in his hand. *He bashful 'baout seein' a gal with no clothes on?* came the curiosity. Nevertheless, she closed the curtain. Most men reveled to espy her nude; again, here was an example of his previous gentlemanliness, of which most male Dunwichers had not a trace.

"'Preciate ya lettin' me do this," she said behind the crude curtain. "And mendin' my gaown."

"'Tis a pleasure . . ."

Sary eyed the shower's pump and lever, trying to renovate in her mind the odd, tall man's operating instructions. *The pump,* she recalled. Her breasts dipped as she bent to go through the proper motions, listening to the modest gush as the sprinkling can filled over her head. Yes, it would be nice to be clean, a condition she rarely got to enjoy. Next, she eyed the lever. *What he say? Pull that, then the water come daown on me?* But as she reached to do so, she at once became aware of . . .

Trailing down her bare shoulders and upper chest she couldn't help but notice the countless minuscule black dots, like someone had sprinkled flecks of pepper on her. Only . . .

The black "flecks" were moving.

Indeed, as if in a mass exodus, these flecks (which only now did she realize were the legion of fleas and lice that took up constant residence in her scalp) were making a prompt departure from their abode. Lice and various other body vermin brought her no shame simply due to the universal fact that nearly everyone had them, and so Sary had for as long as her mind enabled her to recall. The itching one grew used to quite quickly. Yet, now, with an analogous quickness, the vermin were retreating from her. A similar exodus, then, was noticed trailing down her thighs: the multitudinous pubic mites she'd grown so equally accustomed to. It proved the strangest observation, while at the same time, one she was quite pleased with.

"Havin' yew'reself a muddle in thar?" resonated Wilbur's voice. "Forget haow ta work the shower?"

"Aw, no, no, Wilbur. I 'member naow," and then she eased the lever back and shot to tiptoes as the joyously refreshing torrent sprinkled down on her head and ran down her body.

Her fascination with the soap grew childlike when she

glided the fragrant gray lump about, first, skin, then her hair. The smear turned to lovely suds the more she agitated them with her hands. When she was scratching the suds into her recently deloused scalp, Wilbur's heavy and oddly vibrating voice resounded yet again from behind: "I done ment yer gaown, so's naow I'll warsh it fer ye. I got suthin' for ya to whar whiles it's dryin'. I hope ye like it."

"Oh, I'm sure I will, Wilbur. Thanks!"

When nearly the entirety of her body became a suit of suds, Sary caught her hands returning to her breasts to suds them further, then her furred sex as well. A dense tingling rarely felt in her caused her already plump nipples to plump up more, and she felt a strange warmth fill her breasts themselves. More and more, then, she caught her fingers delving as deep as their length would permit into the soft channel of her vagina. The sensations intoxicated her. Inconscient of any forethought, then, she meekly called out, "Wilbur?"

"Ee-yuh?"

"Only place on me I carn't warsh is my back. Could yew do it for me?"

A long pause ensued, then Wilbur's large frame was heard rising, his unduly sizable feet thumping toward the curtain. "Sure, if ye like. I'll just put my hand in so's ye dun't have to open the—" but Sary had already drawn the curtain open, standing naked and suds-encloaked with her back to him. Wilbur released something akin to a pleased sigh. Her small hand reached rearward until his much larger hand took the lump of ash soap. Another pause ensued: she guessed either reluctance or, more likely, another example of his bashfulness, then she suddenly sucked in a breath between her tongue touching the roof of her mouth when she felt her uncharacteristic rescuer begin to glide the soap up and down over her back.

"That feels soooo nice," she uttered.

He withheld any response, just kept gliding the ash soap up and down.

Then, unable to control herself, "Lower please, if ya dun't mind."

"Yuh-yuh-yuh . . . ya mean ye're backside too?"

Sary nodded. Of course, she'd already cleansed this region, but the feel of his strong and unusually long fingers beguiled her to make the redundant request. She leaned forward now, bracing the wood beam which supported the sprinkling can. She parted her legs.

Two long fingers of Wilbur's hand now ran up and down through the groove of Sary's buttocks; and in response, her buttocks repeatedly clenched and released. So long those fingers were—the middle one seven inches long at least, she'd previously noticed, and their companions not much shorter—and this fact only forced a consideration of fantasy: how potent a joy it would be for her to feel one of those fingers slip unhesitantly into her anus while another slipped up into her sex. Thinking of this, in fact, caused her vaginal muscles to pulse in pre-orgasm. The fantasy turned so dense now that Sary felt not quite in her proper awareness, and she was even about to ask him to do this, but—

His huge, sudsy hand withdrew. "Thar. All nice'n clean naow?"

Sary could've toppled over. Heart drumming and the nerves of her breasts and sex asquirm, she replied. "Thuh . . . thank yew, yes . . . "

Her lust-gauzed vision glimpsed Wilbur's hand hanging a plush white towel on a peg. "Ye rinse off naow and dry yourself," and then he closed the curtain behind her.

An actual orgasm was an experience so far removed from her that she couldn't even contemplate the last time she'd had one. The rampant sexual abuse from her father as well as the suitors of her trade delivered no such delights. *But . . . Wilbur . . . ,* she mused. His unnaturally large hands on her, and those impossible fingers running between her legs . . . The sensation left her desperate as a weasel cornered with a pitchfork to bring her own hands to her sex right this moment and make herself climax.

The gums of her missing front teeth clasped down on her lip; her sex continued to beat. Sary knew that if she masturbated, even behind the curtain, she'd generate enough noise to alarm Wilbur.

She slumped in a tingling frustration, pulled the canlever, and rinsed all the suds off.

After drying herself, she wrapped the towel about her body and stepped out of the metal tub. Wilbur now stood nearly stooped over, hanging up Sary's stitched-back-to-rights gown up on a window peg.

"Wow," she said, "yew fixed'n warshed my dress that fast?"

"Warn't no trouble. Hope ye liked your shower."

"I sure did!" she couldn't have replied with more enthusiasm. "I en't felt this squeaky clean since I was real little, when my ma'd scrub me in the tub." The remembrance of her mother brought a great smile to her mauled face, but in a moment more, the smile corroded.

"But now that I think back, lot'a them times my ma were warshing me? My father'd come in then, and . . . " She felt like some flimsy building about to collapse. "Aw, never mind."

"Wun't a good man, I take it?"

Sary shook her head quickly, then sat down on a handmade footstool and began to rub her hair dry. She didn't notice; however, after her brief reference to her father, the look in Wilbur's eyes turned to an aspect of perfect disdain. The sour moment bothered her; she struggled to change topics. "Aw, yew know what? 'T'were the funniest thing. Once I step in the shower, all my body bugs run off me and go daown the drain, even afore I started warshin' myself. Top'a my head dun't itch no more."

Wilbur rummaged in a storage crate set on end, which sufficed for a closet. "Ee-yuh. The bugs most folks got dun't afflict us heer. Likely, ye noticed theer en't no trace of maouse droppin's or rat holes neither, and ye'll never see no spiders and such araound." He seemed to hunt with deliberation for something in the makeshift closet. "No critters outside neither, not fer hunnerts of ells; 'tis why I gotta set my traps ways on aout in the woods."

"No critters outside?" she asked with emphasis.

Wilbur's big crinkly-haired head shook to indicate the negative. "No bugs, no critters, no worms—nuthin'. Nuthin' like that come on the property, and 'tis been that way sinct me and—" but here, Wilbur's speculation held in momentary check, as if he were considering a more desirable choice of words. "Not sinct I were born, my grandsire say. He say it jess might be on acaount of, wal, haow I got me a more powerful smell than folks hereabaouts."

"What abaout that big haouse'a yours that yew use for storage naow? Any varmints in thar?"

"No," Wilbur said in a dry croak as though some inner monitor signaled a sign of dissembled distress. But then he turned, seeming not distressed in the least, and held out on a hanger a long diaphanous black gown that shined unlike any fabric Sary had ever beheld.

A breath lodged in her chest. "That en't fer me ta whar, is it?"

"It sure enough is. 'Twas my mother's . . . Yew'd do it service ta wear it."

Sary was awestruck; never in her life had she seen, much less worn such a beautiful garment.

"And it en't yours jess to wear, mind ya. It's fer ye to have."

Calculating his words took time. This she could not believe. "Wilbur, I could never take this fine dress as a gift."

"'Tis yours naow." He smiled crookedly but veritably, then placed the shimmering gown across her arms. "Why dun't ye put it on while's I go fetch our supper aout the smoker?" and with that, he thunked out of the shed and closed the door.

A corner of Sary's eye effused a single tear. No doubt existed. This was the nicest day she'd ever been blessed enough to live.

(V)

AT THE FINISH of a meal she might refer to as sumptuous (had the word existed in her vocabulary), Wilbur had tended to her remaining ear with some manner of poultice saturated with a mucilaginous medicine that he'd owned, "'Tis'll take the pain right off, and heal them bitemarks up. My grandsire tell me he get this from *his* grandsire, so's ye can bet it's old. Old-time medicine's better'n new."

The pain indeed dissipated immediately. "It's workin', all right—thanks!" Sary said.

Wilbur applied some tape to hold the poultice in place and promised, "Ye'll be fine in a jiffy. If ye're wonderin', this be nothin' scarcely more than some mashed up tar root."

"That's all?" Sary questioned.

"Wal, plus mixed in is a bit'a this and a dab'a that," and he pointed to a glass cabinet full of small old-style medicine bottles. "Locust juice, snake heart, blue iris petals. It wucks, it does. Jess ye wait."

Sary wasn't sure, but she thought she glimpsed a few bottles of preserved toads, salamanders, and bats as well.

With Wilbur's first aid complete, the two of them engaged in further discourse, then, more full-bellied than she'd been in distant memory, Sary yawned. The day still shined brightly beyond the small, high windows, yet Wilbur needed no further clue to sense that she was whelmed by fatigue. He pointed to a mattressed cot beside the high desk. This was obviously where Wilbur slept, for the crude but precisely constructed low table at the cot's end demonstrated the extra length needed for his abnormally long legs. "You're bushed, Sary, I'se kin tell, so jess ye go on'n have yerself a nap while I run some errands."

The idea of a nap, after the luxuriant shower and then huge helpings of exquisitely seasoned smoked meats, sounded lovely to her, but— "Aw, no, that'd be rude after all yew done fer me. I'll help ya with your errands."

Wilbur's head shook in a manner that was not dominating at all but insistent just the same. "Git ye some rest. I wun't lollygag so's ta leave ye alone too long."

Sary yawned again, bringing one fist to her puff-lipped mouth, then stretching her arms in the extravagant black dress. "Wal, okay. Thanks. I am tired all's a suddent."

Pleased, Wilbur took his leave of the shed. Even behind the heavy wood door, his enormous booted feet could be heard thudding the ground. But just as Sary would venture to the long, appended cot, her fatigue was instantly superimposed by an irresistible inquisitiveness. Her feet took her timidly about the structure's cramped interior. She glimpsed some sheets of handwriting in a binder on the desk, and though Sary did have some reading skills, thanks to her mother's diligence, she could make nothing of the unintelligible scribblings. They were more than simply words she'd never seen, but instead, unlike words at all.

Rows of hoary books filled a handmade shelf, and atop a table of heavy oak, amid some scatterings of papers, sat a thick, iron-hinged tome that looked ancient. If there'd been a title on the cover, age and considerable wear had removed all vestige. Although Sary knew she shouldn't— the book was not hers nor any of her business—she gently lifted the stout cover, hearing its hinges grind, and, with some difficulty, read this:

NECRONOMICON
Ye Booke of Laws of ye Dead

As record'd by Abdul Al-Hazred, Mad Arab of Damascus
Translat'd from the Latin of Olaus Wormius
by Dr. John Dee
for Her Majesty the Queen, Elizabeth the First

London
1582

Strips of thin leather marked certain places in the age-plumpened book; she turned to one and found herself on page 751. So ancient was the paper that it reminded her of the softness of felt, yet worm-holes pocked the sheet like overlarge flyspecks. Sary could only read one line before a nauseousness rushed to her stomach:

> . . . be thee One of Fayth, thou shalt hear Their Gibbers from deepe beneath ye Ground and amid ye Stonie Places of Reverence where ye sanctified words hath been spake, and, yea, high up from ye Heavens; if thee be estimat'd to be Worthie of Their observance. Hark! Yog-Sothoth be ye key, and unto ye faythfull, forsooth, Yog-Sothoth wilt smile . . .
>
> Stalwart Venturer, keepe thy fayth, for upon this page be ye secret—yea!—the Dho and the Dho-Hna . . .

THE DUNWICH ROMANCE

Something arcane about the sentences and their fancy winged letters left a sense in Sary's brain that existed with a similitude to the taste left in her mouth several years ago when a man passing through town (Harley Warren, he'd called himself, and said he was from the South) had paid her half a dollar to suck on his anus while he partook in masturbation.

Yuck . . .

She closed the wretched book at once and turned away.

The recollection bothered her most, the page's references to noises "deepe beneath ye ground" and "stonie places."

Next, her eyes scanned the high, elaborate desk, a desk larger than any she'd been aware of. There was a newspaper—the *Aylesbury Transcript*—some manner of fiction magazine—*Home Brew*, dated February 1922—a trade journal from January 1928, called *The Nathaniel Derby Pickman Foundation*, announcing an upcoming expedition to Antarctica, a place Sary had never heard of; plus less distinct curiosa in the form of pamphlets, strips of handwritten notes, and cancelled stamps, including a twenty-four-cent stamp depicting an upside-down aeroplane. While Sary had heard of these inconceivable flying machines, she'd never seen one. Were they designed to fly upside-down? But more of those odd papers of indecipherable writing lay about the sliding top in a more orderly fashion. When she innocently opened one of its miniature drawers, she squinted at a small jar unto whose lid was affixed a string; from the string pendulated a lump of some dark metal, while the jar was labeled, in handwriting, *A. Bierce.* Behind it, a second jar was found, labeled *t.o.m.* She opened another drawer but re-closed it right away with a gasp, for it contained what appeared to be the eyes and nose-cavity of a yellowed skull. No, she'd not be opening any more drawers! Yet the desk and all its Gordian complexity held her spellbound where she stood. All those letter-slots, and letters in almost all of them!

Were they letters Wilbur was writing? If so, the prospect seemed irregular, for Wilbur didn't strike her as a man with many correspondents. More likely than not, they were old family letters. Her curiosity felt as one of perfect innocence when her fingers slipped a few envelopes out . . .

Wal, I'll be . . .

Sary had been wrong: the giant man who'd saved her today did indeed have others to correspond with, for the letters were all addressed to *Wilbur Whateley* of *Dunwich Village,* some dating back as far as 1920. Sary knew her curiosity would have extended too far had she removed the missives from their sheaths and read of their contents, but what harm could there be in taking notice of their return addresses?

Her eyes narrowed immediately. Two were from Miskatonic University in Arkham, a town Sary had heard of and knew to be not far distant. Another from a man in Kingston, New York, named Alonzo Typer; another from a Robert Blake in someplace called Wisconsin; and yet another from someone here in Dunwich, named Septimus Bishop, though she'd never heard of this latter man, what with so many Bishops here and there. An eyebrow popped up when she read the next return address: Innsmouth, from someone named Marsh. Sary recognized the town, for it was the only town she'd ever traveled to outside of Dunwich; her mother had taken her there once to visit a friend whom she—her mother—had grown up with. The next return address owned to no location at all but only revealed: The Church of Starry Wisdom.

So it seemed that fuddlement and nothing more would be her curiosity's prize. *I best mind my own business,* she suggested to herself. *Think I'll have a walk aoutside,* but before she got to the door, she took notice of a block-print map that read THE CAMPUS OF MISKATONIC UNIVERSITY, and crudely circled on it with pen-ink was a square which read LIBRARY. More pen-writing instructed, WATCH FER DOG and 4th WINDOW, EAST

SIDE IZ CLOSEST TO RARE BOOK ROOM. Sary couldn't imagine what these notes might mean. On a small cherrywood end table lay another map, but this was one folded. All she could read of its front print was HARVARD UNIVERSITY, CAMBRIDGE, MASS., EST. 1636, and more scribble, WIDENER and 2nd FLOOR SPECIAL BOOKES & MSS. ROOM. More fuddled than ever, Sary turned, opened the door, and left the tool-house.

Her bare feet glided her across plush green grass, the sun beamed down, and she nearly gasped in delight when she saw how the sun's rays caught the countless glittering flecks that seemed imbued by magic into her black gown's intricate fabric. She fairly beamed herself.

A trace glance showed her several other sheds in the distance, some in bad repair, then she looked again to the well-built, tin-topped smoker-house which had provided her the delectable meal. Instinct warned her to keep mindful of those awful red ants that stung her feet to no end when she walked in the wrong places, but then relief came when she remembered Wilbur telling her that no varmints or insects existed anywhere near the Whateley property. She knew this to be true now more than ever, for not a single mosquito had bitten her yet, even though this time of season they were rife. The shadow of the vast Round Mountain interestingly cast a great darkened curve upon the forest belt beyond. The woods looked so lovely in that half-dark, half-bright line of contrast, but she declined activating her idea to take a stroll amongst the trees, for something seemed . . . unnatural about them. Surely, she'd never observed trees so twisted, stout, and gnarled. Indeed, they appeared over-nourished, glutted, as though they'd grown for their centuries of existence via the sustenance of sour minerals in the soil. Some of the trees reminded her of monstrous figures as of those in nightmares.

Now her gaze surveyed her point of vantage in a wider arch. Beyond the side of the strangely boarded-up Whateley house, she could see the dirt road that eventually took one away from Dunwich, to the Aylesbury pike. It occurred to her to amble to the road, to see if Wilbur might be on his way back—she could greet him—but next, however, it was the dilapidated house that snagged her notice. Did some ugly, dark substance leak from its boarded windows and doors? *Like tar,* she associated. It may have been her imagination, then, when she thought she detected a single *quake* of the house itself, as if something huge within—the main timbers, perhaps—had hitched and settled. Then her memory brought back to her that brief but hideous noise she'd thought she heard earlier, a noise like a monumental *snort* . . .

The great abode, like the book in the shed, caused an unpleasant throb in her belly and a minute headache, so she quickly turned to be out of sight of it. But no sooner had she traversed when she noticed another oddity . . .

Beneath a long, rickety canopy of wood-slats, cords of firewood sat neatly stacked, surely an amount that would take months of a cruel winter to deplete. But the oddity was what sat heaped in a ten-foot-high pile *next* to the firewood.

Building scrap in the manner of a great tumble of house lumber: rafters, beams, doors and their frames, wall-slats, and even great chunks of whole walls. By the looks of the pile, these materials came clearly from *interior* construction, but they'd now become subject just as clearly to an act of *de*construction, as if aspects of the interior had been sundered. *I wonder if Wilbur done knocked out all'a the walls of the big haouse . . .* Whatever it was he stored inside must be quite large. Why a pile of wood-scrap would instill in her a sense of foreboding, she didn't know.

Pursing her lips as if at a rank sapor, she continued her meandering examination of the property.

A number of prodigious drakeberry bushes, in long ranks, diced up the grassy region just beyond the tool-house. Amid the bush by which she walked the closest, she noticed a natural indentation, like a cove of sorts, deep and tall enough for one to enter without being seen by anyone not in close proximity, and it was into this "cove" that Sary's curiosity took her next.

The cove curled inward in nearly a hook-shape, and at its furthest limit she noticed . . .

What's them THINGS?

A pile of singularly curious . . . *things* lay on the ground; Sary's immediate tendency was to divine the impression of pony stools, for they existed as roundish wads approximately an inch wide apiece. Size and shape, however, was where this similarity ended: pony stools, or any excrement that Sary knew of, always bore a rather universal brownish color, while the pile of things she looked at now were far more akin to the color of a peeled banana slightly overripe. This mystery-laden pile stood perhaps two feet in height, tapering as it ascended. Most would find the nature of the wad-like objects as unpleasant or even foul, yet Sary found them only objectively interesting, considering how accustomed her life had made her to the unpleasant, the foul, the disgusting, etc. And it was this curiosity which urged her to stoop and pick up between her fingers the topmost object . . .

A strange slimy texture registered immediately. When she lifted the thing, she expected it to separate from the heap individually, but this was not the case; instead, more of the off-white balls came with the first, and now she perceived that they were in some manner connected, as of a grotesque string of pearls. Fascination finnicked with her. She kept lifting the first ball but found that the entire queue of the others stopped at exactly ten balls. This led her to assume that the remainder of the pile existed similarly: a string of ten slimy balls deposited and redeposited over a period of time, comprising the entire heap . . .

Whatever could the things be?

Fascinated though she was, Sary ended her examination and presumed to continue visually surveying more of Wilbur's property, in which, after taking leave of the bush's hidden cove, she crossed it to look around.

The latrine ditch was what she glimpsed next, along with its tightly lashed frame of logs where one would sit to defecate. It reminded her that she herself needed to urinate, but she'd always been fearful of such waste-ditches, for once, her father had thrown her into one after a particularly vehement session of forced intercourse. She'd been very young at the time—six or seven—and as she recalled, his reaction had not been positive when she'd refused to lap up the traces of his semen which had leaked out of her after his climax. So it was a trip to the bottom of the latrine that was her compensation for such non-compliance.

She picked another ample drakeberry bush behind which to secret herself, then raised with care her luxurious black dress and immediately lowered herself to a squat. It was then that all of the pleasant sensations her skin had been receptive to today . . . had commingled and then intensated to an effect many times more robust: the comfort of being carried in Wilbur's strong arms, then the feel of her own hands caressing the suds of the ash soap all over her body in the shower machine, then—much more so—the feel of *Wilbur's* hands sliding up and down in the cleave of her buttocks and how she cringed for the fantasy of the elongated fingers sliding into her private orifi . . . Even the captivating black gown itself beguiled her in some concupiscent manner, some mystery of its fabric that felt, whenever she walked, as of the hands or even the tongue of some semi-palpable wraith tenderly stroking her skin. Foggy-eyed with these muses, a few moments passed, then her bladder began to void; the stream glittered as it arced out of her and up, and then she discovered her index and middle fingers were V'd at the folds her of sex, opening it; it was such that even the mundane function of urinating pushed more lustful desires into her head. The stream declined, then ceased, yet she remained in her lewd squat, at once finding one hand slipped into the gown's top, fondling a breast; her fingers catered to the already nerve-plump nipple, which sent the most delectable sensations gusting to her privates. Then she imagined Wilbur's fingers there, then his mouth, *sucking.*

Aw, durn, that feels good . . .

She licked the fingerpad of her other hand, stroked the pink nub of her clitoris, once very slowly, then again twice. Her body's reaction to this meager tending was an intoxicating tension; her head rolled around. Two more quicker strokes brought a pulsing outburst to her loins whose density of pleasure caused her to fall over and cringe. She twitched there on the ground, her face overcome by a smile of delight the likes of which she'd not experienced in years. The initial impulse to masturbate had been puissant enough; however, it was the fantasy of *Wilbur's* participation that had set her sexual responses off like a black-powder keg.

Sary lay sidled over awhile longer, pilfering out the last of the after-sensations, but then—

Terror came.

The unmistakable scuff of footfalls could be heard not far off. *Aw, Gawd, please let it be that no one seen me!* She jumped up (hoping that the bush's partial coverage had concealed her from the interloper) and righted her gown as best she could. Either the walker was Wilbur or it was—

Wilbur said he boarded up his haouse 'cos folks sometimes try ta break in . . .

Sary prayed to God that it wasn't some foul-minded Dunwich thief trespassing upon the property. If such a man saw Sary, out here all by herself?

She knew she'd be raped most dementedly.

She peeked around the edge of the bush, yet her eyes only had time to glimpse a figure turn round the hill and disappear behind the sheds, which could only mean . . .

He be headin' for the big house . . .

A daring not typically known to her had her quickly dart from the bush, past the latrine, and to the wall of the smoking-house. It was a deep breath she drew into her lungs, then . . . She peeked around the smoker's corner.

Thank yew, Gawd . . .

Relief assailed her when she easily identified the "interloper" as Wilbur himself. She was about to call out a greeting, but impulse at the last moment caused her to forbear the gesture. Impulse, but also . . . observation.

What's that over his back?

Indeed, a sack of some kind seemed to be slung across the gargantuan man's back as he walked with deliberance toward the boarded-up house. However, Sary now discerned that one of the house's doors stood absent of the nailed planks and beams that sealed all the others and windows. Instead, it was barred by upper and lower iron struts fixed across the egress by two large and ponderous old locks. Wilbur, still not at all cognizant of Sary's vigilance, extracted a key, unfastened the locks, and opened the door . . .

The young woman's angle of observation afforded her a fair view into the domicile's east end, and the sunlight, though partially truncated, showed her only vast emptiness inside. *Whatever it 'tis Wilbur keep stored in thar, it gotta all be at the other end,* she deduced.

She naturally expected Wilbur to enter the leaning abode, but this he did not do. Instead, and most curiously, he remained where he stood outside, and then it looked as though he were *talking . . .*

Who the hail he talkin' tew if thar en't no one livin' inside? The extended distance prevented Sary's deciphering any of what her rescuer was saying.

And next?

Wilbur made the oddest gesture with his hand: at first Sary believed him to be crossing himself the way a priest or minister would, but the motions that were made indicated something far more complicated. It was only a moment later, then, that the colossan unslung the burden across his back and flung it into the house. Then he re-barred and locked the entry.

Sary's plentiful curiosity took on a tinge of something not unlike dread, for in the few seconds before Wilbur had resecured the door, she'd verified that it was no sack at all that he'd tossed within. It was a dead dog.

A dead *collie,* to be more unequivocal.

Same exact dog that awful Hutchins boy sicced on me, she knew, and how could any doubt exist? She'd seen Wilbur blow the barbarous animal's brains out with a pistol.

More strangeness, in a manner by which she could make no deductions.

She expected Wilbur to return to the tool-shed, but instead, he loped straight away from the big house and into the twisted woods. *Whar's he goin' naow?* Sary meandered about the property, looking errantly at the splotches of grass and wild beds of flowers, noting again nary a sign of insect activity, and no bees rummaging for pollen.

"Wal, hey thar!" Wilbur greeted her when he'd reappeared some twenty minutes later.

"Hi, Wilbur. I was gettin' ta miss yew," she said, acknowledging now that his departure, admixed with the inexplicable observations she'd made, had left her vaguely unnerved. But Wilbur's big, angular face seemed to betray a hint of happiness when she'd said she missed him.

"Sorry, I took a tad longer'n I thought. Ran into that bald fella, Kyler be his name—he abaout the only Dunwicher who'll share a good word with me. A *soothsayer* is what he claim he is."

The word perplexed Sary. "A sooth—*what?*"

"One who tell fortunes, like I heerd they got at curnivals. Dun't know haow true it 'tis, though."

All she could think to say was, "Carn't say I'se heerd of him, but I'm glad you got a friend." Her expression cheered. "Wal, naow ya got two friends, me bein' the second."

Wilbur's approach slowed as more inner happiness seemed to dawn within him.

"We'll be friends, always, Sary," he replied in a solemn tone.

Wilbur was so tall that Sary unconsciously stood on tiptoes to see what he had now on his shoulder. *Not another dead dog,* she hoped, but in a moment identified a trap rope.

"So that's what yew were doin' in the woods," she observed. "Checkin' yer traps."

"Ee-yuh." He'd reached her by now and unshouldered the cord, attached to which were several squirrels, a muskrat, and a woodchuck. "A more than midland ketch today," his dark warble of a voice reported. "En't ketched a woodchuck in spell. But like I told ye, I gotta walk aout in the wood a good distance 'cos critters dun't come near the haouse."

Sary naively wondered if he intended to deposit these animals into the big house as he'd done with the dog, but, *'A'course not. They'se for him ta put in the smoke-house,* she realized.

"Hope ye have a likin' for woodchuck."

"Oh, I dew—"

"I got a old family recipe that make it taste like duck . . . ." A pause, then his large dark eyes blinked on an afterthought. "Aw, but ye sure didn't have yerself much of a nap, huh?"

Sary shook her head, admitting to the distraction of how glad she was to see him. "'Tis funny. Tired as I was, the minute yew left, I couldn't sleep a wink, so's I just kind'a walked abaout, lookin' raound yer land. Hope ya dun't mind."

"Not one bit," Wilbur said, but he seemed distracted as well, distracted by her simple presence. His eyes persisted on her: each time he was about to speak, he stalled. "I . . . uh. Aw, durn, Sary . . . "

"What?"

"I'se jess real happy yew stayed. Whole time I was aout, I thought sure ye'd be gone time I got back . . . "

She grinned at the absurd remark. "Wilbur, I wouldn't just up'n leave withaout sayin' goodbye."

The huge man shuffled awkwardly in his big boots. "I know the way I look put gals off—"

"The way yew look's just fine ta me, so's I carn't think'a what yew mean," she tried to allay his faltering esteem. Yes, Wilbur's physical aspect diverged a great deal from that of other men, but Sary only found this trait unique and interesting, not repugnant. She thought, *The way my face look, no ear, all scarred'n pocked, nose mashed up by my pa? It be a blessin' from Gawd Wilbur even turn a glance at me.* Through the self-analysis, however, she realized that not only was she comfortable with Wilbur's appearance, she felt progressively more attracted to him, this latter fact being betrayed then and there as she felt her nipples tingle and begin to stand up beneath the sheer cover of the dress.

I wonder if he notice that . . . However, these ruminations, though they expended only moments, left an uncomfortable silence, so she carried on her perky reply. "Yew been nicer ta me than . . . wal, anyone I can ever 'member meetin', and I'd never be rude so ta jess leave withaout me sayin' so fust. Naow, let me help ya git them critters skinned and gutted. No reason yew should do all this work withaout me liftin' a finger ta help."

Wilbur's colossal physique went from tense to lax. "Nup. 'Tis my job, and I'll have in done in a jiff. Why not ye jess wait fer me in the tool-haouse, take a rest?"

"Okay."

Upon the instant of returning to the shed—and with no conscious mandate whatever—Sary's hands slipped up the inside of her gown to further caress her sex. Even this long after her eruptive orgasm, the exotic pleasure lingered; she even felt as though she could masturbate again. *Jess sumpin' 'baout Wilbur got me hotter'n the top of a Dutch oven . . . ,* but only then did she catch herself and expeditiously withdrew her hands. What might Wilbur conclude were he to walk in suddenly?

Several minutes later, he indeed returned, ducking below the door's transom.

"That's shore a fast skinnin' and guttin' job," Sary observed. Just looking at him, however, had her painstakingly sidetracked. Why this misproportioned giant kindled her so lickerishly, she could not appraise, but she recognized this: *If thar ever be a man I'd want to lay me right daown and fuck me, why . . . it'd be him.*

"Been dressin' critters so long, I kin dew it in my sleep," Wilbur's voice wavered in its bizarre depth. "Say"—he stepped forward—"I bet'cher ear don't hurt naow, huh?"

The question sparked in Sary's head as she realized his assertion was true. "Yew was right, Wilbur. I don't got no pain a'tall no more."

His huge hands rested on her shoulders, urging her toward the cot. At first, Sary's loins made a steamy, spontaneous clench; her crudest impulses hoped he meant to immediately prostrate her on the cot and *have* her, just as per her fantasy—

"Set ye daown right here," he said instead, gesturing the cot. "Gonna check it."

When seated, Sary was surprised by the daintiness with which Wilbur's enormous hands removed the poultice he'd previously applied.

"Thar," he remarked in a manner that seemed proud. "All healed up, jess like I say."

Sary felt her remaining ear and easily discerned that even the dog's bite marks were healed. "That's *amazin'*. I carn't thank yew enough, Wilbur."

"Warn't nuthin'," he said, then loped toward the desk. But something caught his eye on the big table.

"Oh, I see ye took a look at the *Necronomicon.*"

"Huh?"

"The big book with the hinges," he clarified, regarding the creepy tome she'd peeked at.

"Wal, yeah," she confessed. "Hope ya en't mad—"

"Naw." He flipped to a few age-fattened pages.

"Probably nuthin' in it ye'd understant no ways, nor be interested in."

Sary was relieved that he didn't consider her "peek" a trespass into his privacy. "My mother teached me ta read a little, but I couldn't make hardly nothin' aout'a all them fancy words. I just thought it was a Bible."

"Wal, it 'tis in a manner." Wilbur's peculiarly dark eyes remained focused on the pages he scanned. "Been somethin' I study quite a bit. Only problem is there be some flawed incantations."

Sary cast a querying glance. "What's that mean?"

Hinges creaked when he closed the prodigious book. "My grandsire tolt me that when this heer copy be translated inta English, someone monkeyed with the words—on purpose, probably—so's ta take away the book's . . . what was that word he used? *Efficacy,* I think. Ee-yuh. The monkeyin' took off the book's efficacy, which means some'a its best parts wun't work."

By now, Sary's not-terribly-formidable intellect had lost all comprehension as to what the giant man might mean; but, so not to feel stupid, she merely gave a nod and said, "Oh."

Next, Wilbur's large-pored face glanced frustratedly to the map pinned to the wall.

That college in Arkham, Sary recalled. *And sumpthin' wrote on it abaout books . . .*

"So's naow I got ta go back to Miskatonic and get me another look at the unflawed copy they got thar."

"Go back? Yew mean ya already been?"

"Ee-yuh. Onct." In his tone, there came a negative inference regarding the excursion. "But the man runs the library thar, he en't much. Armitage be his name. Treated me like I be scum'n sent me aout."

Sary felt badly for her friend's frustration, but all she could offer was, "Wal, then, ain't it likely he'll send ya aout again?"

Wilbur's look to her might have been called desperate and pleading. But of her question, he added nothing.

Her generally unfired libido still raged betwixt her thighs, yet other questions battled with it, questions she burned to ask. Like: what was Wilbur keeping in the big house, and why had he deposited the dead dog in it? What could account for the extensiveness of the interior planks, timbers, wall- and door-frames, etc. that had been piled outside? And—

What be them weird white ball-things in the crook of the bush?

Better judgment prevailed, however, not typical of her. *Why ask stuff that don't be none'a my business?* And in a moment, she felt her eyelids droop; a drowse was coming on with promptitude.

Wilbur had taken a seat at the big desk with all the slots. "I'll jess be a little while heer," and then he appeared—pen in hand—to devote his attention to the sheets of paper Sary had seen, those filled with writing whose words were constituted in an alphabet she'd never seen. But this was all she remembered observing before her fatigue pulled her down on the cot . . .

In the sweet, scintillant darkness behind her sleeping mind's eye, she dreamed of Wilbur lying beside her, kissing her . . .

Sometime later, when her eyes fluttered open, she could tell by the tiny windows that the sun had moved considerably. She yawned and sat back up, surprised. "Why, I must'a been asleep."

"Ee-yuh," Wilbur replied. He remained scribbling at the monumental desk. "Ye needed it. 'Baout an hour ye was out, I'd say."

She felt energized now, in her mind but also in her nerves. That dream, short and incomplete as it had been, left her nipples more gorged with excited blood than ever; it seemed impossible for Wilbur not to notice their swelling against the material of the fine, black dress. She returned her gaze to the arch-backed, intent figure at the desk . . .

Ever the more now, this man, Wilbur Whateley, was striking her as one of uttermost fascination.

"Must be quite a letter writer," she said from her place on the cot. "All them neat little slots is mostly full."

He replied without addressing her. "Been sendin' and gettin' lots of letters over the yeers. But this heer's just my keepin' a journal fer myself. If ye'd took a glance at it, you'd see it be writ in a secret way. A *cipher* 'tis called. My grandsire teached me so's I could read what he left. Guess that's what I'm doin' too, leavin' a record'a such stuff as pertains to family business, suthin' that not jess anyone could read."

This, Sary hardly understood either. But her eyes held fast on the high desk. "Ain't never seen a desk so big'n interestin'."

Wilbur nodded, his fountain pen scribbling. "'Tis nice, all right. I used ta use that old bureau over thar for my desk, but then one time I were in Osborn's general store tew buy me a valise to hold papers"—without removing his eyes from the sheet, his long, stout finger indicated said valise in the corner—"ta take with me to Miskatonic that fust time I went. But out front, I spied Zech Whateley's wagon a-settin' thar with this desk in it'n a For Sale sign. So's I bought it off him. Naow, he charged me a peck, for sure, but that's 'cos he knowed we got money. Same man used ta sell us cattle, and the bugger always upcharged my grandfather."

Sary found it curious: the reference to money. She'd believed the country offshoots of the Whateleys to be as poor as her own family.

"Never thought much'a Zech; dun't matter he's blood. Lotta the Whateleys en't no good, 'specially's after the way they treat my grandfather. Thiefs, liars, the bunch of 'em. But when I espied me that thar desk, I took a fancy to it, so's I say what the hey, I buyed it." Wilbur frowned in a half-smiling way. "Wun't surprised when Zech charge me *extra* fer takin' it to the tool-haouse in his wagon."

Zech? Sary wondered. "Oh, you mean Zechariah," and instantly, Sary's spirits darkened. "I dun't think mutch'a him neither, nor his son Curtis. One time . . . ," but then her revelation dwindled. Why tell Wilbur something so unpleasant? The fact was, Zechariah and Curtis had once paid her a dime each to partake in intercourse with her near the old collapsed Hoadley house, but when their semen had been drained, they'd then seen fit to drain their *bladders* as well, all over her till she was sopping. Many customers, in fact, had felt obliged to urinate on her in her professional past, an impulse she never understood. "They's talk mean ta me fer no reason," she said instead, "so I say ta Hades with 'em."

Wilbur nodded in approval.

"'N fact," she carried on, "I dun't think much'a any of thems that lounge about Obsborn's store. Can tell jess by the way they look in their face they ain't nice folk."

"Naw, most of 'em en't, I'se afraid." The ciphered scribbling continued. "Suthin' 'baout this whole area seem ta be all growed up with bad folk same way a field's growed up with weeds."

Sary rambled on, as she was wont to do when in the midst of someone she liked (which was woefully infrequent). "I went in thar onct ta buy me some rock candy, which be my favorite, but t'was a penny short, and that awful Joe Osborn say he won't give me none unless I fuck 'em all. Over a dang *penny*."

Wilbur paused again but looked at her this time in a quelled distress.

"I *didn't,* a'course," Sary added with some haste. "Gawd. I know I got me *some* pride . . . Then I tried to buy some another time when that old man Tobias Whateley was workin', and I give him a dime but he only give me a nickel's worth."

Suddenly Wilbur was tapping the end of his pen in some remote calculation. "So 'tis rock candy ye like? Wal, I do too." His long arm maneuvered awkwardly until he was able to reach into a pocket. He withdrew a dollar bill. "Seein' haow I'll be writin' a bit more, why dun't you go on up thar'n buy us a big bag?"

Sary thrilled at the prospect and also Wilbur's excess of generosity. *Why's he so nice ta me but en't tried ta git to my pussy?* The instance seemed unfathomable. "Thank yew, Wilbur!" she expressed, jumped up, and took the dollar.

"No point'n ye settin' heer bored whiles I do this—"

"I won't be long!" and she was already directing herself toward the door. "I en't had rock candy is soooo long! Thank yew double!"

Wilbur turned to look at her; his own delight at seeing her so happy appeared muddied by some private distraint.

But Sary knew at a glance. "And *don't worry!* I'll be back!"

Wilbur smiled an interior relief as Sary scurried out the tool-house door.

(VI)

AFTER SARY WAKE UP, *she git all excited wen I give her a dollar for rock candy. Make me feel real good to see her happy like that. She didn't nap atall when I go out earliur, tired as she was, but dozed off after I take off her bandige. Now she be on her way to Osborn's. Few minutes after she leave, I just had to go out to the bush and have at myself with my hand again. Seein her beauty, an just the way she be, and her eyes and smile, leeve me no choice. Saw the pile of my jack-off look disturbed, though. Couldnt be a animal on account no critter come neer the house. Hope it weren't Sary who found it and diddled with it—can't imagine what shed think. I probably just mistaken is all.*

Was calclating the new Alko passages (I didn't like them at first) I larned as I walked back to the pasture where that fat Rufus boy do all them bad things to Sary. Folks never lern it seems. Also thought hard about what might be wrong with page 751 of the Dee, like exzactly. Cud it be its not the wurds theerselves that was writ in flawed but maybe just the angles of the planes? Frum what I read, the unproper angles would muss up the Dho and the Dho-Hna and make it impossible to send word to the city between the magnetik poles. Just don't know fer sure. Got ta stop worryin and just git reddy.

So anywaye, I get back to that old shitty pastureland whitch used to belong ta Elmer Frye, I think, and pick up

52

Hutchins ded collie and sling it over my back. Had to wunder, though, what ole man Hutchins look like on his face (and asettin in that wheelchar I put him in) when his fat son come in all ablubberin and wailin and holding a empty sack that was previous fulla his balls. Bet ole Elam raged shakin his fist and avowin to kill me like he been dewin all these years. I kind of chuckle at the thought cos he know he cant do nuthin to me even if he possess the curage to try. Tis a rule my grandsire teech me long ago when I first started understanding talk, that bad folks don't nevur turn good, they always be bad, and most of em be cowerds too.

But along my walkin root back home, I run into that Kyler fella—who Sary say she never heer of—and he look at me that funny way he look sometimes and kind of smile and tell me, "Aye, Wilbur. Ye be cheerful today, and I am appraised as to why," so I ast him, "How ye know why—ah," (and then I smile too), "on account you're a soothsayer, huh?" Then he tell me, "The love ye most seek out with thine heart, ye've already just got. Nay?" Funny thing for him to say. Always like him, and just about him only in this cursed place, but it come to me that he must mean Sary, and theer aint no way he could know bout her being at my place. So I just tell him, "I sure hope so, Kyler, cuz youre right, I am a might cheerfull today and it be on account of a gal." Then he just nod, still smyling. Not once did he ask why I done had one a the Hutchins dogs over my shoulder neither, and there aint no way he didnt notice. So I bid him a good day but befor I can walk off, he say, "And it mite pleese thee much to know that what it is ye most strive for, ye shall achieve by way of them ancient books ye keep." I stop right then and their and turn bak, knowin full well that what I strive fore most, even more than Sary, is to open the Gate. Wanted tew ask him why he think that but no words cud make their way passed my lips.

Then he say in the end, "Nay, though ye'll not achieve it by the manner in which ye hope most."

And then he nodded with that smile and that was all.

Got me thinkin as I walk back. Like maybe he be a reel soothsayer and not just pretend. And if this be, I don't keer if I kant open the Gate the way I hope long as I open it one way or anothur. But acourse he is likely not a reel fortune sayer.

Walk back double fast to be agin with Sary, even thogh I figure she be sleepin. First, though, I had to feed that One inside so I throw the ded Hutchins dog in the house. Could sense in my brain how close it is all getting and how smart it become. But my biggist worry still be its size, which is why I ben feedin it smaller food. I did the Voorish Sign so to look at it, and it seem to have grown mutch since last time. Grandsire were right but the proper time still be far off. Mite have to start feedin it hardly nothing cos I cant ferget my grandsire's dyin' words about how it can't be let to bust quarters afore the night.

Then I fetch what were in the traps and see Sary already out awaitin for me. Made me feel good.

Inside, we talked mutch, and I seed she took a gander at the Dee but I know she wudn't ever be able to understand. If she got religion atall, it be the Christian one. Grandfather always say I should mind my tongue about the Old Ones, so I did. I reckon she had even less lerning than me, so how can I spect her to calclate things like what my grandsire call the "Holy Adjudicata and Protocall" bein tampered with purposeful by folks in the past who translayted from other langwiges? When I tell her about how I have to go back to Miskatonic, she say a right smart thing, that sinct Armitage throwed me out that first time, he'd likely do the same a secund, and I got the impression that a stick in the dirt like him wouldnt give me what I want even for alla Grandsire's gold. But I be glad Sary say such, cos it got me thinking bout a better way, and I'm surpized I didn't think on it afore this. But in the name of Him Who Is Not To Be Named, I just HAVE ta git the proper translation of page 751. Ef I don't, like my grandfather warn, it all be no use.

Dang! Whats wrong with me? I ben thinkin so hard about the flaws in that blasted Dee copy, I must uv lost all my sense! Shouldnt never have sent Sary to Obsorns by herself, not aftur she say how they razz her that last time n try to fuck her. I best go there myself right now—

(VII)

IN A MANNER close to childlike, Sary fairly skipped her way towards Osborn's General Store, which—even when not considering the ignoble character of most of its patrons—was a mercantile establishment she'd never cared for. No negativity, however, wielded the power to vandalize her current disposition, (one which could only be construed as one of unbridled gaiety). Not even the present surroundings could inhibit her; generally, when she traversed the more remote areas (especially those in proximity to Sentinel Hill), she always had her cause for trepidation. The aforesaid hill, for that matter, rose westerly of the path she now scurried along at this precise moment: it and the straggly, rock-strewn meadows fringed by the distant line of unnaturally contorted trees had frequently imparted to her a kind of skulking dread, as though such inanimate things were valuating her with sentient aversion.

Not *this* day, though.

I only juss met Wilbur today, and I'se already gettin' good feelin's for him. Ain't never met no one nicer'n him . . .

She walked round the rest of Sentinel Hill's brush-hummocked elevation. She whistled a tune—"Yes, We Have No Bananas"—then offered a cheerful wave to a group of overalled denizens lounging higher among a nearby hill's rock-strewn rise. No response was made to her gesture, just blank, decrepit stares, but Sary didn't care. *Why, ya bunch'a old toads,* she thought. *But I hope yew all have a good day anyways!*

THE DUNWICH ROMANCE

The road—more a trail than a genuine road—straightened through the next meadow, Dunwich Village hulking haggardly in the distance. Sweeps of uncut hay shivered about her, though she perceived not even a wisp of wind. Then . . .

Is that . . . a person?

The thing that she first connoted as a bent scarecrow soon turned out to be a person indeed. No apprehension retarded her gait as she proceeded, yet as she did so, the figure's details advanced in clarity. A man, shaven-headed, stood beside a lone tree, nearly as if awaiting her. He wore a long-tailed black coat, a white shirt with bow tie, black slacks, and leather shoes, but though the apparel clearly had been fine in days agone, they were now quite tattered and threadbare. He stood with the aid of a cane, which seemed topped by some flying creature, and though Sary had never been to a moving-picture show, she remembered the time her mother had taken her to Innsmouth on the bus: when the smoke-spewing vehicle had passed through Kingsport, it had slowed at an intersection. This pause had given Sary time to glimpse a moving-picture theater, whose marquee had read NOSFERATU and had sported an advertisement poster featuring the quite scary visage whose most salient features were a thin face and bald head, large receded eyes, and cheeks so gaunt they appeared as if in shadow. It was this image she immediately affixed to this waiting person.

Closer, she detected the reason for his cane: a severely curvatured spine. Then more eccentric facial details came to her heed. Sary possessed no creative alacrity whatever, yet an onlooker who did might describe the man overall as *cadaveresque,* and with a cast of eye (blue eyes, they were) that suggested an accursed affinity of misanthropic revelation. At alternate moments, he seemed somnambulant, as though not aware of her approach at all, yet other moments, he seemed vibrantly notified of all in his range of sight and even beyond. It was then that Sary took note of sinister artwork on his hands and neck, a process she'd heard of called tattooing. Lastly, and most shockingly, the road-stander harbored a metal ring through his nose, akin to the rings implanted to lead cattle or horses.

But when he at last addressed her directly with his foggy blue eyes, his general aspect of negativity evanesced to something rather the opposite. A precipitant smile, in fact, struck her as humanitarian.

In the most archaic Yankee dialect she'd heard in some time, he voiced, "Young gull, greetin's ta ye on this acme of a day. A day of *wonders,* be this, aye?"

Sary considered the uncharacteristic words, then realized the bald man was correct. "Has been for me, yeah." She blinked, remembering Wilbur's mention of a *bald* man. "Say, are yew that Kyler man Wilbur tell me 'bout?"

"'Tis true," the voice creaked in reply. "I espied him not long ago."

"He tell me yew're a *fortune-teller* . . . "

The man seemed to stand atilt. "Cahn't say I am, cahn't say I en't. But heer's suthin' I *cahn* say: eff'n it's Osborn's whar you be a-headin' . . . " but then the remainder of the remark retroceded like something lost in smoke.

Sary didn't care for the man's elliptical words, nor in the way his brow cocked; she tried to return a skeptical facial gesture and adjoin it with a similar tone. "Oh, so yew're tellin' me I'm in the way fer a bad time in thar?"

Kyler's head gleamed in the sun. "Mebbe at fust. Thing abaout auguries, like many setch bodements, is they hev a fancy ta change jest as a man's heart cahn change."

"I dun't know what yew're talkin' 'baout," Sary said, amused. She planned to return to her trek forthwith, but the road-stander hastened to add:

"Mebbe I ought come with ye—"

"Naw, no thanks—"

"—while ye be in thar a-fetchin' yew're rock candy. 'Tis of sorts a *devoir*'a mine—a *duty,* I mean ta say—ta give a jest'n proper *warnin'*, so's a man's *heart* hev a chance to *change . . .* "

Sary had already stopped and turned. It was not the mention of a *warning* which caused her to halt, nor any of what she didn't understand, but instead . . .

Haow'd he know I'm goin' ta buy rock candy?

The question gave her a motive to add credulity to the man's repute. *'Sides, he a friend of Wilbur's.* "Wal, sure," she invited. "Yew can come along if ya want . . . "

Very few minutes had elapsed before the duo approached Osborn's. Even with his cane-assisted limp, his pace was difficult for Sary to keep up with. Not once did she catch his eyes straying to her physique, and this was an observation that relieved her.

"Thar it be," he intoned minutes later, but Sary had scarcely heard him, for the sudden launch of a whippoorwill from a brown, desolate stand of bushes gave her a disruptive start.

"Could be a bad omen, could be good," Kyler reflected more under his breath.

Sary dismissed the comment, not quite positive what an omen was. Instead, she watched the queer general store seem to grow twice as large with each forward step—queer inasmuch as it occupied the sagging wood-plank shell of the old Congregational Church, which she'd heard had been standing for a long time, since before something called the "Revolution" that took place in a time when men wore three-cornered hats. When the building's looming shadow cloaked them both, even the open air behind them affected an unnaturally darkened hue.

Kyler chuckled waveringly. "Haow's *that* fer a omen?" he said, indicating with his eyes the store's most conspicuous feature: the broken steeple of the House of God this place used to be in days bygone.

Sary twitched at an unanticipated chill but made no reply.

Kyler held the creaking door for her, and they entered

A proverbial cracker barrel sat in the room's front, though Sary had never dared take a cracker—even when making a purchase—since the first time years ago when she'd tried. Tobias, the dismal stick of an old man who tended the counter, had railed, "Get yew're dutty whore hand aout'a them crackers! We dun't care to et nuthin' that's been touched by hands which's ben corn-fingerin' fellas and jerkin' their dutty peters!" and then one of the Langs—God knew which one, for a plethora of them had been born—swatted the back of her head. In fact, Sary braved an entrance to this drear, shelf-crammed place only when an unavoidable necessity arose. Many of the churlish loafers who frequented the store had done business with Sary, and not one of them had ever offered a kind word, while most had talked her price down, knowing full well the extremes of her poverty.

"Wal, jest *look* what fall off the shit wagon'n roll in my store!" cracked the gaunt, whisker-chinned Tobias.

"Ee-yuh!" the Lang man joined in. "It be the hoo-er!"

"Stew Face!" blurted Henry Wheeler, the fence-post digger whose great belly seemed draped over his belt like a lard-satchel. "And look who be with her! The cripple with the balt head!"

All of the men wore rope belts, hand-stitched boots, and clothes whose blemishes had been constantly corrected by make-shift patches. Stains were rife on these clothes, and had Sary commanded a sense of smell, she might've suspected that the denizens' apparel was washed even less than those who wore it. Amid the cramped room sat a card table bearing several illicit liquor bottles, along with evidence of gambling. In a corner was a typical tin water pail sufficing for a spittoon; Sary took uneasy note that its contents of expectorant was half an inch from overflowing.

Tobias leaned over the counter, his high voice aggravating as an unlubricated caster. "Hey, cripple, why'n't yew clip-clop thet thar cane aout'a heer rut naow, and yorself'n yor whore with it?"

"Ef ye insist," Kyler calmly replied, "but haow much sense be made aout'a runnin' off payin' customers, on accaount I dun't espy much in the way'a *business* heer," and then the man produced a quarter. "A wrap'a licorice is whut I fancy."

Tobias glared, but then resigned. He was as poor as most in these regions; any currency seeking emigration into his proprietorship would not be turned away. Crabbed hands begrudgingly filled a sheet of store paper with said licorice, then wrapped it up.

"Thar's yew're blammed licorice, cripple," Tobias declared, his Adam's apple bobbing on his old, thin neck. "Naow git aout."

"Ee-yuh," laughed the girthy Wheeler. "Go'n tell more *fortunes.*"

Kyler tucked his parcel under his arm. "Nay, see, my friend heer got business as well . . . "

Tobias and his ramshackle associates all turned hateful glares to Sary.

Even before this, Sary was conscious of assessments being made of her; the hateful glares also possessed more than a small amount of lust as those blood-shot eyes roved her body. One man—the Lang—openly dandled his crotch.

Tobias yelled, waving a bone-thin hand. "Only kind'a business she do is fuckin' and suckin'! She dun't got no cash money!"

"Aw, but I got me some m—" Sary began, yet the owner's outburst would not license the completion of her statement.

"I run a 'spectable operation heer, and I wun't hev no whorin' fer goods!"

Wheeler's brow rose, then he, too, rubbed his crotch while his eyes narrowed on Sary's form. "Holt on a sec, Tobe. Mebbe we oughta dew some thinkin' on this. Can't hut ta give Stew Face a smidge'a food long as she put a fuckin' on us fust—"

"Ee-yuh," added Lang. Did a tiny spot of wetness

darken his crude trousers as his hand continued to knead his genital region? "Jess the look'a this 'un got my pecker *all* riled up. And haow 'baout them tits shewin through thet shiny dress?"

Wheeler nodded with a grin, remarked, "Let's see thet cut on her tew," then briefly raised the hem of Sary's diaphanous gown with a yardstick, the action of which briefly flashed the mound of plush, dark hair between her legs.

Wheeler and Lang whistled.

"Thar some meat fer the dogs!"

"An' my dog's a-barkin'!"

With a half-shriek, Sary jumped at the start, then righted the gown.

This visual treat seemed to ameliorate Tobias's previous condemnation. He, too, caressed his crotch. "Fuhgot jess what a looker she be onct ya git past thet roadkill face . . . "

"*Thought* yew'd change yer mind, Tobe." Lang made a dismissive laugh. "The pussy on this bitch could put hardwood on a pack'a faggots."

A leering pause caused Sary to shrink; the ill-feeling in her gut gave her a clear impression what was taking place, and it was an impression with which she was all too accustomed. *They dun't even keer that I got money . . .*

By now, erections of various dimensions showed through the pants of the rapists-to-be—even the crackly Tobias, who must've exceeded the age of seventy. "Ee-yuh. Naow's ye all mention it, it been a while sinct my dick had itself a good spit!"

"Any livin' minute this cunt ain't full'a cum be a blammed cryin' shame!"

"And we'll be a-fillin', brother! We'll be a-fillin' it!"

"Gonna get me some shit on my stick too. Mebbe a buttful'a my jism'll make this dutty tramp think twice afore she shew her mess of a face in heer agin!"

Sary was no stranger to such less-than-stately verbal

regards, just as she was no stranger to rape. Often, she'd simply resign to it, for resignation tended to minify the physical damage which often played chaperon to resistance. Today, however . . .

She'd had enough. She made to bolt, but—

"Whar yew goin', gravy boat?" Wheeler's cumbrous form moved with unexpected quickness—right toward Sary—in a manner that left no secret of his intent. The exclamation "Nooo—!" was all poor Sary had time to issue before Wheeler had girded her with his porcine arms. The remainder of her objection was interrupted by the vising of her throat in the crook of the man's elbow; this action produced an immediate reduction of the blood-flow to her brain. Wheeler's other arm wrapped about her abdomen.

Consternation and outrage tried in earnest to break through the force being so brutally administered against her, yet in an instant, her vision dimmed. Her consciousness took on a lolling buoyancy, even as her feet flew off the floor and she was lain roughly on the card table and divorced of her gown . . .

At once, her body raved.

"It be only fit thet I warn ye," Kyler intoned, yet before he could give more voice—

CLACK!

The Lang man kicked the soothsayer's cane out. Down Kyler went, to the dusty wood floor.

All I wanted was some rock candy, Sary thought through her fading sentience, *but look what I get instead* . . . She lay in a torpid daze, and she could see only as if through soiled gauze. As much as she wanted to fight and flee, her muscles made only the most feeble responses to her will. She couldn't move, no, but she could feel, and what she felt was the reality of her physical body being metamorphosed into a smorgasbord of touch-fodder for deviants. Rough hands splayed over her quivering skin, squeezing, kneading, pinching, plucking. Fingers burrowed into her sex; a thumb prodded her anus. Her private hair was stroked adoringly, then abruptly yanked and twisted. Soon it was more than hands she felt molesting her; it was raw, hardening genitals. One penile shaft *pap-pap-papped!* against her lips; another, slicked with spit, was pressed between her breasts and drawn in and out after one of the demented toughs straddled her. A third—Tobias's, she would later presume—was squeezed between her feet. Eventually, mouths sucked her nipples to numbness; someone may have bitten her inside the thigh.

The visual "gauze" betrayed only the most inchoate blots of darkness, but at least she believed her overall range of vision was ever-so-slowly regaining clarity.

Words seemed echoic.

"This gull's body got my dick jumpin' like bullfrog on a skillet! En't no way better ta get a tickle in yer blood and some feist in her joint like mussin' a whore up jess fer the hell of it!"

"Bet her pussy's had more cock in it than I've had hole cutters in the ever-lovin' *graound!*"

"I'll be a-breakin' my eggs on *these* tits, ee-yuh, but not afore I fuck this pussy like I'se charnin' buttuh!"

When Wheeler pinched her clitoris and twisted, Sary's hips flinched, and she managed to mutter, "Eat shit, fat man . . ."

Wheeler chortled. "Wal naow, Stew Face, jess fer sayin' that, I'll make damn sure *you* be eatin' shit ahf-tuh I'm done tarnin' yer cunt inside-aout with my pecker!"

Cackling exploded; Sary moaned. Her consciousness, indeed, was returning, but she suspected this return would take place only *after* the definitive act of rape had commenced; she knew, likewise, that pleading with the men, or offering them her dollar bill as a dissuasion, would prove a profitless endeavor indeed.

Kyler's voice sounded from a lower angle, surprisingly quiescent. "I warned ye onct, I'll warn ye again, fellas. Yew'll regret whut it be ye're fixin' ta do . . ."

Wheeler's voice: "Thet balt-headed gimp's pipin' up again."

And Tobias: "Shut yer maouth, cripple, lest ye want it filled with what's in thet spit-can!"

"Mebbe he'd like ta trade thet cane in fer a wheelchar . . ."

Sary was able to lean slightly up and found her vision clearing enough to see one blurred shape spreading her legs. Then—

clunk!

Her head was slammed back down. A now fully hardened penis was seeking entry to her mouth. Sary had recouped enough coherence to yearn, *Gawd, I wish I had my front teeth,* but still could scarcely move. After a pause, the pasty, foreskinned corona pulled back, then fingers dug past her lips. Her mouth was pried open.

"Luke? What'cha fixin' ta dew?"

"Piss in her maouth, a'course."

"Why ya wanna dew thet?"

A chuckle. "Aw, Tobe, thet ain't the question. The question's *why not?*"

Then came a roar of laughter.

The denizen who'd spread her legs was beginning to mount her, when—

"Whut the—" someone huskily exclaimed.

"Hey!"

And Tobias: "Why, yew big butt-ugly, shit-smellin' freak!" and then the sound of scuffling. Sary still couldn't see, but she could feel that her three molesters had all pulled away.

"Thet witch Levinny's bastert kid!"

Sary received the sense that loud, steady footfalls were making an entrance; then came a *slam!* as a door closed; and at her vision's farther periphery . . . did something hove into sight? *What's happenin'?* she thought. With a significant effort, she was able to lean up on elbows. Why had the men prorogued their carnal fete?

Her vision continued to clear but not enough to discern anything in detail.

"I'se a-fetchin' my gun!"

"Ee-yuh, Tobe. Time someone done away with this buzzard-neck white trash devil."

"Be dewin' justice, mind ye. Ever-one knows it were he who made off with Kelly Bishop!"

"And Lars Low's boy tew! Disappeart last October and en't been seen sinct!"

"And them poor Farr sisters! All they ever faound of them was their blammed *shoes* at the bottom of Sentinel Hill!"

These accusations confused Sary—with some of those names came a ring of familiarity—but something else confused her as well: a *hush* as material as a solid wall that insinuated itself throughout the room. Sary's ears buzzed, while in her mouth, an odd mineralish flavor suddenly fizzed. Pricklish static pelted her skin, and she could positively feel her body hair rising on end from the roots.

Then . . .

The sound which Sary heard next she could not liken to any manner of aural example in her life. An abstractionist, or an audiologist, or perhaps a hebephrenic writer, might describe it as "guttural pressure," something akin to human utterance yet too distantly departed from the combination of the traversional and longitudinal waves that are referred to as "sound" to be called "vocal." Its source seemed to defy identification, and it would strike the intellectually inclined as a mode of pandemonic transliteration via some sensitivity to a phenomenon with no previously recognized ken.

In truth, though, it was merely the laryngeal vibrations of an only partly terrestrial throat.

These sounds that were not sounds only heightened that queer mineral taste on Sary's palate, while the remonstrances of her attackers had ceased altogether. But as her senses grew more revitalized, her confoundment redoubled.

Exactly *what* was taking place?

At last, her vision returned as the blood supply to her brain normalized.

Sary stared.

Alas, Tobias, Lang, and Wheeler were still in the room, but all entertained preposterous poses, as their trousers were at their ankles and their genitals not only exposed but so terror-shriveled as to be pathetic. All three ruffians bore the most strained facial expressions, as if in violent resistance against what they were doing . . .

What they were doing was this:

Lang knelt, his neck inclined forward and his mouth opened wide. It was the suet-white, sack-bellied post-digger Henry Wheeler who stood upright, the withered penis tweezered betwixt thumb and forefinger. Wheeler was urinating unsparingly into the Lang man's mouth, while Lang himself swallowed gulp after gulp after gulp.

But Lang was not the only one consuming a vile substance. Tobias Whateley stood near the corner, his thin forearms shaking as he held in his hands the noxious tin-bucket-turned-spittoon. He'd already raised it to his lips and was—

gulp, gulp, gulp

—swallowing its contents in noisy, grueling increments.

Time seemed to lock in place; the sound of *gulping* held sway over the store. Gulping, gulping, gulping. Eventually, Wheeler's bladder had shed the last of its product, then Lang fell over on his side, curled into a fetal configuration, and began to shiver. But the elderly Tobias . . .

He just kept on *gulping*.

How much time transpired proved impossible for Sary to take account of, but some considerable time it must've been, for it was after only an eternity of staring that the old man finally reached the spit-can's bottom. From his rack-thin frame, however, protruded quite a distended belly, as though a honeydew melon had been slipped beneath his shirt. Then Tobias, too, toppled over, curled up, and convulsed.

When Sary's mortification veered off, she saw that Wheeler had already broken from his previous stance and had quite perfunctorily squatted. Amid flatulence that resembled boughs cracking, the post-hole digger moved his bowels directly onto the floor, to deposit a remarkably weighty allotment of excrement.

Why the heck is he . . .

In spite of the resistant cast of face, Wheeler knelt immediately and began to eat, and it was with no meager zestfulness with which he consumed the self-made meal. When the pile had been transferred entirely into his belly, he licked the floor clean, whereupon, like his cohorts, he sidled over in convulsant misery.

This scene, and the others before it, however, proved *not* to be the strangest that Sary would witness today.

That peculiar sub-aural semi-sound had disintegrated, such that Sary now wondered if she'd heard it at all. Impulse, then, caused her to turn her head . . .

Wilbur . . .

Indeed, her surprised gape revealed Wilbur Whateley as the one who'd earlier entered the ramshackle store. The colossally tall man stood as if in trance, mouth open, eyes aimed blankly at the raftered ceiling. Additionally, his hands were outspread, and from each palm issued a modest floret of flame crowned by a smoke-plume which seemed to possess the oddest chlorotic hue. The flame itself, in fact, was possessed of a similar tint. There was something sickish about it. But in the time it took Sary to blink—

The flames and smoke were gone.

Wilbur stood in typical fashion, his gaze addressing Sary. In moments, he'd come to her, lifted her off the table, and gently helped her back on with her gown.

"Aw, Sary, I'se so sorry. Dun't know what I was thinkin' lettin' yew come daown heer by yerself—I should'a known these low-daown scum'd pull suthin' like this . . . "

But Sary felt invigorated. "I'm fine, Wilbur—"

Towering over her, Wilbur gulped. "Did they . . . "

Sary shook her head with a smile. "Nope. Yew come just in time. Oh, and your friend over theer come in with me." She scratched her head. "Seemed almost like he knowed them crummy men wouldn't git theer way . . . Mebbe he *is* a fortune teller."

"Yew mean Kyler?"

"Yeah, he's right th—" but when Sary turned to where the bald man had been knocked down, he was no longer present in the edifice.

She rebuttoned the gown, her mind abounded in perplexity. The three miscreants remained curled on the floor, moaning, twitching, their trousers down. Tobias actually sucked his thumb through his flinches. Sary struggled to refocus on details but found that an overmuch effort was required; her memory took on a haziness that matched her previous faltering vision. *Did I really see what I THINK I saw?*

Wilbur stiffened when Sary innocuously took his hand. Her eyes narrowed in a deep solicitude. "Wilbur, what the heck juss happened? I could'a sweared I saw . . . " but did she, did she *really?*

Had she *really* seen Lang willingly swallow Wheeler's urine?

Had she *really* seen Tobias consume the spit-can's contents, and Henry Wheeler eat his own feces? And . . .

Did Wilbur really have FIRE comin' aout his hands?

Wilbur's wedge-like face took on an aspect of desperate mediation. Did his hand tremble slightly in Sary's grasp? "All I done is make them ugly fellas think things they'd otherwise not think."

"Huh?"

"It be hard to 'splain. Ever heer'a *mesmerism?*"

"Wal, no—"

"Haow 'baout hypnosis?"

Sary shook her head. The words meant nothing to her. "Was it—was it . . . some kind'a *magic* yew was makin'?"

Wilbur's evident nervousness loosened a bit. "Naw, nuthin' like that really, though I can understant why some'd think as sech. Tain't nothin' really but science if ye look hard, jest a way of *distractin'* a man so's ta make him do whut he dun't wanna. I only make him *think* he wanna."

Science? *Distraction?* Sary wondered. She'd had no proper learning and knew she possessed little in the way of intelligence, but she was aware of what *those* words meant. *So he made Henry Wheeler THINK he wanna eat his own shit?*

"It be best ye juss not think 'baout it," Wilbur said with a different emphasis, and the emphasis told her this: that somehow, through some means Sary could not cogitate, Wilbur had indeed induced those appalling Dunwichers to debase themselves exactly as she'd seen.

The sudden realization brought upon Sary such a potent sensation of delight that she nearly giggled aloud . . .

"Let's git aout'a here afore someone come in," Wilbur suggested. "The state patrol been comin' through Dunwich lately too."

This latter component of Wilbur's information was one that Sary was depressingly aware of. The state patrol had indeed commenced to infrequent patrols of Dunwich since a rash of disappearances had been reported among several of the more remote country-branch families. Sary doubted the efficacy of such patrols but saw them more as an excuse for the officers to travel off their regular beats and, in a number of cases, threaten to arrest her for vagrancy violations unless she could find in herself a willingness to offer them various sexual gratuities . . .

"Yeah," she agreed. "Let's go."

Wilbur led her out into the now deepening dusk, but before heading for the road back—

"Wait a sec," he remarked as if something forgotten

had just alighted itself. "Whar's that rock candy you come fer?"

Sary bristled. "Them poop-heads in there didn't even give me chance ta buy some 'fore they started messin' with me."

Wilbur went back into the store only to return just as speedily, bearing a five-pound sack of rock candy.

(VIII)

WAS GOOD I *got that notion to go to Osborn's cuz just as I thought, them loafers in there were puttin a hard turn to Sary, looking to fuck her against her will and whatever else come inta their dirty heads. But afore they cud have there way, I did one of the Fire Ensorcellments I learned while saying the newest Pnakotic stanzas that corresponted with paragraf 1106 on Al Azif like my grandsire taut me to do. It work better than ever, which tells me I'm getting the right intonations. Did me good to see them men get whats comin to them. Got all distrakted, though, cuz after she get ma's black gown back on, Sary take hold my hand. Was reel nice and made me feel like I never had, had trouble keepin my mind straight. Anyway, she ast me if it be Magick I pulled on them men but I just kinda moseed around the topic. Don't know how shed feel if I told her the whole thing. As for them loafers, I kinda laugh to myself. Theyll be sick for a few days, but I don't calclate theyll bother Sary no more.*

We walk home, and Sary ask me about the disappearances cuz she overheard what them men say, implyin it was me. I didnt lie now, I just tell her I didn't take the Farr girls or Lows boy or that shitty Bishop girl. "Never laid a hand on em," I tell Sary, and that be true cos it were what I called out the air that took em, not me. Guess it was a little lie but what cud I say? She agree anyway that none of em were any good. The Farr sisters were theeves of the first water, as Grandfather yewst to say, and the Low boy and Kely Bishop talk bad and lie bout folks right through there face, me inclooded. I never call the Old Ones on decent folks, but of corse theres not many good folks round here anyway. "Folk like that be best in the bellies of Yog-Sothoths minions," Grandsire say so many times. "En't fit to pick the corn out a my shit."

Was gettin dark by time we get bak to the tool-house, then Sary and me eat a bunch of rock candy, and I cuold tell she like it a lot. She thank me again for my mother's gown and for helpin her gainst them skell at Obsorns and also the Hutchins boy, and for feedin her and what not, but then I got feeling low when she say to me, "Wal, Wilbur, I guess I better be goin now. I takin up enough of yer time and generosity," so I get all flustered and tell her, "Aint no call to leeve, less acourse ya wanna." She tell me she didnt wanna but was afraid she be incunviencing me, which I assure her she wasnt. "I'd reely like for you to stay," I said but felt funny saying it cuz why wud a beautiful girl like Sary want to stay with me? But she come over and take my hand again, which make me all swoony, and she smiled a sec but then looked down, and say like theres something not right in her heart, "Wilbur, I gotta be honest, and I spect you know already but I don't got no larnin or work skills so . . . well, I gotta sell myself to men for money. Believe me, I tried, but I cant find no other way. Im kind of ashamed but there be nothin else for me." Of corse I already knew this and don't keer so I tell her back "Sary, these are bad times, not jess here but everwhere. Barely any money ta be made. Don't matter what folks do to keep clothes on there back and food in their stomach. Long as it don't hurt no one else, least don't hurt decent folk. Now, when a girl gotta sell herself for money, I don't find nothin wrong with that. My grandfather always tell me it aint good to make judgment about folks unless we walk in their shoes first." She seem releeved to hear me say this cos I could see by her face that *a big burden had been lifted from her tellin me that. Then I say more, "But you don't need to leave here now just ta make money," but I didnt feel I had right to say I didn't like her making money that way. Werent none of my business. But I tell her to wait right there a minute and I go out of the shed and run strait to the little family burying ground with the old iron fence round it. I go direct to the big old flat grave marker stone of my great great great uncle Silas Whateley. On the ash tree which grow right close, Grandsire had nailed a wood slat cut from the old Hanging Oak used to be in the town square, and on it he carved the words from the Pnakotic which make for what he call a Imperceptibility Conjuration. Now, Silas Whateley's old stone be almost as big as a coffin lid and be heavier than most men hereabouts could lift, and even if they could, Grandsire knew they'd never try on account how superstitious Dunwichers be and wouldnt dare meddle inna unconsecrated cemetery— t'would be the worst of luck—and specially since Great Uncle Silas were condemmed by what be calt a Writ of Assize and hanged for sorcery in 1749, and folks round here beleeved to the core of em that if you mess with the grave of a condemmed warlock, you be cursed feirce and all your family too. That is why Grandsire put all the Whateley gold underneeth that big flat marker stone; but he still know he couldn't take no chances. That also be why he put up the Conjuration, cos it make it so anyone who might lift the marker stone wouldnt be able to see the gold in there. First I lift the stone with no trubble since I be stronger n most, and acourse don't see nuthin save for the skeletin of Great Uncle Silas, but then I put my hankerchiff over the words on the wood slat so's to block it out and just like that—that coffin be so fulla coins and gold nuggits Great Uncle's skeletan be almost all covered with it. Also in there, in a metal box, is my own folder I been keepin for yeers, which contain all the most importint pages of the Necronomicon, the Remingius, and the Alko n Eltdown which I translate in to English so whoever come after me won't have a tussle of a time understanding. Plus I also stick in my more recint diary payges not writ in cipher, for the same reason. But anyway I grab a few pieces of gold, then put the stone back to rights and take bak my hankerchiff. Wuz going to go bak to the tool-house but stop without thinkin next to the crooked bush. Tis funny how a serious fancy can take a fella over, but see I am so fulla good feelins bout Sary that there I be again goin into the bush to beat myself off, my mind ful of what it be like to make love ta her. Cudnt stop myself, and I dang lost COUNT of how many times I done it just today, and that durn pile of my seed gettin bigger then a cow flop. But I get bak to the shed right qwik, give Sary one of the old golden coins and say, "Here be some money so you don't have no need to go do them things with men I spect ya mostly don't like. Itd be a pleasure for you to stay here long as ya want. I wont bother ya none, and ye can go off n do what you want—just be keerful—and I'll be here mostly doin my writing and gettin ready for my next trip to Miskatonic, what I think I already told you about." She stand there sort of funny, thinkin and lookin a mite odd at that coin which I guess is worth more n she make in a month of selling herself. She look like she WANT to take it but got to hezzitating, then her shoulders drop down and she tells me, "Wilbur I cant take this money, it wouldn't be right. I already took quite a bit of yor good will, and Im not good with the idea of taking money I havnt erned." "Naw, you just take it cos I don't need it and you do, and be honest I didn't earn it neether, 'twas my grandsires," and then I say she can earn it back by doin chores and such, but in trooth I'd never have her do chores, and then I said, "Sides its already dark and there mite be trouble for you ta go walkin home in the dark what with all the scoundrels about," and I got the idea to keep talkin maybe so to change the subject and get her mind offa leevin' and I go on, "By the way, just where is it you live?" She sat back down on the cot, fingering that gold piece, and she tell me to my surprise, "I don't really GOT no place to live now, not for a coupla yeers. I mainly been sleepin under the covered bridges or old basements when the weather's fine, and durin winter, theres some men who—" She stopped splaining but I know that she was gonna say some men who pay ta fuck her let her sleep with them or in their barns or houses and such. Then I just keep on talking to keep her mind distrakted and say, "So I take it yer folks don't live round here no more or maybe died like my ma and grandsire?" Kinda bit my lip sayin that, feering that maybe her folks died bad or something and mite mess about her spirits, but she just said like it was nothin how her mother who she loved a lot died a couple uv years ago. Twas Doc Houghton who said she was took by her heart seezing up. But her father still live off the old Loveman Trail past Deans Corners, in a log cabin. I remember seeing a log-built cabin just where she say, and since there wasnt others like it on the trale, I figger that must be it, but then I ask "So you don't stay there, instead a sleepin under bridges and barns and what not, where its likely to be uncomfortable?" She didn't seem at all bothered answerin, "No, I cud never stay with my pa no more on account of what he been doing to me since I was little." I got all riled deep inside heering that becuz I hear about such things all the time in theese parts, but she just go right on talkin bout it, "yeah, he aint a good man atall. Got to fuckin me when I was real little, like four I guess, and he do it a lot, but then he stop doin that once I get the blood of eve and hair tween my legs, so he make me do him with my mouth instead cos he didnt want me ta get pregnant. Said if he got me pregnant, the baby ud likely be ugly as me and anythin that ugly shudn't live. Yeah, so from then on he'd make do my mouth on his, well, you know, his dick, which he grow to like most of all. Said I did it so good hed make me do it to him four or five times a day, and if I fussed about it, hed wail the tar outa me.*

Twas him who knock all my front teeth out and he break my nose so many times it got crushed flat and wont never be normal again. Looks like a rotten tomaytuh. Broke my arm once too." She shrug her shoulders then. "Always wonder bout what make people so bad like that. Do you know, Wilbur?" I was itchin with "ire" as my grandfather used to say, from what she say her father do to her, but I try not to show it, and say, "Well, Grandsire tell me many times that some folks is BORN bad and twerent nothin in life that make em that way. 'N fact, he speculated that MOST folks are like that, and its why this world be so frightful. Said most folks are so bad and useless and dishonist and such that they aint fit to be here, that theres other things out theer, I mean like in the universe and such, that got more right ta be here than human folk, and I dare say I think he was right." She look a bit confused by what I said, but then she said back, "Yeah, I know, LOT uv bad folks in these parts, and my pa? He be the worst I ever know. Hes just all sick in his head, I think. One time I member I was about 14 and he make me suck him off but I sed I didnt wanna, so he slap me silly till I cant see straight and next I know he's draggin me out in the woods where he got a big hole dug, big as a grave, it was, so then he tie me up and throwed me in the bottum of that hole and first he pee on me and then you know what he did? He start BURYING me in that hole. He start shovelin' the dirt in, yellin' bout how someone ugly as me in the face NEED to be buried just like garbage, and I'm down there cryin' and screaming and he just keep shovelin' in the dirt, fixin' to bury me alive but right when he wus just about to cover up my face, he stop and start laughin and tell me he is just jokin, but next time I say I don't want to suck his dick, he'll bury me for reel. So, well, from then on I suck him any time he say without a tiff cos it just aint worth it. Thats how evil that man be—oh, and heres sompthin else. See, when I wuz 17, my ma take me on a trip, only trip I ever been on. She take me near what she call the Big

Water to a place called Innsmouth where she got a friend of hers she know since she was a child, and we staid there a whole month, and I cant tell you how nice it twuz to be away from my pa and not gettin hit and not having to suck him. I cried when it was time to go back to the log house, and I even think of running away, but I didn't cos I know my pa wud blame my ma and beat her bad. But anyway, when we get back, pa is all outa his wits mad, and first thing he do is lock my ma in the closet, then he drag me to the table ware there's a fruiting jar a-settin, and then he tell me what he done. See, what he done was beat himself off 5 times a day each day I was in Innsmouth, and each time he cum in that jar, then skrew the lid on so his jism don't dry up. THAT's what he done, an I aint zajjerating. 5 TIMES A DAY for the WHOLE MONTH he cum in that jar! By the time ma and me get back, acorse, the jar was more n half filt with his beat off and twas a big jar too. My pa take that lid right off and make me drink it, he did, and he say if I didn't swaller every drop, hed beat my ma and me feerce so, well, I had no choyce, so I drink it, and I tell you it tasted AWFUL it did, worse than normal on account most of it was spoilt. For a whole day I was put up sick with a bellyache like you wudn't believe. And if that wasnt bad enough, last summer I think it be, I see him acrost the river pickin cattails, but I knowed he carn't swim so he couldn't come get me, but he yell over that ever sinct I run away from his house, he been savin up all his beat off in jars and one day he'd snatch me and take me back there and make me drink it all and then kill me. Jeez. I thought about that a long time, him makin me do that back then and wantin ta make me do it more, and it just make me hate him so much, but werse was how I got to wonderin about the difference tween bein bad and bein just plane EVIL, cos I knowed full well then that only someone pure EVIL could do somethin like that." She shake her head.

I was boiling up with angur when she got done sayin

these things, but what I felt worse than angur was a deep down sadness like I never know before, not just from WHAT she said but HOW she said it, like it didnt bother her at all, which I can only figure is cuz shes just so durn used to being treated awful by her father and other folks that she think being treated awful be just another part of reguler life.

But it AINT just another part of reguler life!

So I decide rite then n there that for all Im worth I gonna prove to her that theers better things in livin than bein treated shitty by folks and being beat and hurt and what not. No sir. What else could she do, bein' a young girl and all? Wasn't nothing SHE could do bout it.

But there sure as SHIT be sumpthin I can do about it.

Im still sitting here at the big desk with the oil lamp turned low, as I'm writin watchin her sleep with the moonlite on her face from the high little window. Every time I look at her, she just seem more beautiful then before, and—

Had ta stop with my pen for a sec cos while I was watchin her, she start to turn an toss a bit on the cot and git ta moanin more then a tad. First I thought it must be a bad dream she be having, but then I notice shes kinda smiling and then she gets to rubbin her hands up and down her bodie through my ma's old black dress, and she moan some more louder, then she starts rubbin her bosom with one hand and rubbin her privit place with the other, but I can see she still be asleep. One of her tits fall out the toppa the dress and then she gets to playin with it, and I see the nipple on it grow biggur right before my eyes. So it become pretty clear to me it aint no bad dream she s havin, it's a good one. Wish I cud believe it was me she was dreemin about but, well, itd be plumb stoopid to think sech a thing.

Now shes rockin' back and forth on the cot and really gettin worked up, so mutch that I wudn't be surprised if she wake herself rite up. I will stop writing now, turn the lamp down some more, and watch, an if she wake up I'll act like I fall asleep in my chair.

IT **WAS A** rich mixture of feelings with which Sary awakened so abruptly in the middle of the night, and still more such feelings had dominated her cerebrations before she recalled falling asleep. *Them men at Osborn's,* the memory suffused, and then with it the inexplicable delight that she bubbled with upon knowing that her assailants had been forced, by an operandi she failed to understand, to consume horrific substances. She also remained aware of the unusual peaceablility from that point on, since walking back to the tool-house with Wilbur and sharing the rock candy with him. They'd conversed for some time after that, which had pacified her further, but she'd felt slightly uncomfortable when he'd given her the gold piece. Soon, though, Sary's eyelids drooped; she took Wilbur's suggestion to heart and agreed to stay with him, at least for the night. As awkward as the lengthened cot appeared, she found it comfortable to a luxurious degree; sleep whelmed her in only moments.

She recalled her melange of dreams, then—dreams whose tranquil essentia seemed so inconsonant to her: somnolent images of vast, beauteous pastures whose verdancies filled her spirit with an immeasurable delight; of resplendent and celestial dawns; of grand forests unspoilt by the encroachment of man and his ax for time immemorial, and of the silence of such forests, which could only be described as deific. Moreover, partnered with all this was an all-pervading sense of inner-equitableness the likes of which her heart had never experienced.

What she could not grasp, of course, was the seeming instantaneous *reversal* of the dream's overall mien . . .

Those beauteous visions of pasture, sky, and wood—quite verily—transposed themselves into a shocking and inscrutable opposite: Osborn's General Store and the trio of nefarious debauchers who'd accosted Sary only hours ago; and it was with her dreaming mind's eye that she gazed at the appalling event. However, as the scene replayed, she found a thoroughly different perspective presented to her: not witnessing the assault as a victim but, this time, as an omnipresent spectator; likewise, it was not via her objective *vision* with which she made her observations but via what one might think of as some manner of hideous *camera dementata* . . .

Sary saw the perpetrators—and their respective acts of self-degradation—from various flexures and multiple ranges of proximity. One after another, each of them cranked opened their mouth to unwillingly consume the material of their punition. If anything, this ocular recrudescence seemed to take place in a most unnatural *slowness.* Initially, Sary's component of dream-awareness recoiled at the repugnance of this perspective, as would anyone's, yet . . .

She continued to watch with an undeniable *acceleration* of attentiveness. And what she saw next struck her even more inexplicably:

She saw *herself,* escorted by Wilbur Whateley, leave the derelict general store.

Yet the dream's visuality remained, which enabled her to continue watching, and what she watched would be deemed, by any general canon, as unwatchable.

For a time, the three men had lain shuddering once their stomachs had been filled with unmentionable effluences, and Sary had assumed that the self-inflicted atrocities were at an end.

She was incorrect, however, in this assumption.

It was the age- and wretchedness-wizened Tobias who

first came to his feet, doing so in a straining, wincing protestation, as if being puppeteered by a force of will more malignant even than his own; and in jerking motions, he picked up the spit-can and began to vomit into it. While this rather noisily ensued, under similar locomotions, Luke Lang and Henry Wheeler each staggered behind the old wood counter, rummaged falteringly amongst the aisles of shelving, and then returned, Lang bearing a half-gallon glass bottle and Wheeler holding a large bowl. Lang at once girdled the bottle's opening with his lips and began to vomit Wheeler's urine (along with other digestive debris). Into the bowl, of course, Wheeler regurgitated his feces.

Even in the dream-conscience, Sary found no need to ponder over what might next take place . . .

Tobias passed the spit-can to Lang, Lang passed the urine bottle to Wheeler, and Wheeler passed his heaping bowl to Tobias Whateley, and they all began to consume the contents of these receptacles. Then the process of regurgitation/consumption was repeated until each man had had the opportunity to sample *all* the offerings of the day.

Sary started awake as if a scream had issued directly into her ear, and with parallel rapidity the dream's constituents appeared in her wakened awareness.

If one could gasp *mentally,* Sary did so, and it was a gasp of fitful wantonness. Her body churned on the mattress, buttocks clenching, toes flexing, sex palpitating. Her fingers were twisting a delicious ache into a gorged nipple, while her other hand seemed determined to admit itself entirely into her womanhood's tender threshold. Her sexual fluids ran rampant; her abdomen sucked in and out as her back stressed like an archer's bow pulled to maximum arciform. In her mind, she knew she was awake, yet that simple acknowledgment is all she seemed able to command. What remained was only a fervent—no—an *inexorable* sexual ravenousness, a yearning for orgasm comparable to the hunger of a donjon convict left unfed for a fortnight. The capability of coherent thought was impossible, overtaken as she was with this raw and primitivistic need to be *penetrated,* to be *cored,* to be drubbed by *immediate* and *interminable* intercourse. In fact, if any analytical thoughts did indeed exist in her head, they were merely recollective images of her dream . . .

Not the glorious pastures and atavistic sunrises, but her three antagonists cabalistically forced to consume various bodily waste.

She felt aflame, bolting up in the cot. She could hear the thuds of her heart as her hand bedeviled her sex and her breasts buzzed.

Her eyes snapped wide.

Aw, my GAWD . . .

The logical queries that such a predicament might bid never arrived, queries that considered her sudden, unquenchable, and very uncharacteristic lust, or, in her own backland dialect, *Haow can dreamin' baout men etting shit'n drinking pee'n spit make me so dag blasted horny?* It was a pertinent question, and had Sary been a schooled alienist of, say, the Freudian Doctrine, she might devise that such an excitement came as the result of multiple retrograde symptoms of erotic-reversal revenge totems.

But, lo, Sary was not a schooled alienist.

At any rate, the recollection of nauseating imagery blotted out all else in her mind, leaving only the verisimilitude of sexual appetency and the unheeding drive to slake it.

In labored breaths, she scanned the shed's interior. Only a sliver of light leaked from the oil lamp on the desk, and in this inappreciable illumination, her eyes deciphered the lanky, awkward form of Wilbur, slumped asleep in his chair.

Sary rose as if instigated by Vodou. She walked dizzily to where Wilbur slumbered; then, with no abashment whatever, she skimmed the diaphanous gown over her head and straddled Wilbur bare-groined in the chair. Whether he came awake instantly or not, she had no idea; her focus, instead, had her hands frantic at the man's belt. Several eye-blinks later, his belt was untied, his trousers were opened, and Sary was grunting in an absolutely adamantine effort to haul his trousers down. Wilbur did indeed come awake at this point, and in such a manner as could be likened to outright alarm.

"Suh-Sary! What it be yew're doin', gull?" he exclaimed, and then his hands came to her bare waist to intercept her efforts.

The words of her reply seemed hewn by the heat of her angst. "Wilbur, I carn't 'splain it at all, but I feel jess plumb *out'a my mind* with a hanker ta fuck yew! Got ta thinkin' 'baout all ya done fer me, and 'specially makin' them men do them things at the store and—*jiminee!*—it's got me hornier than a mare in heat!" and with this declaration, she was able to jack Wilbur's pants down several inches.

Wilbur hitched them back up. "Aw, no, Sary . . . "

"Wilbur, please! I dun't know what come over me, but I jess, I juss, I juss GOTTA have yew in me!"

"But-but," and then his large hands finally snapped to her wrists and arrested all movement of her hands. "Thar's suthin' ye dun't understand! See, I'se *different,* is what I'm a-sayin'!"

"*Different?*" she wailed.

"Different from fellas hereabouts!" He broke into an ungovernable stammer. "Different, I mean, duh-duh-duh . . . *daown thar* . . . " and then he tremulously gestured his groin.

Utter bafflement contorted Sary's face in the barely visible lamp-light. "Ya mean . . . yew're *dick?*"

Wilbur froze with the question. "Wal . . . ee-yuh—"

Sary's tautened wits and sexual delirium had no time for this; her hands shot back to his trouser rivet. Yet his hesitance made fuel for thought: the presumption that he was merely bashful was the first possibility to come to mind (though why should a man as large, physically intimidating, and fearless be bashful?); she also considered that perhaps his genital endowment was less than substantial, an instance which was known to infuse in men no small quantum of insecurity. Either way, though, Sary cared not in the least. She was insatiable—she would have her way, and she would see to it that he did not bemoan the result. "Dun't yew worry abaout nuthin'," shot her scorched-whisper response. "Jess yew *relax* naow an' let me do this!"

At long last, Wilbur resigned to her insistences, but not before turning the lamp all the way down. This Sary took to indicate an embarrassment on his part—again, the Small-Genitals Possibility seemed most probable. Or did he possess some genital *deformity* that he expressly wished her *not* to see? The potential amused her. In the time of her professional calling—and the benefit of knowledge *a posteriori,* one could say—she'd witnessed bifurcated coronae, dual urethras, a trine of testicles, penile shafts bent akin to horseshoes, endomorphic foreskins, and even less cogitable aspects of malconformation. As far as penises were concerned: *I've seen 'em all . . .*

No, she cared not of Wilbur's unaccountable reservations—*I'm a whore,* she didn't have to remind herself, *and it's a whore's job to make fellas feel good . . .* Sary determined to do exactly that, but not before making herself feel good as well.

In plenary darkness, she re-opened Wilbur's pants. She was vaguely aware of herself actually *panting* in anticipation of intercourse. Was she drooling as well? Wilbur, however, sat trembling to the bone, as of a puppy ashiver in bitter cold.

His pants were now opened and lowered just enough to grant Sary sufficient access. She could investigate nothing with her eyes but, indeed, her *hands* could investigate, couldn't they?

And investigate they did.

What her fingers reached down and encompassed seemed, forthwith, unrepresentative of the penises she'd experienced, and as for her previous surmise—that Wilbur might be poorly bestowed—this idea no longer held water. It was a bowed, ax-haft-wide appendage that her grasp had found, which felt tacky and queerly cool. At once, she thought of a fresh plucked goose neck. She ringed her thumb and forefinger, then felt upward to the appendage's terminus. No aggregation of foreskin was discovered, nor was there anything semblant of a glans. It was turgid, yes, as of an erection, yet . . . did erections lack any manner of a fleshy domed crown? A licked pinky tip, next, examined the more or less stump-like conclusion of the organ, seeking to identify the urethral exit, but . . .

Thar en't no pee-hole at the end'a his dick!

No. No evidence of any such seminal and urinary aperture.

Nevertheless, and her mystification notwithstanding, with one hand, she proceeded to stroke the fleshy but strangely cool shaft, while her other hand delved lower to cosset his testicles—

No testicles, nor any manner of what might be thought of as a scrotum, could be identified at the shaft's basal root.

Wilbur, she grimly realized, *en't got no nuts . . .*

Instinct impelled her to display no reaction, which came easier, at least, given the stark hardiness of her erotomancy. Unusual or not, Wilbur's genital potential was about to be tested to every limit of thoroughness that Sary could muster. She meant to mount him now by raising the apex of her thighs high enough to license coitus, and in preparing to do exactly that, she opened her hands on his chest to push upward—

As if shocked, she flinched, then froze. Her eyes popped wide in the darkness.

When her opened palms had pressed against his shirt, she felt anything but what she'd expected: the rapid squirming of a mass of . . . *things* . . . beneath the shirt fabric.

Things? *What* things?

What things could there be that *squirmed* beneath a man's *shirt?* She'd only expected to feel the toned chest muscles of any hard-laboring man and the indentations of ribs. Instead, Sary had felt something like an aggregation of thin snakes shifting under the fabric. And just as she had flinched, so had Wilbur, as if reacting to the fact of her discovery . . .

Her lips moved to voice query, but before she could utter as much—

Whoa!

—she flinched once more. One of her hands had lowered most errantly to the inside of his middle-thigh. Here again she felt something quite at odds with what she *should've* felt: something, too, like a snake, only, in this case, an individual snake much wider than the mass of far more slender things that seemed to wiggle en masse. Might it be a stout rope running down the inside of his pant leg? But that was nonsensical! Why would Wilbur place such a thing there? For a moment, she entertained a notion equally ridiculous—that it was not a rope running down his leg at all, but a tail.

But only animals had tails, not men.

Even in the dark, she sensed his alarm. "Wilbur," she began, "what's that yew got under—"

"Shhh," he whispered, and immediately engaged in a distraction potent enough even to quell her questions over such a seeming abnormality. The distraction was simply this:

His middle finger had gently slipped into her vagina, and its entrance brought with it the precursory penetration that she so craved. Gently, yes, but *deeply* as well, for Wilbur's middle finger—she'd noticed shortly after meeting him—extended quite a bit longer than the middle fingers of most men. However, the *extent* of the penetration was not all that bid that initial overwhelming gust of ecstasy; it was also the tactic which was perpetrated. Wilbur deftly churned the finger amid the slippery channel in a configuration similar to a teepee, and this action only aggrandized her pleasures.

Gone, then, was all concern over any physiological incongruities that seemed to present themselves beneath his shirt and down his pant leg.

The most exotic sensations began to spiral upward from the seat of her womanhood to her breasts and then to her brain. *More,* the thought beat like the very spasms of her groin. *More,* and with this, she raised her pelvis high, grabbed his erection, nudged its tip into her vulva, and—

Ahhhhhhhhhhhhh . . .

—sat right down on it.

Where Wilbur's finger had catalyzed her to near-frenzy, she now felt skewered and then summarily ushered into libidinal madness, for his genital shaft was double his finger's length. She quivered in place, her nerves thrumming. She could not think in any level of cohesion but could only follow her craven instincts, instincts which demanded she be *plungered* by him. *I need him ta work my pussy like a dang well-pump!* the crude thought swept her.

The workings of the "well-pump," however, would be short-lived.

Wilbur's hips drew back once, then thrust forward, and just when she expected a session of hard, fast, and very deep penetration to commence—

"Aw, aw, Sary!" came the warbled gasp. Wilbur's body went slack beneath her as though he'd collapsed to exhaustion. "I swar, I en't never felt nuthin' so sure-fire *good* in all my life . . . "

Sary's mouth fell open, and she could've raged. *Fer pity's sake! I been with men who come fast, but never THAT fast!* Indeed, the event she'd yearned so torridly for had ended in less time than it took to begin. A stroke and one-half, perhaps, of his penis in and out of her, and Wilbur had climaxed. She couldn't very well berate him—it was his hospitality that had admitted her here—but still . . .

Of all the dag-blasted bum luck! What could be more mussed up! She'd been led up to a pinnacle and then thrown right off into a mire of crushing disappointment. With Wilbur's failure to engage in coitus for more than a second or two, Sary felt positively stolen from.

Her shoulders slumped at once. *Oh well . . .*

His big hands pressed against her bare hips, urging her off of his lap. "Dang, Sary," he said almost breathless, "that thar be the dandiest."

Sary stood up, tongue-tied for a response. All she could summon was, "Wal, that's good," after which followed the most awkward pause. She felt silly now, standing there naked and not knowing what to do.

This awkwardness, though, ensued for a very short duration. Sary's curiosity had no choice but to bolster with the fact of a very, very incontrovertible observation. She was now standing up; hence, her groin was no longer coupled to Wilbur's.

She asked herself very slowly, *If I'm over heer, and Wilbur's over thar . . . haow come my pussy feels like it still got a great big dick in it?*

This was quite a momentous question, to say the least.

She could still hear his heavy breathing in the almost nonexistent light, and she knew she was standing several feet away from him now. Could she be mistaken? It didn't seem possible, yet her conception of logic left her at a loss to do anything but make certain. She stooped, navigated her hand to where her sense of proximity told Wilbur to be sitting and, moreover, to where she believed his crotch was—

There.

There was his thigh, the heavy denim that it was clothed in more than apparent. Her hand slid higher then. Had he already refastened his trousers?

No! Her fingers felt the opened fly.

Then she reached in to feel the evidence of his penis, but—

All her hand came away with was a length of some wet and very sheer film-like substance which, after a lingering inspection with her fingers, she could liken only to a foot-long sausage skin.

An *empty* foot-long sausage skin.

She stood in more bewilderment, blinking in the dark. *What in gad-zooks happened ta his DICK!?* Indeed, her hand should now be holding a limp penis, but what it held instead was something she could only ponder of as a limp sleeve—in other words, a sleeve with no arm in it.

And if the "arm" was not in the "sleeve," she made the only deduction she could via the evidence of what she felt between her legs.

Yes, the "arm" was now in her vaginal barrel . . .

There was no denying the sensation: something long and over an inch thick continued to occupy her vaginal canal, as if she'd been masturbating with, say, a peeled banana yet had inadvertently left the banana in her when the task was done.

Wilbur turned the lamp up slightly and then appeared as a looming shadow coming to her. His voice resonated in that strange way of his. "Dang, Sary. I know it's more than a fair parcel'a questions ye got. I'll try to my best ta answer 'em," but then, in an abruptness that was at the same time gentle, he picked her up, cradled her in his long arms, and began to step forward, the floorboards creaking.

"But-but whar it be yew're takin' me?"

"Jess the cot, so's ye can have a lie daown. Yew be abaout ta larn one'a the ways I'se different from the other men ye've took up with."

Different? she wanted to protest. *Yew're dang DICK disappeared!*

Something in Wilbur's deportment, however, suggested that *he* knew that *she* knew this, but that she was minding her tongue. The divergences she'd been made apprised of indeed obliterated all possibilities of fancy or suggestion.

Her colossal host set her down nude on the cot. "But fer naow, ye're better to jess lay thar. Won't take more'n a speck of time afore ye get yers."

More, more confusion drew lines in Sary's face. "Git my . . . what?"

"Wal, 'twon't be long 'fore yew yerself'll be comin' . . . "

Comin'? she wondered. The intercourse was over, that was certain. Did his odd words mean for her to masturbate? Or did—

All ponderment ceased. At once, Sary became intensely aware of sensations beginning to bloom deep in her sex. Although something else remained deep in her sex as well, didn't it? The mysterious *matter* that continued to fill the moist passage as though it were a disconnected erection. And then—

Every nerve in Sary's body began to *hum,* for lack of any other way in which to describe it, and soon she was writhing powerlessly atop the mattress. *Aw, my—aw, my— aw my Gaaaaaaaaaaaaaawd . . .*

She didn't notice that Wilbur had loped back to his desk, so entrenched she was with this saturation of lewd sensations tremoring out from her sex to her breasts and then slowly and droolingly spreading about to encapsulate every square inch of her skin. Her sex thumped to the rhythm of her heart, and her breasts thumped similarly. No manner of will could be instigated, only the subconscious commands of her pining sexual instinct. Whatever Wilbur's climax had left burrowed in her vagina, it was reacting in some earthy yet anagogic mystical fashion, piloting her without the benefit of copulation to heights of pleasure thus far unknown, and entreating of her intricacy of nerves every iota of ecstatic potentiality. In moments, Sary's quaking spasms girdled the entirety of her body, every muscle clenching in a most concentrated sexual reactivity; and that is when she transcended the primal threshold of orgasm.

But a characteristic orgasm this was not. Instead, the experience first seemed to unroll and then gushingly *explode*. She could've been an erection herself, spasming, spasming, spasming in plush, opiate bliss; she could've been a minuscule bundle of nerves being sucked akin to a gumdrop in a hot, voracious mouth. Indeed, her vagina itself felt as though it were being expertly *sucked* in order to exploit every carnal nerve, while something equally as immaterial seemed to suck out her nipples and lave her skin with the same expertise. Her naked form churned on the bed, helplessly, convulsantly, as she continued to come and come and come, her climax seeming first a distillation of all possible human pleasure and then an *inundation* of her sexual being. These spasms of flesh-euphoria did not abate after a quibble of seconds as did most orgasms. They did so instead for half an hour.

Upon the experience's fruition, Sary lay in near paralysis: drenched in sweat, eyes rolled back, tongue lolling from an agape mouth. When the most remote traces of cognizance leaked back into her consciousness, she detected very easily that the previous feeling of *stuffed-to-fulness* was no longer present in her vagina. She dopily slipped a hand there for verification, inserted a finger, and found the feminine cavity very wet, very tender, and very absent of obstruction. Her uneducated thoughts then detailed to herself: *I en't never come like that in my whole life!* though what she'd actually undergone was an orgasm precipitated by a para-human constituent. All that her physical investigation divulged of the indicia was a vast region of wetness saturating the sheets between her thighs. She presumed at first that this must be the result of her own womanly fluids escaping during her bliss, but—

There seemed an *awful lot* of such fluids.

She lay like putty amid the sheets and, with some exertion, turned her head toward Wilbur, who sat now at his writing desk, looking on with contentment in his dark eyes and strange visage.

Her lips worked to generate speech, but the initial attempts failed, leaving her able to only mumble a slew of "blub-blub-blub" noises. The monumental orgasm's remnants had her feeling as though she'd been dipped head to toe into warm vessels full of luscious, alien tinctures whose very contact with human flesh triggered pleasures as potent as they were unearthly. In time, though, she regained more semblance of composure and was able to chunter: "Holy *jiminee,* Wilbur. Didn't think it were even *possible* ta come like that."

Wilbur's large head nodded in the shadow-diced lamplight. "I knowed yew'd like it, and am glad ye did. Way it 'twas 'splained ta me by my grandsire's that gulls come a mite fierce, and fer longer, on account'a me bein' different from fellas hereabouts."

Fellas hereabouts . . . the words repeated in her head like stones dropped into hot tar. He'd used that term a number of times, hadn't he? *Yew're different, all right, and I dun't keer none long as yew put a fuckin' like that ta me more'n onct.*

"And I can tell—like I told ye before—yew got yerself a right pile'a questions 'baout *haow* I'm different, but all's I can best suggest is ye jest leave it be. It en't nuthin' but a bunch's stuff ye likely wouldn't understand anyway."

Sary smiled then, like a sated feline, when she recalled the extent of the pleasures he'd treated her to. "Wilbur, I wun't ask yew *nuthin'* 'baout *nuthin'* 'cos yew gotta sumpin' abaout yew that cud have every woman this side'a Miskatonic River chasin' you like mutts chasin' a meat wagon."

The giant man seemed to fall into a muse just then, as if in some mode of personal rapture. Then he said, "It been a long day had by ye, so yew jess go on ta sleep naow. I'll relax back in my writin' char and ketch me some shut-eye here."

Her response was immediate. "If'n yew sleep in that clunky ole cheer, Wilbur

Whateley, I will likely shriek so's ta wake up all the dead aout'a the old buryin' graound, I will."

Wilbur's long, high brow went deep with furrows. "Why . . . what'cha mean, Sary?"

"Yes sir, I will haowl at the blammed moon . . . if'n yew dun't come over heer right naow and sleep with me!" and then Sary slid back to afford more room on the cot and reached her arms out toward Wilbur.

Wilbur rose forthwith and appeased her supplication.

(X)

WITHOUT CONSTRAINT, however, Sary felt inclined to question Wilbur's obvious intention of coming to bed still donned in all of his clothing, yet an intuition—one formulated in previous observation—at once commanded her to make no such query. Wilbur had already demonstrated some preoccupation anent to his physical aspect, so Sary considered, *Why ask him sumpthin' that he dun't wanna speak of?* No, she mustn't needle him, for fear of imparting a displeasure in his attitude as far as her presence was concerned. She conjectured, instead, that if it were Wilbur's wish to sleep with his clothes on, it was his right as well. But when his awkward frame lowered beside her upon the great cot, he gave voice to several points almost as if he were possessed of a qualification to decrypt her own very concerns while they remained solely with the confines of her mind.

Wilbur, sounding drowsy now, said, "Aw, I know theer be lots 'baout me that's got a buzz in ye're bonnet—as my grandsire used to say—and I 'spect that afore, when we was jess gettin' started, ye might'a felt suthin' beneath my shirt and daown one'a my pant legs that struck ye as mighty awry, but it be jess like I been sayin' . . . that not everyone be 'zactly like all folk hereabaouts and what'cha be used to. I'se different, is all, so I don't see that it matters more'n a tittle."

"Oh, it dun't, Wilbur," she was quick in her assurance. "I guess I be a bit nosy sumptimes; 'tis my nature, I guess, 'least my ma used ta say so. So's I'll dew my best not ta rankle ya with silly questions that'd pester ya."

"Aw, naow, dang, Sary," his deep vibrating voice grew lower. "Thar en't nuthin' ye could do ta pester me . . . ," but soon it became apparent to her that the day had stricken Wilbur with a formidable budget of fatigue. *I best juss let him sleep,* her better judgment suggested—though the deferment to her better judgment was quite often not her forte. In fact, even just moments after her monumental orgasm, Sary admitted that another such experience was most notably the object of her desires, and disappointment was not in wait of her.

Again, she was unable to repel this lusty perseverance, and no sooner than Wilbur had begun to snore, she slithered atop him, commenced to abrading her groin to his and to titillate him with her hands in a most urgent manner. However far removed his penis might be from that of other men, Sary did not now care. She creviced one hand beneath her bare belly in order to re-arouse him, but even upon the instant, a foot-long cylinder of turgidity was effortlessly discerned at his crotch. Her breath felt hot as fish broth, and she whined, "Wilbur, I dun't mean ta disturb yew but—"

The behemothic man did not need to be coaxed further; in fact, he seemed just as fidgety for intercourse as she. His huge hands slipped downward, unfastened his trousers, and extracted the sought-after member . . .

Their previous coupling was reprised posthaste and ensued correspondingly. Panting, short of breath, and nearly teary-eyed in anticipation, Sary straddled Wilbur and again impaled herself upon the bizarre, rootlike shaft; and after two or three pelvic strokes, her bedmate was seized by ecstatic convulsions. After several moments came a gasp on his part as his climactic tensions all ran out of him. But now Sary's curiosity thrummed as intently as her craving for more release. That deep fullness was indeed present again in the channel of her sex . . .

Even after she unstraddled him and left no doubt that genital congress had been cessated.

Wilbur's voice croaked, "Aw, honey, that thar was sooooo good . . . " A moment later, he was asleep.

Sary promptly lay back on her side of the cot. First, she let her hand inspect the area just within Wilbur's opened trousers, and unequivocally, her surprising observation of before was repeated. The erection, like a long, raw, and oddly cool pork loin, could no longer be found anywhere amid the man's groinal region; instead, only a sheer film-like length of . . . something . . . had seemed to replace it. Again, Sary's "empty sausage skin" simile came to mind. Ludicrously, she wondered even if Wilbur's erection had *separated* itself from his body upon climax, to remain sheathed in her sex, only to *re-grow* for a future copulative opportunity. But this supposition was too outre to take with any sober regard. Hence, a logical conclusion to the conundrum remained to be speculated, and the question had no choice but to coruscate: *What*, in the name of all notions analogous to Sary's conception of normality, could explain the undeniable material breadth that now existed in her vagina?

Next, she felt about her own private region, admitted a finger, and—

What's IN thar?

For something surely was, and the object seemed to parallel quite closely the dimensions of Wilbur's erection. In fact, the substance's morphology indicated that, with the proper level of adroitness, she might even be able to extract it.

Sary finessed her fingers in a way that such an extraction might be made—

But that is when time ran out.

She was at once stolen away on the rushing tide of another sexual culmination. Her body clenched and quaked, her sex seeming to open and close akin to the mouth of a fish out of water. So *infused* she felt with such impossible sensations, it seemed as though some capacity of her brain had entered into arcane collusion with her sex to unloose the most dense, heady, and intoxicating spasms of uninterrupted carnal delight. She churned mindless atop the cot, grinning lewdly, licking her lips, and molesting her breasts, and even shrieking and giggling aloud as she drooled through one bacchanalic fusillade of bliss after another. The experience throbbed on for no less than thirty minutes' time.

How long afterward she lay stupefied, immobile, and incapable of thought could not be estimated. Even after the orgasmic avalanche, she twitched there on the cot in some raw-flesh *denouement* of pulsing nerve-reactivity. More unconscious than sentient this time, her hand feebled to her exploited sexual portal to verify what she already presumed: the "fullness" within had changed to flux, leaving another great splotch of sopping moisture in the sheets. Whatever the object had been, it almost seemed as though the rigors of her orgasm had caused it to liquesce during the relentless contractions.

And Sary felt liquesced herself; the experience had left her like some *thing* that had melted to semi-solidity. It was long before she could move, so all-consuming that second orgasm had been—if anything, double the potency of the first. *I gotta have this, like, ALL THE TIME,* her mind squeezed out the greedy thought. Through one of the little windows, the moon glowed, admitting a bandeau of ghostly light. The black patch of her pubic hair shimmered tinsel-like, while the cream-white skin of her belly appeared burnished with oil. Wilbur snored quite resonantly beside her.

Later, Sary found she could move and even teeteringly rise from the cot. She warned herself to be cautious so not to waken Wilbur even before she acknowledged to herself what it was she meant to do. *The lantern,* she thought, and she'd manoeuvered herself off the cot with the utmost gingerness. Her bare feet touched the wood floor, then in a calculated slowness, she padded to the looming desk where the oil lamp remained, turned so low as to emit nearly nothing in the way of illumination. The moon's gossamer radiance alone would not suffice; Sary, ever-so-incrementally, eased the wick up until there existed enough luminescence to make a more detailed scrutiny yet not so much as to breach Wilbur's slumber . . .

She crept back to the cot, Wilbur's side this time.

It was not the expected empty "sausage skin" that awaited Sary's next delve of hand, but instead . . .

Another erection.

I juss dun't get what's goin' on . . .

It was indubitable: Wilbur was different, all right, and given the utter numerousness of patrons Sary's profession had convoked, she was unable to deny his unique genital exclusivity. *What a WEIRD dick it be he's got on him,* her muse put it another way. The organ seemed to vanish after climax and then undergo a momentaneous rematerialization. Like her sausage skin notion, another absurd metaphor occurred to her: a stocking'd foot and then suddenly the foot no longer occupied it . . . but then a short time later, a *new* foot appeared within. What could explain this?

Closer attention seemed in order.

Sary had been informed, on a myriad of occasions, that one act she possessed an efficacious proclivity for was the act of fellatio; and it was this act, then, that she began to perform upon Wilbur. But so not to wake him, she implemented great care in not jostling him in any way and not touching him other than with her mouth; and a slow and very dainty process it was. Back and forth her head went, sliding her wet, skilled lips up and down over the queer foot-long shaft; this adroit action did not persist for long, however, before—

Sary lurched backward in an amount of time far less than it would take for her brain to register alarm and dismay. It seemed as though Wilbur's formidable erection had somehow come *detached* and then *launched* itself into Sary's mouth with more than a little force. Her eyes crossed in the shock of it, yet she remained at least subconsciously apprehensive of the need *not* to awaken her mysterious host; somehow, she managed to avoid clunking to the floor from the force of the genitally derived *thing* now jammed in her mouth. As well, she governed herself enough not to gag, as much as she felt inclined, for the object had not only invaded her mouth but also had pushed deep down her throat. The first impulse was to swallow it whole so not to choke . . . but if she did so, she'd never divulge the object's exact nature. Instead, she trembled, affecting a "crab position," and was able to circumvent what would surely have been a very loud hacking noise. She steeled herself and slowly and concentratedly forced the bizarre intrusion back out of her throat and onto her bare belly.

It made a wet *pap!* of a noise.

Thank Gawd . . . Her senses refreshed themselves, and she detected with relief that her shock and her reactive effectuation had not roused Wilbur. The dim lamplight revealed him still inclined on the cot; although when Sary leaned upward and squinted, she saw not a sign of Wilbur's abundant penis but instead just a foot-long squiggle of tissue. But this she noticed via a glimpse, for her attentions had already been drastically diverted by the weighty presence of that which now lay on her belly.

Sary picked the unknown object up in a hand whilst silently manipulating herself to a position by which she could make a more comfortable analysis . . .

This analysis took but a moment.

Her eyes, now well-accustomed to the scant illumination, fairly *bulged* in their ocular cavities. Yes, the object that Wilbur's member had ejected . . . was a manner of substance that happenstance had already introduced her to.

Them . . . thiiiiiiiiiiiiiings . . .

Indeed, Wilbur's penile discharge—obviously the

physical matter of his orgasm, just as semen was the physical matter of a more typical man's—she'd confronted earlier in the day, during her exploratory excursion about the property: the pile of lumpen, off-white things deposited in the crook of the drakeberry bush. *Them weird ball-things,* she remembered, *like string'a white meatballs. They done come aout'a Wilbur's dick—they'se his CUM!* Sary could not possibly cognize ejaculant existing so bizarrely and out-of-aspect from what she'd come to regard as normal, but at least this discovery answered a great deal of her questions all at once, and this she delimitated in her own manner of bucolic discernment: *Wilbur's dick en't nothin' but a flimsy sheath, like a sausage skin, which fill up with these meatball things ever time he gets horny. And when he gets his nut, them white meatballs slide aout'a the sheath!*

The revelation, which was likely to revolt most women, had no such effect on Sary. Instead? She felt quite the opposite: *fascinated.*

Sary, of course, was not at all familiar with the tenets of Aristotlian Syllogism and its sequent components of deduction by means of axiomatic inference, but she *was* able to deduce this: with a typical man, female orgasm was generally effected through the physical action of copulation, i.e., the repeated insertion and withdrawal of an erect penis within the confines of the vagina; but as Wilbur was clearly *not* a typical man, female orgasm seemed triggered by merely the *presence* of his solid ejaculant in the woman's reproductive orifice. And such orgasms . . .

Better'n anything I ever thunk possible . . .

Sary immediately loaded the "meatballs" into her vagina.

It was all she could do not to cry out. No sooner had she manipulated the aggregation of lumps into her sex, she was writhing on the floor in paroxysmal bliss. Her vaginal vault spasmed like the heart ventricle of a hypertensive cardiac patient, and as if lying in a pool of electrified water, she convulsed time and time and time again, each convulsion eliciting quakes of incalculable pleasure which seemed to defy human sexual capacity.

Half an hour later, she twitched limp on the floor, her face contorted by the most lubricious of grins. More relief surged through her upon noticing that Wilbur was quite a sound sleeper; he'd snored through the entire machination. Part of her scrupled to return to bed before her luck departed, but it was a much greater segment of her that propelled her very quietly forward. At the door, she took considerable heed in pressing up the iron latch, opening the door, and then closing it behind her—all without begetting so much as the tiniest sound.

The warm, star-ridden night sprawled above; the moonlight *brimmed.* The craving of an opium-eater caused her to run as fast as she might—sweating, flushed pink, and unabashedly nude—directly to the drakeberry bush with the queer passage-like indentation. She collapsed to her knees before the pile of her new-found treasure and, salivating akin to a lunatic, lewdly opened her legs and fed the first string of Wilbur's discarded seed into her "pussy." Only a second of thought explained why the pile was here: *It's his beat-off! He come aout here ta jerk his dick so's no one see him and leave his nut on the graound! It dun't melt away unless it's in a gal's cunt makin' her cum!* And in the second *after* that, Sary was squirming on the grass as she was wracked by yet another concussive, thirty-minute-long Grand-Mal-Seizure-like orgasm; and when this was done, it was into her drooling sex that she fed the *next* lumpen string, and thirty minutes after *that,* the next.

And so on.

By the time she'd utilized the entire deposit of Wilbur's "beat-off," she was but a whimpering form of lax flesh incapable of movement. She lay spread-eagled, a veritable spate of fluid seeping into the ground between her legs. The experience all but drowned her in a vat of unearthly ecstasy that had worn her orgasmic capabilities out as completely as water wrung out of wet clothing through a wringer. All the while, the orgiastic grin never left her face; she simply lay there staring insentiently up at the sky's illimitable void as evening expended itself into dawn.

When Sary was able to cogitate in a fashion more profound than a slow-dripping leak, she felt a jolt of alarm as the sparkling light of morning bathed her naked body. *I best git myself back in bed afore Wilbur wakes up!* but her energy—after last night's saturnalic extravaganza—was slow to summon. What if Wilbur discovered her out here, lying in the grass fully naked?

What on earth might she offer in explanation?

Only a moment's passage made the question inert. A crunch of dry weeds, a rustle of the bush, and then a towering shadow.

Oh, nooooooo . . . .

"Whut ye . . . ?" The sun blacked out Wilbur's immense, crooked shadow. His head's angle suggested that he was looking down, seemingly, in a brief confusion: first, spying Sary naked and exhausted. Then he noticed the spot where a pile of his strange semen should be—a spot now vacant.

Sary peeped, "Um, Wilbur—I'm, uh—"

Wilbur's next pause gave Sary a chill of dread, but then the gigantesque figure betrayed a restrained chuckle. "Look like ye've figgered aout fast that it's more ways'n one I'm different from fellas hereabaouts." Was he unnerved upon looking more closely at the spot where he'd deposited the wares of his masturbation? "Kind'a embarrassed, I am . . . "

Sary ached when she attempted to move. "Wilbur, *I* be the one who's embarrassed! Yew jess ketched me aout heer buck nekit and . . . wal . . . " She glanced bashfully to where his sperm had been.

"'Tis good ye made use of it"—another small chuckle— "it en't like I could. I jest meant it's a bit embarrassin' sinct ye know naow I been comin' aout heer to this bush to have at myself with my hand." Wilbur's broad, oddly angled shoulders shrugged. "I juss carn't help it, 'specially sinct . . . wal, sinct meetin' yew."

An unrefined remark, yes, but in its unrefinement was only the vehicle of the utmost sincerity. Sary felt a glow in her heart.

Quickly, then, Wilbur bent over and in only a moment had picked her up in his hard, rack-like arms. "I was in a low state I was when I waked up, 'cos I thought ye'd up'n left." Wilbur's enigmatical face shifted as he smiled. "Carn't tell ye haow happy I be findin' ya aout heer."

Sary put her arms about his chest as he carried her— she *liked* being carried by him—and as she did so, she again detected the incongruent element beneath his tightly buttoned shirt. *Does he got ROPES tied abaout him?* she wondered, for that's what it felt like through the fabric which she'd noted earlier. Another question might have struck her as well—do ropes squirm like snakes?—but by now the situation reduced these curiosities to mere trifles. Sary didn't care about Wilbur's physical disconsonances. *He dun't keer 'baout all the ways I'm messed up,* she reminded herself. Instead, she smiled and hugged him as he carried her back to the tool-house.

"Guess ye didn't have ye'reself no sleep atall last night," he presumed.

"Wal . . . no," she said, stretching luxuriantly in the cradle of his arms.

"Naow ya can." He gently lowered her to the cot. "I got some work ta have at. Jest ye sleep whiles I be gone—er, help ye'reself ta whatever ye want."

She looked up intently. "Whar yew goin'?"

"Jest got me some calls ta make'n some odds'n ends," but this was the extent of Wilbur's specificity.

In spite of Sary's exhaustion, some unnamed urgency livened her. "Wal . . . haow 'baout I come with yew? I can help—"

"'Preciate the thought," Wilbur terminated the notion posthaste, "but, no, on accaount it be the sart'a work I needs ta tend tew myself. 'Sides, ye surely be tired as a ploughman durin' harvest moon."

As last night, so, too, this morning: Sary *was* depleted of all energy, yet at once, the idea of sleep seemed intolerable, and she didn't have to wonder the reason. "Wilbur, I'd prefer it *mutch more* if'n yew'd stay heer with me."

While she'd uttered the declaration, she'd moved her hand—without conscious volition—to her sex.

Wilbur nodded with something like abstract joy and self-congratulations intermingled. "I'll be back not far past the noonday . . . then we'll take keer'a what be on ye're mind, and believe me, I'm lookin' farward to it—"

Sary didn't know what she'd do if he left without first conducting to her more intercourse. Her sleek naked body tensed on the cot; her nipples beetled as if from anger. Just as she would urge herself forward to unfix his trouser button, though—

Wilbur, still smiling subtly, whispered this phonetic sequence from the Second Eltdown Translations, "Ssssseerdunnnnmurrrrrikfrantnzzzz," and Sary fell fast asleep on the cot. Her host paused to look upon her, and it was a look founded by much more than primitive lust.

No. It was something whose sophistication and intricacy well transcended that. Then he grabbed his carry bag, into which he placed his journal tablet and some other things, gazed once more at Sary's sleeping form, sighed, and then left the tool-house.

(XI)

PAID RESPECKS TO *my ma's grave on account today's I'm pretty sure her berthday. The grave is unmarked, of corse, one-tenth of a stade in the woods goin north from a 73 degree angle off the first tree at the Cold Glen Crossroads. Even after all this time, I feel bad bout what happened, specially since my ma was dealt a farely poor rasher by nature. All white skinn and pink eyes that was crooked in her head, her hair even whiter, plus it all stickin up like mine, arms and legs not same lengths and all, and one'a her tits stood up high while the other hang down passed her bellybuttin. She was all mazed in her brain too, my grandfather say, on account of how most branches uv the Whateleys be corrupted by ingrowing on therselfs. Wasnt my ma's fault. Grandsire admittd it were a mistake for him to push the old books on her, she didnt understant em—how cud she? Then that fussbudget Mamie Bishop got to pryin and putting stuff in her head against me and Grandsire. Ma just got worse an worse after Grandsire die, and started actin and talkin like she might try to muss up me opening the Gate to Yog-Sothoth. I lernt well from my grandfather that there werent NOTHING more important than opening to Yog-Sothoth, and anyone who try and get in the way, even if it be a blood rellartive, then that can't be allowed, no sir. Had no choice but ta kill her, specially after I was ordered to direct when the ground got to talkin to me on Sentinel Hill.*

Still, it were my mother, and I feel more then a speck low about it.

But nows not the tyme to be thinking low. I got lots to be thankfull for. Last night my dreem come true and I got ta be with Sary. Twas weird how she woke up rite when I thoght she might. And whut she woke up with was a serious hankering for me! Prayze be to Yog-Sothoth! All my feers was for naught! When she find out how my privits was so unlike everone else, she didnt care a smidge! And it turnt out Grandsire was right about the effect my seed have on girls from here. But first I got real scairt becuz Sary put her hands on my shirt and feel my tentaclettes shift, and I could see she was taken abak; then Im pretty sure she feel down my pant leg and feel my probosciduct, but luck be with me again cos all she did was blink and start to say something but then she left it be. Didn't bat a eye neither once she feel my dick and reckon the fact I got no balls like most fellas. If anything she fuckt me, not the other way round! She seem reel disapointed when I cum, on account it happen so fast, but it didnt take long afore my seed get to workin on her privit place. Yes, Grandsire was rite and so was the books. Looked to me that she was gettin way more than she expecked, carried on all asquirmin and ashreekin and atremblin for quite a spell, she come so hard. Made me pleased alot to know I cud make her feel real good like that, and apparently it put qwite a hook in her cos she got all over me again once we were in bed, and then after I go asleep, she sneak outside to the crooked bush and spend the rest of the night stuffin all my old cum inta herself. I seen my mother doin the same thing after I larnt what beatin off was, and she got dang wild about it. She'd git up in wee hours and I'd peep out my winder and see her run outside, lay on the ground, and start ta feedin each loop uv my spent jism into her pussy. Often went nuts with it right then n there, and sometimes Grandsire'd wake up, look out, and just shake his head, cos he knowed my ma had found about it by readin in the special books. Another thing Grandsire say onct is this: "Willy, when a fella make a splittail cum reel dandy, then she be changed for life. It make her all skewed in the head for cummin', and make her dew crazy things ta git it." I was durn yung when he tell me this, so's I'd could guess little about what he was talkin of. Now, acorse, I know REEL well. His wurds would ring true, all right, and I would find that out, yes sir. Yes, my ma was a horny one, all right. Never onct been fucked by a man from hereabouts, bein how ugly she be so's no one had a kindle for her, but Grandsire tell me she sure learnt what cuming was the night on Sentinel Hill when my pa knock her up with me and that Other. After that, she cudnt leave off herself! She'd put all manner uv things up her: eers of corn, kewcumberz, broom ends, gords. One time Grandfather was fixing to make carrot and brown sugar pie so's he need the rolling pin to flat out the dough but couldnt find it nowhere. Sure enuf he ketch my mother in her room buck naykid'n jerkin that pin in an out'a herself. Grandsire hadda mind to trash her but culdn't fer how hard bent over he wuz laughin. Another time, I swar, my ma catched a hognose snake bare-hand, and this be about the fattest snake I ever see, like wide as a reglar fella's forarm, and then she tyed its jaws clozed, slicked it up with sum cowfat, and stick THAT up her pussy, 'tis how hot she was to cum. When that pore snake start ta smotherin, it begin to tussle feerce inside a her, and this just make her like it more, and then she cum like a freight train, as my grandsire used to say. Ma even KEEP the snake a couple days dead so to keep stickin it in herselff. Few times ma even try to make me fuck her when I was little, but Grandfather got wise to that right off an put a hard thrashin to her. But all this be before she figgured out she cud make herself cum mutch better by stickin my seed in her pussy after I beat off. She got crazy in the head with it, and maybe thats what is happenin to Sary. I find Sary just after daybreak layin there with her tongue out and huffin like a herd dog that be all runned out. Wanted me to do it to her AGAIN before I leave the shed, but I sed one of the Languor spells on her cos—dang!—I was just too weared out after the fuckin she put to me.

I guess what happened tween me and Sary was what my grandfather yewst to call a Right of Passage, one uv them things that got to happen to me bfore I become a full man. "Ye carn't force it, Willy, ye jest gotta let it come to yew in the way the Gods think proper. Ye might be tempted ta force it, but then ye likely be tainted by one'a the fair rooker of curses men of the airth got on 'em. See, boy, yew EN'T one'a them men, but only haff, and the other haff'a ye be a hunnert times more importint'n than fellas hereabouts." I wasnt very old when he tolt me this, and didn't quite follow him. Then another time I was washin an Grandsire got a good gander at my dick, which werent filt at all with cum just then, just hangin empty but reel long, and he say, "Good God DANG, Willy! Thet be some fierce dick ye got on ya, boy! Dun't be dispirited thet ye got no balls like other fellas cos, see, yer balls is INSIDE. And when ye get a yearnin in yer head for a gull, wal, SHEEEEEEEEEE-it! That pecker on ye'll load up with yer jism like packin a durn blunderbuss, it will, and'll be stickin up hard an long as a hammer handle. Heed me, boy, heed me true. Onct women get a gander at yer dick, some of em'll head for the hills, but thar'll be others thet'll follow ye to the ends'a the airth fer a fuckin!" I were of the age by then to start gettin them yearnins in my head and was already havin at myself with my hand, but I thougt hard bout what Grandsire say, first about how I cant FORCE my proper becomin a man, but also what he say that day bout how some girls might reely like bein fuckt by me on account how my seed make em cum so good. I like the idea of that, thinkin maybe the girl would wanna be with me. So I member one day not long after, I was comin down Sentinel Hill just after Candlemas Eve cos I liked all the smells up there, and anywaye, I meet up with this girl comin opposite on the trail tween Frye's pasture and the west woods. This girl looked a rite feisty inner sackcloth skirt cut off so's her bare belly show and a top from a old pink blouse with sleeves tore off holdin in a parcel of bosom that my grandsire would say is "formidable," witch I think is the word he used. He wud also call a bosom the likes of this sumetimes "tits aplenty." She had nipples stickin thru that top like they was pipe ends, and I could tell she had a fare plot a hair between her legs too, cuz so mutch there was of it it was pushin out the front of her skirt. The word Grandsire ud use to descrybe this gal I think wud be "fecund," which I guess means she got a look bout her that get a fellas dick up hard right off. The girl turnt out to be Bonnie Sawyer, whose I remember with her brother Jeb used to throw rocks and horse-apples at me when I was little comin my way through the Glen. N Fact I knew what fuckin was back then and how my dick and jism differ from that uv fellas hereabouts due to that self same pair, Bonnie and her brother Jeb, cos sometimes on my walks I see the two a them sneak into the old abandinned Corey stable that hasnt been used sinct alla Corey's horses die from some distemper after Grandfather put that hex on em for dumpin their shit buckets in our yard. I peek over the haff doors and watch them git at each other, Bonnie playin with her bruther's dick till it gets to stickin up and then she take it in her mouth, took his balls inner mouth to, and then shed get on her hands'n knees and hav him do it to her like a dog. Once he pull out and squirt his jism onner back, and I just thuoght Dang, it aint only his dick that be far differnt from mine but his seed too, just kinda white n snotty! Noothing like mine! Couple uv times Bonnie start yellin back at him over her shoulder sayin how he need to put his dick up the hole where her shit come out, and he do that too, witched she seem to like a lot, and there was another time she suck his dick inner mouth and then beat it off on her chest. "Thet's what pa likes best," she said after she done it. Jeb I heard hung himself by the neck in jail that time he got arrested in Aylesbury for trine to fuck some litle girl, and I just thought that was fine. But that be a wile back but now Bonnie she stop me on that old trail next to Frye's grazeland and she act like she don't rmember me and how she yewst to throw rocks, but I swored she really did know. She bring up a big foney smile and say she'll let me fuck her for twenty cents, and it just happend I had twenty cents in my pocket from what Grandsire give me for helping him knock out the downstair walls the day afore. I had sum fire in me that day, on account I was havin what I think is called "puberty" and I was all antsy to pak my dick inna gal's privit place to see what it feels like, so I give her the twenty cents and pull my trousers down, and she just fly into a fit she did when she see my dick already stickin out and fulla my seed, and my pants was low enough that my probosciduct slip out and start reelin about over my head with its mouth openin and closing. Screamed a long while, she did, and then she start to cussin at me fierce sayin such like "My ma and pa was right, yew's one of Lucifer's gargoyles, yew be!" I didnt know what to make a that, no sir. "Be damned ta Hell!" she say. "'T'was the DEVIL thet knocked yer ma up with yew, oh I know, that pink-eyed whore-witch Lavinia, and yer grandpa crazy Wizard Whateley that call him up!" and of all things she take a knife out and come at me with it! I wasnt scairt, I just stepped out the way, but my probosciduct don't follow what be in my mind all the time, so it wrapped about her neck in a blink and lift her up so she hang to deth just like her brother. When it dropped her I just stare, and a mite angree I was cos I wanted bad to fuck her, which she offered anyway on account of the twenny cents she ast for, but I cudn't very well stick my dick inner pussy now she was dead. That woud'nt be nattrull, and it ud likely cauze the Old Ones to look upon me wth disfavor. Thats *what Grandsire ud say, and I larned qwik to heeed his wurds. But there was something Grandsire DIDNT say, he DIDNT say it be unnattrul to set my EYES on a ded gal, nor beat off on her, so's that be just what I did after I open her top so's ta see her big tits sticking up and pull up that skirt to see all that hair on her split, n fact I hadda beat off TWICE on her, and she werent no good anyway so I didnt think it be what Grandfather would call a Transgression. While I was doin this, though, my probosciduct had already slipped up her pussy and took a shit there, a big one. Wished she be still alive a little at least so to be sensable that shit was goin up her pussy. When it was done, I put it back down my pants and get myself fixed up. I knowed then it were best ta always lissen to what Grandfather say. Its bad to FORCE proper things to come to ye, but good to let the gods BRING em. Praise Azazoth. A course I took bak my twenty cents afore I went on my way.*

Right now Im sitting on one uv the smooth rocks down the slope of Sentinel Hill. I guess the word be "nostalgic," but thats how I felt today fur some reeson. I went up the hill previous to gander the big circle of standin stones. Fascinating how they be all set up in a perfect Rhimes circle with six non-Euclidian angles inside. The place smell mighty rich with Their Odor, which be a good sign, and I know if it was closer to a Special Time, the ground would be atalkin without even me sayin a intercession. Then I walk up to the big stone slab which I know was carved from rock not from hereabouts. Acourse, my father werent from hereabouts neether, and this place be wear I was conceeved. Guess thats why I got to feeling nostalgik. I was standin zactly where I come from. When I lefft, I heard the sky rumble like it done so many times, almost like words, and I knew the Old Ones were smilin on me.

I knew I had some big thinkin to do, but I think it best to leave all that out uv my head for now. Sometimes ya think about things too much and wind up foulin up whats coming. Got to keep my Faith, cos Faith is Trooth and Trooth be Power in the Name of Him Who Is Not To Be Named.

Instead I said me some prayers and kiss the soil and the Altar, then go back down the hill with some fire in my eye.

I knew what it be I hadd to do.

Don't know why, but as I was heding for the Corners, somthing told me to walk around the woods by the bridge way. Don't know what wud compel me to do sutch becuase the only thing out that way was Nallers ole potato farm. I never mutch cared fore the Nallers. Was them, Ike and his fat, flat-titted wife Prudence, who filed complaints bout Grandsire with the sheriff in Aylesbury how the cows we bought wasnt seen no more shortly after we buy em. Sheriff didnt do nothing cuz when he come by, Grandfather had already lighted a Obfuscation Candle. Then he put a Tormentus Hex on Nallers wife so to make it so her pussy hurt like it got a thorn branch being yanked back and forth in it for six minutes evry hour from dusk to dawn for a whole moon cycle. Grandfather always kinda laff after that, sayin such like "Gee, Willy, why ye think Ike Naller look like he en't slept in a month?" Well, the Nallers never filed no more complaints aganst us.

Anyway, I didnt know why I'd wanna walk by their farm, but when I do, what I saw refreshed my memry about some things I heard. Standing rite there in the middle of the field was a barn house the likes of which I never dream. TWICE the size of my house, it was, and all made uv fine timber sealed with bug sap, serius roofin, and two hay lofts. It look dang neer brant-new. Then I member that I herd Ike Naller built hisself a new barn a couple of yeers ago, a reel nice one held together with nails insted uv mortice peggs and had tar neath the roof shingles so it'll never leak, so this must be it. Reminded me also about how Ike Naller up and died last fall when one of his plow mules head-kicked him, and more recintly them loafers was jabbering at Osborns when I went in for some whale oil, and they was saying how Prudence Naller was lookin to sell that big fancy barn but acorse there wasnt no one in Dunwich with money.

Shure enough, wen I walk up to that big barn I see a For Sale sign out frunt. Were no lie neether, it was a dang nice barn, and likely the first new building to be put up in Dunwich since the old mill, and durn, that were built way back in 1806, I think. I was standing their admirin it when I heer a rustle and a sharp wommin's voyce, "What YEW want? Git offa my land less'n yew want a trespassin charge!" and I turnt and see it was Prudence Naller, looking twyce as fat than the last time I see her all that time ago. "Juss was wunderin' what ye be askin' for yer barn, ma'am," I tell her. She dagger-glared me hard and say, "I'se askin' five hunnert, but for YEW I'll take a thousand! And I know no piss-poor Whateley got THET kinda cash!" Oh, I had the cash all right, but I didn't say so. Guess I let her poison voice and look in the eye git to me, and I wanted so bad ta whip up on her a pussy-hurting spell that'd last the resta her LIFE instead of just a moon cycle, and theer was another one I lerned that could make her tits go all full up with pus and then bust and rot off. Why she talk to me like that?

And she kepp on talkin, she did, saying I was a low down bastard witchs son, and my ma was a retart, and we was so poor we hadda eat the cobs after we wipe our asses, and my grandsire was a criminal warlock who shuld'a been burnt at the stake and what not, and then she say, "How your retart dirty mama had YEW was by fuckin a blammed GOAT, Wilbur Whateley, and everyone KNOW thet! Cos that be what yew look like, a GOAT!" I kinda smiled wanting to say, Hey yew fat hatchet-face old biddy, my father en't no goat, my father be a GOD, but I didn't of course, and I decided I wun't gonna put no extra pussy-hurtin spell on her neether nor nothing else. She just hateful backwater trash not werth my time and effort, and I walk away. The Old Ones surely spect me to use the wunderfull powers they teech for more than the likes of Prudence Naller. Better she sit and fester all alone with her fat and her hate and her saggin tits and no money.

Then I got back to hedding to my original bizzniss. Deans Corners wasn't but a half mile walk and the Loveman Trail not five skore cubits past that.

It was a shitty lookin little cabin now that I was seeing it again, or maybe my thoughts was colored by knowin bout sum of the shitty things Sary's father did to her in it. Noticed smoke comin out the smoke pipe, so I figgered he must be cookin in there, pole cat probablee judging frum the smell. The doorknoker strike me as qweer, jess a old metal plate showing a face with no mouth nor nose, just two eyes. Ugliest knocker I ever see. First I thought just to push the door open, walk in, and take care of the miscreant, a word Grandsire yewst to say, but then it seemed better that I take off my shirt ferst so to get his blood thick with feer before I kill him. Now my own blood was boiling feerce, so when I take off my shirt my tentaclettes was whippin and churning and squirmin like a mass of twennie blood red coperhead snakes, and their mouths all snapping open showing their liddle needle fangs. I was riled up big to see the look on this fellas face when come I through his door!

But I got it in my mind it be better to sneak in the back rather than bust in. I keep quiet as I can once inside, trine not to step on any uv the trash layin about. Werent much of a cabin, couple rooms, dirt floors mostly covered by old planks, and furniture my Grandfather would have laffed at, so slapped together it was. In the kitchen there was a shelff holding at leest ten fruiting jars, and there werent no fruit in em, no sir. They were full instead of some milky likwid, I remembered what Sary tell me, so I didn't hafta wonder what was in em. I get to thinkin so I take the tops offa those jars and let my rite-side domminent tentaclette *suck all the cum out of em. Then I hear kind of a panting noyse, I thought, while I was moving through the kitchen past the woodstove. I keep my tentaclettes and prosbosciduct perfect still so they don't make no ruckus, and then I peak round the edge of the doorway. And, well—*

There be Sary's father—a skinny, dirty little rube runt, he looked like, scruff faced and mostly bald—settin in a chair, and he was buck naykid sure as I am tall. He sit all tensed up with eyes clozed, one hand pullin on his ballbag like it were a bell rope while beatin off furius with his other hand. Hadda be the funniest thing I ever saw, and oh how I wished Grandsire was still alive to see it! And sure enough, settin right by him is a haff full fruitin jar, so I know just what he plan. I wate there hiding behind the doorway on purpose, so to give him enough time, then he grab that jar and just when it look like he was gonna have out with his cum, I step into the room.

He drop that jar right away, and I never figured a man could scream like this one did, more like a sheep being gutted than a terrorfied human being. He take one lookit me with my tentaclettes all abuzzin, and I sware his eyes come half out his head! I guess the man was so clutched up in fear that it keep the blood up his dick so it stay hard, and it is reel funny seein a naykid man scream, but, well, for some reeson its EVEN FUNNIER when that naykid man be screamin with a hard dick. Anyway, he keep screemin and then try to run off, but one uv my tentaclettes shoot way out and trip him so he fall flat on his face. I pull my trousers down and let my prosbosciduct come out, and when he see THAT I thought he would up and die. I sent its node lickety split rite up his ass and take a shit. Was a ample meal I eat last night with Sary and likewise it was an ample shit. Packed it all right up inta the middle of his bowels, I guess theyre called. Would like to know what thoughts go threw his head when he realize he been filt up with another man's shit. And filt up he was too cos when my probosciduct get done, that piss-ant skinny reprobate scumm werent skinny no more. Belly stuck out on him like Henry Wheeler! "That's for what ye done ta Sary," I tell him, and when he herd the name his mouth fall open, but then I add, "and so is this," and I sent my dominant tentaclette straight down his throte. His belly then get even more bigger cos my tentaclette done empty all that cum from the jars into his stomach. "Ye be et UP with sickness of the head, mister," I told him, "to make Sary drink your jism, and then save it up all this time sinct she leave, fixin ta make her drink it again. What be WRONG with you?" Guess he didn't heer me thogh, cos his eyes go all crost and look like he was goin to swound.

But now was tyme to do whut I come for.

My probosciduct wrap round his chest like a snake and then constrikt, and you could heer all his rib bones crack at once. I know I hadda move fast bfore he get all cut up inside and go unconscious and die. I fold him right over, a-pushin his head inta his lap, and, see, with his ribs all broke he could be made to lean over farther than natural, and that's when I say, "I heer ye like ta have yer dick sucked, so's now ye can suck it yourself, and if ye dun't, I'll take the top off that woodstove and put you in alive."

Know what he did then?

Yes, sir, he start to suckin his dick.

I make him do it quite a while, and his crackd ribs be grindin and he's whimpuring fieerce and a-cryin like a liddle gurl. Gave me a good feelin to see such a evil fella doin this to hisself, but I knew I best finish up heer and get back to Sary. I keep his head down tween his legs so he keep suckin, and then I send two of my tentaclettes each into his ears, and they started gnawing through till they get to his brain, and then they start eatin his brain-meat. He be convulsin' about then—dick still in his mouth, mind ye—and finally the tentaclettes eet up enough of his brain that he die.

That make my heart sing, it really did, cos the way I calclate it, there be a no more proper way for a fella like this to die than to die with his own dick in his mouth, a belly full of his own cum, and more of my shit up his backside than his own.

I found a can uv lamp oil and throwed it all around the place and put plenny on him too, then run a line to the kitchen. The wood stove be too hot for me to lay my hand on of corse, but not too hot for my probosciduct cuz Grandsire say there be no heat nor fire from the earth that can hurt it, so it knock the whole woodstove over and the spilt coals catch, and then that line of oil turn to fire and run rite back to Sary's father, and that be that. Not a minnute later, I'm a-walkin through the woods at a leeshurly pace and that shitty little cabin with the shitty little man in it be all ablazin'.

(XII)

THE ADVENT OF Sary into Wilbur's life and he into hers unfolded as something essentially domestic, and inaugurated into their psyches a sense of contentedness, joy, and synergism that, to objective onlookers, would have seemed, indeed, marital. The broken pieces of one's life were abstractly reassembled by the influence and even the mere presence of the other. To Wilbur, his personal dreams had come to be, and to Sary, she could scarcely believe that life could take place in such a train of wonder.

Though they never utilized the word, they were, for all intents and purposes, in love, and before them both blossomed all the ingredients of a wonderful life together. It was regrettable, then, that such a life would go on for but five more days. Of this, Sary hadn't an inkling.

Wilbur, on the other hand, was in possession of a fair idea that he would be wise to cherish his time with Sary, for time was as of vapor, or of a bird on a wire.

***

It needs to be retailed, however, that the pair's newfound domesticity, contentedness, and compatibility ensued along with a veritable *extravaganza* of sexual intercourse.

***

Though many bridges of dubious safety existed in Dunwich, the one worthy of the most remark was the covered log-spanned bridge just beyond Dean's Corners. If anything of a "landmark" might be referred to in that sordid little carbuncle of a village, this was it. The bridge extended across a more than meager brook which joined the Miskatonic a mile downstream, just as it canted away from the precipitous Round Mountain. In 1694, before the first incarnation of the bridge had been constructed, the men of the settlement's earliest colonists had poisoned the water with carrion and Paris Green, knowing that said water flowed directly through the camp of the aboriginal Pocumtuck Indians, sickening and/or killing scores of squaws and infants, as the adult male contingent of the tribe was out on the hunt. In 1701, the first bridge was built, the same year that the village's original designation, "New Dunnich," had been changed boldly to *Dunwich,* a more direct reference to a legend-cursed hamlet in southeastern England (which had had a fierce repute for black magic and children gone missing) before it was ordered razed in the late sixteenth century by a Court of the Oyer and Terminer; but the accuracy of this information is open to debate. Another questionable rumor persisted as well (regarding the bridge itself, in fact): that the larch logs which comprised its first crossing platform had come from a not-far-off woodland in which still more of the Pocumtucks had been slaughtered via an ambush perpetrated by the next generation of Dunwich men in 1719. Several of the comeliest squaws had been abducted, lashed to the trees of this wood, and barbarously tortured (with much attention paid to their sexual parts), such that their screams had traveled with sufficient tenor; hence, the "bait" of the "trap" had been set. When the warriors had embarked on what they perceived as a rescue, the Dunwich militia had been waiting with flintlocks, pitch and torches, and blunderbusses. This massacre had effectuated the extinction of the Pocumtuck tribe in His Majesty's Colony of the Massachusetts Bay.

The fact that, in after-years, more than a few Dunwichers had hanged themselves from the coupling spikes of the bridge gave further fuel to the legend of its provenance. It was beneath this bridge that the Reverend Abijah Hoadley had performed the town's first Congregational christening in 1746, and in the same water, a year later, that the reverend himself had been drowned quite protractedly. His body, after much violent molestation, had then been fed to swine by what some regarded as the local "coven," presided over by one Silas Ephriam Whateley, a darkly prominent ancestor to Wilbur and lineal progenitor of those of the Whateley Clan who would choose occultism, incest, and fervid isolation over Puritan society; and Lammas Night, Roodmas, and All Hallows Even over Easter, Advent, and the Yule. During the hours of darkness, a fair number of girls, women, and, lo, even a few boys had been raped on the bridge; and more than seldom had been the time when backwater strumpets (such as Sary) had plied the enterprises of their trade, only to receive, as the goes the adage, a bit "more than they bargained for." Persons had been murdered on this bridge as well, by the highwaymen of olden times and occasional transients afflicted by malignancies of the brain. Three men had been gelded on the bridge; and one woman, the wife of a bean farmer named Saltonstall, had been " . . . confront'd b'fore her, while yet behind, and tooke against her Will unto ye Bridge which be know'd as ye *Deane's Corners Bridge,* and then promptlie and with overmuch Violence *strip'd* of all Garment, and thereby forc'd unto Carnal Knowledge with more than several Men not recognizable to her; where next, she be held down whilst severall barking curs be brung to this most Hideous Scene which then did procede, likewise, to engage in *Unnaturall Consorte* most offensive to God and Abominable in the uttermost to Scripture, upon much Goading and Urging, whilst ye Divellish Perpetrators did Hoot, and did make Exclamations of Laughter, and did clappe their Hands in Plutonian Glee; whereupon—horrid to convey!—this Pore Woman, devout'd Servant of God, be by Knife divorc'd of her Naturall Bosom and then—Lord, protect us!—scalp'd in ye Manner of ye Savages, (yet *not* by Savages so did she spake), not of any Hair upon ye Crown of her Head but yet of her most *Privat Hair,* which be then Made Away With amid Laughter and Revell worthie of Lucifer ye Morning Star himself," asserted the criminal complaint filed with the Scrivener and Clerk of the High-Sheriff. The victim, whose name was Charity Saltonstall, survived for more than a year after the excruciating crime, well long enough to bear the child wrought by the rape, a female-child who would be given the name Melany. Melany, later at the tender age of thirteen, would step onto the bridge and cut her own throat from one jaw-corner to the other, but only after setting fire to the schoolhouse, in which five of her classmates perished. Her teacher perished as well, a Mr. Peaslee, whom diary entries would posthumously reveal to have been sexually seduced by Melany for several years.

Sundry other mutilations, emasculations, disfigurements, and less precise mayhem had also taken place on or in vicinity to the bridge, most with no motives whatever; and during the times of the witch-panics, a drove of women (most of whom were perfectly innocent) had been first branded with Our Savior's mark upon the bosom and the privates, and then dunked into the rushing water below, urged to confess. Given all of this, the perpetual hearthside whispers of grandams was no wonder: that the bridge and its surrounding wood was ghoulishly and indelibly haunted.

Wilbur, however, harbored no such preposterous beliefs.

But it is more than incidental to point out that his first *kiss* had occurred on that very bridge, and the sensation of Sary's lips pressed so unreservedly to his may have caused him to actually weep. Sary's heart—indeed, her very *spirit*—revolved around Wilbur as surely as the moon revolved around the God's Earth. For the first instance in his life, Wilbur was held with unflinching acceptance, not repugnance, and this seemed more than he could believe. Yet believe it he did, for the young woman's devotion was so plain that its authenticity could not be questioned. Not only his unnatural height, nor his shocking visual aspect, but far more intricate characteristics had been, one way or another, observed by his young paramour. The presence of his twenty tentaclettes beneath his shirt, for example, and the snakelike bulge of his probosciduct running down his left pant leg: these traits had surely come to Sary's notice, just as his unrepresentative genitals and semen had already, yet she shewed no sign of revulsion, shock, or alarm.

And now, upon the noontime of July's thirtieth day, they kissed quite heatedly under the bridge's rickety wooden awning, which provided but a few openings to permit the entrance of fresh air. When Sary's tongue delved into Wilbur's mouth, it did not hesitate when it came into contact with his own tongue, which was in fact forked. She even moaned when the oral investigation made this discovery, almost as if Wilbur's atypicalities *enhanced* the moxie of her arousal.

It needs to be established that Wilbur was not, by any stretch of interpretation, intellectually challenged, though most took him to be due to his countrified manner, regional vernacular, and speech impediment. On the contrary, aspects of his paternity very much left him equipped to cogitate the length, breadth, and depth of the geometrical sciences, quantum calculus and its inherent syntactic systems, and, indeed, the furthest reaches of even the most combinatoric mathematical thesis—even to the extent that the likes of Wilhelm Gottfried Leibniz and Sir Isaac Newton would feel wholly inept. Similarly, the giant's powers of intellect could be questioned even less due to the fact that he'd taught himself fluent Latin, Greek, Sanskrit, German (along with many participles no longer in use), multiple provincials of Arabic, and also the Alko, Pnakotic, and Eltdown tongues and several more languages with no cradle to the earth. As he'd grown older, in his own personal journal writings—however brilliantly ciphered via an artificial alphabet of his own invention—he elected to scribe in local dialect, in order to leave a shadow of his personality for any who might follow his reverential footsteps, and he had taken up the rather lazy habit of spelling words incorrectly in his haste, but this was but a quibble. The fact remained: Wilbur Whateley was an uncompromised genius of all objective sciences his calling required.

He was *not* a genius, however, in matters less concrete—creativity, for instance—and of the heady variations of romantic and erotic *tactic*, he knew precious little. On this day, though, whilst in the midst of a most pleasurable and affectionate embrace with Sary, the words came to Wilbur's mind, *Wal, durn. Mebbe she want suthin' more than me jess stickin' my dick in her. Wouldn't like it not one bit if'n she start ta git bored with me,* so then as Sary's mouth seemed enthralled by the divergencies of his tongue, he slipped her dress up over her hips, said, "Heer ye go," and hoisted her up so that she sat on his shoulders with her crotch to his face.

The musk scent and intricate morphology of her vagina left him vibrant with wonder, and it was then that he commanded his forked tongue to first "side-wind" about the delicate rose-pink flesh of her vulva. In time, he admitted the tongue directly into the lubricated channel within, with no little fascination. A shriek of pleasure and her hands insistently going aclutch in his hair gave Wilbur every assurance that she was not adverse to the ministration. The tine of each "fork" roved independently, effecting sensations with which she'd never been acquainted; and by the manner in which she panted, squirmed, and clenched her thighs, Wilbur estimated that she was approaching the fringe of climax *without* the introduction of his columniform sperm, nor even his penis. It was here wherein Wilbur's understanding of female sexual reactivity transitioned into what could only be called "gray area," but since her gestures in response took on an invariably positive bent, he simply continued to maintain the oral process.

Next, he allowed his tongue to extend to its farthest physical limit—several feet—and for the tines to part, which his otherworldliness made possible. One he deployed into a minuscule aperture that must have been her urethra (when it penetrated the duct of her bladder, he found the taste within tangy and fascinating), and the other into the even more minuscule ingress of her cervical canal. The activity seemed to incite in Sary a frenzied rising action which she enjoyed to a point of delirium, but after a time, he felt it necessary to see to that action's propulsive descent. This he achieved first by drawing each tine briskly in an out of their respective apertures and then withdrawing them altogether in order to command them to assume a corkscrew, all the while engaging them to swell in girth, a facilitation also allowed by his para-earthly anatomy. Soon, Sary's vaginal vault was filled to excruciating stringency with the mass of spiriferous coils, which expanded and contracted while simultaneously nudging to and fro. The young woman curled into a shrieking ball about Wilbur's head as her climax commenced, and when said climax was at an end, she could only gasp, cry, and quiver in her elevated place. Nothing pleased Wilbur more than to know that she was pleased.

However, by this point, his own arousal was nearly painstaking, so attracted was he to her. He'd already lowered his trousers, which permitted of his probosciduct to rove about in revel, and then he gently raised Sary off his shoulders—his beard aglitter and his mouth full of salty sapidity—only to lower her with great finesse onto his erection.

One thrust inward, and one retraction, and Wilbur went wobbly kneed by the freight of his orgasm, while moments later, Sary went writhing in another of her own, which protracted the opiate spasms for thirty more minutes, this process releasing from the inner covered bridge screeches which must have traveled the whole of the upper Miskatonic Valley.

Wilbur cast nervous glances this way and that, fearing passersby, but when none were in evidence, he began to amble out of the bridge. Though all of his mate's orgasms with him had been very much all-consuming, none had been more so than this. Sary had blacked out, which made it necessary for Wilbur to carry her all the way back to the tool-shed like a limp parcel.

This, he was all too pleased to do.

(XIII)

PERHAPS THE INCONGRUENT yet very welcome issuance of Sary into the quintessence of Wilbur's existence goaded a change in his aforementioned creative deficit. His deportment with regard to her took quite a passionate and romantic turn. Holding her hand whenever they were out became vital to him, and it seemed just as vital to her. And there was no cessation nor diminishment of the joy which now took possessorship of him. They kissed often and pursued many other modes of physical affection that were not at all sexual in motive. Wilbur found he delighted in the mere sight of her, the mere vision, be she even just sitting, talking nonchalantly, or engaged in some mundane task. Since their second night together—though they did engage themselves sexually at least three times per evening—they slept as if attached to one another, so persistent was their bond. Each morning they awoke, Sary would gigglingly insist that he come outside with her at once—she wearing not a stitch!—and then proceed to kiss him just as the sun began to rise, and she insisted upon the same at dusk. On a different night—she did not recall which—it was Wilbur who devised that they venture to the center-point of Frye's pasture and, beneath the majesty of the moon and twinkling stars, make fervent love.

Another time, after making love yet again, they were taking a scenic walk down an arbored lane near Billington's Wood. Sary's mood reflected an unvoiced concern, that concern being: *Good Gawd, what am I a-gonna do if I lose*

Wilbur to some other woman? The prospect, however paranoic, instilled in her a whirlwind of woeful contemplation, for if she were to lose Wilbur, never again would she experience such staggering delights as she had with him through whatever sexual sleight he'd mastered; similarly, she wouldn't likely meet someone so kind, nor someone not repelled by her facial looks. Wilbur, however, was worried himself by what her cast might signify, but he could only guess. "Suthin' clearly worryin' ye, Sary, and I jest become afeared'a what it might be—"

Sary's expression tightened, and she feigned, "Oh, I'se jest fine, Wilbur! I'se not worryin' a'tall . . ."

"I be thinkin' that with all this great fuckin' we been doin', mebbe . . . mebbe ye're worried abaout gettin' made in the way, ya know, in the *mother's* way."

The train of Sary's thoughts snapped like a heavy bough. "Oh, Wilbur! I'ud jest *love* that, I would! I will pump babies aout fer yew as many as I can muster if it be watch'a want!"

Wilbur, with this, saw the lengths of his misinterpretation; and the resultant embarrassment easily showed on his face. "Dang, Sary. I was only goin' ta say that ye *needn't* worry 'baout me gettin' ya pregnant on accaount that I *carn't*."

"Yew *carn't?*"

"Naw, I'se 'fraid not. See, jess as, uh, sarten parts'a me is different from fellas hereabaouts, so's my seed. Way my seed is, is, wal, it en't possible fer it to make a gull have a baby."

Sary's eyes thinned to slits. "Haow yew know?"

"That big book on my table say so, fer one thing, and from what my grandfather tell me back when I was jess comin' ta be a man. The word he use—wal, it's likely a word that en't known ta ye—the word he use was *incompatible*. See, my seed be *incompatible* with the wombs of women hereabaouts. Means it wun't work—my seed, that is."

Sary tried to recite the unusual word to herself but soon gave up.

Wilbur went on a bit of a ramble. "Ee-yuh, Grandsire tell me, all right, he say 'Willy, onct ye stert carryin' on with gulls—and ye can *bet* yew will—ye en't gonna be able to make any of 'em big in the belly with your child,'" but from this point, Wilbur curtailed what remained of his grandfather's earthy monologue, which continued, *Yes, sar, boy, ye can whip aout thet big dick'a yers and ye can fuck all these heer Dunwich jism buckets up one side'a taown and daown the next, but ye en't NEVER gonna knock 'em up. Um-hmm, ye can fill 'em with your nut like a baker fill a blammed CANNOLI with cream and theer en't no more chance'a yew puttin' a baby up her cunt as theer be a ANT haulin' a bale'a cotton! It be on accaount thet your cum's INCOMPATIBLE with gulls hereababouts* . . . Hence, the origin of Wilbur's discovery of the word. "Hope ye en't disappointed, Sary. That jess the way it be with me. Chances'a me makin' a baby with yew . . . wal, thar en't a chance in a quintillion yeers ta the tenth power."

"*How* many yeers?"

"Quintillion ta—er, wal, jess means a long time."

"Wilbur, whether yew make a baby with me or not, I dun't keer," she beamed, "long as I git ta be with yew!"

So much for that interstitial bit of information.

Upon the languishing of the sun on July's final day, however, Sary seemed to sense a figurative cloud spreading over their personal realm, which threatened to overwhelm her joy unutterably, but why she would muse upon this she could not put a finger on. Wilbur spent more time earlier in the day at his desk, writing, and also consulting other arcane papers in his bureau, as well as some books so antiquated that their very bindings were no longer extant. *De Vermis Mysteriis*, she vaguely made out on one title page, and another: *Le Mot est la Vie*. Wilbur regarded these crumbling tomes as though he were viewing a sick loved one. Yet no decrease was observed in the vibrancy of his attitude toward her—if anything there was an *increase*—but betwixt the layers of his undivided attention,

Sary very much perceived the afore remarked cloud—a cloud, for sure, of *worry.*

During an earlier segment of the evening, he'd been seen pacing back and forth outside before the big house, wringing his overlarge hands, and once he'd unfastened the door's antique locks and gone inside. Had Sary heard a muffled but gargantuan *snort,* and then something like a plaintive *mewl?* Of this. she felt sure as she watched through the tiny window, and then she could declare that the mewl reminded her of a domesticated beast in the throes of suffering, so sadly did this aural emission emanate. Then Wilbur had come out, relocked the door, only to turn with what may have been tears in his eyes and an even more intense cast of concern upon his facial aspect. It was indeed an *unbridled* concern, as of one far steeped in a misery of inner-calamity. Sary said not a word when he returned to the tool-house but instead efforted to relieve his unspoken distraint by ministering to his genitals with her mouth. The gesture assuaged him a good deal, but then he regretted that he must leave "fer a spell" to tend to some unspoken-of onus, after which he exited the shed, insisted she lock the door behind him—"None ta worry, but jess a precaution, mind ye"—and loped off in the direction of Sentinel Hill. By now, the man's anguish left Sary quite consternated herself, though she subdued some of this by— unable now to resist, of course—picking up the odd, palish column of Wilbur's spent seed where she'd left it on the floor and inserting it into her private channel. This affected another half-hour of sheer carnal bliss, whose impact required yet another half-hour from which to recover her sensibilities and motor skills alike.

By midnight, Wilbur had not returned.

Nor by two a.m.

The deepness of the night sky lent grim assurance that the carriage clock was to be believed, and therefore, Sary was unable to engage her self-restraint further. Frantic, she dressed, opened the shed-door, and prepared at once to begin a search for Wilbur. But no sooner had she stepped without the confines of the abode . . .

Her eyes stung ever-so-modestly.

Due to Sary's lack of olfactory reception, she did not smell the smoke which had permeated the property like fog; but even in the moon's luminescence, her eyes could very well detect the haze which informed her that a fire blazed not far off. Then she looked west—

She screeched high and piercingly as a steam-train whistle.

A fire burned indeed, from what appeared to be the very spot she suspected was Wilbur's destination: Sentinel Hill. She could even envision the plume of flame wavering behind those queer columns of standing stones where sat the antediluvian slab whispered of by her late mother. An uproarious fire this was not, yet the nexus of its light seemed more intense than any common forest fire should be, while at times, its crackling radiance very definitely gave off flares of the oddest *green,* akin to tarnished bronze. An academic with an intricate imagination and a proclivity for metaphor might describe this hue as *lucifesque.*

However, the entity of Lucifer had no connexion whatsoever. And next?

The *sounds* came.

It was as though the pandemonium of Babylon's demise, the din of the Mongol Horde, and the cacophony of Tartarus entwined and released at once. Had the earth let loose an *a capella* of screams? Was the ground beneath Sary's feet actually *muttering?* From the black sky's void came a *CRACK!* so chaotic and ear-splinting, she would've not believed such a sound possible; she could only, in her terror, assume that the heavens had ruptured. The wake of the infernal crack was filled with a sound, though not as deafening, possessed of an even worse consignment of aberration, yet she would later realize it was, though less amplified, a sound that carried some familiarity. It could be likened to the resonance of a massive rockslide, only a rockslide that was somehow taking place *underground;* and in conjunction, there came an even more abominable sonic accompaniment, something similar to the sound she recalled when she'd heard one of the Grangus bulls dying at Bowen's farm—they'd said that a bovine grippe afflicted the miserable beast, which Sary took to mean something was amiss with its lungs. What she heard this moment—yet from *beneath the ground she stood on*—was a phlegmatic basso flutter with a repugnant *wetness* to it, but yet also what seemed to be a pattern of *structure*. She grew sick in place, for she had indeed discerned a less profound version of the same when happening by Sentinel Hill in the past.

It was as though some hellish subterranean entity were endeavoring to *form words,* though they be words from no language she could contemplate. If such an utterance might be illustrated, it would be as thus: *"NGH'NAAAAAA-EEEE-BRLUB-H'YUH-D'NAH-YOGSOTHOTH . . . "*

Then the sky *CRACKED!* once more. A windless gust slammed Sary flat upon her back, and as still another *CRACK!* rocked the firmament, she screamed, presuming that the event her mother had once whispered of, the Day of Dissolution, was at hand.

In the margin of a blink, however—

Sary sat up, staring.

—a perfection of silence held dominion over all.

Sary rose, boggled. Surely, an experience of such impact could not have been the product of imagination. But her perplexity was not long to last, as the urgence of her mission returned to her mind: Wilbur.

Her eyes flicked back and upward. Atop Sentinel Hill, the fire still burned. She leapt ahead with the dread alarm in her heart, and a prayer in her mind exploded forth: *Please, Gawd! Let it be that Wilbur en't up thar in them flames!*

Sary broke into a hard run—

Only to come to a complete halt.

The figure in the smoke-tinged moonlight coming along the trail was Wilbur.

When previously her screech had been one of fright, she now screeched in exultance. She ran ahead and fully jumped into Wilbur's arms, to hug and kiss him, to latch hold onto him for dear life—indeed, to *celebrate* the fact that he'd come off the fiery hill unharmed.

The giant seemed awestruck by the surprise. "Wal, naow—calm ye daown! Why ye be all a-tremble?"

Still hugging him in utmost desperation, she could only reply in pants, gasps, and fits. "I see the flames burnin' up on Sentinel Hill, and had the awfulest notion that's whar yew went off to!" She burst into outright sobs. "Aw, Wilbur! I was so afeared yew be burnin' right along with them flames!"

"Thar, thar, hon." He let his embrace sooth her. "I be jess perfectly fine, as ye can see. 'Tis true I was up Sentinel Hill, but I made it be that the fire I set couldn't spread nowhere."

"The fire . . . *yew* set?"

"Eee-yuh," he said in a softer intonation. He gently turned her about to head back to the tool-house. A perceptive person might've noted a shift in his character, as if to mollify any trepidation that Sary entertained. Pronouncing the word "worship" as *waship,* he said, "See, fires be the way some folks worship the gods they'se believe in."

Sary's expression suggested cogitation. "Wal, when my ma took me to church sometimes, they inside all dressed up in theer vestments'd light candles afore the sarvice. Is *that* like what yew mean?"

After a pause, Wilbur replied, "Ee-yuh. Same thing, in a manner. And, see, I go up Sentinel Hill on accaount that be to me what charch be for most folks—just that it's a different sort of place to pay tribute to what ye believe in. Not ever-one worship the same, nor on the same days neither." He walked slowly with his arm about her shoulder, and he seemed to take considerable care in the words he selected, as if about to divulge to her some manner of deep, intricate tractate. "Jess as most go to charch on Sunday, and on especial days like Christmas and Easter, there's others, like me, who got a *different* religion that calls on 'em to worship a *different* god, but mind ye, it en't on Sundays, nor on Easter or Christmas but at night mostly, durin' special times like Lammas, fer instance, which be right naow—"

A familiarity sparked in Sary, which gave her reason to make an active remark. "Oh, I know of Lammas 'cos my ma and me heerd the minister talk abaout it onct, back before my father forbid us to go to church. We'd take a loaf've bread and say prayers over it, then burn it so's the smoke float all the way up to God. If I 'member proper, Lammas was haow we thank God for givin' us the fust harvest."

Wilbur nodded resolutely. "'Tis quite true that Lammas fount its way into Christian thinkin' way back, but actually, it be much older'n all that. Same goes fur Candlemas, which be knowed as Roodmas 'raound heer, and 'tis the day I was borned, matter'a fact. And the same for *Beltane Eve,* also called the Walpurgis Night, and then also for Eve'a All Saints, which used to be called Samhain back in olden days they called *Pagan* times, but naow most think of as Hallowe'en. 'Tis funny haow almost all religions on the airth got some link ta them there special days, but what most dun't cal'clate is there be a *reason* they got ketched up with special power that dun't in no way connect to the Christian God nor the Jewish one, nor what folks far off believe in, Gods knowed as Buddha and Allah and such."

Sary was squinting through the information, which she found interesting in spite of her deficit of understanding. "Yew say there be a *reason* them days is special?"

Another determined nod from Wilbur. "There is, surely, and the reason be this: them days is special 'cos of haow the *stars* be arranged."

Sary stared and blinked. "The *stars?*"

"Ee-yuh," Wilbur's inscrutable voice assured. "The way the stars show theerselfs"—he pronounced the next word with much attentiveness—"cosmologically, which I dun't 'spect ye know abaout. Stars like Aldebaran, and Procyon, and Betelgeuse. Has all ta dew with the angles and the planes of their configgerations. S'where the power come from, see? Aw, wal, ye probably dun't, 'cos it be quite taxin' on one's brain and require yeers of study. Took me quite a spell to have a fair understandin'."

At this point, Sary became utterly dispossessed of any hope of comprehension. She recalled none of such things from the church sermons; but then again, she'd always been subject to a less-than-formidable attention span.

Her pace slowed, and she asked the only thing that then occurred to her: "So . . . what it be yew got is a god *different* from the Christian God an' the man named Jesus?"

"That's right. *Different* from all that."

"Wal . . . what be *your* God's name?"

Wilbur's hesitation seemed to grow more complex through each stride, and when he spoke to answer, the reply sounded more akin to regurgitation than speaking:

"Yog-Sothoth."

Sary looked at him. Had she heard something queerly similar just minutes ago, not via Wilbur's voice but pronounced via the impossible mumbling which seemed sourced underground? As she wondered over this, though, she winced, for something, perhaps a natural spasm, or then again perhaps something more foreboding, supplanted in her head an ache that was brief yet pin-point. "Ain't never heard'a him," she said in a shorter breath. "Yew sure he's a real god and not juss make-believe?"

"He be real, all right. I know it. He answers my prayers . . . Do *your* god answer yer prayers?"

"Oh, yeah!" came Sary's enthusiastic reply. "He did jess naow, as a matter'a fact!"

Wilbur's cast of face indicated intense interest. "Jess naow?"

"Um-hmm. I prayed to Him that He make it be yew warn't burnin' up in that fire, and . . . heer yew is!"

"Ye dun't say?"

"Oh, yeah," she continued, "and 'member that day jest a few days ago, when Rufus Hutchins was puttin' up quite a hurtin' ta me? I prayed for Jesus to save me, and"—Sary squeezed Wilbur's hand—"and lookit what happen! Jesus sent me *yew!*"

Wilbur nodded via a pretense to appear convinced. In his own mind, however, the colossal man was thinking, *I got me a funny feelin' it 'tweren't Jesus . . .*

(XIV)

August 1, 1928 late morning

CAME DOWN FROM *Lammas late lass night, and Sary see me. All out of sorts she wuz, thinkin I got burnt up in the Fires. Its funny how things can go so everlivin good and be so bollixed up at the same tyme. Never heard Them speak so clear to me in the passt, and never afore has the manner of my chants work so perfect. I know it be over all this time that the doodads up in my throat that makes for speaking have got well-prackticed and can reech out to the Old Ones far better than any man who be full human and know the same Rites as me. Grandsire tolt me this wud happen, and durn if he warnt right. But of corse with good news there offen be bad, and this be—as Grandfather used to say, I think—"No 'ception to the rool." Earlier I open the house door and go and see that One inside after making the Voorish, and it has got so big it can't barely fit all the way in there. It know now it be eating too mutch, which be why it got too big, but I know it is my fault this happened. I shud've payd more attention, I didnt calclate things right. I felt so bad looking in there and seeing it so starving and misserable. Makes me think bak to that fella Kyler none too long ago, the soothsayer, n how he said somethin like I'll get whut I want but not in the manner I most hope for. Guess he reely is a soothsayer.*

Because I know now I will not be able to open the Gate to Yog-Sothoth.

That One in there know it too.

But there stil be plenty to do. Just cuz I cant open to Yog-Sothoth don't mean someone else can't. Why else wuold the Voices on the Hill say what they said?

So anywaye, when I come down last nite and got Sary calmed down, she start askin about what I was doing up there, and I was serious on the spot for a answer. So when I tolt her the Fires and all just be another way of worship, she got to talkin about religion, and askin still more. Hope what I sed made sence to her. Least I can tell she not be like most everyone else round here, harborin hate for someone who look diffrent and have different beleefs.

But now that I think about things deeper, I see all is not lost. Just got to be smart and make the Old Ones proud of me. THAT be how I prove to them I am worthy of the privilige they offer me and my exhalted heritage.

Yes. I will prove it all to them.

Sary seem to beleeve in the Christian God, like so many othurs round here claim to. All my life I hear a saying they got and the saying be this: "God works in missterious ways."

So does Yog-Sothoth.

(XV)

INDEED, IN A dearth for phraseology more definitive, Wilbur had been well-afforded not only the situation's seriousness but also its *fact:* that this phase of his life would soon be at an end. Yet the example of his existence had hitherto apprized him equally of this: With every end, there came a beginning. This knowledge—for he was *certain* of it—gladdened him to no small measure.

The remainder of the afternoon of the first of August he thrilled to spend with Sary. They ambled the wild brush near Ten Acre Meadows, crossed through fields of stunning flowers, and kissed in the old lattice-work which fronted the abandoned Hyde Mansion. During the entirety of their walk together, only very few moments transpired when they were not holding hands or touching in some endearing way. Wilbur's consciousness, whenever he was in Sary's proximity, felt expanded as if some arcane and impalpable aspect her life-force allowed for him to experience a mode of happiness that exceeded the limit of his brain's qualification to feel it. He was bursting with joy—

—even in the knowledge that he would likely be dead soon.

These "endearing" intimacies—it should come as no wonder—magnified later in the day into activities far more robust, which provided for Wilbur several instantaneous ejaculations, and for Sary, several bouts of half-hour-long orgasms. Wilbur's "seed"—it was now plain to her—proved the vital desideratum for orgasms so potent; in fact, the effect of this oddly shaped material on her libidinal system left her more sexually satisfied than nearly any woman to ever trod upon the earth, since only a handful, in all of human history, had ever experienced intercourse with one as para-worldly as Wilbur. Afterward, with her face imprinted by what seemed a permanent grin of satiation, Sary lay on the cot like something boneless and absent of all vim, though her groinal nerves still pulsed euphorently in post-orgasmic *ecstasis*. The sky was darkening by the time her senses began to resume a semblance of order, and then her previously orgasm-discombobulated vision focused through inconsiderable lamplight; she found Wilbur bent over attentively at his desk, whereto he'd moved the iron-hinged book. His engrossment was undeniable, as he was reading intently; his lips moved in silence as he seemed to recite extracts to himself. Sary wanted to go over there and take an interest in his studies, but the carnal "working over" he'd unleashed left her with not even enough energy to move. Minutes later, he closed the book rather gingerly, so not to allow any undue noise to be made; it was clear Wilbur believed her to be asleep and sought not to wake her. So . . .

Sary made no actions to inform him otherwise: she pretended to be deep in slumber, all the while keeping her eyes closed to slits. His spending the day with her had already diverted so much of his time. She had no right to demand more of it by interrupting him.

But . . . What was he doing?

To the old carven bureau he moved next, opened a drawer, and appeared to engage in some scrutiny while taking stock of something inside. Did Sary hear a few tiny metallic *clinks!* from within? Wilbur took on an expression of frustrated concern, whereafter he paused, then turned carefully and tiptoed toward the elaborate washing chamber. He'd taken the lamp with him and set it down on the other side of the apparatus, then very slowly pulled out what he'd referred to earlier as a "privacy curtain." Sary was touched by his modesty but more so by the care he was taking to keep from waking her. Now the meager illumination glowed behind him (while he stood in front of it) shielded by the curtain; this arrangement allowed her to view him only as a silhouette.

Sary watched with attentiveness then as the silhouette began to disrobe.

She'd known full well that—aside from the disconsonance of his penis—Wilbur's anatomy existed in an extreme departure from the anatomies of other men. That bulkiness, for instance—an often *oscillating* bulkiness—that she'd noted beneath his shirt, not to mention the single hose-like appearance of some evidently organic object that he kept hidden down his pant leg. In the midst of their intercourse on the covered bridge, Sary even thought she may have detected this object's emergence when Wilbur had lowered his trousers—the impression she'd received was that of a girthy multicolored snake roving independently about as she succumbed to his oral succor and genital penetration. Yet her orgasms had been so propulsive and absolute that she honestly didn't care *what* the bizarre appendage might be. The acknowledgment, in other words, was obvious: Wilbur was physically different from typical men, and this atypicality (for whatever reason might explain it) was immaterial to her. Her only concerns were of Wilbur and the cruciality that he understood the thoroughgoing manner with which she cared for him. Just at that moment, her eyes rapt on his silhouette, she mused, *Wilbur could be a durn DEMON and I wouldn't keer. Naw, I wouldn't love him no less . . .*

She saw with no difficulty that Wilbur had removed all his clothing behind the illumined curtain, and, yes, the curious and even writhing *bulk* about his lower chest she saw as well. Likewise, that organic object that ran down his pant leg was now liberated from the confinement of his trousers, and just as she'd thought, it hovered about him as the giant man prepared to wash. This was not the first time Sary would wonder if Wilbur was actually possessed of a *tail*. But as her curiosity heightened, so did her arousal; she *needed* him yet again, to experience still more of that sexual cabalism that he and only he could deliver to her; so an idea sparked at once in her mind and she said, "Wilbur?"

The silhouette froze. "Aw, durn, Sary," came the warbled respond. "I'se sorry I waked ye. 'Twas trine hard not tew."

"Naw, I warn't asleep." She giggled. "I'se watchin' yew 'hind that cartin, and a-gettin' mighty hot, if yew know what I mean. Dang, Wilbur, I'se so *'tracted* ta yew, I could jess squeal. And-and, wal, mebbe yew en't of the sart ta wanna heer words from a gal that's *serious*, but I got me no choice but ta say thet yew're jess-jess, like, *reely important* ta me . . . "

Wilbur's black silhouette remained frozen.

Sary continued, her voice soft and lilting by its enrichment from desire. "I en't never felt so good 'baout a fella as I feel fer yew."

More silence from the wash-cove, perhaps for as much as a full minute. Then Wilbur replied in a strange, stifled half-choke: "And theer en't nuthin' never made me so happy as what ye jest said."

The seriousness of these conveyances seemed to materially thicken the air like broth converting to roux. Sary knew she mustn't overwhelm him with her feelings now, for they were ultimately selfish, and she knew that much was on his mind of late. So she changed the motive of her words: "Would yew like it if I come in theer with ya and help ya warsh? I'd jess be et up with happy were yew ta let me have my hands all abaout ya."

The bulk surrounding the silhouette's lower chest seemed to shift more actively, and the "tail" moved about with more deliberation. But Wilbur's dark voice said, "Mutch as I'd like ye tew, I'm afeered ye'd be reely disquieted by seein' me full naked. Ye already know that theer be a lot abaout me quite different from fellas as ye're used to—"

"Wilbur!" she exclaimed. "I dun't keer, not one bit!"

"—but, wal, I got me a idea . . . "

***

Emotion pulled at Wilbur's *élan vital* as of one whose arms had been lashed to opposing steeds. Wilbur's joy at having been informed of his importance to Sary had nearly caused him to collapse in a tumult of jubilant tears. There'd been nothing of the disingenuous in her voice, nothing at all, while another of Wilbur's otherworldly aptitudes enabled him to detect with some accuracy when one was conveying untruths. Yet the impact of his joy was almost as immediately superseded by a riveting *fear.*

What it be Sary wants right naow is more hobknobbin' and . . . He looked down at his penis, which remained an empty sheath.

Not even a specimen as vastly deviated from humankind as Wilbur could successfully engage in intercourse with such rapidity that he might possess an *instantaneous* sexual recovery. *Dang, all this fuckin' we been doin' has up'n left me limp as a cut-off dog tail;* in other words, intercourse with her just now had been rendered impossible. At once, though, he recalled her seeming ecstasy when he'd tended to her privates with his tongue that day on the bridge. He considered repeating this gesture, but then, a more diverse possibility occurred to him . . .

"Wilbur?" she insisted. "What's this ideer'a yours?"

The curtain, of course, still intercepted her view of him, but he would need to give up this veil. "All right noaw," he said, "what ye need ta do fust is go'n pull closed all the curtains over the little windows."

Her excited movements were easily overheard as she discharged the instructions and came back to the cot. "I done it. What naow?"

"Naow? Wal, jest ye wait a sec," and then he fully turned down the oil lamp's wick. Darkness filled up the room.

"What can ye see?" he inquired.

"Why, nuthin', a'course! 'Tween the cartins closed and yew puttin' off the lamp, it be darker than the bottom of a rabbit hole!"

"Good," Wilbur murmured. Then, completely naked, he stepped out from behind the privacy curtain and began to approach the cot.

"Wilbur?"

"I'se right heer, hon. I'se comin' over—"

"Wal be keerful yew dun't fall! Haow can ya see?"

"I'se jess fine, Sary," he assured, as he *was* able to see, even in such tenebrousness. It might be appropriate to mention that the eyes in Wilbur's head were essentially as normal as those of typic men, and with them, indeed, he could scarcely see a thing. Yet the paternal side of his genetic inheritance had graced him not only with two eyes in his head but also—

Two *more* eyes in his hips.

These were described in Hazred's *Al Azif* as "ancillary ocular organs." Did they appear as human eyes as well?

The answer to that would be an indubitable *no*.

The fringe of cilia surrounding each was nothing akin to eyelashes. Instead these protective hair-like strands were motile, greenish-yellow in color, and possessed of collateral sensory nerves. Each eye, too, was harbored at the front of each hip by a cusp of pink, porous mesenteric tissue which existed quite unlike a typical socket of bone. The eyes were oval, not spheric, and black, not white, with only a diminutive aperture to suffice for pupil and iris. With them exposed like this, Wilbur could see acutely through utter lightlessness, heavy fog, and torrential rain and snow; indeed, he could even see through certain solid obstructions such as clothing, wood panels, and none-too-dense sheet metal.

And just now, he could, to a great and enthusiastic detail, see Sary as she lay awaiting him on the cot, her naked physique cringing for him, her breasts near to pulsing, and the frenzy of anticipation coning her nipples. She cringed further as she tried but failed to resist the impulse to stimulate her sex manually.

"Aw, Wilbur," came her parched, liquid-like whisper, "all's I'se livin' fer of late is ta be made love to by yew . . . "

Wilbur stepped ahead, his tentaclettes all aflutter and his probosciduct elevated and pendulating. "Heer I be," his own facsimile of a whisper returned, and then he leaned carefully over, visually adoring her body with his rudimentary eyes. "Gonna tetch ye naow, but it'll be differnt from what ye expect."

"Dew it, please, Wilbur! Carn't stand waitin' ta feel ya . . . "

As has been aforementioned, the area of Wilbur's body that, when juxtaposed to a human's, would be identified as his "thorax" or upper abdomen/lower chest, was outgrown with exactly twenty boneless appendages. These were similar morphologically to, say, common garden snakes: each being possessed of a yard's length (though further extension was possible) and a width of a half an inch. Each, too, possessed a terminus akin to a cephalopodic "sucker" combined with a mouth and was rimmed by protractible fangs comparable to fishbones in width yet a strength far surpassing any metallic element on the known Periodic Chart. These examples of dentation Wilbur mentally commanded now to retract entirely. Additional mention, however, is thus: only *eighteen* of Wilbur's tentaclettes were as described. Each side of his thorax also possessed one larger and more diverse tentaclette. Wilbur's grandfather had called them the "dominant" tentaclettes, while they were referred to in the Wormius' translation of the *Necronomicon* as the "*tentaculum superiora.*"

It was the pair of these organs which Wilbur's mind now summoned to action.

He wielded them slowly and precisely to adhere their

silver-dollar-sized suckers to each of Sary's nipples; each sucker, it has until now been neglected to add, possessed a much smaller sucker within—a sucker within a sucker, in a sense—so that the smaller affixed themselves to each of Sary's *papillae*, while the more encompassing organ covered the entire areola.

And next, as was their function, they began to *suck*.

The sudden and quite exotic pleasure so immediately generated caused Sary to squirm, tense, and moan just as immediately. Yet this action existed only as the *aperitif* of what Wilbur envisioned. Eighteen more tentaclettes remained to be utilized, and the colossan wasted no time in manipulating the sucker of each to attentively encompass the tender, super-sensitive flesh of Sary's majora and minora, and her clitoral node as well. These, too, began to suck with a steadfast precision. The intricate process, of course, provided for Sary an even more adventive means of pleasure; and the eruption of responses from her sexual nerve-network became plain with the rise of her moans and the extent of her pelvic convulsions. Wilbur, to himself, celebrated his craft in producing such a gratifying stimuli for her.

Still more remained, however.

His probosciduct reared, as if excited itself by the prospect of its next task. This malleable, tail-like appendage could extend to a length of six or so yards and was fascinatingly adorned by purplish emblems of an annular or spiral nature. And though its terminus was indeed fitted by a fleshy duct capable of ingestion and expulsion, Wilbur's extra-dimensional genes provided it not with teeth. It did, on the other hand, come equipped with an exaggeration of a tongue which, where taste buds would be on a terrestrial tongue, sported hundreds of diminutive wedges, better described as being like *larks'* tongues. Wilbur required no great amount of contemplation as how to most creatively apply these minuscule tubules.

He brought the probosciduct to bear, so to speak, down between his own legs, and not quite but very nearly entering Sary's vagina. The appendage would not seek penetration, but its otherworldly tongue would. With a careful slowness at first, the tongue slid forward, delving to the farthest depth of Sary's vaginal canal, then with the same slowness began to protract and withdraw, all the while (since it was expandable) swelling to a girth which far exceeded that of Wilbur's erection, or the erection in fact of any human male. Simultaneously, of course, the myriad of tiny tubules began to lick, revolve around, and otherwise titillate every square millimeter of Sary's interior vagina.

The process elicited the desired effect, as the young woman flew into a delirium of exhilarating spasmodic reactivity. Wilbur then increased the tempo of the back-and-forth penetrations until they reached a cycle more akin to that of the piston of a motor than the carnal thrusts of a man. Meanwhile, he thought he would maximize his suitor's pleasure by unreeling the much more narrow forked tongue in his mouth, tantalize Sary's anus, and thus afford a more complete ornamental stimulus, which he hoped would be of a kind unrealizable to the present experience of women of the earth.

He would be quite correct, as well, as he engaged himself thus, in a manner of metaphor, as an organic "apparatus" whose singular purpose was to entreat as thoroughly as possible the full range of a woman's sexual response.

Thet's a-workin', thet's a-workin' . . .

Sary's orgasms, though not as lengthy as those manufactured by his sperm, did indeed suffice to leave her quaking, shrieking, and spasming with previously unknown pleasures. When her nerves had fully liquidated their capacity to orgasm, Wilbur recalled all appendages, while Sary lay in a near comatose state, so potent were the rigors of her delight.

Thar's the ticket, ee-yuh. She look more happy'n a egg-suck dog in a blammed hen house, he thought. It was a quip his grandfather used to say.

Wilbur could not have been more regaled. He relit the lamp, then briefly left her inert while he washed, dried himself, and donned clean clothes. His own penis, energized by the visual excitement of Sary's nudity, had now assumed a semi-turgid state as his body struggled to beget more of his alchemical spermatozoa. He felt a great assurance that by morning, he would have undergone more than enough refraction, whereupon more proper intercourse would ensue. His grandfather had once said, *Willy, when a fella's wore his pecker out on a gull, he needs ta take TIME afore his dick got more goods ta give up.* Therefore, Wilbur took this simple pearl of wisdom to heart. There would surely be more "goods" available after a sufficient passage of time.

He gathered up his canvas carry-sack, filled with the few things he might need (a small crow bar, for instance, and his pistol). A moment was all that he needed to take pen in hand and scribble a quick note, which he left conspicuously on the desk top.

Gawd, I love her, he mused, his eyes agaze at Sary's sleeping form. He retraced his steps back to the cot to plant a fragile kiss on her lips.

Then he left the tool-house, quietly closed the door behind him, and ventured out into the vast and illimitable night.

(XVI)

T WAS THREE gentle chimes to which Sary found herself waking, with a mist of lamplight filling the room. A second's confusion, then the memory of her previous seizure of pleasure resurfaced, which sired a delighted moan. But a quick sweep of her hand made it clear: Wilbur was not in bed with her.

Whar could he be at THIS hour?

A tickling sensitivity flared within her sex when she rose nude from the cot. Had Wilbur gone out to check the traps? Or perhaps he was tending to the smoker. But the sliver of yellow light from the oil lamp seemed to impart a summons, so she drifted to it . . .

She turned up the wick, to discover a sheet of paper awaiting her on the immense desk. It read:

Deer Sary: Only the Levens know how I about have a fit just bein away from you for even a minnute. But I didnt want to wake you, figuring how tired you likely be. I hadd to go to the generul store in

Aylesbury ta fetch me somethin' them cads at Osborn's don't got. It be a long walk, I know, but do not wurry yourself becuaze you can rest sure that I'll be back by time the sun rise, and will likewise be thinkin about you til then.

Adoringly,
Wilbur

Sary felt a prickly heat of gratuity by the thoughtful last line, as well as the "Adoringly"; but reason did not take long to occur to her. *Why he goin' to Aylesbury NAOW? Their general store en't open, and nor is any other at this hour . . .* As had happened so many times thus far, Sary found that her exhaustion had been surmounted by inquisitiveness. And she didn't like the idea of Wilbur being about so late. He'd implied that many in Dunwich kept him in ill-regard, so the same might be true of Aylseburians. Her svelte shadow crossed the floor as she meandered about the room, then she found herself standing before the carved bureau wherein Wilbur had examined something earlier in the day. As she recalled, it had been in the top drawer.

I know I shouldn't, but . . .

She opened the top drawer.

Beside the decomposed books with no bindings there

sat a square tin whose top read Mavis Talcum Powder. She pulled off the top.

Bullets . . .

Pistol bullets, by the looks of them. One of them she picked up and was barely able to read the numbers *.455* along the rim at the bottom of the cartridge. The bullet was crusty with tarnish, even pitted, and stained darkly from age; an examination of the remaining projectiles revealed an identical state. Had these been the things she'd heard *clinking!* when Wilbur had consulted the drawer?

Sary shook her head, vexed. What her lover felt inclined to "fetch" at this hour, she could not estimate. The image that kept intruding upon her curiosity, though, was the constant reminder as to *just how good* the sex had been before he'd left. *What did he DO?* she wondered. He'd seemed pains-taken to keep the light out; Sary hadn't been able to see a thing. How could the man have possibly administered to her in so many places and so many ways? And all at the *same time?*

When she focused on the quality of the orgasm—

Ooooo!

—her vagina lurched once, very hard, in a shadow-climax itself. The involuntary spasm only reminded her just how much she adored Wilbur's lovemaking and how desperately she wished to have more of the same.

She turned with some force to divert herself from such libidinous thoughts. Now she stood before the big desk and all its fascinating clutter. What Wilbur had most recently been writing revealed itself to be more of the uncipherable script she'd already seen. She allowed her eyes to scan the letter slots, then the neat little drawers, but as if driven by some unknown revenant, she was next focused on the large, hoary book with iron hinges.

It lay open, and she read a passage:

Curs'd be ye Ground wherein Dead Musings doth live Revigor'd and

Oddly Bodied, and Evill is ye Brain which be supporteth by no Head.

Sary stared at the words. When she'd looked at the book that first day, she'd detected desultory nauseousness, but now . . .

She felt . . . *interesting.*

She flipped a page and read another passage:

Negotium perambulans in tenebris . . .

Sary flinched at the ghost of a sensation: very nearly that of an urgent hand cupping her crotch, then squeezing her there.

Another page:

Ye Affair which shambleth about in ye night, ye Evil which defieth ye Elder Sign, ye Herd which stand watch at ye guard'd by-waye each tomb be known to possess, and which feedeth on that which groweth out of ye tenants therein—

Upon finishing the bizarre passage (which she understood *nothing* of) Sary was surprised to find the furrow of her sex slick with lubrication; moreover, her nipples stood out, having given over to a delicious buzz. Her immediate impulse was to pinch said nipples to goad more sensation and to stimulate her sex with her hand. Her eyes, however, seemed to move out of tandem with her brain.

A further passage:

Yog-Sothoth be ye key to ye gate.

A hot gust caught in Sary's chest. She stepped away from the book as if overwhelmed, and though her mind was blank, she could feel her right hand burrowing into her sex to the wrist. Bewildered, she drew it out, and stared at the book. *It's some kind'a magic . . . ,* she presumed, even knowing that she had little belief in such things. Her sex continued to twitch in the weird pre-climatic pulses.

The book was having a tangible effect on her. Sary decided to flip to yet another page and see what happened . . .

Upon ye absence of ye ashe of Jbn Ghazi, a heartfull myrmidon shalt do good, in ordereth to take into thine eyes that whicheth maye naught be seen, thou must needs partake in ye deft practice of ye sign know'd most Especiall as ye Voorish Sign, which maye be done as thus:

And here, the transcription came to a surcease, to depict instead a series of similar sketches whose quality of illustration seemed the work of no unskilled artist. There were five sketches all told. The first was a sketch of a human hand (a left hand) with its ring- and middle-fingers curled downward and the thumb touching the pinky. The four sketches remaining each featured the same undetailed male figure, showing this sequence:

The figure brought its awkwardly configured hand to its mouth.

Then the hand touched the left pectoral.

Then the abdomen.

Then the forehead.

At once, Sary recalled Wilbur making this same gesture the other day! Initially, she'd been reminded of a priest making the sign of the Cross, but then saw the nullifying incongruities.

She could perceive no harm. She stilled herself where she stood, then, consulting the diagram for guidance, manipulated her hand as designated, and then—

Heer goes . . .
—made the antediluvian Voorish Sign.
Wal?
Sary's shoulders drooped several moments after she'd completed the gesture. Nothing untoward became obvious to her; the room remained unchanged. But then again—

What effect did she expect to be made privy to?

A more practical way to spend her time was what occurred to her next; hence, she turned—

—gaped—

—and froze as if caught in the glare of the Medusa.

The lamplight well revealed a very peculiar presence on the cot: the presence of a *woman* (and one apparently impinged upon by a number of congenital defects), lying naked, heaving, glazed in sweat, and spread-legged upon the hand-made mattress. What's more, the trespasser's harrowing *uncomeliness* came as a shock equal to that of the inexplicable fact of her being here. First noticed was her skin, an unhealthy pinkish white with the faintest blue veins coursing beneath. Next, her hair: ash-white, in an unkempt eruption of kinkiness, both upon her head and betwixt her legs. Four toes were evident on one foot, six on the other; and one arm was clearly longer than its counterpart. Weirder were the woman's eyes, which alternately opened and closed from the sensory result of what she was doing: her irises were pink, while the whites shone a pale, sickish yellow. And weirder even than *that?* The right breast jutted plumply, but the left sagged to the mattress like a two-foot-long skin-sock. The nipples of both more resembled plops of chewed jerky. Had Sary been less distracted by the sheer alarm of her discovery, she might also have noticed suspicious configurations of *scar tissue*— as of scars from repeated *incisions*—congregated about the intruder's throat and areolae.

But these oddities, along with the oddity of the woman's presence in the tool-house, were utterly superseded by the activity she now very fervently partook of. She was masturbating with a teardrop-shaped summer squash more than twelve inches in length. The woman engaged in this process in the manner of a ramrod, inserting the squash's widest end first and then dragging it quickly and arduously back and forth. Clearly, her vagina was well-acclimated to the admission of objects of such size. Each thrust forward caused the woman's buttocks to clench and her malformed feet to curl, and each extraction—so wide was the squash—threatened to exteriorize her vaginal barrel. An acorn-sized clitoris protruded with each repetition.

Beside her, arranged in a row, lay more objects which she evidently planned to insert into herself: a pickax handle, a wine bottle, a very fat dead snake.

Eventually, the squash's physical integrity succumbed to the burden that had been wrought upon it and collapsed to wedges within the woman's sex. She hastily withdrew the pieces, then reached for the pickax handle . . .

That was all. The woman disintegrated, just as campfire smoke would vanish at a modest breeze.

What the HAIL I jess see? Sary interrogated herself.

A ghost?

Was she seeing things?

Was she sick?

But the outrageous woman had been as plain—and as real—as day. A dash to the cot and the placement of Sary's hand upon the mattress, supported this contention: there was a minor aggregation of dampness there, and heat, as if someone had quitted the mattress only seconds ago. Then . . .

Wait a minute . . .

She'd seen the woman immediately after she'd made that hand-motion from the old book.

The Voorish Sign . . .

Sary configured the fingers of her left hand, took a breath, and made the sign once more while looking with great intent at the cot.

The anemic woman did not make a reappearance.

Sary went back to the tome, looked up at an inclination, then shouted, "Holy *BULL-flop!*"

It was now an ancient man who stood before her. Grayish-black crinkly hair bloomed about his head, and he had a beard identical to the hair; it was much like Wilbur's hair and beard, along with the recessive chin. But this oldster was short, bow-backed, spindly, dressed not in the laboring-attire of the day but in black trousers, black shoes, and tunic—like an outre priest. About his neck hung a flat metal pendant depicting what Sary could only guess was a malformed head with snakes trailing from it. Spectacular gems surrounded the monstrous effigy, stones like rubies but striated with threads of obsidian-black. Also of note were several lines of scar tissue on his throat, incisions made long ago.

The man looked at Sary crazy-eyed, though there was an undisputable shade of *approval* in his overall cast. His lips moved emphatically yet gave no voice. He was nodding.

Then he, too, disintegrated.

WHAT is goin' ON?

This question, a qualified one, would regrettably be commuted to uselessness in only a moment.

Before Sary could long cogitate the meaning of what she'd just witnessed, she flinched and her heart skipped as—

CRUNCH!

—the sudden sound assaulted her ears. Did it remind her of wood planks being pried away?

A murmur akin to voices followed the noise.

Sary rushed to the small window.

Outside, in moonlight more than profuse, a male figure busied himself before the saturnine house, in his hand a crowbar. *Aw, noooooooo,* Sary thought, for she recognized the trespasser: Joe Czanek, a local idler whose repute was that of a poacher and petty thief. Last year, the man had paid Sary a dime for sex, whereupon he'd kicked her hard as he might between the legs, choked her unconscious, copulated with her to satisfaction, revived her by urinating in her face, took his money back, and tromped off, laughing. The reason for the man's presence here was obvious enough: he was crow-barring the planks off one of the downstairs windows of Wilbur's house, sporting burglary as his motive.

This, however, was not Sary's most salient concern.

Of late, Joe Czanek was seldom seen out of the company of his partner, a drifter and former state incarceree named Manny Silva. Mr. Silva had raped Sary on several occasions, and not without the accompaniment of some diverse violence and appalling degradation. What much troubled Sary was this: *I see Joe Czanek right thar, so where might Manny Silva be?*

BAM!

The shed door broke open by the impact of a large, booted foot belonging to the subject of her last question. "I *knowed* I heerd me suthin' inside this li'l shit-house. And look who it be!" Manny Silva guffawed. "Stew Face, weerin' nary a stitch!"

He was fat, had a lazy left eye and a curious hole in his right cheek. Seeing Sary so abruptly nude transformed his plump face into a portraiture of lust-soused diablerie. Before Sary could move to defend herself, the abdominous home-invader (drooling through the cheek-hole) deployed himself in a tactic which cornered Sary, and then—

THUNK!

Silva had lunged, slamming the prostitute against the wall, an act which deprived her of all energy and air. "Yes, sar! Jess wait'll Joe git a gander'a *yew!*" he speculated, then grabbed his victim by her tuft of pubic hair and conveyed her from the tool-house out into the sultry night. Sary's head and shoulder-blades scuffed along the ground, around the shed, and out to the front of Wilbur's boarded-up house.

"Hey, Joe! Take a look-see!"

On her back, Sary wheezed breath, blinking spots out of her vision. By the time she was vaguely sensate, two moonlight-forged silhouettes stood over her, arms crossed in valuation. She heard black chuckles, and then—

Kurrrrrrr-HOCK

—one of them spat on her.

"Wal, what have we heer?" Czanek, the thinner criminal, posed. "Never thunk *any* gull would have the stomach ta take up with Wilbur Whateley."

"I heerd he en't got *no balls!*"

"Probably no dick neither!"

Dizzy, Sary croaked her proverbial two-cents' worth. "Wilbur be *double* the man'a both a yew combined."

"Yeah?"

"And I heerd yew fellas suck each other, then swap the cum," Sary added.

The men laughed. "Do we, naow?"

Belts came unfastened, trousers were lowered. Right now, Sary needed no capacity for interpreting matters beyond the range of ordinary perception; she was not surprised, in other words, when both miscreants began to urinate on her. Why destiny had seen to insist that Sary be pissed on *so many times in her life* was a puzzle she suspected had no solution. But she knew well that far worse was in store for her tonight.

"Now *thar's* haow it's done," Czanek's black words blared. "En't nuthin' more finer'n pissin' on a gull a'fore ya fuck her."

"Yes, sar!" cracked Silva (whose urine, for whatever arcane reason, tasted *spicy*). "My pa tolt me the same thing yeers ago!"

"Weren't my pa who told me," Czanek recollected. "'Twas my *ma.* 'Tis a good rasher'a kidney juice what make a woman know her place."

Both men maintained their urine streams for a full minute without so much as a decline; to Sary, however, it felt more like an hour. When she summoned some strength and made to lunge away—

THWUP!

—one of the interlopers stomped on her belly.

Sary again was pilfered of all her wind. She could do nothing but gasp and cringe as her two visitors *continued* to urinate with a copiousness which seemed more equine than human. But when they at last had no more "kidney juice" at their disposal, Sary remained sufficiently paralyzed from the abdominal blow. What she heard, with the hard moonlight in her eyes, were sounds akin to those of men undressing in anticipatory haste. Then?

A *causerie,* since the debauched chat which followed could not be dignified by the word "conversation."

"Dang, talk about some dandy luck. Fust we see Wilbur headin' daown the rud toward Aylesbury"—he pronounced the word "toward" as *terd*—"and then we find this 'un buck naked in his shed."

"And with Wilbur goin' all the way aout thar, it en't likely he'll be back a'fore marnin'."

"Plenny a time ta search that big ole pile'a shit haouse of his and find all the gold he got hid in thar."

"Yes, sar! An' plenny'a time ta fuck this *hoo-uh* raw!"

A chuckle. "Wonder what ole Wilbur'll think when he come home'n find his tramp full'a *our cum!*"

This was the manner of colloquy that Sary's dizzied attention rewarded her with. So it was the gold they hoped to find within the house? Sary knew it was not there but instead somewhere in the woods, for that's from whence Wilbur had trekked when he'd given her the coin . . .

She began the grim speculation in her mind, *When they dun't find it in the haouse . . .* but there was no advantage in finishing, for it would be granted that the likes of these two would torture her with an unprecedented vigor in order to be apprised of where the gold might be.

The truth made her feel gypped, as it often did in her life. *Wilbur wun't be back fer quite a spell, and likely as not, I'll be dead when he git heer*. Rogues such as Czanek and Silva would hardly leave a living witness to their crimes.

If only she could somehow slip away long enough to regain the tool-house, secure a knife or other weapon, and at least die fighting.

"I fucked this one a'fore," Czanek remarked. His shadow appeared to be *flapping* its penis.

"Aw, yeah. Me too, bunch'a times. Didn't piss on her, mind ya, but I shore as hail *shit* on her, and rubbed her face in it tew. Then I gave her a boot shampoo as to go with it."

"Watch this," Czanek suggested. "See, what *I* always do 'fore a fuck a gull, see, I give her a good hard kick in the cunt."

"Yew dew?"

Czanek's gaunt silhouette nodded. "Reason ta dew that is on accaount when ya cunt-kick her hard enough? It make her pussy swell all up inside and get'cha a tighter hole up in 'nar for ya to get your dick in."

Silva's silhouette stared still as if the entirety of Immanuel Kant's doctrine on Transcendental Idealism had just been imparted to him with full comprehension. "Why . . . I never thunk'a that."

"Aw, yeah. *Always* cunt-kick a gull 'fore ya fuck her. 'Tis a waste not tew," and with this, Czanek walked around to Sary's feet, bent over, grabbed her heels, pushed her legs far back, and—

"Gander this, Manny. I'se gonna cunt-kick her *so hard,* her baby-maker'll come up her maouth!"

Sary still could scarcely move. The prospect of Wilbur arriving for a rescue as timely as he had at Osborn's seemed to present a very low order of probability. Instead, she resigned to this atrocity, remembering well her short time with Wilbur and how happy he'd made her. She turned her head aside, staring barrenly. Waiting . . .

What she saw, though—and with an unbidden yet insistent focus—was the very window that had been previously vandalized by the talents of Monsieur Czanek. All the boards had been pried away, and the frame itself too. This left a gaping black oblong hole . . .

"Git reddy!" Silva exclaimed as Czanek poised his kicking leg.

"Git set!"

Czanek pulled his leg back farther.

"Aaaaaaaaaaand . . ."

Sary remained too dizzy even to pray, but her bedimmed mind managed a final gesture: *Yew take keer, Wilbur Whateley. Hope ya know I love yew . . .*

The extra second which Silva would require to yell "Go!" would not be provided, nor would Czanek have opportunity to propel his foot forward against the desired abutment of Sary's sexual aperture. Instead, both men seemed to seize in place, their heads cocking toward a faint, even barely audible sound.

Was it a *hissing?* Or more semblant to a *slithering,* as of a snake advancing rapidly?

Sary's eyes remained peeled on the vicinity of the agape window. Just below this stretched a portion of scrub grass, which—

Sary squinted in the moonlight.

The grass was *moving.* As if, indeed, a snake were traversing there.

But in this case, it would have to be an *invisible* snake.

Joe Czanek and Manny Silva, with a suddenness as if catapulted, left their place on the ground and *flew up into the air.* They roved there, not as if flung but as if via some manner of controlled suspension—that is . . . an *invisible* controlled suspension. Screams took little time to issue from both of the airborne gentlemen, screams which might mirror an abstraction as those of human souls held helpless and *ad perpetuum* in the clutches of perdition.

In truth, these two valueless sociopaths were in the clutches of something else altogether.

Into Sary was injected an amount of adrenalin more

than commensurate to efface her pain and bleared consciousness and to locomote her with an excess of speed to the edge of the tool-house. Circumstance left her no option but to stare into the moonlit area before the house and behold the unbelievable sight. Her two accosters continued to belt out blood-spraying screams as they continued, too, to rove about in the mid-air. By moonlight, Sary could see well that they were fully naked, and could see *too* well every depressing detail of their fish-belly-white bodies, their horror-diminished genitals, and the splats of excrement blurting from their bowels. Each scream stepped up as their uncanny hovering went on. Were bones heard cracking? And was some inexplicable distortion suddenly affecting the abdominal regions of both men? Sary felt certain that Joe Czanek's waist *collapsed* for no discernible reason; again, the "snake" parallel came to mind, for many times on her walks she'd witnessed snakes subduing squirrels, rats, and such by constricting about the mammals' bodies. When the snakes unreeled to reposition themselves, their prey displayed midsections that were collapsed in a corkscrew fashion . . .

Manny Silva's more corpulent physique distorted to a degree that might even be called spectacular; suddenly, he was a sack of suet bisected by a tightening string. Whatever was happening here alarmed Sary so much as to becloud her cognizance entirely. Therefore, she wasn't really even aware of what she did next . . .

She made the Voorish Sign.

If her jaw could've actually come detached and dropped off, it likely would have. Sary could now see the invisible "snakes" which had wrapped about the thieves and held them aloft.

But these snakes were an incarnadine color, a foot wide, dozens of yards long, and overlain with what seemed to be countless cup-shaped outdents, which, had Sary any ken with aquatic zoology, she might have likened to the tentacular suckers of octopi and other similar Cephalopoda.

The tentacles seemed to revel in what their capture yielded; they reeled back and forth displaying the duet of prizes—indeed, almost as if to display them *to Sary herself.* More than feces rained down now, but blood too, exiting mouth and anus alike due to the constrictive pressure. Were Czanek's *lungs* actually dangling from his lips? And what wagged wetly beneath Silva's fat legs was a *tail* of intestines. But more curious than any of this was the *point of origin* of these monstrous appendages:

The vandalized window.

At this point, the tentacles began to withdraw back into the ragged portal, taking their human rewards with them. But before they'd retracted fully into the house, they disintegrated to nothingness, just as had the old man and the insatiable albino woman.

Sary knew very little just then, but she knew *this:* however perilous the prospect might be, she would have to see *all* of what was in Wilbur's house. She would have to behold with her own eyes what manner of *thing* existed at the other end of those "snakes."

She very slowly rose to her feet and, in an automatonic state, returned to the tool-house, took up the lantern, and walked back through the moonlight to the house—

To the *window.*

She maximized the lantern's wick and was at once cocooned by licks of wavering yellow light. She thrust the lantern into the aperture, then set it back down after seeing nothing whatever inside. The phrasal idiom *No time like the present* was not one with which Sary had any conversance, but her own unenlightened grey matter managed something correspondent. She stared into the window's Acherontic blackness as she prepared again to make the sign. Something, though, gave her pause.

A feeling. A *notion* whose origin could not be terrestrially identified. Sary sensed—as people were wont to do—the distinct and singular impression of being watched—no, more—of being *gazed upon* with intentness, even deliberateness; but this was stemmed in far more than the commonplace and rather prosaic fear of the unknown. An altogether different persuasion of fear infected Sary as the house interior (and its nearly corporeal darkness) commandeered her gaze. Was it really fear? It seemed so, for her heart raced, she trembled acutely, her molars were chattering, yet these denominators of the emotion in question ended resolutely and were then accompanied by traits clearly *unrepresentative* of the same.

The lubriciousness within her sex—in a single mental *throb*—grew so teeming that such sequent fluids ran openly down the inside of her thighs, and with each contraction of her heart there came an equal contraction of her *genitals*—ghosts of orgasms that seemed part of her natural state at the present time. It was the darkness past the ravaged window, she knew (something not as much a darkness as a *reckoning, audient physicalization*), and some constituent therein proving to be far more than a simple retardation of light. She could sense it thick in the air, while the air—inscrutable as it might sound—seemed surcharged with not only awareness but also some catalytic *attribute* that seeped into her blood. It *histrionicized* her nudity; it fired conduction in nerves hitherto unsparked; it ignited *mycoplasmic triggers* to permit of sensation thus far unrealized and unfelt; it tickled the very *gene markers* hidden deep amongst the neurosecretory *pieces of minims* that comprised every fiber of every living cell. Sary's breasts hummed in reactivity, her ovaries vibrated like hummingbirds caught in one's hand, while hormones transmogrified into *new* hormones and gusted forth from her pituitary gland to drench her libidinal receptors; and the orgasmic spasms of her genitals migrated directly—like an electric bolt—to her brain.

All this, merely by looking into the darkness within the house.

Out of mind now, Sary made the Voorish Sign, thrust the lantern back into the window, and looked—

THE DUNWICH ROMANCE

＊＊＊

Was it some imp of the perverse that decoded the retinal images in Sary's eyes and directed them into her memory? Her first glimpse into the bizarre house brought with it a paradoxical unconsciousness: paradoxical in that she seemed to behold herself and her surroundings as if drifting above her physical body; hence, a consciousness within *un*consciousness. Had her very spirit evacuated her body to move about and to *see?* If so, in what manner of vessel did her spirit now abode?

This question and a superfluity of others would occur to her in rapid succession only to be just as rapidly discarded as inconsequential. Matters of far greater signification were at hand . . .

Her nude body lay dormant beneath her, and Sary noted the clarity in which she saw it, as if through some slightly distorted yet harrowingly accurate lens which revealed every pore of her skin, every razor-sharp black hair upon her head and betwixt her legs, each individual lacteal duct of her areolae, etc. She then raised her head (in a manner of speaking, of course, since whatever now served as quarterage for her sensibilities no longer enjoyed a physical connexion to her body) in order to pilot her sense of sight into the confines of the house.

The two tentacles she'd previously glimpsed absconding with the ruffians were now joined by *dozens* more, each tipped by mouths which snapped open and shut in some celebrative synchrony. Those first two tentacles, however, still reeled about, grasping the now quite dead Manny Silva and Joe Czanek, and had Sary a greater capacity for linear thinking, she would've wondered what the appendages had in store for the two miscreant corpses. Instead, all of her attention fixed on the morphological madness and physical contradiction that existed within.

Did the scores of stovepipe-thick tentacles change from

blue to grey to purple as they also swelled and shrank as if to a premeditated rhythm? Ultimately, the living bulk looked like it had outgrown its shelter to such a degree that very little further growth would be permitted before the house erupted; indeed, so close were the massive thing's boundaries that Sary could scarcely see deep enough through the tentacles to espy what manner of *body* existed to sport the appendages. Might it be akin to the torso of a mammal? The carapace of a crustacean? Or the plasmic sheath of a bacillus cell? Inexplicable, too, was the manner in which the thing seemed to *phase in and out* of various states of being. First came a state of palpable *organum;* then a less composited state, as of jelly or mucus; then a state of distinct semi-solidness akin to compressed vapor.

Was this incalculable creature's physical mass edging into and out of a dimensional realm contrary to that of the known *three* dimensions?

If Sary were to learn this question's answer, it would not be today.

When she looked again, the corpse of Czanek was being dragged slowly in and out of the mouth-end of a broader tentacle, and each withdrawal dissolved or in some way abraded the cadaver's flesh. (One might've thought of a child sucking a popsicle.) Eventually, little remained save for bones, whereupon these, too, were admitted into the tentacular mandibles and swallowed whole. But Sary had been mistaken about the other corpse—Silva, the fat one— which still twitched with piteous life. From the writhing, impossible congeries, a more petite appendage emerged; it wrapped itself about Silva's genitals—just where the scrotum adjoins the crotch—and slowly tore the organ out at the root. This was swallowed, while more such tentacles converged and consumed Silva's physical form one bite at a time. Lastly, the remnants, like Czanek's, were swallowed and digested.

At this point, something changed.

Sary's unembodied senses felt a decline of temperature

and an elevation in proximal air pressure. The incognizable behemoth stilled itself, and Sary interpreted the stasis as an indication of *attention* on the thing's part. Why she would make this interpretation, there was no telling. Nevertheless, she was correct.

The thing, indeed, was *assessing* her.

Then a great many of the appendages which composed its physical form retracted . . .

Now Sary could see what existed as a foundation for the tentacles, the heart of the artichoke, so to speak. It was a mass of eyes, all which looked upon her in fascination and even respect. A mass of eyes, yes, the height and breadth of the largest pine tree on the property. Each eye seemed to be set in nothing at all akin to a socket but instead some gelatinous substance, and . . . did this substance also have mouths, or things *like* mouths, situated throughout? It would be pallid to say that this being—entity, creature, what have you—existed with virtually no alliance to the laws of nature as we know them; and it would be just as insufficient to say it was not of this earth. It was far more—and far less—than any of that.

The thing's body seemed to percolate, it seemed to *bubble* within. Its eyes did not blink, for they had no lids with which to do so, but they did variegate in shape, while their irises went from one astral hue to the next—colors, tints, and shades never before beheld by the natives of this planet.

Horrific? Yes. But fascinating as well.

And next?

The great bubbling mass began to *turn*.

Of course, it did not turn as, say, a human being would, nor did it change its position by means of swivelling or traversing. Instead, the excrescence of its base squirmed and rippled, licensing movement, and said movement could only be voluntary.

It meant to show her something.

When the squirming ceased, the creature had

presented to Sary the side of itself that had been previously eclipsed by the lantern shadows. It was this moment of unalloyed shock and tenebrific revelation that blacked out Sary's gossamer senses and sent her spirit soaring back into her prostrate body. A pair of appendages protracted from the hulk—the same pair, in fact, which had so effectively ended the careers of Messrs. Czanek and Silva— and gently lifted an unconscious Sary from her place just outside the window, then—extending farther—placed her back on the cot in the tool-house. They hovered momentarily, as if contemplating her in some commendable way, then retraced themselves back to the material gibbosity of which they were a part.

The actual sight which so forcefully shot Sary back into stygian realms of unconsciousness was nothing more than this:

The creature's face.

It was a half-face, really, the right side consisting of runnels, bumps, and indescribable contours whose purpose could not be estimated. The left side, however, demonstrated great patchworks of what might actually be *hair,* kinky, black accumulations like sporadic moss; one eye not in keeping at all with the myriad eyes that enshrouded the thing's thorax, complete with lashes and an irregular *brow*; a sagging lipped orifice that the anti-nature of the thing meant for a mouth; a distinctly recessive chin; and patches of some pale, yellowish covering which hideously resembled *human epidermis.* More clumps of crinkly hair sprouted about the mouth and the side of its face—a cheek?—and there was even a macabre convolution of flesh which bore a suspicious likeness to an *ear.*

Overall, however, this "face"—or the atrocious assemblage of impossibility that sufficed for one—bore a suspicious likeness to *Wilbur's* face.

(XVII)

AT A TIME nearly identical to that during which the criminal denizen Joe Czanek had been breaking into Wilbur's house, Wilbur himself was breaking into a mercantile emporium known as Leffert's Feedstock & General Goods, located in the township of Aylesbury. The mechanical nature of the intrusion had been so easy as to unwarrant exposition, and so were the descriptive details of the interior shop. Wilbur lowered his trousers enough to just expose the two ancillary eyes situated in his hips, and with these, he suffered no effort in navigating himself through the shop's utter darkness. A cash-box sat opened beneath the counter, revealing obvious loose bills and change, but the giant occult scholar had not come here with any intention of stealing; his moral posture, in fact, made distasteful—and moreover *unthinkable*—the idea of stealing from someone who hadn't stolen from him. On the contrary, his intention was to leave more than sufficient payment on the counter when he found what it was he needed.

And what he needed was ammunition.

Taking chances—or, worse, taking blessings for granted—was a sin he could not well afford, for tomorrow night, indeed, was the time. He remembered too well the guard dog near the Miskatonic library, and in spite of several physiological advantages, Wilbur knew that the dog was fortified with reflexes which surpassed his own and harbored fangs and jaws that might very well make

169

simpleton's work of his tentaclettes and even his probosciduct. Wilbur, in fact, had been *plagued* by vicious dogs all his life; he could scarcely embark on a leisurely stroll without some such hostile cur, enraged by his scent, tearing after him. Grandsire's big pistol had forestalled many a canine confrontation, much to the displeasure of the dogs' masters.

But not only was Wilbur running out of bullets for the formidable Webley .455, the cartridges his did possess were so old as to be of questionable reliability. Twice now, he'd had to repel attacks only to have the weapon's hammer fall on a defective primer, and though engaging the next round was but a matter of seconds, seconds were insufficient in certain instances. Wilbur was not afraid to die, but he knew that he must *not* die—or be grievously injured—before he discharged his all-important task on the night of the morrow.

Osborn's had stopped carrying the peculiar caliber Wilbur needed, and even when they'd most recently had it in stock, they'd refused to sell to him. "Ya big ass-ugly freak! Yer face looks like the devil's bunghole, and ye smell even *wuss!*" Tobias railed at him once. "Ye think I'm a-gonna sell ammunition to the likes of *ye?* Ya done already kilt half the dogs in the village, ya cockeyed monster! I'll have me no truck with the blood'a Wizard Whateley! Naow git aout!" Wilbur was surprised not at all by his cousin's hostile rant. "Yer bleach-faced ma sucked my dick onct fer a haff-pint'a hooch," the old misanthrope saw fit to add. "I pushed up that trash-cloth dress'a hers and gandered her pussy and—sweet Jesus!—the sight give me *nightmares,* boy! Look like a blammed *woodchuck* with a *ax-cut* in it!" Wilbur was none too pleased to hear such talk about his mother, yet he doubted the rant was invention; hence, it wouldn't have been ethical to hex the old man for mere words.

All that aside, the young colossan could ponder no other resort but to travel hither to Aylesbury to procure the necessary bullets. The piddling lock on the ammunition cabinet came apart with a single tug, then—

Disappointment.

The .455 cartridges Wilbur so desperately needed were not in the store's inventory. And since the establishment sold only ammunition and not firearms as well, Wilbur's trek had been a profitless one.

The gods be a-testin' me, he could only presume, for to exhibit agitation would be to reveal an absence of faith. No time remained for him to venture to another town. *I'll jess have to hope ta Yog-Sothoth that them old bullets I got'll fire.*

Wilbur felt no fear at the prospect. He would simply discharge his task to the best of his ability, or die in the endeavor. Yes, he felt certain beyond doubt: the gods were testing him.

But when the drone came into his head only moments later, he knew that another test was upon him. He'd only just quitted the store and commenced through the woods toward the Aylesbury Pike when he'd stopped to stand stock-still. It wasn't a seizure, nor any manner of ringing in the ears. Instead, this could be described as a *visual* drone, and he knew at once from whence it came.

His brother.

***

Wilbur, awkwardly as he appeared, ran all the way back home. It was the psychic coupling that existed between himself and his twin brother that had heralded his haste, and that same ethereal tether that showed him most of everything which had occurred back at his grandfather's house, to a level of detail as accurate as if he'd been physically present. Wilbur's clumsy trot foreshortened the several-hour walk to a span of under an hour; and when he arrived at the property—winded, flushed, and oozing netherworldly perspiration—he audibly cried out thanks to Yog-Sothoth and his retinue when he found Sary asleep and unharmed in the cot.

He leaned over, teary-eyed, and kissed her on the cheek. He prepared to depute with exigency to the house but found several trace scents afflicting his nostrils. A dank *reptilian* smell? And the tinge of unwashed female genitals of a particular nature as to remind him of his *mother?* Also a scent apart from all of that, much more concise: cologne. Dunwichers were not known to have much use for cologne, but Wilbur could not forget the homemade fragrance his grandfather concocted—with orange-flower oil and lavender—to wear on special occasions. A slow swerve of his head showed him the *Necronomicon* where he'd left it on the desk, no longer opened to Page 751. The ancient sheets of vellum now displayed Page 415 and the transition detailing the proper execution of the Voorish Sign.

That would certainly explain the haunting redolences within the shed.

Outside, the issuance of a chuckle could not be forborne when he discerned no physical vestige of Joe Czanek and Manny Silva. Wilbur envisioned with revel their gruesome deaths, relayed by the connexion betwixt himself and his leviathanic brother and seen through the latter's plethora of eyes, and he could smell their remains being digested therein. It was a rich, syrupy aroma, as often was the case of vile men who'd died inundated in fear and horror. So acute was that psychic cordage that *Wilbur himself* could faintly taste the reprobate scoundrels like after-flavors upon his own tongue.

At the violated window, he made the Voorish Sign and engaged in some telepathic confabulation. His brother smiled at him—a dolorous smile, of course—and Wilbur nodded and smiled as well. The grim acknowledgment flickered between them, though said acknowledgment came as neither much of a surprise nor much of a shock to either of them.

He boarded the window back up, then turned, cheeks still damp with tears, and he gazed at the lopsided moon. The icy light enlivened him. A beautiful world it truly was . . .

He whispered praise and thanks, turning for the shed. His strides were made with confidence and resolve. He knew he would not see his brother again.

❋❋❋

Sary stood tense and wide-eyed when Wilbur returned to the tool-house. The carriage clock's chime-like peals were just now expending four o'clock in the morning. Wilbur was well aware of the graveness of the situation, but the sight of Sary arrested all possibility of him speaking of it.

Never before had he seen her so beautiful than in just that pristine wee-hour moment.

Naked she remained, her breasts alert, even inflamed. Her body's contours could not have been more preeminent if they'd been chiseled by a Michelangelo or a Desiderio. The flat bright-white of her belly, the curvaceous legs, the stark black wedge of private hair—all converged to project into Wilbur an alchemy of ardor, attraction, and of *love* more empowered than the passion which launched a thousand ships. Against the flawless skin, the lamplight wavered, suggesting a sudden complexity emerging within the simple woman. Her hair spilled about her lambent shoulders like ink blacker than any shadow cast upon the earth.

Her lips parted to speak, but a further cogitation stifled them.

She be it, Wilbur knew.

Her wide eyes scintillated; where often they reflected naivety or confusion, they now blazed a *keenness* he'd never noticed in her before, not quite the keenness of cabalistic understanding, nor even of revelation—that would arrive later—but a *thirst* . . .

A thirst to *learn*.

"Sary," Wilbur whispered. This spectacular vision of her parched his throat.

"Sumpin' happened," she whispered back.

"I know it. And I know ye seen it yourself"—his eyes

gestured the opened book—"by larnin' ye haow to do the Voorish."

"I hope yew ain't flustered with me fer meddlin' where I shouldn't have been, but . . . *naow?* I got the feelin' that it's sumpin I *need* to know."

"It 'tis," Wilbur affirmed. "And theer en't no setch thing as meddlin' when it come to one's mind haow they got a *callin'.* A callin' to be part'a suthin' that be bigger'n all of us set together."

To these words, Sary's eyes went ever the wider.

"Them two fellas who come heer dun't caount fer nothin'," he explained. "Mebbe the gods sent 'em special, so to show you suthin'. The gods work that way sometimes. They make us *earn* our blessin's." Wilbur pointed in the direction of the house. "That One in there, wal . . . it be my brother."

This disclosure alarmed Sary not in the least; indeed, if anything, it answered some of her inner queries, of which there must be a multitude.

"It be my twin, come aout'a my ma right after me, on the Candlemas, 1915. See, I en't old as ye must've supposed. The way I be, I grow fast, and that One inside? It grow ever faster. Where I went tonight was to fetch some new—"

"Bullets," she said in a drone.

"Ee-yuh. On accaount them ones I got in the tin be real old setch that some of 'em dun't fire. But that place didn't have none."

Sary's posture fidgeted.

"Dun't worry. I en't afeared. Either Yog-Sothoth'll protect me or he wun't, and if he wun't, it only mean I en't worthy."

"We'll know soon," came Sary's cryptic remark.

This was a good sign. She was learning already, simply through the transpositional effect of proximity to Wilbur's brother. It was esoterica. It was science disguised as occult mystery—a pheromonal transduction of *knowledge*—for human sensibility did not exist broadly enough to understand. It *never* had. "We will, for sure," he said. "I'll tell ye what I can tonight, and if'n things go as I gotta mind they might, ye'll larn plennie more in time. Tonight be the night I gotta go—"

"To Arkham," she uttered. "To the college."

"That's right. I need to be there after midnight . . . when the stars are right."

Finally, Sary moved from where she'd been standing still as an erotic chess piece. She came over and hugged Wilbur desperately.

The words gushed against Wilbur's shirt. "I'm afraid, Wilbur."

"En't no reason to be," he assured her, wrapping his great arms about her. The heat from her naked body seeped into him. "En't no setch things as endin's—Grandsire teached me that. An endin' en't nuthin' but a beginnin' to suthin' else more important—least ways, I mean, for thems that prove themselves desarvin' of the favor of the gods. Them gods? They've *always* been good ta me."

She was shivering. "I'm afraid for *yew*. That somethin' bad'll happen."

"En't nuthin' bad *can* happen ta me," he began to assure her, but then thought it more serviceable to leave off the rest of the doctrinal explanation: the City between the magnetic poles, the Dho and the Dho-Hna, the *Spiritum in Aeternum,* the Yr and the Nhhngr, and the Transfiguration. She would learn it all at the proper time from the book. "Nor nuthin' ta happen ta ye neither," he whispered. "That I sware afore all I hold dear."

Wilbur leaned back and took off his shirt. Sary did not recoil—she *rejoiced*—at this full sight of his writhing, mouth-tipped tentaclettes. She seemed to turn boneless in his strong arms, her sex running with excited fluids. His probosciduct reared, then gently entered her vagina, to pulsate, while a salvo of tentaclettes converged upon her nipples and clitoris to ever-so-gingerly suck.

Wilbur carried Sary to the cot, lowered her there, then turned out the lantern.

***

Most of the final twenty-four hours of Wilbur Whateley's life can only be epitomized via estimation, not documentation. It can, though, be authoritatively intimated that the physical demonstrations of his love for Sary were most copious—indeed, such that for her final few hours she would spend in his proximity, she could barely stand on her own two feet. It was true that Wilbur needed to be inconspicuously deployed near the main library of Miskatonic University no later than midnight on August third, when the Moon assumed a nine-degree ecliptic belt and Antares, Saturn, and Betelgeuse formed a Cavalieri right triangle; this would require Wilbur to part from Sary's company by two p.m. on the second so that he might engage the bus that would permit of his venture to Arkham.

Sary struggled to stand when her lover made this information plain, demanding, "Won't take me a speck of time to get dressed," she asserted, "and I'll come with yew."

But Wilbur had no choice but to disallow the offer, in spite of its kindliness. "Naw, Sary, mutch as I'd like ta have ye with me, it jess carn't be. Yew best stay here, but with any luck, I'll be back tomorrow afternoon, sence them's the ways the bus work, for it only run twice a day."

"No!" she rejected, "I'm comin' with yew! I've got a mind yew plan ta steal a book they got at the college, and I gotta mind tew it'll be dangerous!"

Wilbur was quite taken by the expeditiousness with which she presumed to assist him, yet still he had to say, "I wun't let ye come with me, Sary, for 'tis true, mebbe it 'twill be dangerous, and there en't no way on the airth that I'll allow no harm ta git near ye. And it ain't stealin' I'm fixin' ta do, jess . . . borrowin'."

Fatigued from the previous tumult of intercourse and

sexual variation, Sary nearly toppled trying to get into her dress, but she managed a most indignant glare, pointed a finger, and exclaimed, "I'm a-*goin'*, Wilbur Whateley, and if yew think'a leavin' withaout me, I will pitch a fit far wuss than any storm yew ever see!"

"I got me no daoubt ye would," Wilbur replied, and smiled deeply at her resolve. What a wonder this was. All his life, he never thought the day would dawn when a woman would demand to be part of his life. *Ee-yuh, I love her sooooo mutch. Thank ye, Yog-Sothoth . . .* "Sorry ye carn't have your way on this, Sary," he began, still smiling his love for her as he recited one of the Eltdown Languor Spells, which made her fall asleep so fast she did so on her feet. Wilbur caught her, held her a while, and put her to bed. He looked at her with adoration and whispered, "I love ye, Sary."

Then he grabbed his canvas carry-sack and took his leave of the tool-house.

Sary's perceptivity, however, was quite on the mark. Though Wilbur wasn't *sure* of the evening's outcome, some assistance would prove very advantageous. Out on the Aylesbury Pike, when his awkward form arrived at the bus stop, it was none other than Kyler the psychic who was arriving as well.

"Hey, Kyler," Wilbur greeted. "Yew a-waitin' on the bus?"

"Aye, jest as are ye," the eccentric black-clad man replied. "Though it may not be credited by ye that I am subject to portents mysterious indeed, I've received it of goodly authority that it may be in ye're best interest to have me near."

Wilbur nodded, amused. "I never said I dun't believe yew're a soothsayer—"

The bright sun shined on the lame man's bald head, though his face remained peculiarly shadowed. "For what ye be in sarch of come in the waye of letters."

Letters, Wilbur thought with a pause. Did the cryptic

man with the cane mean letters as of correspondence? Or letters as of . . . the alphabet? Wilbur had no choice but to ponder this with some fascination.

"And for they who venture well into the night? Wal, oft times, when one be not on his proper guard," Kyler went on with nonchalance, "the night comes bearing teeth."

Teeth, Wilbur thought. *That dang guard dog . . .*

After a time, Wilbur said, "I be mutch obliged if ye come with me, Kyler, for I may well need ta ask a favor."

Kyler nodded. "Aye, if I could only ask ye to pay my fare."

"Oh, a'course, I will. 'Tis the least I can dew. As well I can offer ye this gold piece so's ya know the extent'a my gratitude," and then Wilbur offered him a mint-condition Saxon Offa coin struck in 1011 A.D., which would easily bring in ten dollars from a jeweler (but a thousand dollars from a qualified collector or auction house).

"Nay, Wilbur. No money can be took by me from a friend."

Wilbur consented to the wish but would secret the coin into Kyler's bag when he was unaware.

Just down the road, then, a dervish-like cloud of dust was rising. It was the bus to Arkham.

(XVIII)

THIS PORTION OF the narrative, as the finish approaches, might be regarded by some as disproportioned, but this can only be blamed on Fate—as the structure of life itself rarely issues in satisfactory equipoise. Wilbur Whateley did indeed encounter the end of his physical life in the early hours of August the third, in the Rare Books cove of Miskatonic Library. He was savaged by the guard dog which prowls the entire building at night, and evidently some appreciable time had lapsed between the gigantic man's unlawful entrance and the point at which the animal detected his presence. There was evidence of a candle being lit and of Wilbur's effort to *write* something quickly with pen and paper. What this *something* was would remain a fair mystery to the academic trio who discovered Wilbur's body; though one of the three, Dr. Henry Armitage, had the notion that the ungainly intruder had been translating and, hence, transcribing a section of the college's Latin edition of *The Necronomicon,* stanzas that might correspond to Page 751 of the 1582 English edition. However, no transcription was found, so if it existed . . . what had become of it? Armitage could only make an educated estimation.

After the corpse had disintegrated, one of Armitage's associates, Professor Rice, had pointed to a canvas sack askew on the floor and made the supposition, "He must have meant to steal *The Necronomicon* and carry it off in that."

"I'd think not, Warren," came the elder's reply, "for surely a man—or thing—as astute as Wilbur Whateley would have calculated in advance the sack's insufficient size. No, I believe he came here to copy something from the Latin, but I can only guess—since no transcription is present—that a partner of some sort made off with it."

"You mean a *second* perpetrator?" asked Dr. Francis Morgan.

Armitage pinched his chin in contemplation. "It seems so to me, gentlemen." Now that much of the stench had cleared, he walked to an ancillary exit door which locked from the inside. "I unlocked the vestibule door myself, but *this* door?"

Rice and Morgan saw at once that the access had been—

"Unlatched," Rice observed.

"So unless the security man was uncharacteristically lax tonight," Morgan continued, "this door here was indeed unlocked from the inside, by Whateley himself."

"Yes," Armitage agreed, "which might give more credulity to my theory of a second party."

Rice was nodding. "After violating the east window here, Whateley let his confidant in through this door."

Close examination at a later time revealed that Wilbur had arrived with full knowledge of the guard dog's threat, as a large pistol was found near the central desk, its hammer having clearly fallen on a defective cartridge. So swift the watch dog's reflexes had been that the awkward giant had insufficient time to forward the cylinder to the next round.

It was as simple as that.

Not so simple was the aspect of the decedent's body. There were few who disbelieved that an intruder had died in the room, for the repute of the three witnesses was not contestable, even as the details of the corpse remain a matter of private record, not public. It was actually better that way, for what might the masses interpret about the *aspect* of such a dead body? Better, too, in the long run, that the *corpus delecti* had actually vanished via some mode of disintegration before a camera could be procured for recording such evidence.

No description of Wilbur's naked body will be conveyed; it will only be said instead that the dog had attacked the colossal man with the savagery expected of it and ripped off most of the trespasser's attire along with unpleasantly large swatches of his epidermis—if it could be *called* epidermis. Within minutes of the occult scholar's death, no vestige of the man's physical mass remained, save for some morbid whitish liquefaction. This, too, would disappear completely just as the medical examiner arrived. The man—or entity— had disappeared as if he—or it—had never existed.

In the weeks following, no clue would be imparted to Armitage as to the identity of Wilbur's "associate," while all ponderment over the question would disappear as effectively as Wilbur had himself, in the second week of September, when the Dunwich Horror (in the form of Wilbur's twin brother) had erupted from its confines and gone on a futile and even pitiable rampage. After *this,* though, once the Whateley property had been certified as safe to examine, Armitage inspected the premise personally after having received, as per his instructions, all written material, letters, diaries, and books left by the departing giant.

Armitage would spend the rest of his life investigating the horrific affair yet would receive no reward for his effort. This failure would actually haunt the academician, such that he'd often feel he had lost some abstract battle with the dead giant he'd once sent out of his library. The doctor would have wagered his life that Wilbur Whateley had indeed copied Page 751 of the Latin edition and relayed it to someone else. So the question reared with some significance, even to the point of the doctor's own death: who had absconded with these transcriptions?

And why?

***

After wakening from the Languor Spell, Sary slept not at all for the entire night. Instead, she paced, worried, and looked repeatedly out the shed's door in the dim hope that Wilbur might return early.

But she could not wrest away from the conviction that he would not.

At daybreak, having no familiarity with the timetable for the Arkham bus route, she straggled morosely to the crude bus stop post and waited.

She waited some time, until past the noon-hour, in fact. Her heart gave an excited thump at sight of the rattletrap vehicle, then she jittered on her feet, hands clasped in prayer, when the smoke-belching motor slowed and stopped. The door flapped open, but the sinking feeling had already afflicted her—either a premonition or an umbra of pessimism—for she'd felt begloomed since she'd last seen Wilbur yesterday, and this feeling had worsened since a nervous nauseousness had struck her past sun-up, such that she'd reeled from a sudden, persistent headache and had even vomited. Had she been more mindful of symbolism, it might be said that she now awaited a *somatic vacua*, the very *personification* of her feelings.

Only a lone passenger alighted from the bus, and it was not Wilbur.

Over a minute was required to permit of Kyler's safe descent from the bus step, but once his cane was properly planted and his feet on the ground, he stepped forward toward Sary, dark of countenance but bizarrely fulgent of eye. At once, he said, "Aye, fair gull, 'tis to the gods we be all subjected, and with every shadow they may drop afore us, there come a grace ef we be so desarvin'. Of this, I believe, ye already have a bit'a mind."

The verbiage affected Sary with confusion and even agitation. Her spirit demanded that she immediately ask where Wilbur was; however . . .

The words became like a mass of logs clogging a river's course.

The bus blundered away, leaving a wake of dust which, once cleared, left the black-clad soothsayer standing at Sary's other side. Finally, the portent which so darkened her psyche allowed for speech. She said bluntly, "He's dead, ain't he?"

The strange bald man did not hesitate, nor did he mince the words of his reply. "Aye, Wilbur Whateley, ye're devot'd mate, be no more'a this airth, but who's ta say this airth here be the only 'un? 'Twas a dog of a most vicious sart which spell the tall man's end—"

Sary exclaimed with some adamance: "Then where be the grace that's s'posed ta come too! With Wilbur dead, I might's wal be dead myself!"

"Nay, gull, for what ye feel be the end'a ye jess really be the stert."

This was idealism and foolish rhetoric which, even if Sary knew what such words meant, she suspected at once that Kyler was only attempting to dull the blade-like pain that cut into her. No condolence could appease her now, nor any mode of rationalization. Wilbur was dead, and a reversion to her previous life was the only substitute. She would resort to self-annihilation before allowing such a consequence. No more intercourse for money, no more penises in her mouth. No more ingesting semen, laving horrific anuses with her tongue, or submitting to any further manner of carnal degradation.

No more.

"Take heart, gull," the fortune-teller offered, and into her hand he placed a sheet of paper tied in a roll. Then he began to walk away, his cane scuffing the dirt road's surface.

"What's this?" Sary demanded in a clap of a voice.

"'Tis Wilbur's legacy, thet is. And ye're new life."

"What?" she bellowed at the departing figure, but each time she blinked, the lame man's progress away from her seemed to double in an impossible amount of time. Indeed, he appeared to have traversed a mile in just minutes.

Crushed, outraged, and forlorn, Sary looked at the roll in her hand, then trod in her shiny black garment back to the tool-house. It was here she sat for hours, her eyes blank upon the old wooden walls. Certainly, the roll would prove a letter from Wilbur to her which, no matter how affectionate, she could not bear to read. A final letter was nothing but the inscription upon a grave-stone. Sary did not want to be reminded that she'd never see Wilbur again, for the missive would only *verify* that and hence distill her misery. She even considered killing herself without ever opening the note but . . .

Some unknown force countermanded the notion.

Not till sundown did Sary rise from her glum seat on the cot. She struck flint and steel, lit the lamp, then arranged herself at Wilbur's great desk. Some minutes more were expended before she untied the tube of paper.

One sheet was all she expected; what she found instead were several, the top three of which contained unintelligible scrawl arranged in numbered passages, seven in all. The writing seemed different from that of the various sheets she'd seen on his desk. No, this scrawl was penned with a seemingly greater care, as if to afford her a sharper possibility of interpretation, while the strange words were interspersed often with hyphens. She scanned a random line: *6) Guh-narl-ebb, eye shub- negg add-uk zynn nem-blud nie-ar-lat-hotep.*

Sary maintained a glum stare at the sheets. What possible reason could exist for having the bald man deliver to her such bizarre lines of writing?

The fourth and fifth sheet appeared as she'd expected: lines she could read, and tightly composed as if their author were heeding space. Sary steeled herself, then began to read:

Deer Sary: I writ this ahead uv time in case things

turn out less'n the way I wud prefer, which means if yew be reading this, I be dead. I take Kyler to the collige with me so's I'd have someone to bring back this message in case I got hurt or kilt. By now, especially after using the Voorish ta see my brother, ye know well I am not from hereabouts. My father come from a place far off from the Earth, way on up in the stars. It all be part of a plan that is importint, and of which ye be a strong part if ye chooze.

First thing I got to tell you mite not like but I hope yew do. I warn't speakin no lies when I tell yew severul days past that you need not wurry bout gettin pregnant by me on account my seed not be compatible with yor womb. This be true, but, well, it all change after lass night when you went to the winder that them men busted out and then got ye reel close to my brother. See, theres things in my brothers skin and breth that when he get too close to someone hereabout WORK INTA that personz blood and change em, and what it done was it change YOU, it change yer WOMB so's my seed become whut's called POTENT.

This means, Sary, you be pregnant this very second, pregnant from our lovemakin. Hope ye dont be mad, but it just be the way it is. Tis whut the gods want. It be best that we foller what they want cuz they know what is best for us. Acorse if this don't be to your liking, tis yore right ta git a abortion, which is what that man ye know Doc Houghton know how to do.

I hope ye do not do this thogh, on account uv what be in yew now is somethin we make together, and be a expreshion of how I feel for ye.

Sary may have stared at the passage for a solid hour, but from the second after she'd read the passage, her misery had been banished, to be refilled by a joy which felt brighter than the sun. Now she knew the root of this morning's unbidden headache and bout of vomiting— *morning* sickness.

I'm gonna have a baby! WILBUR'S baby!

When she regained control of her emotions, she read on:

What ye need to know rite off is I'm leevin all the Whateley gold to ye. It'll provide for you always and make it so ye never have to get with fellas again for money. It be hid in the liddle fenced cemetary out back, under the slab marked Silas Ephriam Whateley. Ye'll need a pry bar to git up the slab and a rope ta slide it back and forth on account it is very heavy, but what ya got to do ferst is cover the wood plank hangin on the nearest ash tree. It got things wrote on it that make all who look in the grave see nothing but a skeletin, however that coffin really be fulla gold. It's like a spell, called a Imperceptibility Conjuration.

Sary could not conceive of such an endowment. Her destitution had changed to incredible affluence in a single moment . . .

What also be hid in the coffin is a metal box what got in it all the most valuble pages from the books I got in the shed, mostly from the hinged book but also from other books. The payges was all copied by me so to keep em safe. Soon ye will need to start readin these pages so's to lern em. Lotta things in those pages that'll give ye powers like ye never dreemed, and I mean MAGICK powers.

Of this, Sary could scarcely maintain her equanimity. Was Wilbur crazy to say such things? Was there *really* such a thing as magic?

Then she recollected the Voorish Sign and what she'd seen . . .

Of course there was magic!

And now it seemed that Wilbur had bestowed it unto her . . .

My darling, if ye choose to be a part uv all this I am talkin bout, then first chance ye get, you take the biggest chunk of gold in Great Uncle Silas' grave, which be werth a thousand dollars eezy, and ye give it to Prudence Naller so to buy her big fancy barn which be up four sale now. Ye need that barn on account it will be big enough for all ye need. Don't mention none to Prudence Naller bout how ye know me, just give her that bloon of gold and that ole fussbudget will be happy to sell ye the barn.

The information, of course, left Sary rather fuddled. A barn? Why would Wilbur want her to buy a barn when his own livestock was barely existent now?

Buy the barn tomorow, then move right in, on account ye gotta get out of that tool shed an away from my house soon. My brother is fixing to bust quarters shortly and ye can't be anyweer near him when that happenz. Move all ye need from the shed to the barn but leave the big book with hinges and other papers there. There be no need to bother with em on account all you need is already in the copies in Great Uncle Silass grave. That man I told ye about, Armitage, he know I got that big book and if it is not there after I die, he will know someone else got their hands on it. So jest leeve it.

The papers I copy give ya all the power ye need for the future. Once ye read those papers in the grave, ye'll understand why you is importint, and why our BABY be importint.

At this, Sary determined herself. No, she did not understand, but she received the distinct impression that once she read the material he'd referred to, she *would*. The *baby*, now, was most crucial to her.

Ye'll understant more and more as time go on, by what ya learn from the papers and by what ye lern from even the air, once ye come into their graces . . .

Sary continued to stare and stare.

The rest uv the sheets that Kyler give will look amighty strange ta ye, but that be becuz I translated the words from the good copy they got at Miskatonic, which replace the mussed up words in mine. This be the rite way of the words from Page 751. They are chants, what ye say aloud three times apiece on the special days up on Sentinel Hill. Roodmas, the Walpurgis, Hallowe'en. See, I wrote the chants down in a manner that be called PHONETIC, which mean it allow you to READ the words the way they is supposed to SOUND.
    These words uv the chants be the most importint words ever knowed in all the world.

Sary felt an excitement buzzing in her veins. Somehow, crazy as all this sounded, she knew it was true, as if there were some component of *the very air around her* which imparted conviction and trust . . .
Yes. The very air around her.

THE DUNWICH ROMANCE

And there is other things on them sheets which be spells, incantations, hexes, and wards which ye'll learn how ta do. These are things thatll help ye along the way, and protect ye from bad folks and such. It is a tremendiss power ye will have, Sary. Though I be ded in body, I am not in spirit. Soon ye will even be able to see me when ya do the Voorish. It will be not my ghost but what's calt my eidolon, and I'll be able to help guide ye. Don't be confused, my sweethart, just do all what I say, and ye will see! Grate things be comin!

I'll be able to see Wilbur again! her thoughts rejoiced. The same way she saw the old man and that pale-skinned woman earlier, after she'd done the sign! Wilbur would still be with her in a sense!

And what I need to explane now is this: that baby ye got in yer belly? It really be TWO babies, twins. One will be like me, and one like that One in the house, my brother. You will grow to love em both once ye find out what this be all about . . .

Twins? Sary's eyes bloomed. *One like Wilbur and one . . .* Like that gigantic, tentacled monster inside the house . . . Sary rubbed her belly through the diaphanous gown. *It don't matter none that it be like that thing. All that matter is it be from Wilbur . . .*
More and more, she was beginning to understand.

One more thing, then I be off. Once all be done by us that our god need to be done, the world will change for the better, back to the way it is supost to be, and I will get a new body by means of what's called Transfiguration. Yew will too, and we will be together again. Once the earth is cleared off.

*Until this time come, pleese know I love you,
Sary, with all my hart, and I always will. Forever.*

*Love,
Wilbur*

***

Yes.

Once the earth is cleared off.

Sary learned quickly, from the papers in the metal box in Silas Whateley's grave, and from the density of the air in special places where the Words had been uttered, and from the muttering underneath the ground at Special Times.

And from Wilbur's momentary presences when she made the Voorish.

She had bought the Naller barn the very next day, just as Wilbur had posthumously requested. It was a great spacious barn, well large enough for what she now understood would begin to occupy it after nine months had passed. It also possessed several smaller rooms for herself and the other things she'd brought along. She read and re-read every day now, and would continue to, and would practice all the things she was learning constantly. Wilbur's death had given Sary a *new* life to live, not merely waiting for the time she would be with him again but also to be a fine, resplendent mother for the two children she would soon give birth to. This she knew, for all she was worth.

She knew something else as well.

When she did indeed give birth to the twins, she would name the human baby Wilbur.

THE INNSWICH HORROR

(I)

THE MOTOR COACH noise provided an aural mental backdrop: I imagined myself as the Master, and fancied I could see what *he* would see beyond the drab window. Not common fields, unremarkable tree lines, and a typical New England summer sky but scenes much more sinister. Blasted heaths pocking malnourished meadows and dying scrubland, trees twisted and lightning-scarred, and a sky onerous and swollen with menace. And there—yes!—over the rusted iron railing-work of a decades-old bridge, my gaze was commandeered by the sluggish Miskatonic, in whose depths God knew what lurked or lay bloated in death or states *worse* than death. The prosaic bus window was no longer a simple transparent pane but a prism-obscura, a looking glass to eldritch sights, nether-chasms, and leaky rives betwixt dimensions and incontemplatable horrors. Then I blinked—

—and slumped with a smile. It was just the rushing and very healthy Essex River below and, to either side, an endless rise of pine and oak. No, though God had possessed me with an ample grasp for learning, I was not so possessed by even an irreducible fraction of the Master's imagination. I suppose that's why I delighted so in his tales. Imagination, indeed, was a gift better reveled in by true scribes of the fantastical.

Scribes such as Howard Phillips Lovecraft.

I shared the bus with but a half-dozen other fellows, men of hard labor, judging by their appearance; and I dared wonder if Lovecraft himself had ever ridden this same bus. If so: *Which seat? Which window did he gaze past to titillate his muse?* It was a funny thing, such reverence to this manner of fiction. Just as HPL was obsessed with everything from the cosmos to colonial architecture, I, it seems, am obsessed with his work.

My name is Foster Morley, thirty-three years of age, brown-haired and brown-eyed. I suppose Lovecraft might describe me as nondescript and unobtrusive, but he would likely be amused by a certain parallel. Like so many of his protagonists, I come from solid English gentry and family means, wealthy by legacy, and hold an unutilized degree from Brown University. I occupy a 180-year-old manse in stately Providence, near the Athenaeum, where my family bloodline migrated to before the Revolution. That family is now deceased, I the only offspring. Hence, by the grace of my Creator, my days are dreams in which I want for nothing, and when I am not philanthrophising . . . I read. I read Lovecraft, over and over again, for never have mere words on paper been able to transport me to other, more interesting worlds. Worlds not akin to this one at all—with its financial depression and its unfathomable wars. No, but instead worlds of dreadful wonder and daedalic terror.

Oddly, I was never aware of Lovecraft until I read an obituary in the *Providence Evening Bulletin* over two years ago, in March of 1937, commenting on the local academic fantasist's passing and strange career. Curiosity piqued, then, I lucked upon the June 1936 issue of the magazine *Weird Tales* and pored over "Shadow Out of Time." From that point, I was duly habituated, after which I expended minor sums but fastidious effort in making everything the Master wrote a constituent of my library. My obsession was at hand, and more than that—perhaps my salvation. Though content in my companionless solitude, I now had something bereft to me for so long: mental substance, a trip to lost terrascapes every night, rather than counting tedious hours of vacuity.

THE INNSWICH HORROR

I took to re-reading his work at the tree by his grave at Swan Point Cemetery; I strolled weekly past his rooming-house in College Street and would always stop to peer out upon Federal Hill and spy St. John's Catholic Church, his model for his last tale in earnest, the brilliant "Haunter of the Dark"; I'd prowl Angell Street and Benefit, hoping that some psychic lingering of the icon might brush by me—or somehow bestow a macabre, ethereal blessing; I'd even shop weekly at the Weybosset's Store where he so often spent his pittance on food. More than once, too, I railed to New York to stare up in awe at the squalid Flatbush rowhouse where the Master lived off and on with his wife; most recently, I lit a votive at St. Paul's Chapel on Broadway, where they married. I took to traveling where *he* traveled: from Marblehead to the District of Columbia to New Orleans, from Wilbraham, Massachusetts, to Dunedin, Florida—and exclusively by steam train or motor coach, for this afforded me to see what he saw on the same long and clattering jaunts. That process—*seeing*—was most crucial to me, seeing and being where he had been. I once stood at the foot of Poe's grave in Baltimore, only because I knew that Lovecraft had stood there once as well. I even tried to purchase the looming gable-manse at 135 Benefit Street, but the owners would not sell, even for the preposterous price I offered, this being, of course, the nefarious, lichen-enslimed "shunned" house.

Obsessed? Without doubt. An alienist, I'm certain, would label me with some syndrome close to clinical, something analytically Jungian. Through Lovecraft's words, I know that I was desperately in search of something, and I'll only know what that something is when I find it.

Er, pardon me. I should say that I've already found it—in Innswich—perhaps to my eternal turmoil.

I'd left the servants in charge—they were quite used to my junkets of inexplicable travel by now—and had decided to retrace the fictive journey of one of his characters, that character being the unnamed protagonist of my very favorite tale, *The Shadow Over Innsmouth*. HPL's own notes, according to his confidant August Derleth, name the hapless fictional character as *Robert Olmstead,* though the name never appears in the actual story. It is not difficult to see, however, Mr. Olmstead's mirror image to Lovecraft himself: an antiquary and architectural afficionado traveling the depths of New England, always by the least costly mode possible, to pursue his own obsessions.

This, then, would serve as my summer outing. Robert Olmstead departed Newburysport for Arkham on July 15, 1927, with the intention of perusing the witch-haunted town's archives and Colonial structure. Hence, my own desire to duplicate Olmstead's trip, again, to *see* what Lovecraft saw. Therefore, ever the stickler for detail, I commenced with my own sojourn on July, 15, 1939, leaving Newburysport from the same bus stop in front of the very real Hammond's Drug Store for the town of Salem, which was HPL's blueprint for Arkham.

I'd selected the forward-most seat on the coach, on the right-hand side, which afforded a spacious view through the windscreen. Several miles past the Essex now, the scenery seemed to denigrate in a manner that eludes sensible description; suddenly, the woods looked *impoverished,* the vegetation lost its summer luster, and even the road, paved only by crushed oyster shells, elicited the word *sallow,* though I know this sounds preposterously non-schematic. It was something, however, that existed beyond that month's record-breaking drought. An unchecked darkness settled in my spirit for reasons I cannot define.

Finally, through the windscreen, I took refreshing note of some sign of humanity: a rundown wood-slat shack—obviously a domicile—next to what appeared to be a smokehouse. A hog pen, too, caught my eye, bounded by crude chicken wire and surrounding less than half a dozen swine. Something smelled appetizing, though, which I thought could only be from the smokehouse. Lastly, a sign and roadside vending stand came into view. The sign read: ONDERDONK & SON. SMOKEHOUSE—FISH-FED PORK. At the same instant we passed, the driver seemed to grunt.

"Fish-fed pork?" I queried the driver. "I've never heard of that. Have you ever happened to try it?"

The driver's face remained forward, and at first, I thought he had no intention of answering. "T'ain't nothin' I've ever et nor ever will. Same five hogs in that pen damn near year-long. More like fish-fed *skunk,* knowin' the Onderdonks. He and his kid—they'se furren. Don't like 'em, an' they'se don't like us."

A second of cogitation translated *furren* as foreign. I couldn't resist: "Us as in whom?"

"Don't matter!" the driver snapped. "Me, I'm just doin' my job. But them Onderdonks don't dare try to sell past the loop."

By now, I had no conceivable idea what founded the driver's displeasure. "The loop?" I said more to myself.

"They sell that slop you call barbeque to migrants and plain folk who happen to be travelin' from New'bry to Salem, but they never take the loop in to town."

The perplexion steeped. I thought I'd best keep my queries to myself, yet I also knew that the map showed no other town between Newburyport and Salem. "The town? You must mean Salem, but surely, we're still an hour off at the least."

"No," he grumbled. Only now did I take notice of the driver's features—first recounting Lovecraft's story and the motor-man named Joe Sargent, cursed by that "Innsmouth look": narrow-headed, flat-nosed, crease-necked, with unblinking, over-protuberant eyes. Sargent's appearance causes in the mind of Robert Olmstead a spontaneous aversion. This fellow here, however, though surly in demeanor, was just a commonplace workingman.

"Olmstead," he said, "and here's the loop now." He

veered aside and took a fork in the road past a sign that read OLMSTEAD—2 MILES—POP. 361. "This the only bus that goes there'n it's a fifteen-minute time-point."

It wasn't the fact that we were suddenly embarking toward a town I'd not heard of (not to mention a town not displayed on the map) but something else altogether. "*Olmstead?*" I pressed the word. "You're telling me there's an uncharted town called *Olmstead?*"

The question perturbed him. "It's on the time-table. We had a devil of a time tryin' to get the county to let us put in a bus stop; they made us *incorporate,* whatever that means 'sides havin' to pay a fee. Had to do the same to get mail delivery. T'ain't right that Olmsteaders shouldn't have no way to get to the bigger towns, especially the economy bein' the way it is," and then an abrupt thumb jerked over his shoulder to gesture the six other passengers sharing the coach with me. "Weren't for the fishin'," he added, "we'd be sunk."

Though these men must've heard the driver, their faces remained blank. They were unkempt, shabbily attired—fishermen, I saw, for they each had an armful of new fishing rods, plus several rolls of nets. It was clear they'd traveled to Newburyport to purchase these supplies. Still, though, the distraction of these rough but normal men didn't suffice to sway my major focus . . .

This is something. An arcane notion told me that mere coincidence wouldn't suffice to explain this. A town—Olmstead—sharing the name of Lovecraft's very protagonist in *The Shadow Over Innsmouth* . . .

The road narrowed and grew more runneled as my olfactory senses told me we were nearing the water. Suddenly, an excitement usurped all other thoughts. Though Lovecraft traveled extensively his entire adult life, none of his travel logs that I knew of mentioned a town called Olmstead. *Had this town given Lovecraft the name of his main character?* I so hoped. *And if so, what would the town be like?*

The answer would be soon at hand.

(11)

IT WAS AN assailing disappointment that first swept me as the smoke-belching coach stopped in what I presumed was Olmstead's town-center. In fantasy, I thought I'd made a unique discovery: that I'd stumbled upon the true model for the Master's most masterful tale, and that, at any moment now, I'd be envisioning Innsmouth's evilly shadowed alleys, crumbling wharfs, and oddly angled, steep-roofed buildings rife with decrepitude and that "wormy decay" so ably conveyed by the tale's creator.

Instead, I was greeted by nothing of the sort. Olmstead clearly owed its architecture to the utilitarian government blockhouse designs that came with the subsidized renewal projects of the late-'20s to early-'30s. What a let-down! Olmstead, indeed, was generic, not singular.

The bus seemed to hiccough smoke a full minute before the motor shut down. The half-dozen shabby fishermen stood from their seats simultaneously, then filed out, carrying their rods, tackle, and nets.

"Fifteen minutes, in case ya want a breather and a stretch," informed the driver without looking at me. "You're goin' on to Salem, right?"

"Yes, sir. Thank you," I said and followed him off. He headed across the sterile street, toward a shop.

The smell of fish and low tide gushed down the street from the direction I knew must be shoreward. Nothing at all like the aghast *reek* that so nauseated Robert Olmstead in the tale. The town-center left nothing particularized to

199

describe, just block building after block building. Some must be apartments, for out from their windows hung laundry to dry; others must be businesses, though I detected not much in the way of local commerce. Now, I had to smile at my overzealousness. The coincidence of the hidden town's name was clearly just that. *And this place,* I thought, *was no more a creative influence to Lovecraft than it would be an influence to any traveler: lackluster, unfeatured, insipid.*

When rising footsteps signaled me from this juvenile plunge of disappointment, I expected to find the chilly driver returning but instead looked up into the smiling face of a spry, good-conditioned man about my own age, or perhaps slightly younger, sharply dressed in conservative suit and tie, with dark-brown hair neatly combed. He carried a briefcase and wore one of the smart beige Koko-Kooler hats, which were all the fashion rage among younger men these days. His expression seemed, oddly, one of relief, though I was certain we'd never before met.

"How do you do?" he greeted.

"I'm quite good and hope you are as well."

"Sorry to intrude, but it's just that your face seems a bit more welcome than the other men I've met here." His eyes glimpsed the cumbersome coach. "I take it you're traveling?"

"Why, yes. I'm going on to Salem. The name's Foster Morley—"

"William Garret," he returned and heartily shook my hand. Then he whispered, "Some odd ones in this town, eh?"

"None that I've yet noticed," I admitted. "Haven't seen anyone else about, other than you, I mean. You're obviously not an 'Olmsteader,' to use the driver's designation."

"No, I'm not. I'm from Boston, an accountant—er, I should say an *unemployed* accountant. So you haven't seen a blond fellow walking about, have you?"

"I'm sorry, no. I'm just taking a stretch before the coach is off again. Why do you ask?"

Now, his deportment shifted to something more intense. "It's my friend, you see—his name's Poynter. We worked in the same accounting firm but both lost our jobs when this depression—as they're calling it—got the best of our business. He came here a month ago and recently wrote me. He found a job, I should say, but now I can't find *him*."

"Is that so? Did he say who'd hired him on?"

"One of the fisheries down at the point, to keep records," and then he turned and gestured the source of that wispy fish- and tide-smell. "There are several there, but none I've found know anything of my friend, and none are hiring accountants."

"Perhaps your friend Poynter didn't care for his new job and has already left town," I suggested.

"No, no, he wouldn't do that. He was *expecting* me."

My next question seemed the most logical. "Where did he direct you to meet him once you arrived?"

Now, Garret pointed to a multi-storied blockhouse across the street. "The motel there, the Hilman House. I took a room—only fifty cents a night, so I can't complain about *that*—but the strange thing is . . . " He paused, though, in aggravation. "When I checked myself in, the clerk said that Leonard Poynter, my friend, had indeed rented a room there and was currently still a guest. The problem is I can't for the life of me find him."

So obvious was Mr. Garret's enigma, but now I possessed an enigma of my own. That excited fugue-state came back into my head, and I knew that I'd discovered something for sure. First a town called Olmstead and a character called Olmstead, and now?

In Lovecraft's *The Shadow Over Innsmouth,* the protagonist checks into a motel called the *Gilman* House, and now here I stood looking at a motel called the *Hilman* House. I'm sorry, but *this* was more than coincidence. It *had* to be. Something about this tedious town, without a doubt, impressed Lovecraft enough to at least borrow some names from it, and I was suddenly convinced that there must be more influences waiting to be divulged.

Garret peered close, concern in his eyes. "Mr. Morley? Are you all right?"

His voice snapped me out of my mental revel. "Oh, sorry. Something sidetracked me. But you know what? I think I'll be staying on for a few days after all."

"Splendid!" he whispered again, through a tight smile. "It'll be good to know that I'm not the only normal person in town."

I laughed distractedly, but before I could say more . . .

"Hello, gentlemen," a soft voice greeted.

We both turned to take wide-eyed note of a commonly attired yet perfectly attractive woman. She strolled down the walk, arms full of groceries, and grinned more than typically at the two of us.

Garret tipped his hat. "Miss . . . "

"Gorgeous day, isn't it?" I plodded.

"Oh, yes, it is," and that was the extent of our discourse.

"There's a looker," Garret whispered.

"I should say so," I remarked, actually a bit ashamed, for this woman's over-typical good looks gave me cause peer more than I should've. Her bosom could be described as raucous, as she was not only endowed but appeared un-brassier'd. The respect I had for my Christian faith reminded me what Jesus said regarding lust, but not in enough time to avert my eyes.

"As they say in England," chuckled my friend, "there goes the apple-dumpling cart," but then he leaned closer to denote discretion, "but that's another queer thing about this little town."

"That being?"

"I'm serious, man. I've never seen so many pregnant women in one place in my life."

"Preg–" I began, and when I gave myself another yet

more distanced glance, the more than moderate gibbosity of the woman's abdomen told all. "Well, I'll be. You seem to be correct."

"Four or five months at least, and it's not the first biscuit in that one's oven either."

I looked dismayed. "How on earth can you tell *that?*"

He elbowed me with a grin. "You saw the jugs on her. They're still filled up from the last one."

The uncultivated talk was making me uneasy, for it wasn't my bent. "But, really, what did you mean when you said you've never seen so many—"

"This town—I'm serious. I'll bet that's the dozenth pregnant woman I've seen since I've been here, and I'm telling you, most of them have been lookers."

"Really . . . Still, it's a good thing, if you don't mind my opinion. The government is wise to encourage propagation since the Spanish Flu epidemic of '18. We lost half a million in that, they say, and almost all of them young men."

Garret nodded grimly. "And right after losing—what?— another hundred-some thousand more men in that devilish war with the Huns. I agree with you. America needs more birthing, especially if we have to get into this next one with Germany, like so many believe."

I wasn't sure how I felt on this subject; I tended to trust authority. "But the President just declared neutrality in the European War."

"It doesn't give me much comfort, I'll tell you. Right after Germany and Russia signed the non-aggression pact, look what happens. Russia invades Finland. And don't believe that Brit Neville Chamberlain either. Peace in our time? Hitler's pulling the wool over the whole world's eyes. And what are the Japanese doing in the meantime? Invading Manchuria."

"Let's pray God that men can find a diplomatic solution." It was my nature not to engage in political conversation, though the man had some points that perhaps gave me cause to feel naive. "But getting back to our previous, if not a bit too earthy topic, we must be fruitful and multiply—"

"Just as it says in the Good Book, yes. And I tell you," he went on, "I'm not too pleased about Congress striking the Comstock Act—when was that? Last year?"

"No, no, it was '36, and we agree again, William. Barrier prophylactics should remain illegal except when prescribed by a physician for the prevention of disease. An open market for such things really does circumvent nature—"

"And God's will, if you don't mind my saying so."

"Not at all," but then we both looked at each other and laughed. "Not exactly everyday conversation, eh?"

"No, my friend, it isn't, but it's still invigorating to find someone who shares my doctrines," he said.

"Likewise. So now I suppose you'll be returning to your search for your friend, Poynter. I'm going to check in to the Hilman and then take a stroll about. I'll be sure to keep an eye out for your friend. Let's meet for dinner tonight. If I happen to find your friend, I'll bring him. Say, seven o'clock?"

"A terrific idea, Mr. Morley—"

"Call me Foster, please. And where's a suitable restaurant?"

Again, he pointed just across the street, to the small restaurant I'd noticed earlier, Wraxall's Eatery. "It's not bad, and large portions for a slight price."

"Good. Seven—I'll see you then."

Garret walked off, a spring in his step now that he had a "normal" confidante. I, on the other hand, had a new exhilaration to feed my Lovecraftian obsession. Though the town looked nothing like the Master's Innsmouth, what little tidbits of recognition might I find in its details?

I fetched my valise from the coach, and when I returned to the street, the driver stood sullenly before me. The look on his face might be called hateful. "Why ya got your bag? We'll be takin' off for Salem now. Ya t'ain't staying in Olmstead now, are ya?"

"Actually, yes," I told him. "I've changed my mind and decided to stay a few days."

At first, he appeared about to object, as though the prospect offended him. After all, I wasn't an "Olmsteader." It occurred to me just now how small his mouth seemed. The little twist of lips turned. "Now's I thinkin' on it, you might like Olmstead." Then the fleshy twist merged into something like a smile. "And Olmstead might like *you*."

He climbed back aboard the bus and drove off in a smoke-chugging clatter.

So Olmstead might like me? I mused. Of that, I cared little. But clearly something about it had impacted Lovecraft to blend some of its peripheries into his shuddering tale of inbred fish-people and pseudo-occult horror.

Just like in the story, the vested, elderly clerk at the Hilman's front desk seemed pleasant and conventional enough; he was all too happy to let me a room. Without much pre-cognizance, I blurted, "Would a Room 428 be available?" for this—as astute readers will know—was the room Robert Olmstead rented in the story.

"So you've been here before!" the man seemed to delight in a neutral accent. "That can only mean you like our accommodations. See, since the rebuild, Olmstead looks quite nice and's got some fine amenities."

I didn't spoil his assumption by revealing that I'd never previously visited, but instead I evaded by inquiring, "The 'rebuild?'"

"Ah, yes, sir. 1930, '31 thereabouts, government contractors put up all these nice, sturdy block buildings. Fire-proof, storm-proof, like they done lots'a places. When the Great Storm hit last September, there weren't no damage at all. But Olmstead of the past was a sorry sight. Just an old rotten wharf town fallin' in on itself. God bless Roosevelt and Garner!"

This came as no surprise. Soon after the stock market collapsed in '28, the Federal Re-Employment Act hired on thousands of jobless for reconstruction purposes, paying a dollar a day. Many towns in disrepair were rebuilt. Now, however, inspired by the new information, I couldn't help but feel sure that what Olmstead looked like before this rebuild *had* to be the visual picture Lovecraft painted for his readers in *The Shadows Over Innsmouth.*

My work's cut out for me, I thought, thrilled by the promise. Certainly, behind Olmstead's new face, there must remain some vestiges of its *old* face. I was determined to find the crannies and cracks that would lead me to them.

Room 428 proved quite comfortable: well-furnished, a new bed, even its own bathroom, complete with Cannon brand towels. Nothing like the dingy hovel that happenstance had forced Lovecraft's character into. The bathroom, in fact, offered brand new cakes of Lux Toilet Soap, the best national brand. I was also impressed by the RCA Victor Console radio provided as well; it was similar, though not *quite* as fine as the pricier model I owned in Providence. The room's metal-framed windows offered a view of the seaward rise, a formidable sight. If anything unnerved me, it was the room's *newness.* The entire building, in fact, felt barely used, as though it were a facade, feigning an appearance of prosperity that didn't truly exist.

But what an absurd thought!

As I made my exit from the room, I caught sight of a maid leaving another room, but she wasn't pushing the expected cart full of brooms and linens. She was hefting a suitcase. She couldn't be a guest: her outfit left no doubt as to her duties. The scenario simply seemed odd, but what alarmed me right off was her most obvious trait.

She was pregnant.

"Miss!" I called out, rushing down. "You mustn't carry that in your current state! Let me take it for you."

When I'd approached her directly, I was smiled at by a comely, youthful face framed by luxuriant tousles. A more roguish observation might be to say she was one of Garret's "lookers." Shapely legs flexed as she lifted the case, while her gravidness—like the woman on the street—had enhanced her bosom to dimensions that would cause even the most steadfast gentleman to glance more than covertly.

"Oh, that's very kind, sir, but it's not heavy at all," she gently replied.

"I insist. You're with child and shouldn't be carrying—"

"Really, sir." She giggled playfully. "It's light as a feather. And my doctor told me moderate exercise is good for the baby."

I couldn't very well argue. Even pregnant, though, she was strikingly physiqued. She couldn't be much more than twenty, and I guessed her to be late in her term. Something about her proximity to me felt rejuvenating, some impalpable element of her smile, gender, and youth. I considered what she symbolized: vitality, a brimming life blossoming with still more life . . . All which served to remind me of the counter-productivity of my own indulgent existence. Suddenly, my mind raced to maintain conversation, if only to continue in her presence a moment more.

"An acquaintance of mine—Mr. Garret—is searching for his friend, a Leonard Poynter. He's apparently taken a room here. Have you had a chance to see him?"

The maid's eyes suddenly seemed weary in spite of her youth and beauty. "No, I'm afraid not, sir." She spoke more quickly now, her full lips glistening. "It's not my place to learn our guests' names."

"Oh, I see," but still I struggled for more to say. "What's your opinion of the menu at the restaurant across the street, miss? I'm to meet Mr. Garret there later."

"Oh, Wraxall's, it's quite good, and Karwell's opens at eight o'clock, if you're one to imbibe since the repeal of Prohibition. The people there are nice. Our little town doesn't seem very big, but there's actually a good many folks passing through—workers and salesmen—between the bigger towns and cities."

"That's good to hear, and, yes, it is a nice town indeed—"

"But I really must be going now, sir," she hastened. "It's been pleasant talking to you."

"The pleasure's been all mine . . . "

I watched her turn with a downcast smile, yet couldn't escape the impression that she was slightly uncomfortable.

She disappeared down the stairs, and I urged myself to wait a moment before I proceeded down myself; I couldn't have her thinking I was being a nuisance or, worse, caddish. After a minute, however, I entered the stairwell myself. The maid's descending footfalls could be heard echoing in the well; when I peered over the rail, I saw she'd already stopped on the landing and was taking the suitcase through the door. The door's shutting echoed briefly.

Something immediately began to bother me as I took the steps down myself, and I knew what it was when I arrived at the landing she'd stopped at: it was not the lobby door she'd gone into; it was the door to the second floor.

Why would she be taking a guest's suitcase to the second floor?

I tried the knob and found it locked.

A guest had simply changed rooms, I reasoned next. That was all.

Several clerks and presumably a maintenance man busied themselves in the lobby, all quite congenial, and back out on the street now, I spied several shop keepers through windows, a fellow sweeping the cobblestoned main road, and a postage carrier. All smiled and nodded to me. When I strolled down the street, still more local persons met my eye, and not one of them failed to speak a greeting or nod cordially. This forced me to recall Garret's observation: *Some odd ones in this town, eh?*

What could he mean by that? Other than the churlish driver and perhaps the several furtive fishermen on the bus, there was nothing at all odd about anyone I'd encountered. He'd mentioned interviewing for jobs at some of the waterfront fisheries; perhaps that's where he'd been treated oddly. Watermen were known to be a sullen and protective lot as a rule.

I'd brought along my copy of *The Shadow Over Innsmouth,* for after a bit of strolling, I was sure I'd want to re-read it, perhaps beneath a shady tree, or in the park if there was one, or maybe the waterfront. It was a copy of the only hardcover of Lovecraft's work to be bound and published in his lifetime, the Visionary Publications edition. It cost one dollar plus postage. I was almost certain now that Lovecraft had indeed been in Olmstead and had been quite influenced by the place. Knowing this would make the re-reading all the more fascinating.

Now. Find a quiet place to read, I thought.

Across the street, passing a flag circle, a youthful woman bounded by, and she, too, smiled quite generously at me. Her prettiness equaled that of the maid, but there was another similarity: she, too, was pregnant.

Not that there was anything unseemly about encountering three pregnant women the same day, regardless what Garret believed. It merely seemed coincidental.

Coincidences, though, were the cause of my being here, and when I remembered that, my previous zeal was refreshed. Now I could embark on my quest to uncover more topical parities between this very real town of Olmstead and Lovecraft's very fictitious Innsmouth.

I walked over to the Ethyl Gas Company station, whose sign boasted gasoline for 9 cents per gallon, a penny lower than the city. There, I purchased a pack of my favorite Beechies chewing gum with pepsin from a pleasant proprietor but was told that no local maps could be had, just county and state. I was informed, however, that there were benches along the waterfront where I could read comfortably.

A block down, a motion-picture theater advertised Gene Autry's latest: *Prairie Moon.* I now laughed at my fantasies: Lovecraft would've been appalled to find such modern conveniences in the town that was once the model for the crumbling Innsmouth. Before I could cross the street, engine-roar startled me with some suddenness, and I turned to see a sizable truck rumble by. Its doors read IPSWICH FISH CO., and it was clearly heading north, to its city of provenance. The back of the truck—I could see as it passed—was stacked full with iced-down fish. The anomaly sparked at once: why would a large fishery such as Ipswich be buying fish in Olmstead? *It should be the other way around, shouldn't it?* Olmstead didn't strike me as large nor involved enough to compete with the big fisheries, and besides, the papers made it plain that fishing in this part of Massachusetts had dropped off due to silt disturbance from the Great Storm and higher river salinity caused by the summer's drought.

When a finger tapped me on the shoulder from behind, I flinched and spun. Smiling before me in a work apron and plain cotton dress was a bright-eyed, short young woman, no more than thirty. Even more so than the maid, her prettiness radiated, and not even the clumsy work boots and unbecoming hairnet could take from it. The hair seemed caramel-blond beneath the net. "Come in for an ice cream, sir. They're only five cents, and we make it fresh here. See, we've just got our own machine!"

She seemed to communicate the information with an overflow of pride; I was nearly taken aback when she grabbed my hand outright and gestured me into the shop, which only now did I discern to be Baxter's General Store and Postal Annex via stenciled paint on the window glass.

The bell rang as we passed through. "My name's Mary Simpson, sir," she brimmed and rushed around the counter. "I suppose you're only passing through, but you really *must* have an ice cream."

My amusement was intensified by the aforementioned prettiness. "A chocolate, please. I'm Foster Morley, Miss Simpson, and you're correct, I am just passing through, a bit of a traveling holiday, exploring new parts and such.

Plus I'm an avid reader. But I hope to be staying at least several days. I've a room at the Hilman."

"Oh, good. It's a nice motel now, and so is everything else since the rebuild."

"Mmm, yes, so I've been told by the desk clerk . . ." but at once I was seized by an abrupt beguilement: I saw now—now that I'd had chance to make a more definitive visual surveillance—that the bright and bubbly Miss Simpson was not only very attractive and very amply bosomed but also very pregnant. I could detect this quite plainly by the protrusion of her apron. "I'm finding Olmstead most interesting," I continued. "A successful example of President Roosevelt's social refurbishment program."

"Oh, yes, sir. Olmstead was barely fit to live in before that. But now we've got all new buildings, a library, a new warehouse district and fire station; we even have an ice-factory on the waterfront, like what they have in the big ports."

"As a matter of fact, I just saw a truck bound for Ipswich loaded with iced fish. I take it the fishing's in good repair here?"

She passed me my bowl with a spoon. "It's never been better, sir—"

"Please, call me Foster, Mary, and please allow me to buy you an ice cream as well."

This smidgen of generosity delighted her. "Thank you, sir—er, Foster," and then she fixed a bowl for herself. "But the fishing, yes, it's the backbone of the town. We're actually selling fish to many towns, even Boston, while in the past if we wanted fish, we'd have to buy it from them. Fishing's better here now than anywhere else. In Olmstead, you'd scarcely know there's a depression."

Since she'd made the observation, I suddenly had to agree. I saw only clean streets, fine buildings, and smiling people since I'd arrived, not disheartened breadlines, uncollected garbage, and collapsing homes. In addition, I saw another Lovecraftian parallel: Innsmouth, like Olmstead, was an unusually thriving fishing town.

"See," she continued with her professional pride, pointing her spoon to the shiny white machines. "We have Westinghouse meat-keepers too, and our own delivery truck that's almost new. And—"

I waited for her to finish, but instead, her eyes merely widened in silence.

"Is something the matter, Mary?"

"What a coincidence!" she squealed. "Your book, I mean!"

I'd set my copy of *Innsmouth* on the counter when I'd taken the bowl. Her recognition amazed me. "Don't tell me you're a reader of the great H.P. Lovecraft?"

"No, Foster, only because I never learned to read much. I recognize the name because when I was only eighteen, Mr. Lovecraft stayed in Olmstead for a short time."

I very nearly dropped my bowl. "Mary. You didn't happen . . . to *meet* Mr. Lovecraft, did you?"

"Oh, no, I didn't get that privilege, but here's something interesting. Back then, Baxter's was a First National Mart, and my brother, Paul—he was seventeen at the time—he actually waited on Mr. Lovecraft in this very store you're standing in now. Mr. Lovecraft wanted directions about town, so Paul drew him a map."

This shock of shocks almost put my knees out. The attractive woman's brother had *met* the Master! What precious conversation must have taken place. And now this: the reference to her brother's map! Surely, this had founded Lovecraft's early scene in the story where a congenial "grocery youth" had provided Robert Olmstead with just that: a *map* of Innsmouth. Like most writers, HPL had used an ordinary factual occurrence in which to dress the fiction.

"Foster, why, you look—"

"Dumbstruck?" I laughed. "It's true, Mary. I know it might seem peculiar, but the work of Lovecraft is my foremost hobby; I pursue it with a passion as well as any information about his life in general. And this is such a stroke of luck. You could very well help me in my indulgence. Please allow me to take you and your brother to luncheon sometime. Aside from your wonderful company, of course, I'd just like—Paul, is it?—I'd like to ask him a few questions about Lovecraft's visit—" but then the bungle hit me like a physical blow. "Pardon me, Mary, but of course I meant you, your brother, *and* your husband."

Mary didn't balk at the comment; she merely replied, "Oh, I'm afraid my husband turned out to be not much of one. He left me for another woman, ran off to Maryland."

"I truly regret to hear that, Mary. You deserve better than an irresponsible lout like that." It infuriated me that any real man could abandon a pregnant wife.

"Oh, it's all right. It's one of life's lessons," came a surprisingly cheerful reply. "My stepfather says the hardest lessons serve us best."

"How true."

"And I *do* have a good life. I have good work and live in a good town. I feel very blessed."

"A selfless and commendable attitude. Too many these days take so much for granted," I amended.

"And my brother, Paul"—her glance cast down for a moment—"he's not well, I'm afraid, and wouldn't be able to manage an outing."

I didn't know how to respond other than topically. "Oh, that's too bad. I hope he recovers quickly."

"But I'd be happy to talk to you about Mr. Lovecraft at any convenience. You see, Paul quite took to the man and related to me everything they talked about while Mr. Lovecraft was here. "

"Then, please, we must do that, Mary."

She gave the faintest coy smile. "That is if your *wife* doesn't mind you taking another woman to lunch."

"I've never married," I blurted, only now aware of the slightly sticky situation. She was pregnant, after all—with a stumblebum's child.

"You can't be serious!" came her exclamation after another spoonful of ice cream. "A handsome, well-mannered gentleman like you? *Never* married?"

I prayed I didn't blush. "I fear I wouldn't be suitable for any woman," and then I played it off with a laugh. "I'm far too indulgent."

"Oh, I don't believe that!"

"But, yes, I'll stop in tomorrow morn, and you can tell me a time convenient for you."

"That would be fine, Foster. I'll look forward to it."

By now, I felt a bit guilty admitting this attraction to a woman with child, but of course, my only interest was strictly of the platonic variety. That aside, this was a great opportunity. What Mary could convey of Paul's conversations with the Master would be of joyous interest to me. I was about to continue conversation when the bell rang again and the door opened.

"Oh, hi, Dr. Anstruther," greeted Mary.

"Hello, my dear . . . "

"Dr. Anstruther, meet Foster Morley. He's here on vacation."

I turned to face a distinguished, well-suited man with iron-grey hair and beard. "How do you do, sir?" I shook a soft but strong hand.

He grinned broadly. "I'm splendid, Mr. Foster. How are you liking our little town?"

"I'm intrigued by it, sir, a very clean, self-respecting prefect, indeed." I glanced minutely to Mary. "And such nice townsfolk."

"Oh, yes. Perhaps you're not aware, but you're sampling the wares of Olmstead's very first ice cream machine. It caused quite a row when it was first installed."

"God bless such luxuries!" I tried to joke.

"We're prospering where other towns are going by the wayside—quite a feat in these economic times. We've been very fortunate of late." He turned to Mary, handing her a stub of paper. "Dear, check this claim number, please. I'm expecting a delivery of some urgency. Mrs. Crommer should be going into labor any day now."

"I completely forgot," Mary remarked, checking a shelf of boxes, then finding one. "Will it be her tenth?"

"Her eleventh," the doctor redressed. He glanced to me. "Stock for the future, as the President says."

"Uh, yes. So true," I practically stammered. But this information? A woman expecting her *eleventh* child? And thus far, I'd seen several other expectant mothers. *Olmstead is certainly a virile town . . .*

Mary opened the box on the counter, and Dr. Anstruther withdrew its contents: four securely packed quart bottles of caramel-colored glass. Each was clearly labeled: CHLOROFORM.

"No safer anesthetic for difficult births," Anstruther commented, and replaced the bottles.

"American medical technology," I offered, "seems more burgeoning now than ever before. I've read they'd found a near-cure for schizophrenia via electric current."

"Not to mention bone marrow transplantation for patients with blood problems, and coming breakthroughs against poliomyelitis. America's leading the way by leaps and bounds. Judging by the current global political climate, though, I fear we'll be focusing our prowess of knowledge and industry on war rather than peace."

"Let's pray that's not the case," I said. "This man Hitler does seem sincere in his promise to annex no more land after Austria. Plus, there's his pact with the Soviets."

"Time will tell, Mr. Foster. And now, I must go." He shook my hand once more. "I'll hope to see you soon."

"Good day, doctor . . . "

"As fine a small-town doctor as you could ever ask," Mary complimented after he left. "Seems what he's doing most of these days is delivering babies. He's delivered all of mine too."

I hoped it wouldn't be too abrupt a departure from good manners to ask, for the question was somehow irresistible. "How many children has God blessed you with, Mary?"

"Nine"—she errantly patted her swollen abdomen—"counting this one."

Nine children, and with no husband to bear half the responsibility, came my regretful thought. Truly, she was a strong woman. "It must be very difficult for you, being on your own, I mean."

"Oh, my stepfather helps out a lot. It's just that he's getting so old now. And, Paul . . . well—"

Suddenly, there came a thunk from the back room, and what I could only perceive as an accommodating human grunt. "What's he done now?" Mary whined. "I'll be right back, Foster." She scurried through a door behind her.

I couldn't help but overhear:

"Can't you *wait?*" Mary's muffled voice complained.

"Not-not much longer, I can't." A male voice, one in some distress.

"But there's a nice man out front, and he's asked me to dine with him! Now—" A pause, then what seemed a grunt on her part. "Get back in your chair! You'll just have to wait! I won't be long—"

"I'll try . . . "

Mary returned with a sheepish smile, then came close to whisper, "That was Paul, just trying to get attention, I'm afraid." She seemed to be tempering herself against an inner rage. "The reason it wouldn't do to have you meet him is because of his injuries. He's very self-conscious—he had a terrible accident several years ago."

A selfish notion, I know, but it made me cringe to realize that the true-life model for Lovecraft's "grocery youth" was on the other side of that door and not accessible to me. And what of these injuries? There was no genteel way to inquire.

"I let him stay in the back while I'm working so he doesn't get too lonely. Sometimes he even sleeps here when no one can give him a drive home."

"Oh, I see. It's, um, good that you can do that," was all I could muster to say, but what else could she have meant by her insistence, *Get back in your chair*—? That and the remark about drives home?

She could only mean a *wheel*chair.

The moment had struck an awkward note, but it was that same selfishness of mine that sufficed to turn the subject. "Before I'm on my way, I have a question."

She leaned over, elbows on counter, chin in fists, and smiled in a way that struck me as dreamy, though I couldn't imagine that *my* presence solicited the look. "Ask me anything, Foster. You're really an interesting man."

Did I audibly gulp? I hope not! "I've decided to find a quiet place outdoors to read," and then I held up my book. "See, reading the story whose setting Lovecraft formed by his direct impressions of this very town strikes me as fascinating; it's my favorite story of any, and re-reading it here will allow for an entirely new perception."

"I think I know what you mean," she said. "But the Olmstead you're seeing today is nothing alike what Mr. Lovecraft saw when he was here so many years ago."

"That's my point!" I exclaimed of her perceptivity. "Would you by chance have a photograph of Olmstead before the rebuild? I'd love to compare it to Lovecraft's descriptions in the book."

"We've never had a camera, but . . . " She held a finger up. "There is a man you could try talking to. Er, well, maybe that's not such a good idea."

Was she teasing me now? I absolutely *quailed*. "Mary, I implore you, please—"

"There's a townsman who used to be a photographer; he trained in New York even, and took pictures for newspapers. He even took a picture of Mr. Lovecraft standing on the New Church Green with Paul. You can see the entire waterfront in the background, the harbor inlet and lighthouse, the old Larsh Refinery, and the town dock, which they used to call Innswich Point back then."

I could've collapsed by these new parallels! Innswich: obviously a variation of Innsmouth. The dead lighthouse which overlooked the notorious *Devil's* Reef from whence came the batrachian Deep Ones. And the Larsh Refinery: in Lovecraft's grand tale, it was at the *Marsh* Refinery where the gift of gold trinkets bestowed to human worshipers by the Deep Ones was melted down and sold on the market. *I MUST see that picture!* I determined.

"Please, Mary. How can I find this photographer? It's imperative, truly—"

Her chin slumped in her palms. "How can I say no to *you*? I only mean that it's not a good idea. The man's name is Cyrus Zalen. He's about forty, but he looks sixty, and you can' miss him. He always wears the same long, greasy black raincoat. He smells horrible, and he's . . . well, he's just not nice. He lives at the poorhouse behind the new fire station."

Cyrus Zalen. Presumably a breadliner or, to use Lovecraft's term, a "loafer." In Providence, they called them "bums" and "rummies." "An unfortunate turn of fate for a newspaper photographer," I remarked.

"He was a fine photographer . . . before he got mixed up with the heroin. In New York, he got hooked up with ex-soldiers who'd become addicted to it when they went on leave in France, a city called . . . Marcy? I can't remember."

"Marseilles," I corrected. I'd read of these places there called heroin laboratories where they converted the resin from opium poppies into this devastating new drug. "Still, I'll have to find Mr. Zalen."

The prospect seemed to worry her. "Please don't, Foster. He's not a nice man. He'll try to connive money out of you, and he may even be a thief. He's known to do . . . immoral things, but it would be unladylike for me to explain. And this was so many years ago, at least ten, I guess. I'm sure he doesn't have the photo anymore anyway. Really , Foster, don't go there." She leaned even closer. "It's a *dirty* place where he lives—there's probably diseases. A woman died of typhus there several years ago."

I didn't take her warning lightly, actually flattered by her concern for my well-being. But if it was money that Mr. Zalen wanted for his old pictures, then money he would have. My wallet was chock full.

"You needn't worry, Mary. I'm of hardy enough stock. I survived the outbreaks of 1919 and 1923, and in fact, I've not been sick a day in my life. I'll be very careful when interviewing Mr. Zalen, and I can't thank you enough for your guidance."

She gripped my forearm with some determination. "At least make a deal with me, Foster. I think Paul has an extra copy of the photo. If so, I'll get it for you, if you promise *not* to go to Cyrus Zalen's."

I was touched to the point of amusement by the vigor with which she insisted I not meet this man. "All right, Mary. I promise."

She beamed a smile, then gave me a sudden hug which almost made me flinch. The all too brief contact brought my cheek to hers. The scent of her hair was luxuriant.

"And I can't thank you enough," I went on, "for your acceptance of my invitation for luncheon tomorrow. Oh, and here—for your wonderful ice cream." I put five dollars on the counter.

"But it's only five cents—"

"Keep it, please. You can buy a special treat for your stepfather and children."

The moment lengthened. Her eyes held on mine. "You're very nice, Foster," she gushed. "Thank you . . . "

"Until tomorrow, then!" and I was off.

I left in a blissful rush, not only quite taken by the cherubic and lovely girl but also by this new and surprising kindle to my obsession.

I knew at once that I must break the promise I'd made. Her concern was obviously exaggerated, and I couldn't very well deprive her brother of a photograph that must mean a great deal to him. *The poorhouse behind the new fire station,* I recalled, and—there! A sign right before me read FIREHOUSE with an arrow pointing west. A sudden uproar startled me when several more fish-laden trucks hauled around the cobblestoned circle, but when they passed, I noticed that the westernmost road entry was cordoned off and closed—sewer pipe workers were digging—so I thought it best to cut around behind the row of block buildings that housed Baxter's General Store, Wraxall's Eatery, and the others. The alleyway gave wide birth, and I was pleased to find it clean, free of garbage and its attendant stench, and absent of vermin. I was halfway along, though, when I heard a voice so wee I thought it must be my imagination.

I stopped, listened . . .

"Bugger. You did that on purpose. I *know* you did. You want to mess things up for me."

True, the voice was oh-so-faint but unmistakably the voice of Mary, and when I turned, I noticed a narrow window opened just a crack.

It was not my nature at all—please believe me—but something connatural in my psyche *forced* my eyes to that crack . . .

Time seemed to freeze when my vision fully registered the macabre scene within. A thin, haggard man sat troubled in a wheelchair—Paul, no doubt. Either age or despair ran lines down his face like a wood-carver's awl; his hair was a shaggy tumult. But the severity of his overall physical state trivialized the ramshackle appearance and uncleanliness.

I felt wounded appraising him . . .

His legs ended at the knees, leaving sleeves of empty denim.

His arms ended at the elbows.

My God, I thought. I'd never imagined that the accident Mary referred to could've been so calamitous. My spirit was left tamped when the thought impacted me: that this ruined twig of a man had just over a decade ago been the energetic seventeen-year-old "grocery youth" who'd generously prepared Lovecraft/Robert Olmstead with a hand-drawn map of the town.

And what was now taking place was a pitiable site indeed.

The girth of Mary's belly made it difficult for her to bend over, yet bend over she did, after which, she fiddled at Paul's trousers. It was clear now what his problem had been earlier. A bucket in the corner of the office told me that's where he'd been struggling to when he'd flopped himself out of the chair: for the purpose of urinating, a task not easily accomplished given his disabilities. I could only presume that his trousers were left perpetually open for such emergencies.

Distaste plainly stamped on her face, Mary held a tin can betwixt the poor man's legs, into which he now voided his bladder.

Her wince intensified. "For goodness sake, Paul! You go more than a horse! Hurry!"

Another full minute lapsed when, finally, the void terminated, and Mary aversively emptied it in the small sink. "You just want attention anytime you know I'm getting some."

"I do not," he said forlornly. "I had to go, and you weren't here."

She sat with some effort in a fold down chair, cradling the distended belly. "I'm doing all of this for you and step-dad, you know. Working two jobs and carrying another baby. I'm tired of you taking me for granted. You're lucky to be alive, you know, and you *wouldn't* be, Paul, if it weren't for me."

Paul railed, elevating his stumps. "Oh, yeah, I'm so lucky to be alive! Thanks very much!"

"Don't talk like that," she said in a lower and somehow darker tone. "We could have it a lot worse. Both of us."

"He wanted to talk to *me,* not *you,*" Paul objected, spittle on his lips and tears in his eyes. "I knew Lovecraft better than you, and just because—"

"That's enough," came her tempered retort, then she rose from the chair, but before she could exit—

"Mary, wait! Please!" the invalid implored.

"What?" she nearly growled.

"I need you to . . . "

"You need me to *what?*"

Now his voice degraded to a pitiful peep "You know . . . With your hand . . . "

A hot glare raged on her face. "No! It's dirty and sinful! It's disgusting!"

My brows rose high.

Paul's forlorn whine continued. "But it's so hard to do it myself. I get lonely back here, and—"

"No!"

"At least—at least . . . can I see? I've got nothing else, Mary. Please. Let me see, just for a second . . . "

Mary's comely visage was now a mask of disdain. "No! I'm your sister, for goodness sake!" then she left the room in a whir and slammed the door.

First, the blaring sight, then, second, the implications left me agog at the window. Yet when my eyes found their way back to the unfortunate Paul, I heard my very soul groan . . .

He sat now in a desperate hunch, his back to me, his shoulders moving as his forlorn whimpers drew on. I did not need to see to know that he was attempting to masturbate with his elbow stumps.

What a tragedy, I thought.

My secret gaze retreated. Though the situation offended my outer sensibilities, I did not issue judgments, but what a sorry plight life left to so many. *The poor girl, pregnant while having to work two jobs to support an invalid brother and most likely an invalid stepfather. While the poor brother himself has only . . . this as his only accessible mode of pleasure.* The grim reality only served to reflect more of myself back into whatever sense of self-awareness I possessed. I was the indulgent, filthy rich, having never had to work in my life, while these people . . .

I knew that before I left this town, I would do something quite generous for this destitute family . . .

The alley's exit conducted me to a crossroad, where I turned westward and followed the sign. Clean block buildings lined one side of the street; stands of dense trees lined the other. I set my quiet despair behind me to re-attended my task.

I MUST locate this Cyrus Zalen . . .

Sunlight sifted through high branches, while from the east, a gentle surf touched my ears. I wondered if Lovecraft had ever walked this particular street and so hoped that he had. I knew that I was seeing what he saw as his mind worked on the pieces of *The Shadow Over Innsmouth.*

A crunch to my left stopped my gait. I turned, scanned the crush of trees, but saw no one where I was sure someone must be. The sound I'd heard was unmistakable: a footstep crunching down on the drought-withered detritus of the woods.

After several more paces, the crunch resounded again.

"Hello there!" I called when I saw the figure shamble through the trees. A figure, yes, adorned in a long, ruined black raincoat. "Mr. Zalen! Please! I've dire need to speak with you!"

The figure disappeared as quickly as if it were part of the woods. I could only wonder now just how debilitated Mr. Zalen had become via the rigors of opiate addiction and impoverishment. The latter stages of such misfortunes regularly left its victims incoherent or fully mad. Should this be the case with Zalen, my trek could well prove pointless.

A ten-minute stroll left me standing before the new fire station, where several men chatted amiably while they washed and polished the grand, new pumper truck. Not half a block on, I found what could only be the poorhouse.

The single-floored length of small apartments looked

pressed down by adversity, as though soullessness were as salient a feature as the compartments' peeling paint and rag-stuffed broken window panes. From them issued the smells of urine and rotting food. An elderly man sat slumped and glassy-eyed before one dingy-doored room, to the effect that I thought he might be deceased until he shivered once and hacked. An obese blind woman with a white cane sat just as dejected at the next unit. She looked up sightlessly when she'd no doubt heard my passing, then rose from the milk crate she used for a chair, tapped back to the doorway, and went in. The door slammed.

The end unit struck me as darker than all the rest, though the sunlight here shone evenly across the entire length of apartments. A doorless postal box revealed no occupant's name, and I noticed a grease-stained garbage bag sitting roadside filled with stubs of burned down candles, expended flash bulbs, and empty food cans aswarm with flies. A cracked walkway led me forward until I stopped, forced to eye a curious door-knocker mounted in the beaten door's center stile, a queer oval of tarnished bronze depicting a morose half-formed face. Just two eyes, no mouth or nose, no additional features.

I wrapped hesitantly with the knocker, staring uneasily at the name plaque posted just above: C. ZALEN.

(III)

WHAT THE DOOR opened to show me was more of what I expected: a thin, pallid man demonstrating every sign of physical squalor. He still wore the ruinous black raincoat, which hung open to show him shirtless, sunken-chested, slat-ribbed. Frayed trousers torn off at the knees were what he wore below the waist, as well as rotten shoes. His already sunken eyes appeared nearly non-existent by the smudge-like crescents beneath them. I made every attempt to smile and seem unfazed.

"Ah, Mr. Zalen. My name is Foster Morley. I saw you cutting home through the woods, but I guess you didn't hear me."

The man frowned. Longish black hair had been slicked back off his brow by either tonic or, more likely, the natural oils from his scalp that had accreted from not washing often. "What do you want?" he asked in a voice that sounded more hardy than I would expect from such a dilapidated unfortunate.

"You're the photographer, correct? The newspaper man, or have I been informed in error?"

"That was a lifetime ago, but I guess if you've been *informed* about me, you're either police or a client . . . and you don't look like police, so I guess you better come in."

So he must still have some clients for his photography business, I reckoned. Which meant he had *some* money coming in. He invited me inside to a living room in worse repair than the exterior: a legless couch, the sparsest furniture, and one of those large wooden cable spools on end to serve as a table. A chemical scent in the air suggested the solutions of photo development. Before he closed and bolted the door, he peeked both ways outside, as if suspicious of something. He oddly reached *behind* a bookcase whose shelves dipped at their centers, and withdrew a simple folder.

"Fifty cents each, Mr. Morley," he told me, and handed me the folder. "I can tell by the way you dress you're not on the outs like a lot of folks these days. You want to buy, not sell."

I couldn't imagine what he meant, but I could tell by viewing the folder's side what it contained: a hefty stack of photographs. An instantaneous thrill made my nerves buzz at the prospect. Mary, even in her disapproval of the man, must've called ahead to tell him what it was I sought. I nervously took a seat, and flung open the folder . . .

What a horror the times have turned this world into. I could've gagged at the repellent images that leapt up at my eyes from the glossy surfaces of the photographs. These were neither pictures of Lovecraft nor of Olmstead in days past. It was, instead, outright pornography.

The scenes depicted in the few sheets I looked at need not be described. I can only say that the photography itself was strikingly vivid and every bit of expert.

"But the ones with the white girl making it with the colored fellas are a buck each," he continued. He skimmed off the tattered raincoat and hung it up on a nail in the wall. "If you're into kids, they're two bucks each."

I thrust the evil folder back to him. "This is . . . not . . . what I came for."

"Oh, so you're a seller? Well, you gotta pay me up front for the film and developer, and I get half of what I can sell 'em for. But keep in mind, if they ain't pretty enough, I won't bother 'cos I can't sell the pictures. And the more you can talk 'em into doing, the more I can sell 'em for."

Through a dazedness of incomprehension, I merely replied, "*What?*"

He shot me a glare sharp as a dagger. "It's the business, man! You got a couple cute daughters and you want me to snap 'em nude or fuckin' guys, right?"

I stared. "No," I croaked. "I have no children."

"Then what do you want, Morley?" he suddenly yelled. "I need *money,* and you're wasting my time! Get out of here!"

Bleary-eyed, I gave him a ten-dollar bill.

"What's the sawbuck for?" his rant continued after snapping the bill from my fingers. "I don't turn tricks, man! I'm no swish! You want to fuck a *girl,* fine, I got one here, but don't bullshit around! You're starting to scare the shit out of me—" and then he yelled at what was presumably the door to the bedroom. "Candace! Come out here!"

Before I could object, the door opened, and out stepped a timid and very naked woman in her twenties. One hand covered her bare pubis; her other arm attempted to cover two very swollen breasts. What she couldn't cover at all, however, was the belly stretched out tight and huge from a state of pregnancy that had to be close to the end of its term. Obliquely, I made out a radio tune from the other room, "Heaven Can Wait," I believe, by Glen Gray.

The girl smiled crookedly at me through a gap in the hair falling over her face. "Hi. We-we could have a nice time together, sir . . . "

More of the real world I didn't care for at all. By now, I'd managed the shock of this horrendous miscalculation and produced a frown of my own, which I directed immediately to Zalen. "I gave you the money so you needn't feel your valuable time is *wasted.* I'm not interested in prostitution nor pornography."

Zalen chuckled. "Come on, Mr. Morley. You ever had your tallywacker in a *pregnant* girl? Bet'cha haven't."

"You're a profane vagabond!" I yelled at him.

"And it's not like you can knock her up."

I wished that looks could kill at that moment, for my look of utter loathing would surely have shorn him in half.

"I'm interested in a *particular* photograph I'm told you're in possession of, and if this is the case, I'll pay you one hundred more dollars for it."

Zalen looked agape at my words, then flicked a hand at the girl to shoo her back into the bedroom. "A *hundred dollars*, you say?"

"One hundred dollars." Now I noticed what first appeared to be splotches of pepper inside the man's elbows, but my naivety wore off in a moment and told me they were needle scars. "My patience is growing thin, Mr. Zalen. Do you or do you not have a photograph of a writer by the name of Howard Phillips Lovecraft?"

For the first time, Zalen actually smiled. The couch creaked when he sat down and crossed his thin, white legs. "I remember him, all right. Had a voice like a kazoo, and all the guy ever ate were ginger snaps." He jumped up quickly and slipped something from the bookcase. He showed it to me behind his gap-toothed smile.

It was a copy of the Visionary Publications edition of *The Shadow Over Innsmouth*.

I removed mine from my jacket pocket and showed him likewise.

"I didn't think anybody even *read* that guy, but I'll tell you, after this came out, a *lot* of folks did, and they weren't too happy with what he had to say about our town. Most of Olmstead back then was moved down to Innswich Point, so the guy changes the name to *Innsmouth*. Christ. Changed all the names but only a little, you know? Like he *wanted* us to know what he was really writing about."

"For God's sake, Mr. Zalen," I countered. "He merely used his topical impressions of this town as a setting for a fantasy story. You're practically accusing him of libel. All writers do things like that." I cleared my throat. "Now. Do you have the photograph?"

"Yeah, I got it, but only the negative. I can have it developed for you tomorrow." His smile turned slatternly. "But I'll take the hundred up front."

I am not a man given to confrontation or brusqueness, but this, I would not stand for. "You'll take *five* dollars for processing fees, and the remaining ninety-five when I have what I want," I told him and thrust him another five.

He took it all too eagerly. "Deal. Tomorrow, say four." His eyes turned to cunning slits. "Who told you I had the picture?"

"A friend of mine," I snapped. "A woman named Mary Simpson—"

An abruptitude pushed him back in his seat; he nearly howled. "Oh, now I get it! She's a *friend* of yours, huh? I guess you're not the goodie-two-shoes I pegged you as."

I winced at the remark. "What on earth do you mean?"

"Mary Simpson used to be the town slut. Now, this town was *full* of sluts, but Mary took the cake. She was a *whore*, Mr. Morley, a whore of the first water, as my grandfather used to say."

"You're lying," I replied with immediacy. "You're merely trying to incense me because you're resentful of people with means. I see your frowsy smile, Mr. Zalen, but I've a mind to wipe it right off your face by canceling any further business with you and seeing my way out of this den of drugs and iniquity you call your home."

"But you won't do that, *Mr.* Morley, because guys like you always get what they want. You'll be back tomorrow, and you'll have the rest of the money. You just don't want to know the truth."

"And what truth is that?"

"Not too many years ago? Mary Simpson was the top dog dockside whore in all of Innswich. Christ, she's had, like, eight or ten trick babies, man. She made a lot of money for me."

Now it was my turn to smile at the bombast. "I'm supposed to believe you're her panderer? Er, what do they call them now? Pimps?"

"Not is, was. About five years ago, the bitch got all highfalutin on me."

"I still don't believe you. She enlightened me of her plight, regarding her husband who abandoned her. Certainly, the man was of less repute even than you."

"Husband, Jesus." He shook his head with the same grin. "If you believe that, you probably believed that *War of the Worlds* broadcast last October."

Of course, I hadn't believed a word of it; I'd read the book! But for what Zalen was inferring now? *It's just more of his loser's game,* I knew. "And now I suppose you're going to tell me she was a drug addict, like you."

"Naw, she never rode the horse; she was just crazy for cock." He raised a brow. "Well, cock and money."

"And this I'm supposed to take on the authority of a drug addict who would stoop so low as to sell pictures of innocent young pregnant women to degenerates."

"There are a lot of 'degenerates' in the world, Morley. Supply and demand—*there's* what your capitalism's caused." He looked directly at me. "You'd be surprised how many sick fellas there are out there who like to look at pregnant girls."

"And you're the purveyor—to support your narcotics habit, no doubt," I snapped. "Without the supply, there becomes no demand, and then morality returns. But this will never happen as long as predators such as yourself remain in business. You sell desperation, Mr. Zalen, via the exploitation of the subjugated and the poverty-stricken."

This seemed to ruffle a feather or two. "Hey, you're just a rich pud, and you got no right to make judgments about people you don't know. Not everybody's got it easy like you do. The government's building *battleships* for this new Naval Expansion Act while half the country's starving, *Mr.* Morley, and while ten million people got no jobs. Redistribution of wealth is the only moral answer. What an apathetic military industrial complex forces me, or the girl in the back room, or Mary, or *anyone else* to do to survive is nothing *you* have the right comment on."

An unwavering sorrow touched me with the self-admission that, on this particular point, he was correct. Perhaps that's why his truth urged me to despise him all the more. Though obviously a proponent of Marx and Ingles, Zalen had quite accurately labeled me. *A rich pud.* I didn't bother to point out my many acts of philanthropy; I'm sure an alienist in this day and age would diagnose my acts of charity as merely attempts to alleviate guilt.

Eventually, I replied, "I apologize for any such judgments, but for nothing else. Even if what you accuse Mary of is true, I could hardly blame her, for reasons you've already stated. I believe that she and millions of other downtrodden . . . and even *you,* Mr. Zalen, are essentially victims of an invidious environment."

"Oh, you're a real treat!" he laughed.

I knew I must not let him circumvent me, for that would only refresh my despair, in which case, he would win. "I'm here for business regarding my pastime. Let us stick to that. I'll also pay—say, five dollars apiece—for any quality photographs of this Innswich Point that you may have taken before the government renewal effort."

His insolent grin returned, and that cocksure slouch. "You *sure* that's all you want, Mr. Morley?"

"Quite," I asserted.

"But, why? Back then, all of Olmstead, especially the Point, was a slum district."

"Though I'd never expect you to understand, I've an interest in seeing the town as Lovecraft saw it when it sparked the creative conception for his masterpiece."

"So that's your *hobby,* huh?" he mocked.

"Yes, and one, I'd say, quite harmless when compared to yours."

He laughed. "Don't knock *my* hobby, Mr. Morley. You know, pretty soon, I'll have to take a bang." He slapped the inside of an elbow. "You should stick around to watch. It'd do someone like you good to see something like that, to look real hard right into the face of the only salvation that capitalism and all its hypocrisy leaves the poor."

"Stop blaming your weakness on the American economic program," I scoffed at him.

"And this book—" He held up *Innsmouth* again. "Pretty damn stupid if you ask me."

"The likes of you would probably say the same of 'The Rime of the Ancient Mariner,' Mr. Zalen."

He clapped in amusement. "Now you're talkin'! Coleridge was a junkie too! But Lovecraft's *Innsmouth* tripe? He got the town all wrong."

"It wasn't about the *town*," I nearly yelled back. "It was an intricate and very socially symbolic *fantasy*."

"And he should've at least done a better job changing peoples' names."

I sat up more alertly. "Why do you say that? I thought it mostly the names of *places* he altered."

"No, no, damn near everyone in town he insulted with all that. Remember the bus driver from the story, Joe Sargent? The real man's name was Joe *Major,* for God's sake. And the town founders, the Larshes, he changed to the Marshes. And then there's always Zadok Allen. What did Lovecraft call him? A 'hoary tippler'?"

"Zadok Allen was the piece's most preeminent stock character, a ninety-six-year-old alcoholic who knew all of Innsmouth's darkest secrets."

Another grinning stare. "You're not very perceptive, are you? The real man's name was Adok Zalen. Does that last name ring any bells?"

The implication astounded me. "Zadok Allen-Adok Zalen, and . . . your name, too, is Zalen."

"Yeah, he was my grandfather. Lovecraft got him drunk near the docks one night with some rotgut he bought at the variety store behind the speakeasy. My grandfather died the next day—of alcohol poisoning from the booze your hero Lovecraft gave him."

Could this be true? And if so, it begged the further question: how much of Lovecraft's invention might be the actual invention of Adok Zalen?

"Did the world a favor, though," Zalen prattled on. "Christ, my grandfather was older than the hills and not worth a shit. He was a liar and a thief, and it was time for him to go."

"I commend you for the respect you have for your relatives," I said with a thick sarcasm.

"Lovecraft was a hack. Seabury Quinn was a *much* better writer."

I could've hemorrhaged! "He was nothing of the sort, Mr. Zalen!" My shout of objection sounded near-hysterical, for now Zalen's deliberate hectoring was taking its toll. This was my literary idol, after all, and I would not stand to hear his name and talents sullied by this denizen pornographer. "Now do you have the pictures of the old town or do you not?"

"I got 'em. Wait here," and he got up and loped into the back room.

The nerve of him, I thought, truly riled now. What could *he* know about quality fantasy fiction? The more I speculated, the more I preferred to dismiss his accusation that Lovecraft may have contributed to Adok Zalen's demise. *He's simply asserting these lies for the purpose of a negative effect.* No different from his lies about Mary.

I nearly moaned when my stray glance showed me a slice of the bedroom. He'd left the door open, and what I first noticed was a large-format camera on a tripodular stand. And then . . . something else . . .

Sitting awkwardly on an unsheeted bed was the pregnant prostitute—Candace, I believe he'd called her. She remained naked, and the mammarian effect of her pregnancy had stretched her areolae to pale pink circles. The great, gravid belly only added to the difficulty of what she was doing . . .

A cord girded her upper arm to distend the veins at her elbow's apex, and into such a vein she was now injecting something through an eyedropper fitted with a hollow needle. *The devil of a man's got her addicted as well, to maintain his exploitation of her . . .*

Zalen, though rummaging out of view, could easily be heard. "You're doing too much," he complained to the girl. "It'll ball up the kid. Remember what happened to Sonia?"

"But I can't help it!" she whined.

"If that kid comes out dead, you're in a world of trouble . . ."

I didn't even *want* to conjecture what he might mean by such a statement. They probably planned to sell the baby to an adoptionage.

The scenario and its implications were sallowing my spirit. I was *not* in my element, and I hoped this would be a lesson to me.

Reappearing, he pulled the door closed behind him, bearing another manila folder. "All I had were these five, *Mr.* Morley," he continued to impudently emphasize. "But it's a hundred for the lot. Take it or leave it."

"I won't be extorted, *Mr.* Zalen," I assured him. Such leverage was to be expected, though. Now that he knew *my* addiction, he would seek as much remuneration as my indulgence would tolerate. "I said five apiece, so it'll be five apiece, and that's *only* if they're precisely what I'm looking for."

"If you like 'em, then pay me what you feel they're worth. How's that?"

"Fair enough," and then I opened the folder.

The first photograph took the wind out of me: a seaward panorama of the town which showed a declining sweep of sagging gambrel rooftops, half-collapsed gables, and smokeless chimney pots. Closer to the sea rose a triad of lofty steeples, two of which were missing their clockfaces. *My God,* I thought. *It's nearly straight from the text: Robert Olmstead's first glimpse of Innsmouth from Joe Sargent's bus window.* A second photo depicted the crumbling waterfront, its half-fallen wharves, fishing boats with ruptured hulls, and mountains of disused lobster traps. A row of sullen factories and processing plants—long abandoned—rose behind this scene of decrepitude and neglect, but again, it was straight from HPL's grimly vivid description in the book. The third photograph showed a low-roofed stone building surrounded by Doric pillars; its outer walls looked eroded by age. Two large double lancet doors stood open, showing depthless black.

"That's the old Freemason Hall," Zalen informed.

And then it hit me. "Of course! It was this building that Lovecraft fancied the Esoteric Order of Dagon, where the crossbred priests held services of worship. They wore flamboyant raiments and tiaras of gold."

"Now turn to the last picture," he goaded.

But the next photo would be the fourth, and I'd thought Zalen said that *five* comprised the lot. Nevertheless, I turned to the next and was stunned by the vision of a macabre sunset over the harbor inlet. The effect made the water look molten. Past more decayed wharves and flanks of leaning, boarded-up shacks whose roofs looked fit to fall in was a vista of the sun-touched channel and what barely noticeably existed a mile or so beyond: an irregular black line just above the water's surface. A dead lighthouse seemed to look northward.

"Lovecraft's Devil's Reef," I knew at a glance.

"Um-hmm. Nothin' devilish about it, though," Zalen said. "It's not really even a reef. It's just a sandbar." He rubbed his hands together. "But they're good pictures, right?"

"They are," I admitted. "It's a pity how you've chosen to vitiate and hence debauch such a laudable talent for the art of photography."

I still felt rocked by the impact of the photos—the truth that they assured in their depiction of the town so long ago. "When, exactly, were these taken, Mr. Zalen?"

"Summer of 1928, July, I'm pretty sure. The only reason I took them was because Lovecraft wanted them. I did it gratis because I thought maybe he'd recommend me to some of those freaky pulp magazines he wrote for. Never did, though, the cheap bastard."

Knowing this even spurred my interest to a new height, and as such, they were worth considerably more than five dollars apiece. But I was offended by this attempt at extortion. "I'll give you fifty dollars for the set, but not one hundred."

"It's a hundred," he stood firm. Then came that frowzy smile again. "But you haven't seen the last picture, *Mr.* Morley."

"Oh. That's right." I flipped to the final photograph.

I stared down, unblinking. Many seconds ticked by like this. Then I closed the folder, rose, and gave Zalen a hundred-dollar bill. "Good day, Mr. Zalen."

"Tomorrow at four, then?"

"Rest assured I'll be here."

"With another hundred for the Lovecraft picture."

"Another *ninety-five.*" I headed for the door. "Please don't disappoint me, Mr. Zalen."

He laughed. "They only way I could do that is if I shoot up a hot shot tonight with the horse I'm gonna buy with the cash you just gave me. Leading cause of death for junkies, you know."

"If you're going to die via an overdose, Mr. Zalen, please don't do it by tomorrow." My hand found the dirty doorknob. "But the day *after* tomorrow would be fine."

"That's the spirit!"

I stepped out of the fetid, chemical-smelling room and felt welcomed into the overly warm light of day. Zalen's squalid apartment had been as dark as his heart.

His near-emaciated form hung in the doorway. "Going back to your room now, huh? To pursue your *hobby?*"

Even in light of what I'd just purchased, the implication via his tone couldn't have offended me more. "My hobby, Mr. Zalen, as you know, is the work of H.P. Lovecraft."

"Right. So I guess you'll walk around town now . . . to *see* what Lovecraft saw."

"That's precisely what I'm going to do, not that it's any of your business. I'm going to Innswich Point."

"It's pretty dull now, Mr. Morley. Just block buildings and a cement pier." Did he snigger? "But don't go there at night."

I frowned on his moss-blotched front step. "Really, Mr. Zalen. The Deep Ones will get me? The acolytes of Barnabas Marsh will offer me up to Dagon?"

"Nope, but the rummies and fugitives will have a lot of fun with a guy like you. Drug runners hole up there."

"Good friends of yours, no doubt."

"They bring it in by boats." The ungainly man scratched the inside of an elbow. "And my grandfather wasn't lying when he told Lovecraft about the network of tunnels under the old waterfront. They go back to the 1700s. Privateers and smugglers would use them as hideouts."

This was of interest, though I didn't let on.

"And if you want a real treat, take a hike up the main road north and have a look at Mary's place," he snidely continued. "It's a real *slice of life*. It's just shy of the Onderdonks'."

My wince communicated my inconvenience, but suddenly, I *was* curious as to where Mary lived in her life of travail and the burden of so many children she was raising all without the help of a man. "Onderdonks'," I repeated. "Oh, the roadside stand I saw?"

"Yeah. And try the barbeque," though this time, I wasn't sure how to decipher his belligerent tone of voice.

I was determined to leave now, I would allow no further badgering, but as I commenced, he added, "And you might want to read that book a little more closely too."

I turned on the cracked walk. "Surely, you don't mean *The Shadow Over Innsmouth*."

"What did you think?"

"I've read it dozens of times, Mr. Zalen, with great attentiveness. I can likely quote most of its 25,000 words verbatim, so whatever do you mean?"

The sun highlighted the coarse details of this utterly

corroded man. "In the story, what happened to outsiders who did too much nosing around, *Mr.* Morley?"

I walked away, almost amused now by this final cheap attempt at melodrama.

"And tonight?" he called after me, "when you're fucking Mary for a couple of bucks? Tell her the father of her third or fourth kid says hi . . . "

So much for my amusement. The man was intolerable, and perhaps he was working on my psyche with a bit more effect than I'd care to admit. The only thing I hated more than him was what his manipulation had caused me to do.

When I found a secluded recess of trees, I opened the folder and looked at that fifth picture beneath the photos of the town. It was a photograph of Mary, of course, in depressingly expert resolution and lighting. She was naked, yes, and—worse—pregnant, yet even in this state, she managed a gracile posture for Zalen's wretched lens. It was some horrendous collision of opposites that had triggered my instantaneous purchase. But I *knew,* I knew for the life of me and for the love of *God,* that I WAS NOT one of Zalen's degenerate clients. It was the shock of the aforementioned collision that forced me to buy it: loveliness wed to a revolting design, the grace of beauty hand in hand with the balefulness of womanhood subjugated. It occurred to me now that Mary was so beautiful I could've cringed. I would've guessed her to be five years younger in the picture, but if anything, her current beauty shined even more intensely. So what if a portion of Zalen's salacious slander was, in essence, fact? Even if, in dimmer times, she *had* been a prostitute, who was I to judge?

I would *not.* For time immemorial, women have been exploited within the grips of a man's lustful world; Mary's past deeds mattered none to me because I know that God forgives all. I could only pray that He would forgive *me.*

Back toward the town's center, I found a bargain shop which had precisely what I needed: a small briefcase. I made my purchase from yet another amiable Olmsteader, a Mr. Nowry, who was very gracious over my tip. "Where might I find the most direct route to the waterfront?" I asked.

"Just follow the main cobble out front, sir." He pointed. "That'll take ya straight to the water. And a beautiful waterfront it is."

"Yes, I'm certain, and thank you."

"Just make sure," he rushed to add, "you're not there after dark."

The kind warning didn't set well. "But Olmstead hardly seems—"

"Oh, yes, sir, it's a fine town'a fine people. But any town, mind ya, has got its bad apples."

True enough. Before I left, I noticed whom I presumed must be his wife in a back office, scribbling on papers.

Her overlarge frock-dress made no secret of the fact she was pregnant.

Another woman with child, I thought, and I tried, with difficulty at first, to cogitate my concern. True, I'd encountered what seemed to be an undue number of pregnant women in the little time since I'd arrived, but then I had to remind myself I was essentially a cosmopolite in a new and quite blue-collar little village. In truth, I supported the government's initiatives to encourage population growth. These small townships were more close-knit and, obviously, more conceptive, which was all for the greater good in the long run. Remembering this, I reconsidered my initial reaction to the number of expectant mothers I'd seen. Surely, it was not as *undue* as I'd thought.

As I leisurely approached the waterfront, though, I noticed a short open blockhouse in which I could see a full dozen women contentedly shucking and canning fresh oysters. Most of them were pregnant.

Zalen's assessment of the town's industrial hub rang too true. I saw at once, in spite of the gorgeous, surf-scented vista of the harbor, that Innswich Point was indeed a very dull sight to behold. But, oh, to have seen it as Lovecraft did! At least Zalen's photo would allow me a facsimile of the privilege. Now all that remained was the partial name that the Master had borrowed. More disappointment struck me when I gazed out to the reef but then recalled that it was no reef at all but a ho-hum sandbar. Workers about the Point's many fish processors and boat docks were mainly strong, plain-faced men, much like the few I'd shared the bus with. I wouldn't say that they glared at me, but their cast was not particularly welcoming. This, for sure now, was the impetus for Garret's condemnation of the male populace; he was referring to these surly watermen.

The blockhouse of the ice-making facility clattered and roared, loud trucks coming and going. From a higher window in one of the fish plants, though, a pretty-faced woman smiled at me, and as I left, several more women in another open blockhouse smiled at me as well. They sat at long tables, repairing fishing nets.

Most of them were pregnant.

I left the innocuous scene and its everyday toil behind me. An appetite had built up since my ice cream with Mary, and suddenly, I was so looking forward to my luncheon with her on the morrow. Nor had I forgotten my dinner appointment with the high-spirited Mr. William Garret, though I regretted I had gleaned no news of his misplaced associate. When a distant bell tolled three times, I knew I'd never last another four hours till dinner, so next, I found myself strolling north up the main road, exiting the town proper.

By now, the day's heat got to me. I placed my suit jacket and tie in the briefcase, then continued along. Like Lovecraft, I was accustomed to walking considerable distances daily. *Perhaps the Master strolled this same road as well,* I pondered. Trees lined both sides of the lane. The scenery's tranquility was much welcome after the unpleasant affair with Cyrus Zalen.

Ah! I thought, noticing the mailbox at the end of a long dirt drive on the westward side of the road. The name on the box was Simpson, and all at once, I was tempted to follow Zalen's queer advice and go and introduce myself to Mary's stepfather and children, but then thought better of it. Mary had implied that her stepfather wasn't well. *Better to wait,* came my sensible decision. If destiny would have me meet her stepfather, Mary should be present.

Perhaps the sudden seclusion created the notion, but as I continued along, I received the most aggravating—and most proverbial—impression that I was being watched. Through the woods on the shoreward side, I could see quite deeply; I could even see the edges of Innswich Point, but easterly? The woods loomed deep and dark. Just at the fringes of my aural senses I could *swear* I heard something moving, enshrouded. Just a racoon, more than likely, or simply nothing more than imagination, but immediately, the most appetizing aroma came to my nostrils. The roadside stand and smokehouse was just ahead, and now the ragtag sign beckoned me: ONDERDONK & SON. SMOKEHOUSE—FISH-FED PORK. Large penned pigs— five of them—chortled as a youth in his early teens filled their trough with boiled smelts and other bait fish. I was happy to see several bicycles and two motor-cars parked on the roadside, their owners standing in line at the stand. It was always good to witness a prospering enterprise.

When my turn came in line, I was attended by a weathered, overall'd man wearing a crushed train-worker's hat, whom I presumed to be the business' namesake. "What'll be, stranger?" came a gravel-voice inquiry tinted with European accent.

I saw no menu board. "It all smells so wonderful. What items do you offer, sir?"

"Pulled-pork sam-itches, or hocks with greens. What most folks git're the pulled pork. Best yuh've ever et, and if it ain't, it's free."

"A worthy confidence!" I delighted. "Let me have one,"

and within a moment, I was handed a sandwich heaped with said barbeque and half-wrapped in newspaper.

"Take a bite 'fore ya pay," Onderdonk reminded. "Then tell me it ain't the best yuh've ever et."

One bite verified the guarantee. "It's *pre-eminent,* sir," I told him. "I've sampled pulled pork from Kansas City to the Carolinas, and even in Texas, and . . . *this* is superior."

Onderdonk nodded, unimpressed. "'S'what a fishman's gotta do when he can't fish proper. I think the word is *ingenuity.* It was me who thought'a feedin' the swine fish. Makes the meat moister, so's you can smoke it slower and longer."

"It's certainly a recipe for success," I complimented. I insisted he keep the change from my dollar for the twenty-five-cent sandwich. "But . . . you're formerly a fisherman?"

"Like my daddy'n his daddy and so on." The roughened man suddenly soured. "Can't get no fish no more. Ain't right. But this works just fine."

My curiosity was fueled. "You can tell, sir, I'm not from these parts, but what I've noticed in Olmstead—the Innswich Point area—is that fish seem to be more than abundant."

"Sure, it is—for Olmsteaders, which me'n my boy *ain't,* even though we've owned this bit of land since way back." The topic had clearly struck a bad chord. "We'se outsiders far as they're concerned. Anytime me'n my boy been out for a proper day's fishin', they run us off. Rough bunch, some'a them Olmstead fellas. Can't have my boy gettin' beat up over fish."

Territorialism, I knew at once. It was more widespread than most knew; in my own town, lobstering families were known to feud, and clammers too. "It's regrettable, sir. But the proof of your *ingenuity* has created an alternate market that I'm sure will prosper."

"Mmm," he uttered.

"So I take it this matter of territory forces you to buy the fish with which you feed your pigs."

"Naw, that we can catch ourselfs—see, every night, me'n the boy sneak out to the north end'a the Point, throw a few cast nets, then sneak back right after. We ain't more'n ten minutes on the water, then we're gone. It's only enough time to pull up a bucket or two'a bait fish, but that's all we need for the swine."

"Well, at least your system is working," I offered.

"Yeah, I s'pose it is." The man's young son, at this point, came to stand by his father. Onderdonk patted his shoulder. "He works hard for a little shaver, and I want him to learn right. It's the American way."

"Indeed, it is," I said and smiled at the boy, but then to Onderdonk, I asked, "I happen to be quite given to pork *ribs* as well. Are they ever on your menu?"

"Ribs? Aw, yeah, but we only do 'em twice weekly. They sell out in a couple'a hours. You come back two days from now, and we'll have some up." He gestured the pig pen. "Soon the boy'n me'll be puttin' Harding in the smoker. Harding's that fat 'un there."

I presumed me meant the largest of the pigs. But I had to laugh. "But you haven't named your *pig* after America's twenty-ninth president!"

"That I did!" the working man exclaimed. "And am damn proud of it. 'S'was Harding's lollygaggin' and that Tea Pot Dome business that done led to the stock market crashin' and leavin' all of America the way it is!"

Of this I could hardly argue but was still amused.

"Took an *honest* fella—Calvin Coolidge—to give respect back to the nation's highest office, yes, sir!" He winked. "Ya won't see none'a my swine named Coolidge, now. But in that sty, we also got Taft, Wilson, Garner, and that socialist FDR!"

My. The man certainly had political convictions, odd for a rough-handed working man. "So, " I jested, "I'll return day after tomorrow to sample some of *Harding's* smoked ribs!"

"You do that, sir, and ya *won't* be disappointed!"

I bade my farewell, then patted the silent boy on the head and gave him a dollar bill. "A gratuity for you, young man, for doing such good, hard work for your fine father."

"Thank you, sir," the boy peeped.

"A good day to ya!" Onderdonk reveled, and then I walked off.

It did my spirits good to see the working class persevere even in the low economic times. The man was to be admired. Being unfairly barred from the plentitude of local fishing, he'd contravened the obstacle, to succeed nonetheless.

Back down the road I strolled, a mixture of thought now elevating my mood. Certainly, the fine meal, and the equally fine day; the knowledge that tomorrow I would own a rare photograph of H.P. Lovecraft; the likelihood of another fine meal tonight at Wraxall's Eatery (for fresh seafood—even more so than pork—was an appreciated indulgence); and just the simple gratification that I was indeed walking where Lovecraft once walked.

And there was one other thing too, which founded my elation.

Mary.

Mary Simpson, I mused. So beautiful. So kind and genuine and hard-working. A uniqueness, even if she *had* once suffered degradations in her unfortunate past. Pregnant with no present husband, still she worked to fulfill her responsibilities. I admitted only now that I was falling in platonic love with her, and platonic it would have to remain, for I could not fathom anything more, no matter how urgently I may have wished it.

And I would see her tomorrow for luncheon.

I spun, my heart bucking in my chest. The surprise had taken me with the most unpleasant manner of suddenness.

From the westerly woods I had, for sure, heard a noise.

I was not at all suited for imbroglio, but—now—I knew I was being spied upon, and I was determined not to be harassed.

I peered intensely into the wood, then may have heard a twig snap. "I hear you!" I exclaimed, and did not hesitate to step through the curtain of trees. "Show yourself like a man!"

Several more twigs snapped, as my stalker had clearly embarked deeper into the trees. I wasn't sure why, but I continued to give well-gauged chase.

Fifty yards into the woods, a dappling of sunlight betrayed the stalking entity.

For only the briefest second, I glimpsed the figure, not his face but his attire: the long, greasy black raincoat and hood.

"Really, Mr. Zalen, this is no way to treat a paying customer!" my voice surged into the trees. "If it's thievery on your mind, I can assure you I'm well-armed!"

This much was true, and from my trouser pocket, I'd already withdrawn the small hammerless semi-automatic I'd bought at the Colt Patent Firearms Company in Hartford. It was a Model 1903, which I'd read had been the weapon notorious bank robber John Dillinger had carried the day he'd been gunned down. I was not a crack shot, but with a full magazine, I was crack enough.

Zalen stood still but had clearly heard me. At once, he bolted and let himself be swallowed by the woods.

"I'm disappointed, Mr. Zalen!" came my next call. "But, thief or not, don't forget our appointment tomorrow!"

The density of trees soaked up my voice. A shy, retiring sort as myself might be shaken by such a near-confrontation, but I felt nothing of the sort. I felt calm, confident, and unwavered, and I had no intention of avoiding Zalen tomorrow. He had something I wanted, and I would pay for it as planned. Now that he'd been apprised that I armed myself, he'd be uninclined for any untoward behavior.

When I turned to reverse myself from the woods and regain the road, I saw the house.

Mary's house, to be sure.

Only the dimmest sunlight penetrated the intricate

umbrella of high boughs. The region's all-pervading lack of rainfall had reduced the forest ground to a carpet of tinder. I first dismissed what I was seeing as a hillock, but then a more concentrated scrutiny showed me small single-paned windows amid a long, vast sprawl of ivy. Eventually, I detected corners that had not so been overrun, as well as a slate roof and chimney made of the old tabby bricks from the pre-Revolution period. Beyond the squat and ivy-covered abode, though, stood a clearing radiant with sun, and there, a lone, wee figure seemed to frolic. As I peered closer, I saw that it was a young boy firing arrows with a crude and more than likely hand-made bow. The arrows were those made for children, with rubber suction cups at their tips, and with these, the lad determinedly took aim at an old propped-up window frame which still contained glass.

So this was one of Mary's older children. Odd, though, that only one would be enjoying these splendid outdoors. This close to the house, I expected to hear and see evidence off all eight of her children. *She implied that her stepfather looked after the younger ones,* I recalled. Yet the house sat in an almost palpable silence.

At once, I felt encroaching, even trespassing. It was only the pursuit of Zalen that had led me this deeply into the parched woods. Nevertheless, however impelled to leave, I remained, staring at the leaf-enshrouded house. The impulse to look in a window was very strong, but then I had to chide myself. Not only would that've been the act of a cad—which I was not—it would've been illegal. *I have no right to be here, so I must leave.* But I had to wonder about the motives of my deepest subconscious—or what Freud called the Id.

Was it Mary that my I'd hoped to spy upon?

When I turned to leave, I almost shouted.

There, standing immediately before me, was the boy.

I recovered quickly from the start. "Why, hello there, young man. My name is Foster Morley."

"Hello," he replied blushfully. He was thin, bright-eyed, and had that look of so many children: curious wonder and ripe innocence. He looked tenish—it was so hard to tell with adolescents—and had been dressed neatly but in threadbare clothes. One hand held the makeshift bow; the other a quiver of the suction-cupped arrows. After a moment, he said, "My name's Walter, sir."

"Walter, it's a pleasure to meet you." He timidly shook my offered hand. "Now, would your last name happen to be Simpson?"

He seemed to quell surprise. "Yes, sir."

"Well, how do you like that! I'm a friend of your mother's. I spoke to her just this morning at Mr. Baxter's. You should be proud to have such a hard-working mother."

He seemed quietly astonished by this information. "Yes, sir, I'm very proud, and so is my gramps."

His "gramps" could only be Mary's stepfather.

"He's asleep now," he went on. "He's . . . old."

"Yes, and for the elderly, we must always have respect." I glanced at his twine-and-tree-switch bow. "My, Walter, you're quite the archer. Practice makes perfect"—and then I pointed to his window-frame target, from which several arrows had attached themselves—"and by the looks of your impressive skills, you may one day find yourself on the Olympic archery team."

"Do you really think so?" he asked with excitement.

"Of course, if you remain diligent and continue to practice. When you're older, you'll need to train with a real bow, but I'm sure a careful boy such as yourself needn't have to wait much longer for that."

"My mom said I could have a real bow when she makes enough money to buy one. But I can only use it when she's watching."

"That's good advice, son. 'Honor thy mother,' like it says in the Bible."

"Are you here . . . to see her?" he asked. "She's still at work."

I didn't want to lie to the youth, yet I couldn't very well tell him I was pursuing a stalker nearby. "No, Walter, I was merely having a nature walk when I happened upon you and your house. These woods are quite a treat for me, for I spend most of my time in the city. In Providence."

"Oh. I walk in the woods a lot too, sir." He pointed just behind the house. "There's a neat trail right over there that goes all the way back to town through the trees. That's how my mom walks to work every day."

"Why, I'm grateful for your advice, young man," I enthused. "I'll be sure to take that trail back myself. But tell me. Why are you out here all by yourself? Surely you have brothers and sisters old enough to play with."

His eyes blankened, as though the question were a stifling one. "I have to go now, sir, to help my gramps."

"Of course, and what a fine young man you are to be so attentive to your grandfather." It was all I could say, for it seemed that to press him about my previous question would only put him on the spot. Still, I had to think, *Mary's got seven more children. Are they all in the house?* "But before you're off, Walter, let me give you a present." I was probably out of bounds by doing this, yet I couldn't resist. "And I'm sure your mother and gramps have quite wisely advised you not to take gifts from strangers, but we're not strangers, you and I, are we?"

"No, not really, Mr. Foster," though the mention of a present had clearly throttled his attention.

"What I'd like you to do is take this and buy yourself a better bow," and then I gave him a ten-dollar bill. "And with what's left, wouldn't it be nice to buy your mother some flowers?"

"Oh, yes, sir, it would!" he almost shouted with glee.

"And when your mother asks where you got the money, just say her friend, Mr. Morley."

"Thank you, sir! Thank you a lot!"

"You're quite welcome, Walter. I hope to see you again."

I smiled as he scampered off to the squat house, entered a barely seen door, and disappeared.

What harm could there be? I only hoped I'd made the lad's day. I set to locate Walter's path just behind the house, but again found myself thwarted . . . as more questions occurred. Where exactly *were* the other children? And why had Walter been so reluctant to answer my inquiry?

I skirted round the back of the house, toward the clearing, yet while doing so, I deliberately kept an eye out for windows. The last window that would be available to me before I made the clearing was almost entirely ivy-covered.

What could I possibly say for myself should the stepfather see me peering in?

Yet peer in I did, unmindful of the very awkward risk, and why I did this, I'll never be sure.

I only know that I wish I hadn't.

Through the bleary fragment of available glass I first spied a close, brick-lined middle room surrounding a modest fireplace, an additional woodstove, and furniture that I must describe as makeshift. If anything, I was glad that they'd improved the utility of their poverty by reusing items—such as boxes, crates, and unattached bricks—for alternate purposes. Several crates, for instance, formed the foundation for a bed, and evidently, a great sack of burlap, stuffed with dried leaves, sufficed for the mattress, over which typical sheets had been lain. A cupboard housed not drinking glasses but reused tin cans for the same purpose. A table, whose top was fashioned by wooded wall slats of irregular length, had legs actually made from stouter tree branches. This glaring squalor injured me . . . and in my mind, I was already calculating how much my wealth would be able to help this destitute but fully functioning family.

I ducked back, when in the moment previous, a door within had opened. Young Walter first appeared, and what followed at his side was a faltering figure and a tap-tap-tapping sound. It was only the sparest daylight through the minute windows that afforded any light at all. The figure, as I squinted, seemed to be using crutches, and though it was through a wedge of darkness that this figure walked, my detection of long, grey hair told me this could only be Mary's stepfather; Walter was helping him along toward the makeshift bed.

The oddest noises of protestation resounded when he finally got to the bed and, with great difficulty, managed to lie down in it. I could make out almost nothing in the way of details, but the broader scope of his afflictions—some massive form of arthritis, I presumed—was quite clear by the crookedness of his limbs. Was the hand that picked up the piece of cardboard to use as a fan . . . missing fingers?

"Here's some water, gramps," Walter said and brought him one of the tin cans. My angle showed me little, only Walter carefully tilting the can for him to drink out of. The over-loud chugging sound caused my brow to rise.

"Um, gramps," Walter began. "There was this man outside. He's a friend of Mom's, and his name is Foster Morley . . . "

The horrendously palsied figure seemed to lean up, and in doing so, I saw a tragically unnatural curve to his spine. But it was Walter's words that had caused him to lean closer.

"And-and . . . he gave me this." The youth hesitated, then showed the ten-dollar bill. "To buy mom some flowers."

The stepfather's reaction to this information is something I'm sure I will never forget.

He lurched forward, deepening the arch to his back, shot out a hand that clearly was deformed, and then emitted a vocal objection in no language I'd ever heard: a high, almost bearing-like squeal underlain with suboctave grunts and what I can only call a mad tweaking, rising and lowering, and an accommodating sound that reminded me of something wet spattering somewhere.

The suddenness—and *unearthliness*—of the man's vociferous objection affected me almost physically, akin to a ball bat across the chest. I lurched backward, yet my eyes remained on that partial window-view, and all I can say about what I *think* I saw is this:

Something *shot* forward from the haggard mass of shadows that comprised this infirm man. What that *something* was I cannot accurately delimitate. It was either a length of rope or a whip, flung forward with a clearly stated maliciousness toward the boy. That's all I can say: it reminded me of a *whip*.

This whip, then, snapped out with a moist but resolute *crack!* and seemed to take the ten-dollar bill from Walter's hand, then draw it back to the afflicted oldster.

An attendant gush of a mix of those dreadfully low suboctaves, and the squeal, and then that awful phlegmatic splatter followed this action, after which, the boy, paling before my eyes, turned and dashed from the room.

A tremendous malady, indeed, had accursed this poor elderly man, not just in body but also in mind.

I could witness it no longer, and then I fled myself to the clearing behind the house, fairly bursting into sunlight and a flurry of butterflies, and ran outright until—half-crazed— I spotted the nature trail the boy had apprised me of.

Of congenital defects and progressive disease mechanisms, I knew precious little, and though my sense of pity and empathy was sound, I had to forcibly banish the image of this demented and inauspicious man from my mind . . .

As I tramped down the lad's path, I was scarcely aware of its features for several minutes. My heart seemed to hammer in the aftermath of my witness, and my breath grew short. Eventually, I slowed to regain my senses, then stooped, hands on knees, to rest.

The rapid exodus from the maledict house left me in a dirt-scratch of a trail lined by man-tall grasses. Insects chirruped, and the sun blazed.

It was the darkness of the huddled house, I thought, and the potency of suggestion that so grotesquely appended what I saw.

Of all people, I thought again of Cyrus Zalen and his all-too-true implications regarding my status in life. *A rich pud.* My unearned station of privilege had shielded me from such tragic realities heaped upon the less fortunate, and this simply wasn't right. I needed to *know* these direful realities—*and* their consequences—to be the better man that I'm sure God wanted me to be. My empathy must not be staged, nor my pity manufactured. I fancied myself a philanthropist—a willful *contributor* to those who had sorely less than me.

I knew that I must contribute *more*, and more, too, than simply money.

Soft voices severed my thoughts. When I turned my head, a great glimmer flashed in my eyes; through the tall grass, I saw a modest lake full of floating sunlight. But the voices . . .

It was necessary to shield my eyes to annul the glare. There, sitting at a short pier's end, were two women, one honey-blond and the other obsidian-haired. Both were naked, chatting animatedly as they rowed their feet in the water. I saw a small bottle serving as a buoy farther out in the lake.

The girls' bare white backs gleamed in the sun, but the tranquil scene did not parallel the apparent mood of the coal-haired one, who snapped, "I just *hate* it, Cassandra! It sickens me—their condition, I mean. And I have to go again tonight. Oh, God, I dread it *so much.*"

"So you're not in the way yet?" queried the other.

"No, I don't think so. They make me go—every night—until they're sure." The girl seemed to hack. "And I have to be with several of them! One's not enough! It's got to be at least two each night, and I heard they've gotten two more. What's that now, seven all together?"

"Six, I think. Remember, the one died, and that curly-haired man couldn't . . . you know. You never know when one might not be any good all of a sudden. Sometimes, they wind up like Paul."

Paul! the name immediately struck me. A common name, yes, but could they be referring to Mary's invalid brother?

"Well, shit!" exclaimed the black-haired waif with a surprising profanity. "One per night should be enough!"

"It's like the doctor said, Monica. The more you do it with, the better chance of success . . . "

What on earth are they talking about? I wondered, puzzled. And . . . the *doctor?* Did they mean Dr. *Anstruther?*

"That's why he tests them every so often," the honey-blonde continued. "To make sure they haven't lost their . . . I forgot the word. Portense? Er—no, potency!"

I stared at these strange words, my face lengthening.

"But they're just so *ugly* like that!" the dark-haired one, Monica, nearly squealed in objection. "It gives me nightmares."

The honey-blonde, Cassandra, took Monica's hand to offer a consolation. "It's like they say, you've got to get the right frame of mind. It's not about pleasure; it's about something much more important. To think like you're thinking is to be selfish. And they *have* to be the way they are—for safety's sake . . . "

"Ugh! It's just *awful* . . . "

"You don't have to tell me, Monica. I've had six babies so far. It's just the way it is here. It's better for the future."

"I don't know how you could've done it *six times!*"

Cassandra answered dreamily. "You just close your eyes and think *nice* things, Monica. You pretend you're with someone else, someone handsome and strong and sweet and—"

"Someone normal!" Monica upheld her complaints. "Not all girls do it *their* way."

"No, but their way keeps us in their favor, like the doctor says."

Monica seemed to be near tears. "God, why can't I have a real man just once? Sometimes, I'm tempted to leave."

"Shh! Don't talk like that!" chided Cassandra. "We both know what happens to girls who try to leave . . . "

I couldn't have been more bewildered as I listened to the arcane discourse . . .

"I better check the trap," said Cassandra, and she hopped down into chest-deep water. She was wading out toward the makeshift buoy.

Meanwhile, Monica stood up to stretch, hands behind her back. She did so turning, which afforded me a side-glance of her physique. She bore a stunning, willowy beauty in her youth, and couldn't have been more than eighteen. Next, she turned more and was facing me as she continued to stretch. The shining black hair rose in a brief breeze off the water. She was an exotic sight, petite-breasted, long-legged, and flat-stomached. I meant to turn away, for my inadvertent glimpse of her seemed invasive, but then Cassandra returned. She climbed up the pier's ladder to the deck, hoisting with her a small wire trap filled with crayfish. Unlike Monica, Cassandra was nine months pregnant if she was a day.

"Look, it's full!" she enthused over the trap full of skittering things.

Monica came over. "Wow, that is a lot." She tested the trap's weight. "It must be ten pounds! We'll have chowder for *days!*"

As I listened further, my closer attentions lapsed . . . and my hand slipped. I dropped my briefcase . . .

The sound was all too obvious; both girls snapped their inquisitive gazes in my direction. Could they see me? I didn't move a muscle.

"I think someone's there," Cassandra suspected, then she brought a fretful finger to her lips. "God, I hope it's not *them* . . . "

"Look! There!" Monica pointed directly at the stand of grass I hid behind.

"Is it . . . ?"

"No, it's a man! A *real man!*" She strode naked off the pier. "Hey, wait! Come here!"

I grabbed my case and slipped out.

"No!" wailed Monica. "Don't go! *Please!* We can make you real happy! COME BACK!"

I had no intention of complying. My feet took me swiftly down the close path, and I could only hope that neither girl had seen enough of my face to recognize it later. In the distance, I heard Monica's final grievance. "Oh, SHIT! He ran away!"

My pace did not abate until I was back at the town center and gratefully entering the Hilman House . . .

❋❋❋

Secure in my room, I sat on the bed to regain my breath. I turned the RCA on, for music would remind me of normalcy, and I immediately relaxed to "Our Love" by Tommy Dorsey. But this would be followed by the hourly news broadcast: a labor strike is ruled illegal by the Supreme Court, General Francisco Franco conquers Madrid with his fascist troops, a scientist named Fermi warns allied governments that a process now exists which can split atoms and thus harness a terrible destructive force. None of this news sounded hopeful; I switched it off.

The distraction I hoped for was sabotaged. *What exactly HAPPENED today?* I queried myself in some disillusionment. I tried with diligence to find a common logic in what I'd seen and heard but, in the end, failed. I could make no sense of it, but I considered that in my current expended and excited state, it would do me good to calm down to resort my thoughts. The day's heat as well as the mad sprint had left me grimy and saturated with perspiration, so I had a cool bath in the private tub. I tried to clear my thoughts . . .

But a sudden fatigue left me drowsy even in the cool water. I drifted in and out of a half-sleep. Snippets of dreams harassed me: images of not only perplexity but also repugnance.

The man in the squalid house, deformed by some catastrophic arthritic symptom, unleashing wet, gushing invectives in no way intelligible, and then lashing at young Walter with that whip, or whatever it might have been.

And the two nude girls on the pier, one pregnant and then one evidently fearing pregnancy with an appalled resignation . . . Their cryptic words slipped in and out of my half-dreaming mind:

—it sickens me—their condition, I mean—

—so you're not in the way yet?—

—they make me go—every night—until they're sure!—

—sometimes they wind up like Paul . . . —

The words blended, then, with a razor-crisp recollection of their physical bodies, their gleaming nude beauty, their shimmering white skin, and their private feminine features so forbidden—and so wrong for me to have willingly looked upon—yet so exotic . . .

I may have slipped into a deep doze when these vivid images were singularly banished . . . by the image of Mary . . .

First, the loveliness of her face and simple honest manner, and even some of her remarks:

—a handsome, well-mannered gentleman like you? Never married?—

And then a devilish meld: my first captivating image of her working at Baxter's slowly contorting itself into the image on the nefarious and wholly exploitative photograph I'd bought from the despicable Cyrus Zalen: Mary, laid out bare and pregnant and thrust-bosomed as the visual photographic fodder of degenerates . . .

The finality of that image shocked me from my doze, and I'm sure I audibly groaned. The sudden anxiety was one—I'm ashamed to say—of unquenched physical desire of the most sinful sort. It left me carnally evoked, and though in the past I'd always done better than a fair job of abstaining, the primal necessity now could not be extinguished. I need not go on in detail save to say that my frenzy forced me to do what solitary men are *known* to do in such moments of weakness, after which—steeped in shame—I prayed God's forgiveness for this venal and most insolent offense to His grace . . .

Embarrassed after the fact, I languished in the claw-footed tub, but then my eyes shot wide—

I'd heard, with some distinction, a sudden and undeniable sound: the desperate hitching of a single breath into one's chest. It was a lush, wanton sound, more than likely female.

I stared at the opposing wall to at once be inundated by the notion that I was being observed remotely. But if so . . .

From where, exactly?

I jumped from the bath, donned a robe, and, like a paranoiac, actually began to examine the opposing wall and the ceiling over the tub. But no "peepholes" were chanced upon; minutes later, I frowned at myself for the foolish overreaction. The sound I thought I'd heard was most certainly a remnant from the dream-fragments and a fatigued body and mind. *For goodness sake!* I mocked. *Who would be spying on me, of all people?*

My new Pierce Chronograph wristwatch showed me my dinner appointment was fast approaching. I talced myself, brushed my teeth with a new product called Listerine Tooth-Cleaning Paste, then dressed in my evening suit. Though I was looking forward to dining with Mr. Garret, most of my thoughts focused on a different appointment: my luncheon date with Mary tomorrow. I oddly felt that I'd sullied her by my previous act of debasement and self-abusiveness, an absurd abstraction, but such was me. Nevertheless, I would not leave until I'd done one simple thing.

I sat at the small writing table the room provided and opened my briefcase. From it, I withdrew the folder I'd purchased from Zalen, and from the bottom of the assortment of old photos within, I slipped out the shot of

Mary. It was with a plummeting grimness that I allowed myself to look at it . . .

The photo's sharpness, contrast, and overall clarity seemed even more precise than before, and again, I was stifled by the sense of fusion that joined Mary's objective physical beauty with a revoltingly exploitative design: that graceful and exuberant pose, all for the visual consumption of unholy men given to perversity. Every element of the photograph seemed to beckon me to lust—Mary's bottomless, sparkling eyes; her sighing smile; the high, dark-nippled breasts burgeoning with milk; the toned, shapely legs. I noticed now that every inch of her impeccable nudity either shined in profuse sweat or had been deliberately glazed by some kind of oil, the effect of which caused the entirety of her image to shimmer as if alive within the borders of the photographic paper. But I would not succumb to the lust that this image tried to seduce.

Only love.

A monstrous world, to allow this, I resolved. *To enslave the poor and the desperate for the most jaded of intents.* I took up a small pair of folding shears from my travel kit and began to shred the photo, from the borders in, until all that was left was the tiny square of Mary's beauteous visage. The shreddings, I discarded; the square, however, I hid in a pocket of my wallet.

Down the stairwell, then, I went; as I neared the entry level, though, the door to the atrium opened before I could reach it, and suddenly, I was faced by a slim, attractive young woman in a nice but simple frock gown that so many preferred in the warmer months; she was on her way up as I was on my way down. She lent me a meek smile, then nodded as we converged.

"How do you do?"

"Hello," was all she said, as if shy. When she passed me, I was stung by a tremulous shock; it had taken me this long for the girl's willowy figure and obsidian-black hair to register.

Monica, I felt sure. *One of the pier girls . . .*

She'd obviously not recognized me as the interloper she'd been so ardently pleading with just a few hours ago.

Certainly, she's not staying here . . . Perhaps she was employed here with the housekeeping service. But, really, why should I be concerned?

I heard her quiet footfalls as she mounted the steps, then passed myself into the atrium, but as the door was closing behind me—and I'm not sure why I noticed this, but—the aforesaid footfalls seemed to terminate very quickly. Nor was I sure what compelled me to my next gesture . . .

I went back into the stairwell and looked upward.

No evidence of Monica could be discerned, but then—*click!*

The sound registered quickly enough to bid me to glance up at the door on the second-floor landing. It clicked shut before my eyes.

The second floor, I thought. *The LOCKED floor.* Monica, for whatever reason, clearly had access to it.

My frown returned me to the atrium. Why this addled me, I couldn't guess . . .

The congenial bellhop and desk clerk greeted me as I passed. Of the clerk, I had to inquire: "If you don't mind, sir, I'm curious as to the reason for the second floor being locked."

It may have been imaginativeness on my part, but his standard smile and good nature seemed to snap off for a moment. "But, you're on the *fourth* floor, Mr. Morley. Why would you—"

"Of course!" I tried to sound dismissive. "I should've preambled that I just now mistakenly took the second floor for the first." I would not quite call this a lie but, say, a modest divergency from the truth.

But the man's good-natured expression had already restored itself. "Ah, well, the floor's being kept locked for the time being. Renovations. The work shouldn't take more than a month."

"I see. Well, thank you, good man, for satisfying my fairly useless curiosity. I should've guessed!" and then I bid him a good evening.

Across the street, then, to Wraxall's Eatery, where an appetizing aroma awaited. The establishment was spotless and appointed with simple chairs and tables, plus a none-too-surprising nautical motif: photos of old, rain-slickered watermen proudly displaying sizable fishes, a ship's wheel and a ship's glass, fishing nets with floats adorning the corners. I supposed it possible that, before the government renewal, this very eatery may have been the dismal cafeteria in which Robert Olmstead begrudgingly dined as unwholesome loafers cast strange glances.

Brass lanterns quaintly housing candles ornamented each wooden table. My eyes thinned, though, when I noticed that Mr. Garret was nowhere in sight. Only one table was occupied, by a soft-speaking couple.

When the hostess turned, bearing a menu, she was struck speechless.

I couldn't have been more pleased! It was Mary . . .

"Why, Mary, what a pleasant surprise." I tried to contain my joy.

"Foster!" She smiled and pressed a hand to my back to urge me to the corner. "Take the window booth. The view's lovely as the sun sets. I'm so glad you could come."

"I had no idea you worked here as well."

"Oh, I just fill in sometimes. But the money's not bad, now that our wonderful president has signed the Minimum Wage Act."

I'd read of this: a rather scrimy forty cents per hour. But then I had to keep reminding myself that chance—and my father's hard work, not my own—had handed me a status much more fortunate than that of most.

She filled my water glass as I took a seat. "Did you find a nice, quiet place to read your book?"

"Oh, *The Shadow Over Innsmouth* . . . " I'd almost forgotten that had been my original goal. "Actually, I was so busy gallivanting about town that I never got round to it. Tomorrow, though. After our lunch date, which I dearly hope is still on."

Suddenly, she sighed, then drooped her head dramatically. "Are you kidding? I can't wait. It'll be my first afternoon off in weeks."

This disconcerted me. "Mary, there's nothing more admirable than a hard-worker," and then I leaned close, "but I wish you didn't have to put in such hours while you're with child."

"You're so sweet, Foster." She grinned and squeezed my hand. "But hard work is what made America, isn't it?"

"Yes, it is," I said, if a bit guiltily.

"Besides, Dr. Anstruther says it's fine to work until the eighth month, just nothing too strenuous."

I'm sure this were true, but it still bothered me. When she leaned over to hand me the menu, I could detect a bit of her bosom's valley, then recalled, first, the jaded photograph and, next, the split-second glimpse I'd caught of her breast in the back room of Baxter's. Then there it was again, that perfect valley of flesh.

I nearly ground my teeth as I looked away. God! I hope she hadn't noticed . . .

Another distraction was needed, but this time, I needn't manufacture one. A brass ship's clock on the wall showed me I was five minutes late. "Say, Mary? Has a respectably dressed man, perhaps in his late-twenties, been in? Brown, short hair? His name is William Garret."

She shook her head. "No, Foster. Mid-week is always slow—like they say, Friday is Fish Day. There'll be a rush later, when the watermen come back from the docks. But I'm afraid I haven't seen the man you're describing."

"I was supposed to meet him," I began, but then shrugged it off. "No matter. He's either running late or maybe he secured himself a position. He's an accountant."

"Well, they might need accountants in the wholesalers," she offered.

"Yes, I'm sure that's it." It was obvious. He'd probably located his friend Mr. Poynter and managed to get a job. I truly wished the best for him.

Following some more small talk, I got about my order, which Mary had recommended: chowder, fried Ipswich clams, and striped bass stuffed with rock crab. I'd always delighted in such fare and felt bad that Lovecraft himself, a New Englander too, could never share in these delights due to a repugnance for shellfish. My eyes, however, struggled to keep averted from Mary as she went about her table-waiting. *She's just so . . . beautiful,* I kept thinking. Eventually, the other table left, then a man from the back exited the restaurant as well, seeming to head down the block. Next thing I knew, Mary was sitting across from me, with two Cocamalts.

"I love your company, Mary, but might not your employer—"

"Don't worry about Mr. Wraxall," she excused, and sipped her drink. "Every night at seven, he goes to the bar—Karswell's—for at least three boxcars. So I can take a break too while your food's cooking."

"How delightful," I all but exclaimed.

Even in her nonchalance, her eyes cast a glitter akin to diamond chips, and I could see the richness of her dark-blond hair now that it had been freed from the hairnet she wore in the general store. When I caught myself watching her lips surround the drink-straw, I almost cringed at the sudden eroticism of it.

"So, how was your gallivanting?" she asked.

"Splendid, Mary. I'm sure I toured most of the town proper—"

"The docks?" she cut in.

"Oh, yes, the docks too."

"Don't be put off if the watermen weren't overly friendly," she informed.

"Actually, my friend Mr. Garret warned me of it, but in truth, I scarcely noticed any such workmen."

"It's only because they're . . . what's the word?" A fingertip went to her mouth. "Possessive."

This seemed curious. "Possessive? Whatever do you mean?"

"They don't like strangers, Foster," she went on. "Strangers shouldn't be in our harbor; they should stay in their own. We don't send our boats to Rockport or Gloucester. Why should they be allowed to send theirs here?"

Now it made sense; this was the territorialism of which the man Onderdonk spoke of so bitterly. A "stranger" from another port town could easily take note of where the Innswich fishing boats were casting their nets, as well as their time tables. "It seems a fair rule of thumb," I said, "and I'm happy that the town's fishing industry is doing so well." I reflected on a pause. "I only hope that *you're* doing well too, Mary."

"Oh, me? I'm fine. I'm making more right off the bat with the new minimum wage, and since I turned twenty-five, I've been receiving a monthly dividend from the town collective."

"The town . . . collective?" I chuckled half-heartedly. "It sounds a bit socialist."

"No, it's just a profit-sharing plan for residents who work and contribute to the local economy," she explained. "Most of it comes from the fishing. I've been getting it three years now, and each year it goes up a little." She lowered her voice. "I'm ashamed to say, but we don't even have any real furniture at our house, but this year, thanks to the collective, I'll be able to buy some."

The remark sunk my heart; I recalled from my brief visit to her house the makeshift oddments that Mary's poverty forced her to use as furniture. "You're a determined woman, Mary, and with all those children? Plus your brother and stepfather to care for? Your resilience is quite remarkable. I must confess, though, I actually met your son Walter today. What a fine lad."

This admission seemed to hold her in check. "You've . . . been to my house?"

I had to choose my phrases carefully. "Not really. I was simply walking by, returning from the barbeque stand up the road."

Her words faltered. "And . . . you met . . . Walter?"

"Indeed, I did. What an industrious young man. He was practicing—quite deftly—his archery skills. I'd only a moment to speak with him, though."

"But you didn't . . . see my . . . stepfather?"

"Oh, no, no. I was just passing by," I reiterated. "I like Walter very much, but I'll tell you, I didn't see hide nor hair of your other children. You've a total of eight, right?"

"Yes, but they're younger. They were probably napping."

"No doubt, on such a hot day." The temptation dragged at me: to simply write her a cheque for $5000 and give it to her, for a *new* house, with *real* furniture, to ease her squalor.

But I feared how that might be taken at this point . . .

"And I hope you're not terribly disappointed with me, Mary, but circumstance forced me to break my promise of earlier," I went on. "I did pursue an interview with this Mr. Cyrus Zalen earlier today—"

"Oh, Foster, you didn't!" she exclaimed.

I raised a reassuring finger. "It was of little consequence, really. You see, I simply couldn't deprive your brother of his photograph with H.P. Lovecraft; it didn't seem right. And as good fortune would have it, Zalen is still in possession of the negative, and I've arranged to purchase a copy from him tomorrow. But you were quite right about one thing," I said with a chuckle. "He's one of a shady lot indeed."

Mary's sudden downcast expression instantly made me regret volunteering this information. But I plainly didn't like the idea of keeping it from her.

"He's a bad man, Foster," she implored. "And it's a filthy area he lives in. He's a drug addict and a con man."

"I've no doubt, now that I've met him."

"And he preys on people—on *women,* Foster. Poor women."

"I can imagine," I said.

Now she gulped. "And I'm sure . . . he told you about me."

Here, I had no choice but to lie, to spare her feelings. "Why do you say that? He had nothing at all to say of you."

She reached across and touched my hand again. "Foster, I have to be honest with you—because I *like* you so much—"

The sudden comment rocked me . . .

"—but a long time ago, I was one of the women he preyed upon," she finished and then looked right at me.

There was no hesitation in my response, nor with my smile. "Mary, there are times when we *all* take an erroneous path in life, and when we do unethical deeds out of desperation, we're only being human. These are not grievous sins, and what you must believe is that God forgives all."

Her eyes were a blink away from tearing up. "Does He really?"

"Yes," I assured her, and now it was my hand that took hers. "The entails of motherhood are burdensome indeed. The past is behind you now, and any of your past misgivings are behind you as well. The same goes for all of us, Mary. The same goes for me. You're doing the right thing now, and you have a wonderful future that awaits you."

She was choking up, squeezing my hand. "I'll just have out with it then, because I can't lie to you." And then she croaked, "Before the town collective admitted me, there were times, in the past, when I'd had to resort to acts of prostitution."

"But that doesn't *matter*," I replied, unfazed—for this I already knew. "You're a moral, honest, and very hardworking woman now. *That's* all that matters, Mary."

She looked at me so strangely then. "I can tell by your eyes—it really doesn't bother you, does it—I mean, what I was in the past."

"It bothers me not in the least," I told her with all my heart. "I'm only interested in what you are now: a wonderful, beautiful person."

She hitched on a few sobs as a bell rang and someone yelled, "Order up!"

She wiped her eyes, smiling. "Foster, the first time in years I've felt good about myself is right *now*—thanks to you."

"You have every reason to feel good about yourself, and I hope you *always* do."

"I better get your dinner before I start on a full-blown bawling spell," and then she was up and rushing into the back.

I sat, now, in a platonic ecstasy. This lovely woman seemed to be genuinely fond of me, something rare in my life of indulgent seclusion. What made me happiest was knowing that my words and earnestness had helped give her a more positive conception of herself.

When my dinner was brought, it was an aproned cook and not Mary who'd brought it. "Sorry, sir, but your waitress is indisposed for a moment. All tearing up about something."

"Allergies, I'm sure," I said. "And thus far, she's done a marvelous job in attending to me."

"Enjoy your dinner, sir."

"I'm certain I will, thank you."

As I dined on this sumptuous feast, I noted varnished plaques mounted on the walls—they were name-planks for old ships. HETTY, one read, and the others: SUMATRY QUEEN and COLUMBY. I couldn't be sure why—and perhaps it was the diversion of the ambrosial meal—but . . . did those names ring a bell?

The chowder proved superior to the standard Providence recipe, and the striped bass may have been the best I'd ever sampled. Toward the meal's end, I felt like the most sinful of gluttons, especially in times when food was scarce for so many.

Mary returned—freshened up now and recomposed—and after she cleared the table, she sat down again opposite me. I couldn't have complimented the meal more. But her look told me something still troubled her.

"What you said earlier, Foster," she began, "about Cyrus Zalen? You said you're seeing him *again?*"

"Yes, tomorrow at four." I knew she wasn't comfortable about me being in this cad's proximity, so I meant to assure her. "It's purely to purchase a copy of the Lovecraft photo so that your brother won't be deprived of his. Zalen needed some time to process the negative. But after that, I give you my guarantee, it will be the last time I ever cross paths with the man."

"That's good, Foster. He has a bad way about him—he's a conniver."

And also the father of one of your children, the darker thought flashed in my head. *But he'll never connive you anymore, Mary. I'll see to it.* "A conniver and then some," I went on in a more light-hearted voice. "I caught the man actually stalking me twice today, once before I met him and once after."

"Stalking you?"

"Slinking about from the woods, tailing me. I'm sure robbery was what he was considering. I'd walked up to the Onderdonks' stand for a sandwich, and it was on my way back that Zalen began to follow me more overtly. I went in the woods after him to show him I wasn't afraid of his kind."

"Foster, you shouldn't have!"

"The man knows I have some means, so I guess he figured robbing me might yield more profit than my purchase of the Lovecraft photo. But I made it quite plain to him that I was well able to defend myself. He'll not be doing that again, I'm sure. But this unpleasant incident occurred not too far from where young Walter was engaged in his archery session—that's how I came to meet him. Zalen was long gone by then." Naturally, I neglected to add that it was Zalen who revealed the rough location of Mary's ramshackle house.

"The man's like a blight," she bemoaned. "It's rare that I see much of him, but when I do . . . all it does . . . it reminds me—"

I squeezed her hand in reassurance. "You must disregard any negative memories that are triggered by Zalen. He counts for nothing. Revel, instead, in the promise of your future. I assure you it will be a bright one."

She looked sullenly at me. "Oh, how I wish that were true, Foster."

My only response was a smile, for I'd decided to say no more. It wasn't necessary because at that moment, I already knew what I was going to do . . .

After a bit more small talk, I rose and prepared to excuse myself. "Well, by now, it's certain that Mr. Garret won't be making an appearance, and I'm a bit fatigued from a day of travel. But please know, Mary, that spending this little bit of time with you was the highlight of my day. You're a lovely person."

She blushed and blinked another tear away. Then she glanced about to see that no one was looking and kissed me quickly on the lips. I shivered in a sweet shock. Her lips came right to my ear. "Please come and see me at the store tomorrow. I'm off at twelve."

"I'll be there. We'll have a fabulous lunch somewhere."

Then she hugged me in something like desperation. "Please don't forget."

I chuckled. "Mary. No force on Earth could make me forget."

Another quick kiss and she pulled away, then picked up the fifty-dollar bill I'd left on the table. "I'll be right back with your change." When she hustled away into the back, I quietly left the restaurant.

The sky was darkening in a spectacular fashion as I made the main street. The sinking sun painted wisps of clouds with impossible light over the waterfront. The street's quaint cobblestones seemed to shine in a glaze; neatly dressed passersby strolled gaily along, the perfect human accouterment to an evening rife with tranquil charm. At that moment, it occurred to me: I'd never felt more content.

It was a shrill siren that ripped the evening's placidity. I turned the corner and noticed a long red and white ambulance pulled right up on the sidewalk, with several uniformed attendants bustling about. Several residents stood aside, looking on with concern.

What's this all about? I thought, then felt my spirit plummet when I noticed that the commotion was centered around the bargain store I'd visited previously. At the same moment, a stretcher was borne out from the shop, and on it was a very still and very blanch-faced Mr. Nowry. In the doorway, the man's expectant wife sobbed openly.

Oh, no . . .

"Poor Mr. Nowry," a small voice announced to my side. "He was such a nice man."

I turned to see an attractive red-haired woman standing next to me. "I-I hope he hasn't expired. He was as congenial a man as you could ever hope to meet; why, I spoke to him just hours ago."

"Probably another coronary attack," she ventured.

"I'll go and see," I said, and made my way to the receding commotion. "Sir? I'm sorry to intrude," I asked of one of the ambulance men, "but could you confide in me as to the status of Mr. Nowry?"

The younger man looked bleary-eyed from a long day. "I'm afraid he died a few minutes ago. There was nothing we could do this time—his ticker finally went out."

I bowed my head. "I scarcely knew him, but he was a good man, from what I could see."

"Oh, sure, an Olmsteader through and through." He

forearmed his brow. "But it's been a strange day, I'll tell ya."

"In what way?"

"Small town like this, we don't get more than two or three deaths a year, but today? We've had *two* now."

"Two? How tragic."

Now the stretcher bearing the decedent was loaded into the rear compartment of the vehicle. The man to whom I was speaking pointed inside. "A young girl too, not a half-hour ago. One of those not in with a decent crowd, but still . . . She died in childbirth."

I looked to where he was pointing and noticed a second stretcher.

Instantly, my throat thickened.

It was a thin, lank-haired girl in her twenties who lay dead next to Mr. Nowry, a sheet covering her to the chin. Even in the pallor of death, though, I recognized her face.

It was Candace—one of Zalen's ill-reputed photo models and prostitutes. But the great, swollen belly was gone now, only swollen breasts showing beneath the white sheet.

"Please, tell me her baby survived," I implored.

"The baby's fine," he said matter-of-factly.

"Praise God . . . "

The man looked at me in the oddest way, then closed the long back door of the hospital coach and went on his way.

I returned to the woman I'd been talking to. "I'm afraid Mr. Nowry has passed away. We should be sure to remember him in our prayers." I took a doleful glance to his poor widow, still sobbing in the shop doorway. "I pity his wife, though."

"She's expecting any day now," the woman told me with something hopeful in her tone. "You needn't worry; the Nowrys are long-term town members. The collective will provide for his widow."

Another reference to this collective. My initial

impression had been less than positive due to unavoidable insinuations, but now, it seemed, I may have been hasty. The initiative, instead, sounded like a very serviceable system of social/fiscal management and profit-sharing. It was heartening to know that Mrs. Nowry wouldn't be left on her own. As for Candace's newborn . . . well, I could only assume it would be cared for by family members or placed in a fosterage program.

"You're new in town," said the redhead with the most traceable smile. Then she sighed. "Just passing through, I fear."

"Why, yes, but why do you put it that way?"

"The handsome men *never* stay long."

The flattering comment took me off guard. "That's, uh, very nice of you to say, Miss, but I must bid you a good evening now." I walked away quickly. Being complimented so abruptly by women always left me tongue-tied. At least it left me, however selfishly, with a good feeling. I'd certainly never thought of myself as *handsome*. I smiled, then, when I recalled Mary making similar comment.

The desk shift had changed when I was back at the Hilman House; a stoop-shouldered older woman tended the desk.

"Ma'am, I'd like to write a note to one of your guests, a Mr. William Garret," I told her. "Would you be so kind as to pass it on to him?"

A moment of fuddlement crossed her eyes. She glanced at a ledger. "Oh, dear, I'm afraid Mr. Garret checked out several hours ago, along with another associate of his."

"Would that be Mr. Poynter?"

"Why, yes, sir, that's correct. They caught the motor-coach to the transfer station. Headed back to Boston, I believe."

"I see. Well thank you for your time."

That explained that, though I regretted not seeing Garret again, if only to bid him good luck in the future. At least he'd re-found his friend Poynter. It was too bad they hadn't secured positions here.

Back upstairs, I passed a cart-pushing maid in the hall. She smiled and said hello. It took a moment to recognize her.

It was the maid I'd spoken to upon checking in, the pregnant one, though now . . .

She no longer displayed any signs of gravidness.

"Why, my dear girl!" I exclaimed. "I see you've borne your child . . . "

"Yes, sir," she said rather flatly. "A boy."

"Well, congratulations are in order but—really!—you should be resting, not working!"

She stared at me, head atilt, mulling her thoughts. "I'm just picking up a bit, sir, then I can go home."

"But it's unacceptable for an employer to insist you work so soon after—"

"Really, sir, I appreciate your concern, but I'm feeling all right. I'll be to bed very soon."

"I should hope so." This was mortifying. And with all the new labor laws in place to protect against such exploitation. "Where's the baby?"

An odd pause stalled her. "Home, sir. With my mother . . . " She gave a meek smile that struck me as forced, and went on with her cart.

Off all the things, I thought. All the more reason for Mary to be out of here. Town collective or not, workers—most especially *pregnant women*—shouldn't be used as an objective resource. Certain medical conditions must always be given leeway.

I'd already decided that I was going to take Mary and her entire family back to Providence with me. Should it turn out to be a mistake, then so be it. At least I will have tried. My only fret was how and when to make my desires known. It was of the utmost importance that she know nothing was expected of her in return, which might be difficult to convince her of, given the darker aspects of her past.

I will remove her from her burdens, I determined, *and give her the life she deserves. And maybe, just maybe . . .*

One day, I'd have the privilege of marrying her.

So much for my "platonic" intents, but it was imperative that I be honest with myself. Of course, my idealism was strong, and I knew that things didn't always germinate into what we truly wanted.

But I knew what *I* wanted. I wanted *her. And I will make every effort to be the man she longs for but has thus far never had.*

I knew that I had to buff not only the edges of my outrage over the young maid's exploitation but also the sad mishap of Mr. Nowry's coronary attack—I needed to let my mind stray elsewhere. I decided to relax, then, in the clean room's quietude, so I sat up in my bed and opened my most cherished book: *The Shadow Over Innsmouth.* It would not be a concerted re-reading, I'd decided; that would come tomorrow when I found the perfect place, perhaps in view of the harbor. Though the buildings were different, the inlet itself and the mysterious sea beyond was the same that Lovecraft spied when the worms of his masterpiece were first coming to mind, a brilliant amalgamation of atmosphere, concept, character, and, ultimately, horror. Evidently, Lovecraft had been so irrevocably impacted by Irwin Cobb's sophomoric yet deeply macabre "Fishhead," and also Robert Chambers' flawed but image-steeped "The Harbour Master," that he'd seized the basic seeds of these stories and taken them into ingenious new directions, to weave very much his own superior tale of symbolic—and wholly monstrous—miscegenation. In it, when narrator Robert Olmstead accidentally stumbles upon the crumbling and legend-haunted Innsmouth seaport, he discovers, first, that the townsfolks have long-since assumed a pact of sorts with a race of horrid amphibious sea creatures first discovered by one Captain Obed Marsh, a sea-trader, while venturing through the East Indies; and, second and worst, that this monstrous and greed-driven pact involved not only human sacrifice but also the rampant crossbreeding of the creatures—the Deep Ones—

and the human populace of Innsmouth. Any page I turned to led to an image or a line that I could easily deem my favorite.

Here was one, a line of dialogue spoken by none other than the "ancient toper" Zadok Allen, whose real-life model had been Zalen's grandfather, Adok. The line read as thus: "Never was nobody like Cap'n Obed—old limb o' Satan! Heh, heh! I kin mind him a-tellin' abaout furren parts, an' callin' all the folks stupid fer goin' to Christian meetin' an' bearin' their burdens meek an' lowly. Say they'd orter git better gods like some o' the folks in the Injies—gods as ud bring 'em good fishin' in return for their sacrifices, an' ud reely answer folks's prayers."

Naturally, I was amused by the convenient parallel: the "good fishing" that the Deep Ones brought to Innsmouth in exchange for bloody oblations. I had to chuckle at this very *real* town's own abundance of local fish. I nearly laughed aloud!

Something that I suspect as being subconscious caused my errant page-flipping to stop, and next, my eyes were locked down strangely on another line of Zadok Allen's drunken ramble: "Obed Marsh he had three ships afloat—brigantine *Columby,* brig *Hetty,* an' bark *Sumatry Queen . . .* "

A vertigo accosted me as I stared at the words. Then: *Of course! I knew I'd seen those names before! They were right here all along . . . ,* for now I recalled these same names from the decorative ship plaques in the restaurant.

So not only did the town of "Innsmouth" exist, though under its true and none-too-different name Innswich, but so did these trading vessels exist somewhere in the town's dim past. I couldn't help but admire the assiduousness of Lovecraft's research efforts—something he was quite known for—to plumb such minute details of reality and infuse them into his fictional landscape.

I re-read parts of several more scenes, all with much chilling delight, then put the book up with the heated anticipation of re-reading cover to cover tomorrow. But there was one more even greater anticipation regarding tomorrow . . .

I must make every effort to look my best, I realized, then shuddered when I opened my suitcase and found my best suit in a crumpled state. There'd be no place open this hour to get them freshly pressed; hence, I could only hope . . .

When I glanced into the closet, I saw I was in luck! There, leaning, stood a collapsible pressing board, and atop the high shelf sat a steam-iron. I knew next to nothing of such procedures, but how difficult could it be? I took out the pressing board, looking for some sort of locking pin in order to extend its legs, when—

"Drat!"

—it slipped from my fingers and banged against the back wall of the closet.

"Oh, for pity's sake!" I complained aloud when I saw that the meager board had struck the wall with such impact that it actually left a hole. *The management will be none-too-pleased over this,* I thought. *Until I pay them double the repair fee.* I stepped inside to retrieve the board, then lowered to a knee to inspect the damage. Bits of plaster lay about, while the insult to the plasterboard looked a foot long and several inches wide. This was flimsy construction, to say the least, yet of the bungling accident, I could only blame my own carelessness.

Before I could pull away, though—

When I put my eye to the rent, the tiniest thread of light seemed to hang in the darkness beyond the plasterboard. Quick calculation told me there must be a small hole in the sidewall, which could only be the wall to my bathroom. When I hastily got up and went to the bathroom, I saw that I'd inadvertently left the light on earlier.

A hole, came the plodding thought. *In the wall . . .*

A *peep*hole?

The notion seemed absurd, but I could not forget my earlier impression: when I'd been bathing, I not only could've sworn I heard a human gust of breath *from behind the wall,* but I'd also been filled with the suspicion that I was being spied on . . .

No true logic could explain my next endeavor. Careful as ever—while back in the closet—I pulled chunks of the plasterboard away. The damage was already done, so damaging the wall further mattered little; I'd be paying for it regardless of the size of the hole. I suppose my motives at this earlier point were subconscious, but after I pulled away several more pieces of the wall and shined into the hole the beam of my pocket-flashlight, I detected an area of space beyond that could easily be taken for a narrow walkway. Of course, it must be only a service passage, for access to pipes, electrical wires, and whatnot. Still . . .

I pulled away some more pieces until the hole was sizable enough to admit me, and then I crawled in.

Back on my feet, inside now, I approached the threadlike beam. Instinct, of course, put my eye to it posthaste.

I was looking directly into my bathroom.

It IS a peephole, came my first thought, but then, *No, that's ridiculous!* The Hilman was obviously a respectable lodging-house. The hole could be explained by a number of circumstances: a simple construction flaw, or a nail-hole where a picture had been hung.

Deeper in the murk, though, I noticed *another* thread of light.

Taking every precaution not to misstep, I proceeded to this next light beam and found, to my dismay, another hole, which looked directly into the bedroom of the suite next to mine.

I was at a loss for what to think just yet. A modest clatter came to my ears, and with my eye pressed to the hole, I noticed movement.

It was the maid I'd just spoken to, who'd only just this morning been pregnant. Solemn-faced and dull-eyed, she lethargically went about the task of making the bed and picking up. On a chair by the door, however, I noticed a small valise, which sat opened and showed that it was full of clothes. And on the dresser?

There sat a neat, beige Koko-Kooler hat, identical to that which William Garret had been wearing just this morn when I met him. Near the door, too, sat a briefcase that appeared all-too-similar to his.

But Garrett and his friend already checked out, I remembered.

Once the housekeeper had finished with the bed, she jammed the hat into the suitcase, closed it, then took it and the briefcase out of the room . . .

Only the baldest, most objective pondering occupied my mind now. I believed there were two more rooms on this side of the floor, and when I peered down—sure enough—I spotted two more of the tiny beams of light, signaling the existence of two more peepholes. Then, in the opposite direction of this hidden walkway, several more such beams could be discerned . . .

I kept my pocket-flash aimed down on the floor. If this walkway did indeed exist for some ill intent—either for perversity or remotely gaining knowledge of a lodger's potential valuables—there must be some mode of unobservable access. At the very end of the passage, on the floor, lay what could only be a trapdoor.

I opened it, spotted a rail-ladder, and without much conscious volition, found myself next taking the ladder down to the hotel's third floor . . .

Black as hackneyed pitch, this climbing-way was; I thought of the esophagus of some Mesozoic creature into whose belly I was venturing. A doorless aperture signaled the hidden passage paralleling the third floor, and it was through that I stepped to face a similarly dark hidden passage. A thread of light marked each of the floor's rooms, but when I quickly looked into them, I noted only untenanted hotel rooms.

So—to the next floor I descended upon the ladder. The

second floor. At the aperture, I stepped into another hallway clogged with darkness made incomplete only by more intermittent threads of light. Here, though, I vaguely detected voices.

I let my shoes take me as slowly—and quietly—as possible to the first of the peeping-holes.

My vantage point only allowed me to view a wedge of the bland, clean room within, where I saw shelves of canned goods, sponges, buckets, towels, and other such items. The voices were distinctly female and seemed nonchalant. Several young women sat in the room, while I could only see slices of them; they appeared to be sitting on several couches. All were in some stage of pregnancy.

"—from Providence, I think, and he's quite handsome," one said.

"Oh, I know the one—he's kind of shy," observed another.

"And kind of rich! That's what I heard. That's why they won't take him."

My mind stalled as my eye remained to the hole. Could they . . . be talking about *me?*

A third, barely visible, contributed, "Oh, I know who you mean." A giggle. "I was upstairs looking in the peep-holes and saw him—you know—playing with himself!"

"No!"

"He pulled himself right off! In the bathtub—"

The other cackled, while I, as might be expected, felt my spirit wilt. It could *only* be me they were talking about . . .

"—and you're right, he's quite a handsome one, but I liked the two others much better."

"The Boston men?"

"Yeah. I wouldn't have minded being made in the way from one of them."

"But, Lisa! Neither of them are very handsome now!" and then more giggling broke out.

I could only stare, more at my own bewildered thoughts than the scene within. This was outrageous, women who were more than likely maids spying on hotel customers. It was certainly actionable, and I most certainly had a solicitor who'd be more than happy to sue, but . . .

What's the reason for all this? I had to wonder through my embarrassment and shock. Women weren't known to be Peeping Toms; that was an aberrancy reserved for men alone. And the reference to two *Boston* men could only mean Mr. Garret and Mr. Poynter. *Neither of them are very handsome now?*

"God, it's just so depressing having to do it when they're like that," came another observation. "I'm happy to be pregnant."

"Yeah. And they're not going to keep the Providence man."

"Why?"

"I told you, he's rich. The others are always fly-by-nights—no one knows they're here—but the Providence man—"

"He's no fly-by-night if he's rich. Someone would come looking . . . "

Even to contort my imagination to its maximum could not account for the words I was hearing, nor the outrageous evidence my curiosity had led me to uncover.

I moved to the next hole . . .

God in Heaven . . .

. . . and found myself looking at the most macabre scene I'd ever witnessed in my thirty-three years of existence . . .

Several bed mattresses lay on the floor, and in the corners were a few metal pans. "God, I hate this," snapped a woman's complaint. It was yet one more pregnant woman, this one rather dowdy and older. She'd perched herself on her knees to tend to a man who lay on one of the mattresses.

Or, I should hasten to correct: the *remnant* of a man . . .

He lay dismembered, naked, scars at the bald nubs where his arms had been removed at the elbows and his legs at the knees. He was lean, pallid-skinned, and bearded, and what the pregnant woman was doing was crudely washing his groinal area with a sopping sponge. Her expression of distaste could not have been more vivid. "They just stink so! And, oh, the lice! I just hate this *so much!*"

"*You* hate it!" complained a second woman. "You don't have to *do* it!"

This objection had come from the forward-most mattress, on which lay a man in an identical state as the first, only he was clean shaven and blond-headed. I saw stitches showing at the nubs of his injuries. But the woman was not washing this one—she was engaged in an act of overt sexual congress, a look of loath on her face . . .

But this was a face I recognized:

Monica, I realized, *from the pier.* I'd just seen her a short time ago, in the stairwell and entering the perpetually locked door to the second floor.

Now I knew why that door was always locked.

What form of madness could explain what I was viewing? These unfortunate men had clearly been *made* into invalids. For them to have suffered *identical accidents?* Impossible. And their symptoms of amputation mirrored exactly those of Mary's brother, Paul. What foul auspication urged me to believe that these men had been *purposely* and *premeditatedly* invalidized for this obscene purpose?

The farthest edge of my vantage point showed me a third mattressed victim, and perched vigorously on his groin was another thin, young woman with her skirt hoisted to make her privates accessible. "Hurry, you stinking bastard," she muttered.

"This one shits himself too," added the pregnant woman in her disdain. "He does it on *purpose.*"

"I do not!" blabbered the victim she was bathing. He seemed stricken with a vocal impediment. "I can't help it—"

"You know where the pans are!" the woman shrieked.

"Maybe we'll stop feeding you for a while! See how you like that!"

"Leave him alone, Joanie," suggested the young woman with the hoisted skirt. "I have to do him next, and if he's upset, he won't be able to. He'll wind up like Paul."

Like Paul, my mind droned.

I watched in the utter horror of it all, surely a scene from the Abyss. When this Joanie had finished with her congress, she grunted and rose, glaring down at her crippled purveyor. This poor man, after a minute or so, grotesquely rolled off the stained mattress, belly to floor, then hopped up onto the savaged ends of his limbs, after which he awkwardly ambled—doglike, on all fours—to one of the metal trays to urinate. Meanwhile, the blond man began to gasp in something akin to tortured bliss while his unwilling partner, Monica, looked at him in a meld of bitter hatred and nausea. Indeed, it seemed some carnal warren in Hell that my eye had happened upon. *Incalculable,* I thought in the deepest despair. *Monstrous . . . ,* for the intent, macabre as it seemed, shone all too clearly.

It must have been some imp of the perverse which forestalled my immediate desire to extricate myself from this evil chasm—and from the very building itself—and just simply flee, when, next, I found myself looking instead into more of the appalling peeping-holes. Similar scenes of incomprehensible obscenity were my reward for this effort: men reduced to naked torsos, either lying inert on sullied mattresses or traversing the room on their butchered limb-ends. One lapped water from a bowl, again, like a dog. Room after room glared with these unfathomable scenes of grotesquerie. But in the next peeping-hole . . .

God, deliver me, I prayed.

This was no chamber of forced-conception. Instead, I spied a room clinically adorned: medical supplies, IV bottles on stands, several elevated beds. Unconscious men with bandaged limbs occupied two such beds: one jibbered, drooling, in the clutches of nightmare, the other lay open-mouthed and utterly still. The man appeared youthful, yet I could clearly discern he had no teeth.

But the forward bed concerned me most.

On it lay Mr. William Garret, limb-ends similarly bandaged from his recent amputations. A tray of bloody surgical instruments, including a bone-saw, occupied a nearby tray, plus bottles clearly labeled CHLOROFORM. *This is a surgery suite,* I knew now, *hidden in the hotel on this floor which is always locked.* Cotton clogged Garret's mouth, and when suddenly he began to blink and shudder on the bed, a pregnant attendant came to his side to comfortingly pat his shoulder.

"There, there, you'll be all right," she calmly regarded him. "It's all for a reason that's more important than any of us." She tried to sound chipper. "And just think of all the pretty girls you'll be enjoying!"

Garret mewled beneath the cotton in his mouth. The cotton had tinged scarlet, and it was then I noticed a smaller stainless-steel tray full of recently extracted teeth.

"He's coming to, Doctor," claimed the pregnant nurse. "He'll need more pain antidote soon."

"Prepare the injection, please, Lucy."

The voice had arrived out of view, but next, I was not surprised to see a lab-coated Dr. Anstruther step up to the surgery bed. "It's best not to struggle, Mr. Garret, and far better to accept your new fate. Discard any yearnings of your former life. You'll get by much better, I assure you." He took a hypodermic from the nurse and eventually emptied it into an isolated vein. "The morphine sulphate is quite effective, and it will be administered regularly until no longer necessary—only a matter of days, really." With forceps, then, he removed the cotton from Garret's mouth. "And, as you've already deduced, I've extracted all of your teeth."

Garret's wasted expression turned to the doctor. "Whuh-whuh . . . why?"

"In time, you'll come to understand. Oh, and I'm happy

to relate that I've examined your semen under the microscope and found an impressively high sperm count and excellent motility. You're a preeminent candidate for sirehood."

Garret just stared, as if into an unreckonable cosmic gulf.

Anstruther turned to the nurse while jotting something on a board. "Lucy, the gentleman in Bed Number Two has unfortunately expired. He'll need to be disposed of, along with Mr. Garret's limbs."

"Yes, Doctor."

"In a few days, you'll be feeling much better," the doctor re-addressed Garret. "And like Lucy has already said, for some time to come, you'll be enjoying the company of many, many women, most of whom are possessed of some considerable desirability. Such is the lot of a Sire, Mr. Garret. Do yourself a service and maintain the proper mental perspective. For so long as you remain virile, you will remain alive, and in your quiet times, I'd advise you to solicit whatever god you may believe in."

The surgery-shocked and now toothless William Garret blabbered, "Look what you've done to me! Yuh-yuh-you're a *monster!*"

Anstruther smiled sedately. "No, Mr. Garret. You're fortunate in that you will never have to see the *real* monsters . . ."

When I forced my eye away from that Tartarean hole in the wall, I felt like a 100-year-old man. I staggered wide-eyed back the way I came, to the climb-way, where I had every intention of ascending back up to my room, securing my personal effects, and leaving this God-forsaken place posthaste. But when I got to the aperture which housed the ladder—

My heart slammed in my chest.

I heard footsteps. Climbing up.

Trying to cut the intruder off and make it up to my room undetected possessed no probability at all. A subconscious directive, instead, took me back across the near lightless channel to its opposite end, where I guessed—or prayed—that there might be an identical climb-way. *Please, Lord,* I beseeched in a mental groan.

Either my prayer had been answered or simple luck was with me, for, yes, there was another climb-way. I stepped in, grabbed the rungs, but before I could proceed upward—

"You, there," a voice called from the other end.

I didn't turn to look but instead tried to hide within the climbing-way's murk.

"Who is that? Nowry? Peters?"

I did not waste mental time considering why the male voice might be calling the name of a dead man, but it would be easy to suppose Nowry had other clan in town. Instead, I made my move. I did not climb up, I climbed down, for to return upstairs might sever any chance of escape. A similar hidden passage paralleled the first floor; I knew I needn't bother examining any of the peeping-holes here. *But there must be a way out, and I've got to find it!*

No door, though, or any other passage, became visible in the light of my pocket-flash . . .

Then I heard the footsteps coming down the ladder I'd just quitted.

To the passageway's opposite end I hastened, for where else could I go? I reasoned there had to exist some exterior access to these hidden crannies. For instance, how had my current pursuer gained the climbing-ways?

A door! I prayed. *There must be a door!*

But when I'd made this opposite end, I found no door; meanwhile, the footsteps echoed more loudly.

It was the sole of my shoe that found it: not a standing door nor access panel, but a hinged plate-metal hatch. I opened it in relief but then gasped as my flash-lamp revealed details of the ungainly egression—a climb-way of ancient brick, fitted with a slime-coated iron ladder, leading straight down. It was with the staunchest resolve that I lowered myself down into its methanous depths, closed the hatch above me, and descended. My position forced a procession in total darkness; I half-expected at any moment to be lowering myself into an open sewer and the stercoraceous smells and matter that companioned them, but when my feet settled on solidity, I relighted my flash-lamp to find myself in still another passageway. My panic had skewed my bearings, but an instinct told me the brick-lined access proceeded north and south. For a reason unbeknownst to me, I took the southward way.

Flash in the lead, I walked for at least one hundred yards in the ill-smelling murk. I knew now, however, that this passage was not an out-of-service sewer line; no signs were extant of the expected residuum. *It's a tunnel,* I knew then, and as surely as if the words had been spoken aloud, *Zalen's* words seemed to echo in my head: *And my grandfather wasn't lying when he told Lovecraft about the network of tunnels under the old waterfront . . .*

I needn't define the extent of the chill that moved caterpillar-like up my spine. And of the hellish scene I'd witnessed back at the hotel, I could only assume that virile men with suitably favorable looks were being forced to inseminate local women, whose newborns were then sold to some illicit adoptive initiative. Why, though, was I more perturbed by what Zalen had told me, especially his cryptic final monologue: *In the story, what happened to outsiders who did too much nosing around?*

Now, it seemed, the most dreadful of circumstances had transposed my very self into Lovecraft's fictitious Robert Olmstead, the out-of-towner hellbent to escape the horrors of Innsmouth.

I could go to Zalen now, tonight, it came to me, *if I could only find the exit to this blasted catacomb . . .*

Minutes later, fate or God handed me said exit as a gift.

The tunnel emptied me near a rock jetty along the harbor's edge. A spectacular frost-white moon hung behind intermittent clouds; the water in the harbor sat still as glass. Gazing out over the twilit port beneath the violet night proved a supernal sight, but all else I'd witnessed was anything *but* supernal. More *phantasmal* than anything else, or more *iniquitous.* The very-normal-appearing harbor, after closer scrutiny, was flecked by arcane maws. Mouths of rock-hidden grottos, and tunnel-exits exuding strange smells. No human instinct could prevent me from entering of such a maw . . .

More lichen and niter-crusted catacombs awaited me, several branching off from the main. I had to harness my sharpest sense of awareness, lest I easily be lost here. The leftmost tine in the fork was the one I chose. I kept my footing sure, only turning on the flash in brief increments in order to conserve its batteries. I didn't have to proceed far before the most hideous death-stench assailed me; a handkerchief to my face barely stifled its sickening noxiousness. Eventually, the tunnel emptied into vast cavern, the first glimpse of which nearly caused me to shriek and flee.

But how could I? I had to find out what *this* was . . .

A charnel house, I thought. *A makeshift sepulcher . . .*

It was mostly skeletons that heaped the obscene, dripping cavern, piles of them, some still dressed in scraps that had surpassed the effects of human decomposition. The bone-piles at the farthest end seemed the oldest, while those making their way—I believe—northwest had been more recently deposited. Mid-heap, I found fewer skeletons and more bodies mummified. This was a *hillock* of human corpses that providence had seen fit to show me; hundreds, easily, had been left in here rather than in proper burying-grounds. *Why?* I choked on the question. Who could be responsible for this? The time-emptied eyes of skulls seemed to hollowly watch as I moved along the wretched boundaries of the mound, and when eventually I'd staggered to its end, I could've collapsed amid the stench and the unholy insinuation.

These—dozens of them—were obviously the

sepulcher's most recently contributed corpses, and while most of the previous had been more or less "whole," the state of the constituents of the rotting, gas-bloated pile needed little conjecture as to their origins.

What primarily composed the ghastly heap of rot-covered bones, flesh-peeling skulls, and worm-rilled half-flesh were the evidence of *dismembered* human beings, each missing arms from the elbows and legs from the knees. Scraps of clothing lay among the human stacks like haphazardly tossed flags. I glimpsed too many suitcases and valises. A smaller pestiferous aggregation of severed arms and legs lay in vicinity.

An undercroft of corpses, a murder repository, I realized. And how long it had been here, I couldn't guess . . . and would never *want* to guess.

The sound of distant scuffling locked open my eyes and snapped off my flash. I back-stepped, praying I didn't fall, for the unmistakable sound of footsteps—and a more arcane unbroken grinding sound—seemed to be making its way toward the sepulcher. *But from where!* my thoughts demanded. My own path of entry lay behind me, while this sound came to my front. I ducked down behind a bunker of half-mummified cadavers just as a bobbing light could be seen.

Another entrance, I realized, from yet another of the stygian tunnels. I hid myself as still as the dead bodies about me, when eventually, the light from an oil lantern bloomed and the interloper appeared from an egress unseen till now. The figure pushed a wooden wheelbarrow whose contents was to be expected: the nude, stump-bandaged torso of the unfortunate post-surgery victim who'd expired in Dr. Anstruther's suite of horrors. Its half-limbs jiggled as the barrow made its way, and stacked upon its dead belly were several sets of other severed limbs, plus several suitcases. Then the barrow stopped and the lantern was set on the ground. The suitcases, first, were flung onto the pile, then the limbs, and then, with a flat grunt, the torso. Of the interloper himself, I could only discern the frame of a man, and I could see he held no handkerchief over his mouth and nose. How he tolerated the charnel stench, I couldn't imagine . . . until he raised the lantern once more, and the sizzling light revealed his face.

It was Mr. Nowry, whom just hours ago I'd glimpsed dead in an ambulance.

What ruse might explain this, I didn't care to ponder, but when I first saw his pallid face in the light, I did, however minutely, gasp.

The figure froze, then turned. I froze as well, praying and preparing to reach for my pistol . . .

The lantern swept this way and that, and by the grace of God, its rays did not reveal my crouch. Eventually, Nowry returned to his wheelbarrow and exited the way he came.

I waited a full five minutes before even budging, then I rose and turned, snapped on my flash, and briskly marched for my own exit, but as I did so, I couldn't help but notice another oblong maw along the rockface. Yes, another tunnel.

Under no circumstance will I allow myself allow enter, I made the self-command, but even before I was consciously aware, my feet were deputing me into this next rock-hewn entry. In spite of the grievousness of all I'd thus far seen, I had to wonder if Lovecraft himself had ventured into any of these tunnels, and then realized that he must have, for from where else could he have derived similar subterrene networks in masterpieces such as not only *Innsmouth* but "The Festival," "The Outsider," "The Rats in the Walls," and so on. I was now walking in the midst of a Lovecraft story but knew the obscene butchery taking place at the Hilman and the cavern of horrors I'd just exited was no "story." Nevertheless, the indulgence of my curiosity outranked my capacity for reason.

I had to see what was at the end of *this* tunnel . . .

As my intermittent flash led me on, another odor

assailed me, but thankfully, it was not one of death nor noxiousness. It was a strong odor with a distinct heft. The more deeply I traversed the tunnel, the more familiar the odor became:

The unquestionable odor of *fish.*

I lost my breath when the tunnel opened into a subterrestrial chamber many times the length and depth of the previous, and herein were many times the number of corpses.

These, though, were different . . .

Why no stench of rot and natural corruption? I pondered. *Why only the smell of fresh fish?* But when my eyes registered the *details* of what my retinas were registering, I felt sicker here than in the previous sepulcher.

The body mound stood *huge*—fifteen, twenty feet high and a hundred long. My sense of perception began to bend, though, as I squinted at the morass of bodies. *They-they . . . they're not altogether human,* I realized. *Some more, some less . . .* Almost all had been stripped of clothing, and their dead, nude skin seemed wax-white with tinges of an unwholesome green veined beneath the pallored translucence. Grievous physical deformities had twisted the lion's share of the corpses into outrageous misshapes; most were balding, but all were possessed of wide-open and mostly blue-irised over-protuberant eyes. Closer inspection, then, showed me hands and feet in various states of elongation, while fingers and toes were clearly—

My God . . .

—webbed.

To the touch—and what compelled me to *touch* one of the things, I can't imagine—the skin felt strangely moist, enslimed, and rubbery, semblant to the tactility of frog skin. But the most chilling verification came next: at least half of these transfigured decedents had rows of slits along their throats. Like gills.

Just like the story, my thoughts grated. Could this

possibly be true? *Madness,* I thought instead. Surely, subterranean gasses known to accumulate in caverns and tunnelworks such as these could germinate hallucinations. It was my subconscious brain, tainted now by such leakages, that had me believing Lovecraft's greatest work was based on some fashion of biological fact. I stepped back from the gruesome heap of agape mouths; unblinking glassy orbicular eyes; pale, bone-bowed limbs; and ears that seemed to have partially or fully shrunk on hairless, semi-human skulls. Injuries, clearly, had been the cause of death for these malformed victims: wounds almost exclusively to the head and chest, and there was suggestion that a predominance of the wounds had been inflicted via gouges and punctures via talons and teeth.

I was too waylaid by this most monstrous and unbelievable sight to ponder any further. I had no choice but to hold my sanity in grave doubt, but next, just as in the first chamber of death, I heard the sounds of someone encroaching . . .

Again, I doused my light and ducked behind a flank of piled half-human corpses when a light—no, several—were discernible. But voices as well this time, two at least; and from the chamber's farthest cranny, the coming light enabled me to detect another rearward egress. By now, I had to reason that the tunnelworks were extensive indeed. Two figures, then, one short, one taller, emerged, each bearing a candlefish torch. The sputtering, smoky flames threw cragged shadows everywhere like a grim, kaleidoscopic nightmare.

"Gotta make it quick, son, like we'se always do," came a roughened, accent-tinted adult voice. "Ya never know when one'a their sentinels is liable to be snoopin' around."

"I know, Dad," replied the obvious voice of a young boy.

"You cut out the biceps'n calves like I taught ya, and I'll hack out the ribs'n bellies. Let's try'n get a whole lot in a little time, heh, son?"

"Sure, Dad."

The smoky light easily revealed these new interlopers: Onderdonk and his young son. They must have discovered a tunnel of their own that gained them access without being visible to the town proper, where they clearly were not welcome. With a considerable skill, the boy flopped several corpses off the pile and, within seconds, was deftly butchering the meat off their arms and legs. Meanwhile, the father, with cleavers in each hand, systematically hacked lengths of ribs off more corpses and neatly cleaved out the abdominal walls. After they'd each administered to half a dozen or so of the dead half-human, half-batrachian monstrosities, they switched. Minutes later, they'd loaded the butchered wares into burlaps sacks.

"Good job, son," Onderdonk praised the lad. "Bet we got here more'n a week's worth'a meat for the smoker."

"I hope we make a lot of money, Dad."

"That's my boy." The adult proudly smiled and patted his son's head. "It's God's way'a lookin' after God-fearin' folk like us, seein' to it that these half-blooders got the taste of fish'n good pork together. What choice we got, seein' how them devil-lovin' Olmsteaders won't let us fish proper in their waters?"

"Yeah, d
Dad. I'm glad God looks after us like this."

"We'se quite fortunate, son, and can't never forget it. Times're tougher for so many."

"But, Dad?" The boy looked quizzical through a pause. "How come they don't rot and get to stinkin', you know, like in that other place?"

"It's 'cos them bodies in that other place is all pure-blood humans like us, but these here?" Onderdonk patted the slick greenish belly of a dead female whose face and bosom looked more toadlike, complete with warts. "All'a these here are 'least half-full'a the fish blood, like this splittail," and he callously cradled a wart-sheened breast. "This 'un here is likely fourth generation along with a whole lot of 'em—the one's ud already turned. But even first generation, boy, is enough to keep 'em from rotting proper, and bugs'n varmints don't go near 'em. It's their fish blood, see? That's what makes 'em never go to rot 'cos they cain't die, not unless they'se kilt deliberate or by accident."

"Oh," the boy replied. "That's kind'a . . . neat."

"Um-hmm. Now, help me fling these leavin's back."

With a drooping spirit, I watched from my discreted location as the pair heaved the butchered remnants up and over the mainstay of the piles, evidently to prevent any "sentinels" from ascertaining what had been done here.

"There," Onderdonk's whisper echoed. "Let's skedaddle . . . "

In the fluttering light, I watched them leave, sacks of pilfered meat flung over their shoulders.

But the sickness in my gut had long-since seized me: the stealings from this preternatural corpse-vault were clearly what Onderdonk passed off to unsuspecting customers as "fish-fed pork," a small portion of which now occupied my digestive tract. When safe to do so, I staggered away, all too aware that this was *not* the effect of hallucinotic gasses, and after retracing several yards back through the tunnel I'd entered in, I regurgitated the entire contents of my stomach.

Back on the rocky crags where the tunnel emptied, I fell to my knees in the relief of the fresh air and the simple sight of the normal world: the moonlight, the harbor, the boat docks and waterfront buildings. *The normal world, yes.* I thanked God, for I knew now how thin the veil was between that normality and utter, unnamable malignity. Who knew what other aberrant atrociousness the world hid just below its surface? I sat against the rock, listening to the water lapping against pier posts and shore—part of me quite paralyzed by my witness, not just *what* I'd seen but what it all *meant.*

I let the salt air flutter against my face and fill my

lungs; I knew my body and my mind needed a few moments' rest before I could calculate the entails of my next move. I stared dumbly out into the pier-ringed inlet, watching silent boats rock gently in their slips, when my eyes found the barely noticeable rise of the sand bar . . .

Lovecraft's Devil's Reef, I mused. At least *that* had been pure invention. But who would believe the rest? And did *I* believe it?

At first, I thought it must be a fleck of something in my eye, but the more I stared, the more convinced I became of something minuscule disturbing the late-night harbor's stillness.

A boat, I thought.

It was merely a small rowboat, and there appeared to be but one person aboard, oaring silently into the inlet. For several moments, I profaned beneath my breath when some clouds of deeper depths roved across the moon to darken the cryptic scene. It was likely only a crabber, or someone checking buoys, but I couldn't fight the temptation that it was more than that. When the clouds moved off, I saw that the meager skiff had been rowed deliberately aground on the longest finger of the sandbar, and its one-man crew had already debarked . . .

He's walking along the sand bar, I saw at once. *And . . . what's that he's carrying?*

Indeed, the distant figure was belabored by what seemed to be a sack that he was dragging along behind him. At that point, the veils of clouds moved fully away from the moon's radiant face, and suddenly, the entirety of the harbor glowed in crisp, ghostly white light.

Even this far off, I could now see enough. The trudging figure wore what I was very sure had to be a long, greasy black raincoat and hood . . .

Zalen.

His progress halted when he came to the bar's point of greatest girth. Then he just stood there for many minutes, his head tilted down as if—

As if he's waiting for something, it morbidly occurred to me. *Waiting for something in the water . . .*

And then, from that same water, something did indeed emerge.

A figure, yes, but one unclothed and gleaming in a bump-ridden off-green hue. It stood lanky and lean, but long-limbed and with a head almost flattened and a face angled forward to a sharp point. Even from this distant vantage point, I could fully detect the *hugeness* of its unblinking eyes; like crystalline globes, they were, aglitter from some stolid menace beneath. Eventually, two more primeval faces rose slowly from the water to reveal their full physiques to the moon, one decidedly female, for it was well-breasted and much more widely hipped than the other two, whose maleness hung bumped and long at their groins. I was grateful that the distance did not afford me any further clarity of physical details.

The first one reached forward and took the proffered sack from Zalen . . .

I didn't need to be properly informed of the sack's contents, for when the thing opened it up and looked in, the tiniest sounds eddied out, tiny, yes, but all-determinant.

The anguished wails of newborn babes.

More and more, it was all coming true. How could I deny what my eyes were seeing? In all this ghastly insanity, what sane explanation could be winnowed out? On the sandbar, the three monstrosities took their human booty and returned to the watery depths, while Zalen reboarded his small skiff and rowed away, and next—

thump!

I'm sure the sudden shock forced me to shout out. It was a spindly yet aggressive weight that landed on my person from above the outcropping where I sat: all blanched-white skin and a thin, vicious face but strangely dead-eyed and veiled by an aura of long, dark, wispy hair. A thin hand snapped at once to my throat and began to squeeze with a strength greater than my own. It was the horror of the assault's suddenness in flux with my previous revelations that diced my thoughts. Instinct more than decisive mental computation triggered my own defensive maneuvers, feeble as they may have been. Only the merest sliver of volition registered, but I was able to discern that my banshee-like attacker was neither one of things I'd seen soliciting Zalen on the moonlit bar nor a living example of any of the part-human, part-monster hybrids I'd found in the earthworks. This instead was a hostile and purely human woman tearing at my throat with one hand and gouging at my eyes with the other. White teeth snapped open and closed an inch before my appalled face, but when I took closer note of *her* face, I screamed again, all that much more loudly. Surely, the scream had been heard by anyone in proximity to the waterfront; it echoed cannon-like across the dark water.

The naked, feral thing clambering over me was Candace, the formerly pregnant prostitute who served as one of Zalen's obscene photo models. Divorced now of the bloated belly, her milk-swollen breasts looked too large for so thin a woman. Her post-childbirth death had darkened streaks under her eyes like tar-smears and left her distended nipples the color of bruises.

"I saw you," I choked, "in the ambulance! You're dead!"

"Am I?" came a dry and strangely hacking reply. No gust of breath vented from her mouth when she'd said this, but worse was her facsimile of a laugh when she squeezed my throat even harder and reached back with her other hand to molest my groin.

"We-we could have a nice time together, sir . . . "

Of all the abominable things—she gently caressed my crotch with the gentleness of a lover, while the fingers of the other hand dug so deeply into my throat, I feared at any moment she'd be unseating my trachea and fully yanking it, Adam's apple and all, out of my neck. It was obvious to me that death had enlisted her into the role of the aforementioned "sentinel."

If my screams had not alerted the whole of the waterfront's population, the ensuant pistol-shot most certainly did. This rejuvenated cadaver that had not too long ago been a wayward young woman named Candace was fully thrashed aside against the rocks. It had been a death-impulse that had unconsciously supervened my terror and slipped my hand into my pocket to withdraw the small Colt .32 repeater. The blind shot had struck at the vicinity of her left ear and took out a fair section of the right side of her cranial vault. I gasped in lungfuls of air as I watched the nude corpse impact the wall of rocks to our side. The report left me spattered with cool hanks of her convoluted gray matter bathed in ill-smelling blood, which appeared blackish, not red, but traced faintly with threads of some alien constituent that glowed in the faintest pale green. In all, it smelled like heavy motor oil and fish.

The reckoning to make exit came immediately, for lights were snapping on along the waterfront edifices. Yet even having been divorced of a moderate portion of her brain, Candace falteringly rose and began to stumble after me, but not before I'd gained enough ground to render her chase futile.

I hastened along the rock line, hoping for camouflage amongst dingy boulders and irregular light. Eventually, I crossed the service road, slipped between a pair of drab-brick fish processors, and escaped that eldritch waterfront into the woods.

God, protect me, God, protect me, the vain prayer spun round my head. Only patches of moonlight managed to filter in to the fringe of woods; I daren't slip in too deeply lest I be blind—I didn't want to potentially reveal my position by having to rely on my flashlight, whose batteries were already growing dim. But as disoriented as my experiences had left me, I felt reasonably sure that my stilted progress was northerly—the direction necessary to lead me, first, to Mary's, and then, ultimately, out of town. I knew it would be miles of desperate walking to get to the next, safer, town. If only I could find a telegraph office—some were known to be operational twenty-four hours—or a rare telephone. But as I wended between stout trees, sometimes only inching along for lack of light, I knew there was a place I *must* go before any of that . . .

I should be getting close, it came to me after a half an hour's progress, and when I squinted between a pair of shabby buildings, I thought I spotted the cobbled lane before the fire station. *Yes!* There it was with its opened bay, yet oddly enough, not a soul could be seen in proximity. Just another twenty yards, then, and I knew I was collimating the unlighted rear wall of the building which housed Cyrus Zalen and his penurious neighbors. In fact, I could even smell the despair-compressed apartment row from the woods.

Dare I advance to the front door, or would it be better to tap on a rear window? Neither prospect enlightened me, but I knew that I *had* to confront this man. Zalen's apartment occupied the age-stained building's end; I crept ever-so-slowly around the side but then froze as if turned to a pillar of salt like Lot's wife Edith . . .

Behind several twisted, century-old trees out front, I could see the shadowed edges of *men.*

My heart could've burst when, from behind, a hand rough as sandpaper clamped over my mouth and I was yanked back into the woods as if jerked by a tether. One of their "sentinels," no doubt, had espied my encroachment. Smothering, I wrestled in vain against a wiry yet ferociously strong shadow. All my breath jettisoned from my chest when I was slammed to the ground.

"Don't make a sound, you fool!" shot a sharp, desperate whisper. I managed to extract my pistol, pointing it upward, but then the faceless shadow continued, "You pull that trigger, we're both dead."

I knew at once, from the voice, it was Zalen.

"Shhh!"

The shabbily-raincoated form didn't fear my weapon

at all; instead, he left me where I lay, to peek stealthily past the tree we were both, in essence, hiding behind. When he returned, his whisper seemed calmed.

"You're lucky they didn't see you. Shit, we both are."

"What are you—?"

Quiet anger. "They're staking out my room, man! They're waiting for me, and they're after you too, you idiot. You almost gave us away, and by now, I probably don't have to tell you what they'd do to us. You wouldn't be hiding in the woods yourself if you didn't know."

The frantic slugging of my heart began to abate. "Sentinels. That's what Onderdonk called them."

"Anyone part of the town collective is in on it," Zalen whispered. "They serve *them.*"

"I saw you!" I whispered back as fiercely. "You're telling me that Lovecraft's story is all true! What's more—*now*—is I *believe* that!"

"How could you not?" Did the slinky figure chuckle? "You must be coming from the waterfront, where I *told you* not to go after dark. Between your snooping around and my big mouth . . ."

"Now I know why so many women here are pregnant— I saw what they're doing on the second floor of the Hilman!" I grated. "They're crippling men and using them to—"

"Sure, think about it. Anstruther's one of the big wheels. He cuts off their legs so they can't run away, cuts off their arms so they can't fight, and pulls their teeth so they can't bite the girls. The initiative is to keep every woman in the collective perpetually pregnant. Whenever some guy's passing through, if he's young, from a good bloodline, yeah. That's what they use 'em for. That's what the things want—newborn babies . . ."

"For sacrifice! It's abominable!"

Zalen rolled his eyes in the moonlight. "Oh, man, you're really dense. This isn't some occult witchcraft thing. It's *science.* That's all Lovecraft wrote about when you read between the lines. The more newborns the town can give them, the happier they are. So they reward the collective."

"*Reward?*"

"This is a *fishing* town, Morley. They reward us with an abundance of fish. Before the New Way, back in the old days, they'd also give us gold."

I stared. "Just like in the story."

"Just like the story, man, yeah. They don't do the gold anymore because it got too conspicuous. The town doesn't need it. All the gold did was make people lazy. Now it's all the resource, *fish*. For the last ten years, this little pissant fishing village has become the most profitable seafood port in the country. We give them what they want, they give us what we want: prosperity. And anytime out-of-town boats try to sneak in and throw nets or drop lines—" Zalen chuckled again. "The boats sink and the people on 'em are never seen again. Hate to think what they do to the poor bastards . . ."

The ramifications now were sinking into the very meat of my soul. "They," I sputtered in disgust. "Lovecraft's Deep Ones, the Dagonites."

"Naw, that's just a bunch of names he made up, Morley. We don't know *what* they're called"—he shrugged—"so we just call them fullbloods, or the *things*. Lovecraft learned enough, though. He was first here in '21, but he didn't find out anything, but in '27?" Zalen's vagabond grin beamed in the dark. "You're kind of like him, you know? He came here 'cos he liked the sights, but then he started snooping. They let him leave because they didn't really know who he was. But that goddamn *story*." He sighed futilely. "They've been here ever since Obed Larsh brought some of the crossbreeds from the East Indies. And he summoned the fullbloods with some kind of beacon the islanders gave him before they all got wiped out."

Beads of cold sweat trickled down my face like bugs crawling. I could only stare at the horrendous gravity of what he was saying, and what I had no choice but to *believe.* "In the story, federal agents and naval vessels destroyed them, so why—"

He cut me off with an offended smirk. "That's about the only part he made up—drama, man. Yeah, I know, they torpedoed the reef, but you already know there never *was* a reef. What Lovecraft got right—*too* right—was the history. It was a true-life tale of social decadence and moral collapse. They have their own power hierarchies just like us; our leaders change and so do theirs. For the longest time, they encouraged crossbreeding between their species and humans, but it was all just for the sake of lust. A human with mixed blood would change over time—things in every cell in their bodies—and eventually, they'd become so similar to the things that they wouldn't die. They had all the poor saps in town believing that after they'd changed over completely, they'd go to the water and live in harmony with them forever, but all the things really did was use the crossbreeds for slavery. But even after they'd changed, they were still part human, and they'd bring their human flaws with them. Addiction, dishonesty, treachery. It got to the point where the part-human crossbreeds began to taint *their* society. So what did they do? Same thing we did after Herbert Hoover, same thing Russia did after the corrupt Czars. They changed their power hierarchy; they cleaned their own society up by getting rid of the corruptive element—human blood. There were no *federal* troops that ever came here to wipe out all the crossbreeds. The things did that themselves—it was a wholesale slaughter, about 1930, I guess. They came up out of the water one night and murdered every single person in town who had any of their blood in them." Zalen paused on a reflection. "Lovecraft would've loved it. They were *doing* what he believed: wiping out the living products of sex between races—or, in this case, between *species.*"

As I put my frantic thoughts to words, they seemed to grind out of my throat. "The first cavern I found via the tunnelworks you told me of, it was full of rotting, dismembered corpses. *Rotting,* I tell you; it was *pestiferous.* The air was nearly *toxic.*"

"That cavern is for the Sires that die."

"*Sires?*"

"The guys they dismember and hole up on the second floor. Every woman in the collective comes in there every night until they're pregnant, but you've already figured that out. Well, they don't live forever, you know, or sometimes a Sire becomes impotent. There's no use for them, so the town elders kill them and let their bodies rot with all the others."

More and more things were making a revolting sense. "And the largest of the grottoes, full of so many more bodies, are the crossbred victims of the genocide in 1930?"

"That's right. They don't rot because their flesh is pretty much immortal. Even if you kill them by violence, they never decompose. Where do you think that weirdo Onderdonk and his kid get all that fresh meat?" and then he, ever-so-faintly, laughed. "Come on," he whispered next. "Let's get out of here."

Why I suddenly felt allied to this man—this baby-killer—I had no clue. It was all circumstantial, I suppose. Through dapples of moonlight, I followed him well away from the back of the apartment row until he came to a barely perceivable trail. I had no choice but to follow. It occurred to me that Zalen's primitive interpretations reflected some of the most recent scientific breakthroughs all too chillingly. Certainly the last decade had trumpeted the works of the Darwinist Englander William Bateson, who'd founded and named this remarkable new science called genetics: the idea that microscopic cellular constituents pass on *hereditary* traits within a species, and other constituents known as *mutagens*, be they accidental or deliberate, can alter said traits. In addition, famed laureate microbiologist Hattie Alexander had just this month proven the viability of a miraculous anti-pneumonia serum through the manipulation of what she calls a *genetic-code* found within the viral cells themselves. If the fund of human knowledge was only now making such discoveries, how much superior might Zelan's *things* be with regard to similar sciences?

I was too afraid to contemplate the notion further.

We appeared to be veering northwest now, and for the first time, the woods felt safe. But in Lovecraft's story, there *was* no safe, and his own version of Sentinels could be hiding anywhere, ready to overhear forbidden talk—

And ready to report back . . .

"How many were killed all told?" morbidity forced me to ask.

"The crossbreeds? About a thousand, I think," Zalen said. "Lots of them were fourth and fifth generation. They were living in the ruins along Innswich Point—the old waterfront. When the government *did* come, the whole town was squeaky clean. No riff-raff, ya know? That's how we came to qualify for the federal rebuild."

Something even *more* morbid spidered along my awareness. "Where," I dared to ask, "are Mary's children? She told me she's had eight—and expectant of a ninth—but I only witnessed *one* child around her property."

Zalen huffed as he proceeded. "No women in the collective are allowed to keep *all* their children. They're only allowed to keep one—their first."

"I already know what happens to the others," I all but choked. "But I need to know *specifically*."

"Oh, do you, now?"

"You called me dense for assuming the newborns are sacrificed in an occult rite. If that's not the case, then what exactly *are* these things doing with all those newborns?"

"How do I know, man?" He smirked back at me. "I'm not one of them, remember? I was never allowed into the town collective—I'm considered an outcast."

But not so much an outcast to be excluded from serving these things, I reasoned. I loathed this man—for what he was and what I'd seen him do—but I knew I mustn't rile him. His information was too valuable, and it may well serve to help assist my escape. An escape I was determined to make with Mary . . .

"The babies that don't come out right," he went on in grave monotone, "I guess they use for food. Candace's kid, for instance. She had it today, and it was all messed up from the horse she was shooting—I warned the bitch—but she lucked out in the end. She died while she was having it."

"Only in a manner of speaking," I begged to differ. "That *dead* girl almost killed me on the waterfront tonight."

"Oh, so that explains the shot I heard—"

"Indeed, it does. I killed her, but she was already dead. I also saw Mr. Nowry disposing of bodies in the first cavern. He was dead in the same ambulance with Candace only hours before."

Zalen shrugged. "They don't do it much, only when they need extra workers—"

"You're talking about raising the dead!" I exclaimed.

"Keep your voice down!" he sneered back at me. "And I'm talking about a lot more than that. You better pray you never have to see one of the fullbloods, but don't be fooled. They may *look* primitive, but they're superior to humans in every way. And, yeah, they have some sort of reagent that can restore life to people who've died under certain circumstances. They've always had it. It's more of that cellular stuff . . . "

More genetic science, I realized, but my thoughts kept deflecting. I simply couldn't get her off my mind. "How long . . . has Mary been part of this town collective?"

"Five years, maybe, six years. Who cares? And speaking of your precious Mary . . . " Zalen slowed amid the woods and urged me westerly.

Suddenly, my eyes bloomed in frosty moonlight; I was looking at something I'd already seen . . .

Where the modest lake had earlier gleamed in sunlight, now it shimmered in the light of the moon. I glimpsed figures along the lake's shore.

Zalen held me back behind some trees before I had chance to blunder forth. "Not a sound," Zalen warned.

Verbosity couldn't have been further from my mind; instead, it was *witness.* Several dozen women stood in a semicircle just at the water's edge, and I must say, this first glimpse of them made me think singularly of occultism. The late hour, the moonlight, and the location only exacerbated a namelessly sinister provocation in my mind . . .

The women wore primal robes whose color was indistinguishable in the intense moonlight, but what *could* be distinguished were fringed panels of fabric segmented by lighter-colored stitchwork. Within these segments, more elaborate embroidery could be seen: symbols quite glyph-like and the oddest designations of geometry that, when looked upon to stridently, caused my head to ache. Were the angles of the horrific geometrics actually *moving?* Each woman, too, held a candle before her—a candle whose flame burned *green*—and I thought I could hear the faintest chimes, the notes of which instilled in me, to the core of my very guts, a feeling of uncontemplatable dread via the idea of utter *absence.* Absence of light, absence of benevolence, absence of morality, absence of all things *sane.* Even more softly than the sourceless chimes, there came to my ears a vocal diaphony that made me want to fall to my knees and be sick: a discordant and cacodaemonically unstructured sequence of words which sounded like:

"Ei . . .

"Cf'ayak vulgtuum . . . "

"Ei . . . "

"Vugtlagln, sjulnu . . . "

"Ei, ph'nglui, hkcthtul'ei . . . "

"Wgah'nagl fhtagen—ei . . . "

"Ei, ei, ei . . . "

THE INNSWICH HORROR

The perverse chants seemed to grow lighter rather than louder, but for some reason, the more difficult this evil song was to hear, the more impact it had on my mind, a veritable *pressure,* a *tactuality* against my face. Yet as sick as I felt, I felt something else concurrently: a most powerful carnal arousal.

"Keep back," Zalen whispered. He forced me to crouch lower. "This lake empties into the bay . . . "

The solemnity of that information didn't at first occur to me. My vision, instead, remained hijacked to these macabre, robed women. The chorus was chanted again when all the women at once dropped their robes and stood nude.

Nude, I had no choice but to observe, *and pregnant.*

All the while, the chant seemed to compress my brain within the confines of my skull. It was sordid and erotic, seeing this in such a manner that I could not look away—indeed, it was evil. Most of the women appeared in their twenties, but I did make out Mrs. Nowry and some others more middle-aged. All of them, then, one by one, tossed their queerly green candles into the water, and I could take an oath that as each stick of wax sunk beneath the surface, the green flame was not extinguished, and at the same time, my eyes seemed to acclimate more intensely to this tinseled night: the moonlight grew sharper, brighter, and with this, my vision grew more acute. Even from this considerable distance, I could make out refined details of each gravid woman. I could see the pores on their white skin, the minute line between each iris and the whites of their eyes, the papillae of each and every nipple, and the fine traceries of venousity within each milk-soused breast. Eventually, all of them lowered to the muck of the lake shore, and what took place then I'll only distinguish as an obscene bacchanal of the flesh, a libertine debauch intent on mutual satiation akin to the Isle of Lesbos. I shouldn't have to specify, either, that one of these concupiscent attendants was Mary herself . . .

My eyes held rapt on the orgiastic scene, and for a time, I thought that even a gun to my head couldn't make me look away, even in the self-knowledge averting my eyes was the only Godly thing to do. But it was Zalen, not God, who urged my surcease.

"It's coming out now—"

"It?" I questioned in the slightest whisper.

"We're not going to be here to see it. Believe me, Morley, you *don't want to see it . . .* "

He hauled me back into the woods just at the same moment a figure began to rise from the lake.

My head thankfully cleared with proximity. "What—what *was* that, Zalen?"

"It was one of them—what did you think?" the long-haired, greasy-coated man chided.

One of them, I thought. *A fullblood . . .*

"One of the hierarchs, but there could be others about too."

I winced at the madness. "That was an occult rite we just witnessed, Zalen. After all I've learned and everything you told me that happens to be true, there has to be more . . . "

"Of course there is," the spindly vagabond retorted. "But all that shit out there by the lake?" He seemed amused. "It's just tradition, Morley, it's just ritual; it means nothing. All it proves is how much *lower* mankind's mentality is. The only way we could ever really relate to the fullbloods—even back in Obed Larsh's time—is through ignorant ritualism like this . . . "

"Just a veneer," I speculated, for so much occultism in the Master's work was just that. "Is that what you're saying?"

"You hit it right on the head. What looks like devil-worship and simple paganism is just the icing on a very different kind of cake."

The analogy, trite as it may have been, validated my assurances now. I followed Zalen unknowingly for a time, my mind too active with a plethora of conjectures. "But all societal systems ultimately have a defined purpose," I insisted. "If this occultism is veneer—or 'icing' used to cover something else up . . . what *is* the something else?"

"You ask too many questions. I warned you about that," he said. "We have to get out of here, that's all. You've got money and a gun, and I've got the way out. If we're lucky, we might make it."

"Don't tell me you've got a motor-car," I nearly exclaimed.

"Sure, I do—er, I should say, I know where we can get one," he supplemented with a chuckle. "The Onderdonks have a truck. That's where your gun comes in."

For whatever reason, this decidedly promising news did not reduce the regard of more of my questions. "You could've stolen their truck anytime in the past. Why is escape on your mind *now?*"

"I told you . . . " He smirked back in spattered moonlight. "Because they're onto us now. Someone overheard me talking to you earlier—"

"So that's it, a breach of the secrecy everyone here must adhere to," I surmised. "More, more of the story."

"Because Lovecraft's story wasn't really a story. I told you that too. Most of it's true. And now we've got to live with it—or die."

I continued to follow his footsteps, still confounded and—why, I'm not sure—enraged more than terrified. The smell of slow-cooking meat waxed dominant; it sifted down the narrow trail to tell me that Onderdonk's property drew near. I was appalled to admit that the aroma—even in knowing as I did the origin of the meat—was delectable. It also appalled me that Zalen, an inveterate thief, criminal, and, worse, one who was a willing party to infanticide, represented my greatest chance of escaping with Mary.

"Mary," I said next. "She must go with us."

"You've got to be kidding me!" he snapped.

"I insist. I have a great deal of money, Zalen. It would behoove you to accommodate my indulgence. Mary, her son, her brother, and her stepfather will be joining our escape."

At this, he actually laughed. "Her and the kid, maybe. But Paul's deadweight; he's a Sire who went impotent. Only reason he wasn't killed and taken to the tunnels is 'cos she begged the hierarch." His next chuckle could've passed for a death-rattle. "And the stepfather? Haven't you been listening?"

"I can't fathom you, Zalen. Mary's stepfather is aged and rife with infirmities. It would be un-Christian of us to abandoned the old man."

"The stepfather is a crossbreed!"

I gawped at words as though they were fragments of shrapnel. "But-but, I thought—"

"Crossbreeding between the two species was made illegal by the new hierarchs, so—"

"So all the existing crossbreeds were exterminated in the concerted genocide," I'd already gathered. "Which doesn't explain why Mary's stepfather is still alive."

Zalen stopped to face me with that nihilistic grin I was now all-too-accustomed to. "You'll love this part, Morley. But are you sure you wanna hear it?"

"Don't toy with me, Zalen. Your psychological parlor tricks are quite juvenile, if you'd like to know the truth. So kindly tell me that—the *truth*."

"We don't know exactly how their political system works, but we think it's several of them in charge and there's one who's more powerful than the others."

"It's called an oligarchical monarchy, Zalen. The senior hierarch would suffice as the sovereign, akin to the Soviet Union of today, or this man in Germany, Hitler."

"Yeah. The sovereign. The sovereign's hot to trot for your wonderful little Mary. How do you like that? He's got kind of a *thing* for her. That was probably him back there at the lake. Don't worry, it won't fuck her—it's not allowed to—but it'll probably do everything else."

The information sickened me but also made me feel

haunted. Thoughtlessly, I seized my handgun and turned to head back to the lake.

"You really are an idiot, Morley," I was told amid more laughter. He'd grabbed my arm and thrust me back. "Even if you did get a clear shot at it, there'd be a hundred more after you in two minutes. They'd *sniff* us out. We wouldn't stand a chance"

I leaned against a tree, gripped by a harrowing despair. "You're telling me that Mary's stepfather was spared from the genocide because—"

"Because Mary begged the hierarch not to kill him. She agreed to keep the old stick in hiding at her house." Zalen nodded. "Hate to think what she had to do to get *that* favor."

I could've killed him on the spot for saying such a thing, but I knew there was truth behind it; desperation led to desperate acts. Instead, I collected my senses and continued to follow him. "What about those who aren't in Olmstead's town collective?"

"Rejects, like me, are left alone as long as we don't tell outsiders what's going on here, and as long as we don't leave."

"Those things can't possibly be everywhere," I declared. "With a modicum of forethought, I'd suspect that escape would be easily achievable."

"Sure, you'd *think* so," he counted, "but why do you think nobody does? Why do you think Mary's still here? It's not because she wants to be, I can tell you that. None of us do."

"Fear, then?"

"Uh-huh. In the past, people—mostly women—have tried to escape. They just can't handle giving up their babies. But every single one has been brought back"—now Zalen's expression turned cold—"and made an example of. There are a whole lot more of those things than anyone can guess. If you leave, they'll track you down the way a bloodhound catches a scent, Morley. They travel along any existing waterway, and they're very fast."

I had no choice but to postulate, "So even if we do manage to get out of here, you don't deem our chances of success to be very high."

"No, but when they're on a rampage like they are now, if we *don't* try, we're dead by morning for sure."

Waterways, hunting a scent, I thought. If we made it back to Providence, I'd install Pinkerton's men round the clock. Either that or I'd relocate to a place so far removed from any waterways.

"There's the truck," Zalen whispered just as the trail had navigated us to an opening in the woods just behind Onderdonk's property. The aroma of slow-cooking meat hung dense. Several shacks sat teetering in shadows; betwixt two of them, I spied a pickup truck that looked as dilapidated as everything else. The only sound that came to my ears was that of pigs chortling.

"Onderdonk's had those same pigs for years," came Zalen's next snide remark, "but they're just for show. I'll bet that hillbilly and his kid haven't really cooked pork for a decade."

"But where is he?" I queried. "The place looks abandoned."

"They probably went to bed after they put the meat in the smoker," he suspected, and pointed to the rows of propped-up metal barrels which sufficed for the cooking apparatus. "That's good for us . . . but get your gun out just in case."

I obeyed the instruction and followed him into the overgrown perimeter. We ambled forth with great care so not to snap a single twig. Moonlight and shadows diced the various shacks into wedges of light and dark; several sets of small eyes glittered at us when the pigs in the sty took note of us. An owl hooted, then went silent.

"That seems irregular," I commented of the burlap sacks near the smokers. "Those sacks appear to be full. I saw Onderdonk with my own eyes, carrying the sacks out of the cavern after he and his boy butchered a number of the crossbred corpses."

Zalen opened a sack; in it were hanks of freshly butchered meat. "Yeah, and if the meat's still in the bags, then what the hell is . . . "

The question didn't necessitate completion. I suppose, deep down, I already knew before we raised the lids of the smokers. I shined my flash inside, then we both recoiled.

Smoke billowed up from Onderdonk's pink-blistered face, while tendrils of it hung off the hair on his scalp. More smoke, as well, issued from the mouth agape in horrific death; the eyes had curdled cloudy white. A powerful pork-like aroma spread a ground fog throughout hodgepodge of shacks. Another smoker sealed the fate of Onderdonk's boy—a pitiable sight, indeed. The lower body-weight, and the probability that the boy had been "cooking" longer than his father, was demonstrated by the fact his eye sockets were filled with bubbling humors. Steam from the poor lad's poached brain keened from his sinuses and ears.

"God save us," I croaked.

"The fullbloods got to them," came Zalen's hopeless appraisal, "which means they may still be here."

The prospect seized my heart like a vulturine claw and squeezed. We all but slithered in the direction of the motor, eyes never blinking. But, still, my questions remained in a maelstrom. "Previously, you told me that women made pregnant were allowed to keep their firstborn, but the others must be relinquished to the fullbloods."

"Yeah? So what?"

"But you also told me that you yourself fathered Mary's third or fourth child. What kind of a treacherous cretin could deliver *his own child* to those things in the water?"

"I didn't have anything to say about it, Morley. We don't have a *choice* here—don't you get that? If I'm 'treacherous,' then so is your beloved Mary."

I wouldn't hear of it. I *knew,* I knew to the marrow of my *soul,* that Mary's misgivings were levered upon her; if she did not comply, her son, brother, and stepfather would be made fodder for the fullbloods.

"And the kid we had was an accident," he went on. "I suppose, back then, I actually loved her—before she joined the collective."

I winced at the excuse. "Only the un-Godliest of men could proclaim to *love* a woman he was prostituting out like a commodity."

"You don't know what you're talking about," and then came a snicker. "And I don't believe in God anyway."

"I should say that's obvious—"

"So if your God really exists, you're gonna have to do a lot of praying to get us out of this." We both arrived at the truck; in the back bed stood two cans of petrol. Ducking down, Zalen took one and carefully emptied it into the vehicle's fuel tank. "And," he went on, "you can *pray* that this hunk of junk starts . . . "

"One last question first," I importuned and gripped his shoulder. My curiosity burned like a brand-iron. "Answer what you refused to answer before."

"Come on, Morley, we have to—"

"I insist! You said that the ritualism is just veneer founded in ignorant traditions of old: occultism used as 'icing' to cover something else."

"Yes!"

"So what about the babies? What about the sacrifices? If the sacrifice of newborns isn't an *occult* oblation, then what else *can* it be?"

"It's not sacrifice, for God's sake. They want the newborns to study them—to study *us*. Their brains, their cells, their blood—everything, to see how they grow. Like what I said before—the microscopic things in every cell that make us what we are—*that's* what they study, *that's* what they experiment with."

"Their understanding of the genetic sciences must outweigh ours a thousandfold," I said. "So that's it."

"Yeah. Sacrifices to the devil? Black magic? It's just a bunch of what my grandfather used to call codswallop. Ornamentation, Morley, to fool the ignorant masses: *us*."

It was with little positivity that I contemplated the potential of his explanation. Based on the little I'd read, I knew that, in theory, the study of human genes (particularly human genes still in developmental stages such as infancy) could not only enhance understanding of human life but could *alter* human life. I was forced, next, to ask, "What is the purpose of their studying us on a genetic level, Zalen?"

"That's the worst part," he said. "They hate us, Morley. They want to wipe us out, but not by brute force."

"With what, then?"

"With disease, deformity, sterility."

"Of course," I croaked, aware now of the ramifications. "Via research and experimentation on the newborns, the fullbloods could identify our biological vulnerabilities and produce viruses, malignancies, and contagious disease mechanisms that could lay waste to the human race from a multitude of angles."

"That's right. That's what they want to do eventually—"

"And you're helping them!" I snapped.

He frowned in the moonlight. "I thought I was helping *you*. I'm helping you and your precious Mary escape. Remember that." He turned then to the bedraggled vehicle. "Start praying, Morley. Pray to your God that this has a starter button instead of a keyed ignition . . ."

I actually did pray for that, but before the prayer was done, I'd leapt back, yelling in fright, for when Zalen opened the truck's dented and paint-faded door, he didn't *lean* in, he was *pulled* in—

—by a pair of long, thin, bizarrely jointed and musculatured arms with hands more resembling the forepaws of a frog but with slick, webbed digits nearly a foot in length. I never saw its face, though I clearly understood what *it* was by the pungent smell which gusted from the truck when Zalen opened the rusted-patched door. It was the smell of a *fish*-pile tinged by the earthy stench of creek scum. Creek scum, too, was what the thing's skin looked like. It took moments in these wedges of shadow for me to compose reactive thought. I did seem to see its bump-pocked sickly green skin *shine* as if wet, and as the commotion ensued within the truck, I also heard wet *sounds*, *slopping* sounds, and then sounds which were more refined and more ghastly.

Only the word *evil* could describe what I heard next, though to make direct simile, I'd have to say it sounded like someone dislocating the joints of a raw chicken, only the "chicken" in this case was Zalen. A heftier tearing sound followed, after which came a great, wet *splat* as all of the long-haired malcontent's internal organs were tossed out of the truck, and after that came the addict's destitution-worn black rain jacket.

Then came the arms, uprooted at the shoulder sockets.

Then the legs.

It's taking him apart piece by piece, I realized.

And last came the torso, though Zalen's genitals appeared to be absent from the groin. I could only hope that the chewing sound I heard from the truck was my imagination.

I do not consider myself a coward, however, for not attempting to intercede with my pistol, for what you must understand is that the above dismantling of Cyrus Zalen expended only a matter of a few seconds. Instead, I rolled behind a rotted tree stump of considerable breadth. Reflex more than my conscious brain directed my positioning; I lay on my belly, both hands outstretched gripping my weapon, doing my best to establish a firing lane over the area I knew the creature must venture into if it were to pursue me. Shooting eye lined up over the weapon's small sights, I waited.

And waited.

Come out! I pleaded.

No significant movement could be detected within the truck, though I believe I noticed *minor* movement. A moment later—and for *only* a moment—the faintest greenish luminescence seemed to fluoresce within, and I could only judge that it was coming from the passenger side of the vehicle's interior. A second later, it was gone.

What guided me to re-examine Zalen's torso, I can't imagine, but as I did so, I made the sickening revelation that the cad's head was no longer in connection with his neck. Why had the batrachian monstrosity within ejected everything but the head?

Something arched in the darkness, thumped, then rolled to answer my question.

Zalen's head.

The head grinned in a manner that mirrored Zalen's snideness to perfection. The whites of its eyes, in a faintness that was less than minute, glowed with the same greenish ghost-light I'd noticed in the truck. "Think about what you're doing, Morley," came Zalen's corroded voice, yet a wet, slushy titter now companioned the words. "You don't have enough bullets to take them on, but you *do* have choices."

The dead words wracked me in a near-paralysis. Zalen's head chuckled when I shakingly aimed the gun at its brow. I noticed too that the torn and bloody stump of the neck glowed phosphorically with the thinnest tendrils of whatever netherworld-elixir had been administered into it—the reagent, I presumed, that had also reanimated Mr. Nowry, Candace, and Lord knew how many others.

"What . . . choices?" I finally managed.

"Join Olmstead's town collective—"

"Bombast," I said in spite of my revulsion and fear. "I will not be a party to infanticide, nor will I aid and abet the enemies of my race."

"Jesus, man. If you don't join them, you're dead. Oh, sure, you might take down a few of them with that peashooter of yours, but they'll get you eventually." The severed head winked. "And when they do, it won't be a pretty sight."

"I'd sooner shoot myself."

"Well, that's the only *other* choice you have. If you're not gonna join them, then you better do yourself a big favor and put that gun to your head right now and pull the trigger, Morley. That thing in the truck just pulled me apart in less time than it takes to bat an eye. You have any idea how much that *hurt?*" and then the dead mouth bayed wet, mushy laughter.

When I looked up, I spotted the silhouette of the thing standing just outside the truck now, staring at me in great attendance. The eyes which shined in the darkness were gold-irised and seemed the size of adult fists. Its evilly webbed hands hung down well below the joints that sufficed for its knees.

"Of course," the wretched head continued, "if you're gonna kill yourself, you'll need to kill Mary first—"

"Mary?" I exclaimed.

"If you don't join the collective, they'll do things to her that will make the Holy Inquisition look like a couple of kids playing in a sandbox. They'll torture the daylights out of her, Morley, with their chemicals and their tools, and then they'll kill her, and then? They'll bring her back just to do it all over again."

"Shut up!" I yelled and put the gun to the head's eye.

"But none of that'll happen if you join the collective. You'll have your Mary, happily ever after."

Tempting as they may have been, I knew that I could not fall prey to his promises. If I agreed, they would kill me just the same for what I knew. I prevaricated, biding time— there was still the fullblood at the truck to deal with. "Let me think about this," I delayed—but then I looked back to the truck and saw that the heinous, scum-skinned creature was no longer there.

"Too late," Zalen intoned with a chuckle.

If was from behind that the slime-gloved hand came round and encompassed my entire face; I was hauled back, unable to breathe, and my pistol fell out of my hand. The foot-long fingers encased the full of my head, and thin as they may have been, they exerted such force that I knew only seconds would be required before my skull burst like a pressured gourd. Zalen's execrable head continued to cackle as my struggles grew more enfeebled; worse, the aberration's other flagitious hand was slipping its way beneath my belt and into my trousers. What I suspected it had used Zalen's genitals for were about to be duplicated with my own.

"Looks like your God hit the road, Morley," hacked another splattering laugh of the evil head. "Can't say that I blame Him . . . "

It was almost merciful the way my consciousness dimmed just as the marauding hand clasped my genitals and began to twist. Would my skull erupt before I ultimately smothered? I felt the thin, boney fingers tightening, slickened by frog-slime. It seemed to temper itself then, as though it would uproot my privates and collapse my head simultaneously; but as I felt what I was certain were my last heartbeats, the abomination released me as if electrically shocked, leapt upright onto its hideous feet, and released a bellow so cacophonous and inhuman I thought I'd go mad merely from the sound.

A sound like a rising and falling shriek intertwined a wet, slopping-like splatter.

I thudded to my side, desperate to recover breath. Moving clouds over the woods unmercifully afforded more moonlight at the same instant I looked up . . .

The awkward-jointed, shuddering thing had somehow been staked to a tree via one of Onderdonk's iron stoking rods rammed into one of its orbicular eyeballs. As the impossible vocal protest wound down, it convulsed with an added sound akin to wet leather flapping.

A dark blur, then, and rapid footfalls snagged my gaze as I plainly saw a figure gliding away into the woods.

Who had saved me? *Mary?* I wondered, but, no, if so, she'd have said something, and no woman in her stage of pregnancy could've moved so nimbly. Or perhaps a townsperson in conscientious objection to the collective's ghastly initiatives. Or . . .

Could it have been young Walter?

The madness of the previous minutes released my senses. I was still on a mission: to save Mary and her son, to see to their escape from this macabre, clandestine netherocracy. Distant thrashing in the woods told me my savior was heading west, across the road . . .

Towards Mary's house.

Recovered now, I reclaimed my pistol.

"Kill her," Zalen's head said. "Then kill yourself."

With more than a little loathing, I picked the head up by its greasy hair and—

"Don't you dare, Morley!"

—dropped it into the smoker which was slow-cooking Mr. Onderdonk. Reclosing the lid, I could still hear its muffled remonstrance. "Ain't nothing but a rich pud . . . "

"But a rich pud still in possession of his head," I replied. Then I ran off—after the shape that had spared my life.

It was chiefly blind faith that guided me through the night-shrouded thicket and labyrinth of gnarled trees. Fireflies constellated the darkness. Eventually, I sighed in relief to see the squat, dark form of Mary's overgrown abode, the faintest candles glowing in the tiny windows. And—

There he is!

It was before one such window that I spied the obscure figure, the person who'd saved my life. But before I could take even a single step forward, the figure whirled, and it whisked away into the trees deft as a wood-sprite. My first impulse was to call out, but then I remembered the necessity of inconspicuousness. Who knew how many other fullbloods lurked near? Nor did I run after the figure, for that would result in complete diversion to my goal. Instead, I peeked into the wanly lit pane that the figure had just quitted, and there I saw, on a pitiful sack filled with leaves and dead grass, Mary's young son Walter, asleep. It was the candle-stub and holder sitting on the crude dirt floor that gave the room its diminutive light.

I had no time for contemplations; softer and more erratic footfalls alarmed me from the southward side of the house. Pistol at the ready, I covered myself behind a tree, holding my breath . . .

The figure that stepped into a sprawl of moonlight was Mary.

She trudged forward with difficulty, obviously returning from the forced bacchanal at the lake. Wearied, then, she gasped, then buckled over and was sick. I rushed to her as she retched in misery.

"Oh, Foster!" she sobbed. "I prayed that you'd still be alive—"

"Your prayers have been answered," I said and took her up in an embrace. *But we'll need more than prayer, I'm afraid,* came an amending thought. She wore the esoteric robe of earlier, with the confounding configurations embroidered within its fringes. Her warm, heavy body trembled in my arms. "I've come for you, and your son—"

She bolted from the comfort my embrace had given her. "We must get inside, and we must keep out voices very low."

"Mary, I—"

"Shhh! You *don't* understand!" and she took my hand and pulled me into the squalor-embalmed house through a narrow, uneven door. Total dark and a dense mustiness suddenly cocooned me; it was only her warm hand I had as a guide.

She piloted me to another low-ceilinged room lit by one candle alone, make-shift furniture in evidence. I helped her sit on a milk crate-turned-chair, and when she finally caught her breath, she looked up at me with the saddest eyes. "Oh, Foster, I'm so sorry. You've jeopardized your life by coming here."

"I've come here, Mary," I asserted, "for you and your son."

Her flushed face fell into her hands. "There's so much you don't know."

"Calm yourself. I know everything now."

Astonishment forced her gaze upward. "You've—you've seen the things?"

"Yes, earlier at the lake, during the regrettable ritual that your circumstances have forced upon you, and also minutes ago, at the Onderdonks'. One of the fullbloods nearly killed me."

"So . . . you *know* about the fullbloods?"

"I know everything. I know what's going on at the second floor of the Hilman House; I know about the dual corpse repositories in the caverns beneath the waterfront. I know why your brother Paul is infirm, and I also know that your stepfather is a crossbreed between their race and ours and that he's the only one of his kind allowed to live after the mandated genocide of years ago." I took her hand. "And, Mary, I know why they're forcing the collective's women to remain perpetually pregnant. The newborns aren't sacrificed, they're *utilized* for research intended to lead to the demise of humankind. Several hours ago, I witnessed Zalen handing over several such newborns to the fullbloods, out on the sandbar."

She hitched on another sob. "Zalen? But, my God, you must think I'm a fiend for allowing my babies to be used like this."

"I think nothing of the sort," I snapped, "for I also know that you are *forced* into this perverse servitude. Should you refuse to comply, you and your family would all be slaughtered." I quieted and gripped her hand more tightly to assure her. "Mary, I know also of the servile tasks you were pressured to perform in the past, out of desperation, under Cyrus Zalen's pandering influence and pornographic endeavors."

She nearly gagged, tears now literally plipping from her eyes onto the dirt floor. "Then how can a moral man like you even stand to be in the same room with me?"

My verity left no margin for hesitation. "I'm in love with you, Mary. It would wound my heart forever for you to not believe this."

Her face went back to her hands. "That just makes it worse . . . "

"Why!" I demanded, perhaps too loudly. "I don't expect you to love me in return, but I can pray and live in the hope that one day you will, and should that never happen, then I will *still* love you just as much."

Now she hugged me quite suddenly. "Oh, Foster, but I *do* love you; I have since you came into the restaurant today—"

I could've collapsed in the rush ebullience that inundated my spirit. At that moment, I knew that in my life of plenty, I actually had nothing—until now.

Now, I had everything.

"Then why on Earth do you say our love makes us *worse?*" I pleaded.

"Foster! Think about it! Lovecraft's story is *true,* and I'm living right in the middle of it."

"What Zalen didn't tell me I found out for myself."

"But, Foster—Zalen is the reason that the fullbloods are on the hunt. They're on the hunt . . . for *you.*"

"When I was at the old Innswich Point tonight, I was forced to shoot one of their reanimants, a prostitute of Zalen's," I told her, then remembered the most disturbing point. "I didn't really kill her, for she was already dead. But my shot detained her long enough to broker my escape. It's quite possible that one or more of the fullbloods saw or heard this, and even more possible that Candace informed them directly after I'd fled."

"That's not the reason, Foster," she went on, a hand to her belly as if discomfited. "It's because of Zalen, much earlier today. Sentinels are everywhere. Every single townsperson reports back to them. And some of them, like Candace, are already physically dead. One of them overheard Zalen telling you about the tunnels beneath the waterfront of Innswich Point. No one can know about that, Foster. It's one of their greatest secrets, so anyone who learns of it . . . is hunted down."

This was moot, though I should've recalled Lovecraft's story with more exploit. Even the most guarded whispers were overheard, if not by the degraded townsfolk, then by the Deep Ones themselves, whose auditory faculties were super-normal. But a paramount point collided with my deductive processes now that I'd gleaned this data. "I take it, then, we're not safe in your house. We must leave at once."

"They won't come here, Foster," she said with downcast eyes. "One of their leaders . . . has taken a fancy to me."

"You needn't be ashamed," I assured her. "Zalen mentioned this. He called them 'sovereigns,' but he also mentioned that sexual intercourse, even among these hierarchs, is banned via their new laws. I also know that the reason your brother and stepfather have been spared is due to this same sovereign's fondness for you. "

She began to speak but then bowed forward with a grimace.

"Mary! You're in pain."

"No, no, I'm all right. I just need a short rest." She reached up. "Help me, Foster, to the bed."

I took great caution assisting her; she appeared exhausted, worn, and aching all at once. A glance to the "bed" forced a grimace on my part, for it existed as no more than the most primitive of straw mattresses. *With a little luck, she'll be sleeping in a REAL bed tomorrow, likely for the first time in her horrendously burdened life.*

A happy sigh escaped her lips. "That's much better, Foster. Thank you. Dr. Anstruther says I'll be due in another week or so."

"Anstruther," I sputtered the name with venom. "I've seen *his* handiwork. I take it he's a senior member of Olmstead's collective."

She nodded. "He's the one who runs everything here—for *them.*"

"I should've known."

She lay back, sedate now, and—I pray God—banishing the profane foray at the lake from her tired mind. "Here, Foster," she murmured; she took my hand and placed it at the center of her swollen belly. "Feel the life inside."

It did so with great wonder. *A blessing,* I mused. *Each and every life is a blessing . . .*

"I'd like so much to keep it," came her next murmuration. Tears welled. "I'd give anything . . . "

"You will keep it, Mary—this I vow." The great bolus of flesh beneath the occult robe seemed to *beat* with heat. "You stay here and rest while I return to the Onderdonks' to retrieve their motor. In less than an hour's time, I'll be transporting you and Walter away from here, to the security of my estate in Providence—"

"You just don't understand," she moaned in frustration. "If I try to leave, they'll come after me. No one in the collective can *ever* leave."

"We'll see about that," I replied but still mindful of what Zalen had implied of the fates of those who had tried. "Leave it to me. I will drive you to safety or die trying."

When she looked at me, I noted something behind her eyes that could only be the desperate joy of hope.

"It just makes me love you more for wanting to do this for us. But I can't let you. We would never make it out; we'd all die."

"I'm willing to take that chance," I told her with no hesitancy whatsoever. "Are you? Would you take that chance for Walter to finally have a good life and attend good schools like other boys? Would you take that chance"—I gave the gravid belly a momentary caress—"to give this unborn child the chance to live and to behold the beauty of the world, and to save it from the blasphemous death that awaits it otherwise?"

She sobbed, gulped, and nodded. "Yes! I *will* take the

chance! Even if we all die, then at least I'll get to die with you . . ."

"Wait here," I told her, choking up. "I'll return presently," and next, I was out of the house and back out into the moon-spattered night.

I did not allow myself to entertain thoughts which might divert my focus, but what a luxury that would have been. I wended back toward the Onderdonks', eyes proverbially peeled, my Colt pistol slippery in my sweating hand. The woods were profuse with night sounds now, where they hadn't been before. It made me wonder. If these full-blooded monstrosities were indeed on the hunt for me, I saw no hint of them all the way back to Onderdonk's ramshackle compound.

The smokers were gusting; I ignored the rich, savory—and unmentionable—aroma. Only from the corner of my eye did I allow myself a glance at the dead creature staked to the tree. The prospect of seeing one of these abominations in detail did not incite my curiosity. Closer to the truck, I had to step around Zalen's innards and body parts, a fairly daunting task in itself, though I did spare myself one mental levity: *It couldn't have happened to a finer and more forthright gentleman.*

Good Lord! came my next distasteful thought, for when I slipped into the time-weathered vehicle, my buttocks grew immediately sopped from the deposit of Zalen's blood which had been let during his evisceration and dismemberment. I sat still a moment to slowly survey my immediate surroundings through the windscreen and saw nothing—absolutely *nothing*—out of the ordinary. *If these fullbloods are hunting me, they're exhibiting a less-than-fair effort thus far.* A grim reminder assailed me next, however: Zalen's earlier concern about the truck's starting mechanism. I was an antiquarian and philanthropist, not a car thief. *If it's a keyed ignition, then I'll have no choice but to drag Onderdonk's half-cooked corpse from the smoker and search his pockets for the key*

. . . I withdrew my pocket-flash, closed my shooting eye to preserve its night-vision, then, for just a split-second, turned on the flash before the dashboard.

My heart fell like a stone.

What my flash illumined was a cylindrical keyway mounted in the dash.

"Here's the key, Mr. Morley," the small but sudden voice whispered just outside the open truck window. Where my heart had just sunk in the worst despair, it nearly jettisoned from my mouth in the coming shock.

It was young Walter who stood beside the vehicle.

"In Heaven's name, son!" I snapped a whisper back to him. "You nearly stopped my heart!" but then my eyes flicked to his adolescent hand and proved what he claimed was true. "How . . . How on earth did you—"

A modest smile of pride touched his face. "Mr. Onderdonk would always keep the key beneath his door mat. I've seen him put it there a lot, sir, during my hikes through the woods."

"Not only a lad of proper manners," I gushed, "but one of industriousness." I blinked. "But you were asleep only a short time ago."

"I woke up and heard you and my mom talking, so I came out on my own to get the key for you."

This was certainly a gift I could never have anticipated. "You're a fine boy, Walter, and a very brave one. But it's unduly dangerous out here. Do you know about . . . ," but then the sentence deteriorated.

"I know all about the fullbloods, sir. I've seen them a few times, but tonight, I've seen a whole lot of them."

And it's my fault, I reminded myself. Walter's courage was commendable, but it did indeed put him in great danger. "Get in next to me, Walter. We're going to pick up your mother so I can take you both to live with me."

"But you'll need help, sir," he added. "It would be best if I position myself in the back of the truck. I can't get a good aim if I'm inside with you."

"A good *aim?* Walter, whatever are you talking about?"

He raised his handmade bow. "They may try to block the road back to the house, but I'm a pretty good shot."

I smiled in spite of myself. "Lad, you're surely the bravest boy to ever walk these parts, but I'm afraid that suction-cup arrows will do little good against the fullbloods."

Then he showed me a handful of *real* arrows.

"See, Mr. Morley? We better go before they come."

What could I say to such youthful ingenuity and unhesitant bravado? "All right, Walter. Get in back and be vigilant . . . And keep your fingers crossed that this old vehicle starts."

The boy hopped in back. With wide eyes, then, and a trembling lip, I inserted the key into the cylinder, uttered a prayer that seemed dismally anemic, and turned the key.

The rusted hulk hitched, gave off a loud metallic whine that made the tendons in my neck stand out, then rumbled to a start. I ground gears in my attempt to get it in first, gritted my teeth at a long grind, then we were finally moving. The vehicle was indeed roadworthy, but in that evidence, the noise its starting had made could surely be heard from here to town.

I pulled out and turned posthaste, gravel and oyster shells popping beneath worn tires. "Keep a sharp eye!" I called to Walter when I considered the necessity to leave the headlamps off.

"Yes, Mr. Morley!" he replied, and when I glanced back through the hole which had once housed glass, I saw the lad positioned in back, his crude bow at the ready. I knew that at an identical age, I'd have been in possession of not one-tenth of the boy's courage.

I'll raise him as though he were my own, I vowed, *and be the father he'd never had, and the same for Mary's baby . . .*

Rusted springs ground when I throttled the archaic vehicle across the rutted road to town. The moon seemed to spray its light upon us for the few seconds that the road exposed us, such that the road itself and the trees and vegetation lining it seemed iridescent, and this made me think of Lovecraft's masterpiece, "The Color Out of Space," said to be his personal favorite. Though my fear levels jumped from this brief exposure, it enabled me to view the road both ways. Where I expected to glimpse enemies, I saw, again, virtually nothing in the way of detractors.

Strange, I thought. *Unless they're lying in wait . . .*

The enfeebled truck rocked when I traversed the wheel and navigated into the long, heavily wooded dirt-scratch lane which would lead us to the house. Suddenly, darkness swallowed us, only minutely dappled by the moon, for the boughs of overhead trees nearly connected with one another from either side, transposing our route into that of a tunnel. I had to retard speed considerably now, for the reduced visibility.

Walter's wan face peered in to the rear hole. "Mr. Morley? Maybe you should turn on the headlamps. I can't see a *thing!*"

The light-discipline of a soldier surely had tactical exceptions, not to mention that I was nothing remotely similar to a soldier. *Just a rich pud,* I recalled Zalen's slight, but he was right. I fancied I could hear him laughing at me now, even as his odious head continued to cook. But now, I would *have* to be a soldier, and I would have to take chances in order to achieve success. I took the lad's advice and switched on the headlamps.

The boy shrieked, and so did I.

Figures rushed forward out of the bramble-carpeted woods. Before I could even make transitive reaction, I saw a queerly robed figure—but one with a clearly human face—lunge forward but then buckle back, his hand shooting to his face as an arrow caught him right in his opened mouth.

"Good shot, Walter!"

When a hand—a human hand, not the webbed

extremity I expected—shot into the passenger window, I thrust my pistol-filled fist toward it, then—

BAM!

The lucky shot caught the marauder right in the Adam's apple. Bubbly blood shot from the wound as the robed predator screamed.

And it was a man I recognized. *Mr. Wraxall, the restaurant owner . . .*

These were not the monstrous fullbloods I anticipated to be set for ambush but townsmen, all dressed in those same robes with esoteric fringe. More snatches of faces were revealed: the hotel clerk, the maintenance man, the diner who'd been lunching with his paramour at the restaurant, and others. When two more shot out from left and right, Walter struck one in the shoulder; the aggressor unwisely hesitated where he stood, then was bellowing as the vehicle's wheels drubbed him beneath the chassis. The second assailant tried to climb into my open window, where I easily fired a shot directly into the top of his head. He fell away, but not before I could recognize the face in the hood's oval: Dr. Anstruther.

Sin or not, I chuckled at the cad's death and considered the splotches of his grey matter upon my shirt a unique badge of honor.

The rest of the road to the house was clear.

Where I'd expected the opposition to be formidable, I found only sheepshank weakness in its place. The squat house now came into view at the end of the headlamps' beams.

"This was almost too easy, Walter," I called out behind me. "And that troubles me quite a bit." I killed the motor, hopped out. "We must hurry now and fetch your mother. Between the engine-noise and my pistol, there'll be more after us . . ."

I sprang to the vehicle's rear bed to lift Walter out, but—

Oh, my God in Heaven, no . . .

The only objects occupying this space were the boy's meager bow and the final can of petrol.

I glanced out into the woods but saw and heard nothing.

How could I have let this happen? I condemned myself. *The town collective snatched Walter out of the back . . . and have taken him away . . .*

(IV)

A **HALF-HOUR'S DESPERATE** search in the woods yielded no positive result, and to search longer would only jeopardize the possibility of getting Mary and her unborn out alive. Hence, I trudged back to the brick-and-ivy-netted hovel like a man on his way to the gallows. What could I tell Mary? Her son had been abducted and most likely was dead already—all under my charge . . .

The very normal sound of crickets followed me back inside, but then came another sound, one which actually deflected my all-pervading muse of despair:

The sound of a baby crying.

I plunged out of the foyer's ink-like murk into the candle-lit room, where the sound of infantile crying hijacked my gaze toward the heap of a mattress. "Mary!"

There she sat, bearing an exhausted smile as she sat upright among makeshift pillows. In her arms, pressed to her swelling bosom, was a newly born babe, swaddled in linens.

"I went into labor just after you left," she said, rosy-cheeked. "And then it happened only minutes later." She turned the infant for me to see.

A miracle, I thought. It was as perfect as any babe I'd ever beheld. The moment it took notice of me, it quieted and looked at me wide-eyed.

"See, he likes you, Foster. Just the sight of you calms him." Mary rocked him as best she could.

"What a wonder," I whispered. "I'm only sorry I wasn't here to assist when the time came."

"Each time, it's easier," she informed. "There was barely any pain with this one." She glanced hopefully to me, eyes aglint in the candlelight. "But we must name him right away, in case—"

In case we die trying to leave, I finished for her.

"I'm going to name him Foster," she said.

I went speechless, a tear beading in my eye.

Then her hopeful glance turned hard as granite. "And they're *not* going to get this one. Only over my dead body . . ."

The joy of this notice crested in my heart but then crashed to the most stygian depths.

She still didn't know that Walter was gone.

"Mary, I . . . I . . ."

"I love you so much, Foster," she interrupted, teary-eyed herself. "I want you to marry me. I want to spend the rest of my life with you, and raise this child with you . . . and make love to you every single night . . ."

The words, greater than any gift I'd ever been given, only dragged my spirit deeper into the abyss of black verity.

"You, me, and Walter," she mused on, breast-feeding now. "We'll be such a happy family."

Sorrow sealed my throat like a strangler's gasp. I could barely hack out, "Mary, you don't understand. It's about—"

"I know what it's about," her placid voice came to me. "It's about Walter."

I stared.

"I never got the chance to explain earlier," she went on, modestly covering enough of her bosom to forestall my view. "Earlier, you said that you'd witnessed Cyrus Zalen at the waterfront, delivering sacks of newborns to the fullbloods."

"But-but . . . but Mary, what—"

"Don't *worry*, sweetheart. You were simply mistaken."

"Mistaken?" I asked, but by now, my mind was thoroughly disarranged. "No, no, Mary, I saw him, it was Zalen."

"You saw a man in a black raincoat is what you saw, Foster. Right?"

"Why . . . yes."

She looked right at me. "Foster, the man stalking you in the woods earlier today wasn't Zalen."

The comment took me aback. "But . . . I thought sure."

"And the man you saw out on the sandbar tonight wasn't Zalen either."

"Who, then?" I demanded.

Mary squirmed in her seat, candlelight pale on her face. "It was Walter's father—"

"What!"

"Foster . . . turn around."

The cryptic command reversed my position, and my eyes blossomed at the surreal sight.

It was a man tall and gaunt who stood in the opposite corner. The black raincoat seemed several sizes too large, and its hood draped most of his face. More important was the minor burden in his arms: it was Walter. At first, I feared the boy was dead, but then I noted the rise and fall of his young chest.

"This is Walter's father," Mary told me in the struggling light. "Those times you mistook him as Zalen stalking you, he was actually coming here to catch a glimpse of his son."

I suppose I already knew via some blackly ethereal portent, even before the figure retracted the hood to reveal the face of Howard Phillips Lovecraft.

I stood, lax-jawed, dizzy—staring at the icon as if beholding a vision from the highest precipice of the earth . . .

The voice which issued from the thin lips sounded high but parched, an exerted whisper. He hefted the living weight. "My son is in no danger, sir; he's merely fainted from the shock of his abduction by several of the town's collective members. Please rest assured that these self-same abductors are no longer among the living."

"You killed them?"

The thin face nodded. "Just as I killed the fullblood that was after you at the Onderdonks'. And as Mary has informed you, *I* was the ferryman you glimpsed on the sandbar tonight." The voice teetered now between cracking and high-pitchedness, hollow yet somehow exhibiting depth at the same time. "In the amalgam of my damnable onus. This nefarious deed has been my province alone since the sixteenth of March, nineteen hundred and thirty-seven."

The day after his death, I knew. The Master's words sounded ruined, like thin-membraned things blown through fence-slats in the wind. The obscene circumvention of death left his narrow visage pallored as if old mortician's wax had been applied to a skull. This semi-translucence caused me to shudder, as did his eye-whites, which more resembled dirt-flecked snow-crust.

"And as you've already been partially apprised," he grated on, "the detestable creatures which I fictionalized as 'the Deep Ones' are in possession of aggressive philtres which re-synthesize nucleotide activity within a certain helical infrastructure that exists in every human cell. This ingenious—and diabolic—process has the power to, among other things, reconstitute life in the dead. Hence, sir, my damnation and the recompense for my sins."

"Your . . . *sins?*" I questioned. "But you've been known throughout your natural life as an atheist. The concept of sin is one you don't believe in."

"Not *my* conception," the haunted man intoned, "but *their* conception."

"Whatever do you mean?"

"I penned *The Shadow Over Innsmouth* close to a decade ago, but, lo, in its flaw, it was never published, and in its not being published, word never traced back to the fullbloods of its existence . . ."

"But that all changed," I hazarded, "in late-1936, when the Visionary Publications copy became available to the public. And word got back—"

"—back to the eternal monstrosities who hold sway over this place, yes. But they didn't endeavor to pursue me then—it was already known that I was suffering from a terminal affliction. Several months later, however, when I died, word of my decease riposted back to them as well. The night after I was buried, a troop of the accurst things came up out of Narragansett Bay, exhumed me, and re-enlivened my pitiable corpse. Since then, I've been forced to serve them in a number of abominable fashions, whose details I'll spare you. The nexus of my punishment, though, and I should think it quite perceptible now, is the delivery of all newborns to the fullbloods' soul-dead machinations."

My throat suddenly shriveled. "They brought you back for that. To be a servitor for them."

"That and far, far worse, sir. But an unwilling traitor to my race, and the devil's package boy. The only way to protect the life of my son was to perform as I'm commanded and deliver the innocent newborns into *their* appalling clutches." The dead eyes looked to Mary and her now-sleeping baby. "It is a task I shall never discharge again." He placed Walter down alongside Mary, then returned his attention to me. "And of you, sir, I must beg a favor."

"But I owe you my life," I exclaimed. "The beast at Onderdonk's was only moments away from killing me before you intervened—"

"Do as you have promised," the ghost-voice quavered, "and deliver Mary and my son to safety."

"I will. This I pledge—"

But in my own hesitation, I recalled something crucial, while on the same hand, Mary's attitude seemed suddenly crestfallen.

"Your brother, Mary. And your stepfather," I commenced with the dark implication.

"I know," she acknowledged. "Paul's not here. He sleeps in the backroom at the store."

The looks we all shared told all.

"We'll have no choice but to leave him. A rescue attempt would grossly reduce our chances of safe escape with Walter and the baby . . ."

"I'll see to the task of relieving him of his misery myself," Lovecraft offered. "The fullbloods will kill him once they learn that Mary has fled the collective, and they'll do so in a manner most grueling and torturous. I'll be certain to get to him before they have occasion to. He'll suffer not an iota of pain."

"My stepfather, though," Mary half-sobbed. "He's in the next room, and I'm afraid . . . "

She needn't finish. He would have to be euthanized, and since I was the one with the gun—"This room here?" I asked of the crude and slightly tilted wooden door to the side.

She gulped and nodded.

"All right, then." I withdrew my handgun, edged toward the door.

Mary struggled to her feet to come near me. "But, Foster, you must understand. My stepfather—he's almost completely gone over by now."

"Gone over?"

Lovecraft picked up the explanation. "The metamorphosis which afflicts the crossbreeds not only taints their physical features but, I regret to impart, also their *mental* faculties. It's a certain eventuality that such hybrids in advanced age such as Mary's stepfather become hostile with time and adopt aspects of the mentality, attitudes, and sentiments of the fullbloods."

"It's true, Foster," Mary added. "He's worse now than ever. If you go in there, he'll attack you."

Then so be it, I thought, but as I approached the door, Lovecraft stopped me with a hand to my shoulder. "You are not expendable, sir, but I am. It's a much more difficult event to kill a dead man than one who's still living."

"But I feel it's my responsibility," I uttered.

"You mustn't take the chance," he insisted. "You're Mary and Walter's only hope. Save your ammunition." He took the gun and returned it to my pocket, then, from his own, extracted a razor-sharp fileting knife. "When I'm not detained for other, more monstrous duties, the fullbloods force me to filet fish in the workhouses, and it just so happens"—he shuddered at the thought—"I *hate* fish." His ruined eyes addressed me more directly. "Go now. Take them out of here now . . . and fulfill your pledge to me."

"But-but," I stammered, still not quite reckoning the fact that it was Lovecraft in my actual midst, maloccluded jaw and all. "You could come with us."

"No, it's time for nature to take its true course," his voice wisped. "My existence has perverted death for too long. Tonight—I'll see to it—I shall be dead for good," and then he picked up the still-unconscious Walter, placed him in my arms, then assisted Mary and the baby toward the door.

Mary tried all she could to stifle her sobs as we stepped back out into the teeming night. Lovecraft bid nothing more as an adieu; he merely cast a final glance at the boy in my arms, then quietly closed the door.

I stowed my passengers all in the front of the vehicle but was stalled by a sudden and very grotesque coercion. "Foster!" shot Mary's diminutive whisper. "Where are you going?"

"Just . . . one moment," I told her, and then it was this coercion that prompted me back to the hovel of a house.

To the back window . . .

I *had* to look in, for earlier in the afternoon, I'd only glimpsed the fringes of Mary's stepfather as it sat back in shadow. My eyes now held wide on the drab glass pane when the room's utter darkness was broken by the inner door opening, and Lovecraft undiscouragedly entered the room, candlestick in hand. That is when I saw Mary's stepfather in detail . . .

The thing lay sidled over on the floor, breathing with a sound like bubbles being blown under water. When it noticed Lovecraft's presence, a head that looked squashed down flinched. Mary had said that her stepfather had now fully "gone over," but I could see that the metamorphosis was not yet totally complete. One eye was indeed froglike in that it existed half out of its socket with a glistening green-black lid. A gold iris glittered amid the great peach-sized orb; however, its other eye appeared far more human, and the amalgamation of these opposites only heightened the grotesquerie of this living result of breeding between two separate species. Two mere holes functioned as the nose, fissures that could only be gills pulsed at its throat, and overall, the skin seemed a queer combination of toad and man.

Then the wide rim of the creature's mouth snapped open and—

ssssssssssnap!

—out shot a sickly pink cord which could only suffice for its tongue. Immediately, I recalled the details of my glimpse through this window earlier in the day, where the same deformed and disjointed figure that Walter referred to as his "gramps" vollied the same cord that I'd then mistaken for a whip. But now I saw that it was no whip; it was a narrow yet heavily veined tentacle, rife with minute suckers which pulsed beneath a repugnant glisten. The appalling boneless appendage was deftly forestalled by Lovecraft's wrist, whereupon he sliced the tentacle off with his knife.

Its pain was readily apparent as arms only vaguely human sprang up in protest. The lopsided head shuddered, the great rimmed mouth locked open in order to release a vociferation that could only have been born in hell: a whistle like a tea kettle interlaced by the slopping, wet, spattery scream I'd heard a facsimile of earlier. When it tried to rise on joints that flexed backwards, Lovecraft came more definitely forward with his fileting knife . . .

I trotted away, unable to bear any more of this dismal execution. When the tenor and volume of the crossbreed's scream quadrupled, I knew the grim task had been done.

With a blank mind, then, I started the rickety vehicle and pulled off. Smoke gusted and springs creaked, but now the truck was barreling down the road away from the awful house that Mary would never again have to enter.

The road south seemed the most direct shot, and its first quarter mile stood miraculously clear. Around a bend, though—

Mary and I screamed in unison.

It was a veritable barricade of monsters which occluded the pass. Fifty of them? A hundred? The logistics scarcely mattered. The sweep of our headlights compounded the sight to an utter vision of chaos: green-glistening skin pocked by brown, toadlike bumps, eyes jutting from compressed, earless heads like balls of black glass. Though they all stood upright, they showed white, runneled underbellies and legs corded with strange muscles. Dangling, horrific genitals told me they were predominantly male. Their height fluctuated between five to seven feet, though even in their upright stances, most were half-hunched over, so God knew their *true* height. Dare I barrel forward in an attempt to mow them down? Were I alone, I may have risked this, but with Mary and her children in my charge, I knew I couldn't.

The sight froze, maximizing the horror of what we beheld. The mass of abominations stood there, flexed on corded muscles, and as the headlamps blared, they all leaned back, tilted their heads upward, and then, as if on psychic command, their hideous rimmed mouths all opened at once and they began to shriek.

The sound caused the very woods to vibrate: a phlegmatic keening blended with the sound of a thousand men marching quickly through muck. If sound could cause physical impact, this was surely the case, for the cacophony now made the truck visibly rock. I'm sure I was screaming myself as I threw the decrepit vehicle into reverse, but even at the top of my lungs, my own utterance of fear could not be heard over the unearthly mudslide of sound which was being vaulted at us. Mary had already passed out, so she did not have to see what I glimpsed in that last half-second before I could turn fully around . . .

With the fullbloods' screams of objection, the tongue of each and every one of them jettisoned from their mouths. Unlike Mary's stepfather, whose hybrid tongue was but a single pink tentacle, each of these monsters possessed a tongue comprised of at least a dozen of the same, glistening and sucker-pocked appendages. Each clump of deranged tongues seemed to twist into a single fat, pulsing column and shivered there in mid-air throughout the entirety of their vocal display. These columns of detestable flesh *had* to extend at least five feet.

I fully depressed the accelerator pedal when I'd managed to turn around to a northward heading. Did my eyes deceive me when I dared to take one glance in the rearward mirror? I could've sworn they were pursuing me now—the entire mass of the things—and some seemed to be leaping forward at bounds of twenty feet, which barely afforded the speeding vehicle any distance ahead of them. It took me a half mile, in fact, to gain any comfortable ground, but just as I'd realized this—

I screamed again and slammed on the truck's brakes.

At least twice as many fullbloods blocked the northward way out. *My God, what can I do now?* When I looked over my shoulder through the truck's former rear window, I could see the first of the southern detachment coming round the bend, bringing their vocal storm with them, but I noticed something else as well . . .

The can of gasoline that had been in back previously was no longer there.

Where it had gone to, I hardly had time to consider. Now, it seemed, I had no choice but to try to plow through this mass to the north. The baby was wailing now, and Walter finally roused too, only to glimpse the horrific sight before us.

"Say your prayers, Walter," I urged, and then the fullbloods ahead of us began to shamble forward. In less than a minute, I knew, we'd be converged upon from north and south.

As I would utter my own last prayer and plunge the accelerator in a feeble attempt to plow through the monstrous blockade, young Walter pointed left and cried out, "Mr. Morley! Who's that man there?"

Man? my shattered faculties managed, but when I looked, I saw the black-raincoated form of Lovecraft waving assertively at us. He was urging me to veer the truck left, into a narrow trail that looked barely able admit the vehicle's width.

I saw, too, that it was *he* who'd taken the fuel can from the truck's rear bed. The can hung from his hand.

When I pulled onto the trail, I saw the northward mass of beasts shift into the woods themselves, as if to try to cut me off before I could drive to wherever the road would take us. Shortly thereafter, the southern mass poured into the trail behind us. The sound they made caused the forest to tremor: the wet, slopping gush detailed by wave after wave of inhuman caterwauls. At this point, the forest was verminous with the shambling, bump-skinned things.

Then the woods began to shift with crackling light . . .

"A fire!" Walter shouted.

I could see it all too easily now as I pressed the feeble truck to the extent of its mechanical possibilities. A virtual *wall* of flame spread through the woods just behind the encroaching ranks, and when I looked desperately south, I saw another wall spreading. Lovecraft had obviously walked a line of petrol on either side of the trail, igniting them only when the dual masses of ichthyic creatures had proceeded deeply enough to be trapped. This month of steadfast drought had turned the forest floor and brambles to a tinder-dry state, and now, it was all combusting almost simultaneously. Orange, wavering light pressed us in now, and the sound of crackling woods soon overcame the volume of the fullbloods' wretched howls, their unearthly battle-cry quickly transposing to sounds of utter consternation. In only a minute or two, our entire surroundings were aflame.

Our adversaries were trapped in the woods now by two encroaching walls of fire. The things were trapped, yes.

But so were we.

Each fire line seemed to follow the truck's progress. The most stifling heat surged inward, and when glancing to either side, I saw mad, inhuman figures thrashing, flopping, convulsing in the ignited woods, dressed in suits of fire. The rearview showed me the narrow trail completely engulfed and with ghost-shapes of blistering *things* as they were incinerated alive. Just as the fire began to engulf the truck . . .

I could've swooned at the sight.

The trail disgorged us into a moonlit clearing.

"We're out!" Walter shouted.

"We made it," came my own disbelieving whisper. I maintained my headway, though, for fear that some of the fullbloods must have escaped the conflagration, but when at a safe distance, I idled to a halt and looked back on the fiery scene . . .

Walter's gaze joined my own. Now, the fires were spreading outward, smoke pouring off treetops and billowing in the sky. The macabre, bellicose howls of hundreds of fullbloods now wound down to pathetic and periodic squeals. It was the crackling of massive flames that drowned out all else.

"What . . . What happened?" Mary asked, bewildered, the baby asleep at her bosom. "It looks like the entire woods are on fire."

"They will be if we don't get away from here now," I realized, and back into gear the truck went, and we were off.

Walter's fortunate knowledge of the area, due to his nature walks, took us to another narrow trail, which emptied us out onto the main road into town in only minutes. All that followed us now was the most eerie silence.

"Mr. Morley?" Walter inquired. "That man in the raincoat saved us."

"Indeed, he did, Walter."

"I know I've seen him in the woods before, many times, but I never got very close to him. Who *was* that man?"

I took Mary's hand. "One day, Walter, your mother and I will tell you . . . "

Not too long after that, a sign gave relieving notice that we were about to exit onto State Route Number One. With a smidgen of luck, we'd be in Providence by dawn.

(V)

THE PASSING OF six months has brought me many joyous changes. The sale of my Providence mansion—to a Standard Oil executive, no less—has left me even wealthier than before. A dead man's words—Zalen's— never left my cognizance: *They travel along any existing waterway, and they're very fast.* Now that God had granted my new standing as a family man, I relocated, only days after that night of incogitable horror, to a place where there existed *no* waterways for fifty miles in any direction, in the 36th state of the union, Nevada. My fortune built us an impregnable adobe house situated in the middle of the region's most arid land, just south of the state's dead-center point. Alkaline mud-plains, sand-swept desert, and endless square miles of sagebrush and tumbleweed provide the vista anywhere one might happen to peer.

And—to reiterate—there are no waterways.

I bank in Carson City, over a hundred miles northwest, and from there, fresh water for drinking and bathing is trucked in weekly. Also trucked in weekly are shifts of Pinkerton guards, who live at the house and keep watch round the clock. They believe I'm merely a successful businessman leery of enemies of the trade. Naturally, I've never told them exactly what it is I fear may one day encroach the house in the middle of the night.

As for Olmstead and its waterfront sector formerly known as Innswich Point, I can only recount what I'd gleaned from the newspapers: the great drought-stoked

343

forest fire had scorched thousands of surrounding acres. Of the 361 registered residents, none were known to have survived, many having been incinerated in ill-fated evacuation attempts, and the rest having died from smoke-inhalation as the fires, as devastating as they'd been, had not actually burned the town's new block-and-concrete architecture. How had the fires commenced? Lightning, the sources said. But the region could sigh in relief, since a rainstorm the very next day had prevented the conflagration from spreading to even more devastating ambits. Curiously, a final paragraph mentioned federal inspectors examining the town's remains days later, but no explanation was rendered for such inspections. Nor was any quantity of information offered for the government's demolitioning of certain sectors of the town's waterfront. For safety reasons, was all they said. And no mention, of course, was made of any dead person found to be wearing a scrimy black raincoat . . .

Mary and I were wed very shortly after relocating, and the life I've always dreamed of is now at hand. Live-in tutors educate young Walter, and I couldn't be more delighted to relate that he's taken on a similar academic and creative bent to his father. A nanny, too, was hired on, to assist Mary with the rearing of the infant that she'd so complimentarily named Foster. Whichever Sire consigned to that accursed and evil-saturated second floor of the Hilman House had actually fathered the child, it mattered not. *I* was now the infant's father, and it was a station in life I felt blessed to have.

Hence . . .

Happily ever after, as the old cliche goes. Except, perhaps, for the nights, where I sleep less than soundly with my Colt Hammerless beneath my pillow and find myself rising at odd hours to scan the all-encompassing scrubland with my field glasses and to check on the night-guards to satisfy myself than no unmentionable marauders had surprised them under the cover of darkness . . .

Mary is pregnant again, in her sixth month, the doctor estimates. My celibacy had ended quite passionately on our wedding night, and her zeal for my body as well as my love only gives me cause to thank God all the more for such a blessing. But this, dear reader, subsumes my only potential calamity.

You'll likely be asking yourself what could possibly be deemed *calamitous* about wedlock in the eyes of God and the sequent wonder of the miraculous union which brings forth new life.

At the very least, I'm reckoning it quite well, I believe. You see, it wasn't until after our marriage that Mary, with quite a bit of trepidation, admitted that only minutes after having given birth to Foster—and whilst Walter and I were out fetching Onderdonk's truck—her genetically deranged stepfather had raped her quite fastidiously. But whether it was my own seed that impregnated her or the tainted seed of that crossbred thing . . .

Only time will tell.

TROLLEY NO. 1852

Providence, Rhode Island
1934

I**T WAS THE** spectral hump of Federal Hill that held the solitary man's gaze in capture, as oft it did, whene're he took to his work-desk in hopes of a Muse's whisper. The westward panes framed this inexpressible sight, which rose two miles distant and, for reasons the lean, stoop-shouldered man could not explicate, beguiled his aesthetic senses as if to whelm them most utterly. Near dead-center of the roof-crowned rise stood the blackly bedrabbed hulk of St. John's Church, whose cold Gothic revival windows seemed to stare back at his gaze in a knowing despair. The man felt certain that one day this morbid and singularly sinister edifice would ignite the fuse of a new tale, yet as so often happens to the creatively inclined, there could be no tale without an accommodating catalyst.

The same could be said of his present scribbling, cursorily entitled "The Thing in the Moonlight," not a tale of itself but some rather desultory notes for one. It gravitated around a salient and very haunting image that had stricken him in a dream not far agone: a decrepit trolley-car rusting on its iron rails, slack power wires hanging overhead like dead umbilici. Ill-hued yellow paint mouldered around the vestibuled car, a colour akin to jaundice. A black and rather faded stencil identified the vehicle: *No. 1852.*

This dream-image disconcerted the man to no end, that and the image of the car's motorman, who turned in shifting moonlight to display a heinous face that was nothing but a white fleshy cone tapering snout-like to a single blood-red tentacle . . .

Like the Gothic pile of the church, the blear-eyed man yearned to harness this image and then rein it in to a tale of weird substantiality. But, lo, he knew without the proper catalyst, it would never be more than a page of fallow cacography. Such was the curse of a poor and aging scribe.

However, the door-slat's clatter alerted him to the arrival of the day's post, and instead of a nettlesome bill or—his worst fear—an eviction, he found a manila envelope awaiting. The upper-left corner bore no name but just a New York City address. From inside, his long, thin fingers extracted a handsomely designed if not suspiciously suggestive magazine. Eloquent letters spelled its uncanny epithet *EROTESQUE* and a sub-heading: *Tales for the Selectively Bizarre.* A woodcut, quite byzantine in its elaborateness, comprised the cover in a style that seemed reminiscent of Frank Utpatel.

The *style*, he observed, yet hardly the content.

The woodcut shewed what—after a studied glance— could only be the silhouette of a winnowy, well-busted woman, undeniably nude and pruriently posed.

A neatly typed cover-letter read as thus:

Dear Mr. Lovecraft:

Forgive the intrusion of this unsolicited invitation. EROTESQUE is a privately- circulated periodical offering fictional fare of the most outre, iconoclastic, and unrepresentative, with eroticism as the central motif. Our readership demands sexually inspired fiction by the very best and most innovative authors of the day— authors such as yourself. Tales incorporating supernaturalism, experimental, da-da, alternate-history, and anti- authoritarian are most encouraged. Should you accept our offer, you will need to furnish a double-spaced typescript of no less than seven thousand words.

You need not worry about the potential controversy of your work appearing in a publication such as EROTESQUE (nor any attendant censorship ramifications); your contribution will be published pseudonymously, and we keep all pseudonyms under the most severe confidentiality. You may be surprised by how many of your peers publish with us on a regular basis.

We pay well above the industry standard; likewise, we understand that authors of your admired caliber need not "audition" for inclusion, which is why we make the first-half payment in ADVANCE. Please find the enclosed cheque for $500.00. A second cheque for an identical sum will be rendered upon delivery of the ms. There is no deadline.

Should you not be interested, or are too pressed by your busy publishing schedule, simply return the cheque in the also-enclosed self-addressed, stamped envelope and accept our thanks for your consideration.

We here at EROTESQUE would be honoured to have your preeminent work in our pages.

Cordially,
F. Wilcox

It would be superfluous to convey the extent of the writer's surprise and exuberance. With a $500 draft in hand and another promised upon delivery? These sums singularly exceeded any in this poor scribe's professional history!

With all that filthy lucre? he pondered. *I could pay the rest of my aunt's hospital bill AND cover our rent for a year!* When the offer's full weight sunk in, he actually shouted out a hackneyed and very ebullient, "Oh my God!"

He visibly trembled, then, when he sat down to read . . .

The magazine, as was manifest, existed for subversive readers indeed. The man found the tales therein professionally rendered, adroitly and engagingly plotted, and flamboyantly conceived; however, it could not be denied. They were pornographic. Hence, the periodical's "private" circulation, for fiction such as this would be deemed illegal most anywhere. Desperate as he was for finances (this past winter he'd never been closer to the bread-line) he had to make the self-admission that he hardly approved of pornography; yet on the other hand . . . *Who am I to make judgments?* A violation of the law? More than likely. But he had to admit also that most of the contents of *Erotesque* displayed works of notable craft and fascinating imagery (however lewd that imagery may have been), and he had to admit likewise that the reading's wake left him aroused in a most primal and unmentionable manner—hence, the effect of the skills of the contributors. How quickly he decided to accept the offer he could not consciously say. Would he be prostituting his wee talents for money? Quite emphatically, he told himself, *No.* He saw this offer as a challenge, and no writer worth his salt ever turned down a challenge . . .

This was all ballyhoo, of course, a cheap rationalisation. The writer had no verve to write pornography, but he *needed the money,* damn it, and he was so tired of eating cold beans and week-old cheese!

So . . .

He thought the following soliloquy: *In my life of staggering travail, I've suffered humiliations and failures untold. Hectored as a child, forced to wear girls' smocks until the age of eight, socially stifled such that I was unable to graduate high school . . . For pittances, I've ghost-written for dolts and stoked their vain egos by allowing them to put their names on my prose and poetry. I bungled my way to termination as a door-to-door salesman, and I stuffed envelopes for mere pennies. I've stood like a lackwit drone in an unheated cubby selling movie tickets to snide, chuckling human vermin. Now, at the least, I would be something much of note:*

A pornographer!

But before he would scruple to live up to this F. Wilcox's adulatory opinion of his talents, he hunted through his fairly recent New York City telephone directory (which he kept on hand due to his frequent journeys there); naturally, there was no listing for *Erotesque* in the business segment; however . . .

Amongst the long string of Wilcoxes, he was encouraged to find a listing for a Wilcox, Frederick, at the same address as on the envelope. It made some sense that a publication of ribald literature would not have an official office, opting instead for the editor's home residence. He stroked his over-protuberant chin, thinking, *I suppose I could call Mr. Wilcox from the telephone at the boarding house across the way* . . . but a second's contemplation deemed the action unnecessary. Instead came the resolve, *My writing is cut out for me* . . . and what an energizing resolve it was!

Ah, but then exactly *what* would he write?

He'd already selected his *nom de plume;* it would be Winfield (his father's first name) Greene (his former wife's maiden name, which seemed splendidly appropriate for the author of pornography. The woman had been insatiable! She would impale herself on his groin in his sleep as though he were some nocturnal vending machine for her pleasure!). His tale's plot, though, was something else. Forcing conscious thought upon a creative target, he'd long learned, always resulted in an abject uselessness that drained the artist's confidence. He took to the streets, then, to stroll as he frequently did and hope that Mr. Freud's *sub*conscious might offer assistance. Some assistance, too, from Dante's Ladies of the Heavenly Spring might then soon follow, or so he aspired. No sooner had he turned down Benefit than some inklings began to kindle. There could be no utility whatever of his "Great Old Ones"—to do so would rupture the tale's pseudonymity!—but he could most appropriately re-apparel what his friend Little Belknap once called his "Cthulhuean Arena" with new garments of occultism. This ploy would not only camouflage the author's identity—and, hence, leave his personal repute uninjured—but also allow him to flex unused aesthetic muscles. As he usually did, he would create a protagonist who mirrored aspects of himself but then plunge him headlong into a most *un*usual concupiscent peril.

He chuckled—an annoying, high-pitched chuckle.

What fun the endeavor suddenly seemed!

Ah, but his success would demand more than an energized endeavor. *Blast! I need an idea!*

The generous bank cheque would take over a week to be honoured, but he did have a dollar or so on his person, and given that this was, of sorts, a celebration, he would so celebrate by rewarding his good fortune with a can of Heinz beans—quite satisfiable cold, he could tell you—and a can of Postum pre-ground coffee. (The other brands tasted like a cacodaemon's bile! *Ugh!*) So into the little Weybosset's shop he ventured, and made his purchases with pennies to spare from the shrewd-faced proprietor (quite a disestablishmentarian), who was blaming the government for the sudden rise of gasoline to seven cents per gallon and gold to nineteen dollars per ounce.

He smiled in silence with a nod and took his parcels just as a dour but well-attired man on the corpulent side stepped up and passed the rankled proprietor what looked like a pharmaceutical prescription, for there was a small apothecarium.

TROLLEY NO. 1852

The proprietor scowled, disappeared into the back, then returned momentarily with what was undeniably a package of barrier prophylactics. He could even read the name-brand: GOODYEAR & HANCOCK—VULCANIZED CONTRACEPTIVE SHEATHS. The buyer seemed embarrassed to make this purchase and appeared doubly unnerved by the writer's presence as witness.

Though there was endless government talk of repealing the fifty-year-old Comstock Act (which banned the sale of these nefarious devices), he was heedlessly opposed to such a repeal. Violations were deemed a federal offense and carried a punishment—quite rightly, in his estimation—of five years imprisonment and hard labor. After losing so many young men in the Great War and then a half-million more souls—oddly, mostly men—in the ghoulish Spanish Flu Epidemic, what was more ghastly than *encouraging* lustful hedonists to perpetrate their carnal traffic without any responsibility whatever? Certainly, America's strength came through the hard work and innovation of its *people,* and circumventing necessary new births in the interest of bed-play seemed a howling affront to not only logic but a central morality. By law, these things, sometimes called "condoms" or, in the vernacular, "skins," were only to be used by couples properly wedded for either the prevention of a pre-existing disease or to allow normal sexual congress between the husband and a wife likely to suffer medical complications in the event of pregnancy.

The embarrassed customer, after paying for his package, hurried his bulk toward the exit, but not before the vociferous proprietor called out, "Don't you be using those on any of them harlots out there, man! It's against the law! And them dirty women are full up with poxes that dissolve those things!"

The buyer couldn't have left in any more haste.

Next, the proprietor turned his scowl to the stooped writer. "You agree with me, don't'cha, mister?"

"Indubitably," he replied and left.

This, he was saddened to prehend, was what the "cracker barrels" of the good old days had become—unpleasant and often hostile rants. Confrontations were not his forte. But the proprietor could not be accused of exaggeration on one count: the gradually rising number of "harlots" plying their trade on these once-fine avenues. Back on the street, as the sinking sun commenced to flame across the roof-pocked horizon, he beheld the rancorous man's meaning. Visible at several corners loitered women of the illest repute, drab-faced and gaudily dressed waifs with hungry eyes. These pestilent and immoral urchins had grown in number to a dejecting degree, it seemed. Victims of President Hoover's economic failures or simply female loafers looking for easy earnings, he struggled not to judge. One thin, bonneted creature with a vulpine grin beckoned him with her finger to cross the road. He did not oblige, of course; then another, brazenly brassiereless and sashaying in the uncomplimentary look of a Flapper, slowed her gait as she passed and asked if he had a dollar for some of her company.

He assured her he did not.

Where are the constables when you need them!

As he stood in wait at the corner for several motors to putter by, he heard a trolley's bell clanging several blocks over, and then . . .

Then . . .

The moment strangely seized him. He stood immobile; a fugue seemed to drone in his head, much akin to the mad flute-pipings of his messenger-demigod Nyarlathotep; and all his powers of conjecture and mental function stalled in what could only be called utter aposiopesis . . .

Barrier prophylactics, the words thudded in his head, and then—

The toll of a distant trolley bell. Then—

Prostitutes . . .

These three images (two visual, one aural) shivered in

his mind and gave root to an unmediated joyousness that caused him to actually shiver in place.

Why? you may ask.

They provided the creative lightning bolt so yearned for and so rare in a writer's life. These individual images lay in his hands, the *catalyst* he'd been so desperately struggling for.

And it was in that irreducible division of a second that Howard Lovecraft had his story for Mr. Frederick Wilcox and the clandestine periodical known as *Erotesque.*

Within minutes, he was back in his chamber, coffee on and pen in hand, writing his new tale . . .

TROLLEY NO. 1852

by Winfield Greene

(I)

MY NAME IS Morgan Phillips, and I am recounting this experience in hopes that, by doing so, I might unburden my mind—and whatever beneficent memories I have left—of some of the venomous and imponderable images which stalk me ever still . . .

. . . for however long the earth shall last.

My relocation to New York (that denizen-abyss of stridence and foul smells) had been by necessity and not—I re-emphasize, *not*—due to the divestment of my position at Brown, as a professor of mythology and ancient histories, two years ago. The latter had been the work of this bungling and greed-induced calamity they are now calling the "Great Depression," whose attendant turmoil left no room for teachers of subjectivities. Only academicians skilled in mathematics, industry, and the sciences could be retained in such troubled times of bread lines and twenty-five-percent jobless rates. For the rest of us (history, literature, the arts), the coffers of higher learning were closed.

Instead, I ventured hither, to this mephitic necropolis of concrete, dirt, and clamour, in the steadfast hope of ascertaining the whereabouts of my sister and only sibling,

Selina, who'd relocated here some five years ago for a $14-per-week accounting position with the well-known Monroe Clothiers chain. She would be twenty-eight now (seven years my junior), and with her youth had come the zeal of wanderlust. "I want *new* horizons, Morgan," she'd implored five years afore with her over-bright eyes and buoyant enthusiasm. "*New* places to see and *new* people to meet, and *don't worry,* I'll write you every week!" So she had, for three years, until her unforeboding and quite energetic missives in the post had dropped off all at once in an eerie silence. Either Fate or the god Selina believed in but I did not had seen fit to parallel my sister's disappearance, nearly to the day, with my own woeful dismissal from Brown. I took the ten-six, with no hesitancy whatever, to Penn Station and have been here ever since.

Or at least, in a *sense* . . .

It was in stifled shock that I first beheld this labyrinthine canyon of crime and leering, stubbled faces; shock that palsied my gait and numbed my mind—a seething urban *mass* of filthily attired bodies of clearly all ancestries save for the Anglican, bodies that moved shiftily through garbage-heaped streets pressed on either side by grimy concrete towers so spiring as to obfuscate the light of day—indeed, a noisome Babel of movement, ill-will, and malodour, of sweat-shined foreheads and menacing scowls. Squalid ghettoblocks stretched shabbily betwixt skyscrapers too dizzying to look upward at; and the smell— the unsurceasing and absolutely maleficent *smell*—which imbued itself in my clothes and, I often suspected, my very pores. This—city—was not for my sensitive kind, but circumstances offered me little choice. I scrupled at once to take my place in the human *crush* so erroneously named for James II, the Duke of York, lest I be swallowed whole by its incogitable machinations.

That *Selina* had been so swallowed remained my most teeming fear.

Degradation after degradation pursued me posthaste—

things I cannot, must not recount. Here, squalor and hatred reigned supreme, for if the flume-like streets proved this evil urban pustule's veins, then surely the ignoble masses served as its blood. I will not say how my first pitiable meals came to my mouth, nor how oft misfortune nearly left me bloodied and broken-boned by mongrel hoodlums in nighted alleyways.

But my bounden duty to find Selina steeled my perseverance. Amid the stinking crowds of pick-pockets and fugitives, and amongst cramped, sunless thoroughfares sided by drear-paned walls zigzagged by clattery iron fire-escapes, I travailed first to secure 30-cent-per-hour employment at a reformed scrivenry, and an unutterably pestiferous "room" on 28th Street for a half-dollar a day.

Time acclimated me to most of my inner horrors and my loath for what I could only metaphor as the societal elephantiasis in which I lived. Selina's rescue, in the very least as my strained mind envisioned it, was all that gave me the will to forge on. I fared well at my new post (a man of erudition? A university professor?) and rose up the few ladders of advancement that were extant, whereas I soon was promoted to night-office manager, whose undesirable hours rewarded me with a modest pay increment. The enterprise, namely Bartleby & Sons, L.T.D., occupied the top floor of a rather Dickensian building that harkened from the middle of the Nineteenth Century, in the lower "meat-packers" borough. Of course, they'd long-since refitted materially with modern typing-machines (chiefly, Remington Model Ones, on which I'd grown adroit at Brown) and, more recently, curious devices of almost supernatural capability, called Mimeographs. My status quickly charged me with the overwatch of the night-staff: all stalwart men and women possessed of acceptable typing skills and an accurate eye, who'd been discarded from better posts by the all-pervading economic gloom. It was, for the most part, elder holographed documents of financial and governmental importance that we were charged with transcribing, from seven o'clock in evening to three thirty or so in the morn.

As for Selina, however . . .

It necessitated less than a week's time to discern that the illustrious Monroe Clothiers chain was illustrious no more; the abrupt sign on the front doors announced that the enterprise had gone on "Holiday" much the same way as most banking institutions—in a more accurate manner of speaking: bankrupt, and all employees let go. Worse than that by far, however, was my horror in learning that Selina's apartment building in the West Side had burned to the ground; though I was relieved to be informed by the New York Office of Public Safety that no deaths or injuries had been reported.

Next, my forlorn sojourn through the mephitis piloted me to the local police precinct's Missing Persons Bureau. Here, to my abject despair, I was informed that said bureau was no longer operational due to budget decreases and the simple unserviceability of such a function. "You got any idea how many people 'disappear' with the economy the way it is?" my complaint was chastised by a surly sergeant at the desk. "Well, do ya, bub?" Ultimately, of course, I could comprehend his point; in such dismal economic times, people moved on to unknown pastures they hoped would be greener but oft were not. *But Selina would've written me had she elected to relocate,* I knew full well. The granite-faced sergeant was unkind enough to add an acerbic statistical datum: "Lots'a women have took to sellin' thereselfs, ya know. What else they got when there's no jobs and bread's up to a dime'a half-loaf?" Then, another datum: "Oh, and, bub? You do know that the murder and suicide rate's doubled since the Crash in '29, don't ya?"

When not tending my duties at the scrivenry, then, I walked . . .

Walked, I say, through every chasm, byway, and alley

in vicinity to Selina's former home and place of employment; walked through the harrowing and ill-scented masses—that loathly, dead-faced human sprawl—thrusting forward my only photograph of Selina to random passersby and shop-keepers, coppers and vagrants alike, refugees and natural-born citizens—indeed, *anyone,* with the plea hot in my voice, "Have you seen this woman?"

None had.

When I'd covered the most logical geographical propinquities, an absence of alternatives forced me to proceed in depressingly widening radii. First, what remained of Manhattan, then Queens, the Bronx, then ghastly Flatbush and the horrendous Brooklyn and its appalling appendage Red Hook, full of leaning tenements and unrestrained hooliganism; Staten Island and its waves of cretins, then across the blackly gushing Hudson to Hoboken, Union City, and beyond. All, all to no avail. In no time, however, I became deft in all modes of travel (ferries, trolleys, motor-carriages) and, during my scouring of the stolid, grey Brooklyn borough, even traveled in the impossible underground trains that had commenced in 1904, in particular this BRT Line and then the reeking, flesh-packed 9th Avenue Line—these being deafening, subterrene contraptions they now called the Subway.

It was all I lived for, for I had nothing else: my indefatigable certainty that somewhere, out thither in this once fecund and beauteous Ilse of Manna-hata that the White Man had paved over with modern horrors called Progress, below the once-resplendent pristine-blue sky now soiled by hostile chatter and coal-smoke; *somewhere* amid all of this, Selina still lived and breathed.

Somewhere.

And though we're taught in our youth of the virtue of tenaciousness and faith (indeed, the very *Godliness* of it), I found instead of solace a soul-poisoning and ever-cresting cynicism that more and more graduated to outright nihilism. I became convinced that Nietzsche's chief tenet seethed in undeniability, that there was no objective basis for truth. Here I was, standing in the middle of that pestilent, dirty-handed verity, the summation of all that mankind has risen to in multiple-millennia of evolvement; yes, yes, *this:* human feces in the open street; the vomit of vagabonds filling gutters like abscessed, putrid evil rainwater; women so bereft of morality (and men too) that they'd sell their sex for a half-dollar, a dime, even a nickel; blood turning brown on unending concrete walls; thugs beating the maimed and the elderly for pittances in raging daylight; police turning quickly away from those most in need; one alley after the next, urine-imbued and clogged like demon-dens with cadaverously thin addicts puffing blank-eyed on opium or even injecting narcotics into their bodies through their veins; rats, rats, *droves* of them; and the lines and the lines and the lines of the dirty and the wretched and the sin-stained. Indeed, the pinnacle of mankind's knowledge and endeavor for ten-thousand years; this ghastly, irrevocable *horror.*

Too often I mused that if the stone-faced sergeant were abstractly correct, and that my faultless sister had reached the psychic saturation-point and succumbed to self-annihilation, I, too, might well soon follow.

Days of useless searches bled into smoke-sullied gloaming, for another night of monotonous labor which, after interminable hours, would then bleed back into days of more useless searches. I'd ride grim trolleys and wretch-piloted coaches, scouring every passing flinty face and scowling countenance in the dead hope that one would be Selina; walked soles off my very shoes searching still more, only to be rewarded by slipping on a bum's blood-marbled sputum or being bumped, shoved, and cursed at in a dozen hateful dialects by scores of hateful faces. Even the churches closed their doors to the uncontainable throng . . . God, indeed. What true *god* could turn his back on a woman as goodly as my sister and allow her to be sucked up, swallowed, and digested into this irredeemable abyss of stench, cacophony, and illicitness? How could any "Supreme Being" exist so coldly and unconscionably as to relinquish kind and life-praising souls as Selina to this metropolic spittoon of human wretchedness? Where eyes in my beloved and stately Providence shined in hope and kindredship, hither they only glimmered dully in turpitude and greed.

After two long years, then, my spirit was all but done. Evening time closed over me like a casket's lid, where then I labored in my cubby till my fingers raged in pain, only to know that the coming dawn would bring no surcease. Day after day, the clocks ticked in a semblance to dripping blood, and I felt as though my soul had metamorphosed to the blackest sand, spilling ever away through some morbid existential hour-glass that had no bottom.

When I slept, I dreamt of the hangman's noose.

At my place of employ, I took care to befriend no one but instead oversaw the nightly duties of all with a stolid, vigilant face; anything less would be fraternisation and hence unprofessional. On the same hand, my deflated spirit left me in no desire for comradeship. There was one soul, though, with whom I did feel something of a connexion: the sullen building's custodian, Robert Erwin. Thirtyish, I'd estimate, a great ox of a man yet amiably demeanoured, Erwin (brief after-work chats and the shared walk to the B-Line trolleys) would most often leave me uplifted via even his most stray comments. Many were the occasions when his simple positivities left me prickly with guilt, for here was a man who never had anything less than a smile to offer, even after having lost his wife to a malignancy, then one daughter to tuberculosis and a second to murderers.

"You can be sure, Mr. Phillips," he regarded me once, "that every day I wake up and the sun's still shinin' and the world's still turnin', and I've got a job when millions of others don't—*that's* a day to give thanks for. You see, Mr.

Phillips, every day is a celebration . . . " The tenor of his voice left no denying his conviction, while most days I stewed in sentiments opposite, becoming poisoned now by my own misanthropy and self-inflicted gloom. We both lived in the district's west end—hence our sharing the B-Line. "Truly it's a great God that can see fit to shine His light on me," he said once. "You're a religious man, I take it?" came my dark question, but he answered, "Not religious enough, but I don't s'pose anyone can be, not tainted as we are by Original Sin. All we can do is repent, right? We're all human bein's and we're all sinners. Yet God gives me my job and my beatin' heart, and you too! So I do my best to give Him my faith."

Such evangelical spouts I tried to avoid, yet something about his soft-spokeness, still, made me heed the words in spite of my resolute *dis*belief in his god. How could I, with my righteous sister likely dead?

But conversely . . . how could *he,* in all his tumultuous loss?

On the night in question, Erwin and I chatted innocuously after-shift as we walked to the trolley-stop. Somewhere unseen, an old iron-striker bell tolled four a.m., a plaintive, dismal sound. At this hour, as was usual, the ill-litten streets looked abandoned, and no rabble-rousers or "rummies," as they were called, were afoot, which always relieved me. A silence that seemed nervous, though, held dominion within the foetid air that hung between the leaning, rust-streaked edifices on either side. It had been a grueling shift, with my company's transcription quota rising to defray incremental costs. Erwin, likewise, had been passed over for a modest raise, for synonymous reasons. I couldn't help but poke some implied fun: "Could it be that your god's light isn't shining brightly as it once did?"

With a scoff, he replied, "Brighter! Are you kidding? Neither of us, Mr. Phillips, got cause to complain. Did you know that in Russia, they don't make but a nickel a day?"

I should've known! More of his positivity.

"But, you know," he continued, "I got to admit, maybe I didn't get that raise 'cos I'm bein' punished. God's way of reminding me who's boss."

"Punishment?" I questioned as we stood beneath a bleak town-gas lamp at the stop. "You're about as free of error as anyone I've met."

The pallored gas-light seemed to drain his ever-optimistic expression. "I can't be a hypocrite, Mr. Phillips. I've done my share'a sinnin'—always been sorry afterward, but still . . . Been thinkin' about it lately, to tell ya the truth."

I laughed aloud on the nighted, trash-strewn street. "Really, now? So if I may ask," I mocked, "what *grand sin* have you been contemplating?"

His seriousness, tinged by guilt, did not waver. "Sins of the flesh. What else?"

He must mean either salooning or whore-mongering, two activities I'd never partaken in. But I maintained my good-hearted chastisement. "Succumbing to the desires that your Creator gave you? Surely, Mr. Erwin, your god can't be so disingenuous as to refuse to forgive *that*."

"Oh, He forgives it—the pastor says so—but only to those *worthy* of His forgiveness."

"And how on Earth does one gauge *worthiness*?"

Suddenly, he looked lost. "I don't know."

But his words had me thinking, not his words of forgiveness from sin but his *implications*. "So you mean you frequent the speakeasies, Mr. Erwin? The rot-gut some of those places pass off as illicit liquor can make one blind's what I've heard. Only days ago, I read of one such den that served up devilish bad rum, and several died. There's that risk, compounded by the simple risk of being caught by violating the laws of the Eighteenth Amendment. Federal men are all over the city, I hear."

"Oh, I don't mean speakeasies, Mr. Phillips," and then he gulped. "Spirits are a vile polluter of the God-given human body. What I'm talking about . . . are the Red Houses . . . "

I nodded while keeping reins on my personal disapproval of such iniquitous havens. Though I recognised immorality when I saw it, I was also thoughtful enough to refrain from judgments, and I could even compel myself to overlook Erwin's obvious hypocrisy: the stalwart Christian but one tainted by a weakness for ladies of the night. Of my own case, I'll say that so-called sexual congress caused me to harken back to the wise quip of Lord Halifax: "The price is damnable, the pleasure is momentary, and the position is ridiculous," which bespoke my views as well. I myself had thankfully never suffered from a high state of libidiny, but I could hardly condemn others affected by more heightened—and notably *normal*—states. How was a good man such as Erwin expected to satisfy his natural primordial drives with a wife long dead? At last, I commented, "I must say, I can hardly picture a moral man as yourself frequenting such places."

"I can't say I frequent them, Mr. Phillips." He shifted his stance within the feeble shelter. "In fact, I've only been to one particular house ever, and only three times total."

It was not even a conscious thing that so grotesquely piqued my interest; it was the inundating pragmatism stoked instead by *unconscious* considerations. I was prepared to accept *any* circumstance that might lend credence to my hope that Selina was still alive. The unkindly booking sergeant's words creaked back like old ship timbers in my memory: *Lots'a women have took to sellin' thereselfs, ya know* . . . Had such a demeaning fate been my sister's lot? Certainly she was well-figured enough to be viable for such a trade, her figure, yes, and, most notably, her bosom. I only hoped that this might actually be, for if it were, it meant that she'd still be among the living and hence retrievable.

A sudden surge in the coal-gas intensified the streetlamp's brightness just as the idea had surged in my mind: *I could go to this brothel . . . and investigate . . .* Indeed, and not that I suspected Selina might work in this *particular* bordello, but surely there stood a more-than-minute chance that some of the women therein had seen or even knew of her. I could show my picture around whilst maintaining the appearance of a "john," as I believed the suitors of prostitution were called.

For the first time in months, I had hope!

But, lo, even as the trove of my hope may have just trebled, simple realities proved another matter. Came my whisper, "I'd be interested in attending this 'Red House' with you, Mr. Erwin, but I'm afraid I've precious little money for such indulgences." My fingers fished through stray coins in my pocket. "How, uh, how much would be requisite on my part for, say, minimal services?"

Erwin's face loosened in a manner of relief. "Thank you for not disowning our friendship, Mr. Phillips. I thought sure you'd think me a cad for admitting this—"

"Not at all. We all have our occasions for urges oft beyond our force of will. But, hear me. How *much* will I need?"

He paused at the distant bay of a foghorn from the harbour, a seemingly unearthly dirge of murky, falling notes; but when it passed, he answered, "Well, the place I've been to, it's called the 1852 Club, and it's a strange place, I've got to say. You see—and you'll find this hard to believe—it's *free*."

I eyed him in the wavering pallor of gas-light. "Did I hear you right? Free?"

"It's free, all right, Mr. Phillips," he assured in a whisper. "I been there three times, like I said, and haven't spent a penny."

How could I not scoff now? I argued, "That makes no sense whatever. Any commercial enterprise, licit or illicit, exists through the conduction of services or merchandise rendered in the exchange of some monetary source! A bordello that doesn't charge for the services of its women would be the uttermost negation of logic."

"You'll get no argument from me, Mr. Phillips." He maintained his whisper as if in fear of being overheard on the vacant street. "I'm just tellin' ya how it is. I know it sounds like a tall tale but . . ." and then all he did was shrug.

A tall tale, yes, but I trusted in my judgment of men to be convinced that Erwin was no such teller. "Well," I said next. "Where exactly is this 1852 Club located?"

Erwin spread out his hands. "To tell you the truth, I'm not sure. Sometimes, I think it must be near Old Greenwich, and other times, it seems it must be Lower East. It's the trolley that takes us, see—maybe a ten-, fifteen-minute trip, but the *route* . . ."

"What about the route?" I insisted.

"It's all this way and that, and up and down, and through alleys I never seen before. It moves through these courtyards that look so *old,* and, and . . . Even a tunnel, where there's no light at all. Gettin' on by mistake one night's how I even found out about the place."

"That's very . . . strange," I uttered.

"Well, like I first mentioned, it's a strange place." Suddenly, he looked dreamy even in the smudged darkness. "The women, Mr. Phillips, it's just one looker after the next, and they don't wear nothin' about the house, I ain't kiddin' ya." His whisper grew heated. "And they do *anything* and'll have ya as many times as you can go."

"All, as you ensure, for nothing," I reiterated.

"For nary a red cent."

By now, the proposition seemed farcical, but I simply refused to believe Erwin would lie so cockamamily. "In that case, I'd like very much to join you tonight."

He seemed to shudder. "I just feel so . . . guilty, Mr. Phillips—"

"Oh, for goodness sake!" I complained. "*Guilty?*"

"It's hard enough staying on a Godly course, and I *do* try, but sometimes . . . sometimes—" He shook his head in remorse. "It's been more than six months since I've . . . well, you know . . ."

Six MONTHS? I thought all too stridently. *It's been more than six YEARS for me!*

Erwin composed himself out of his conflicting sentiments. "I only do it when I *have* to, but I see I've brought you right along into it. Not only are *my* sins on my hands but *your* sins too."

I was losing patience now with the fulcrum on which Erwin's self-perceived "sin" teetered. But I *needed* him now. "I wouldn't worry about it, Erwin. Nature, just the same as your god, is what made us *men,* with the *natural proclivities* of men, so don't get yourself in a swivet. Now, when does the trolley come? Surely, it's not the B-Line—"

"No, no. And it doesn't come every night, but when it does"—he consulted his pocket-watch with a squint—"it would be very soon." Another diverting pause cruxed his expression. "But that's another thing 'bout this place, Mr. Phillips, another *strange* thing, I mean." He stared off into drab darkness. "Time."

"Time?"

"I don't know how to explain it"—he rubbed his brows—"but each and every time I been, it's seemed like I been there for *hours.* I could get on with three or four different girls too, and when I get out'a there, I think it's got to be noon at least . . . but then I look at my watch and it's scarcely four-thirty in the morning or quarter till five."

I staved off a chuckle, for Erwin was permitting his oblique sense of abstraction to supervene the much more primal reality that he must not be possessed of much sexual endurance! Then again, how much endurance would *I* be capable of given the sheer infrequency of my own sexual experience? *Laughably little,* I suspected, for so long ago it was that'd I'd been married.

Several more minutes passed, and my current hopes passed as well. The B-Line would be arriving shortly. "Drat," I said. "It appears that tonight's not our night, Mr. Erwin," but no sooner had I spoken the words than Erwin turned with an enthused lurch . . .

TROLLEY NO. 1852

At the end of the street, like something first semi-tangible slowly materializing from the dark's secret ether, a bulk shape began to form. Crackling sparks grew less dim (no doubt the sparks of electric transference from the ever-present power wires looping overhead), companioned by a faint and very ghostly circle of yellow light at the shape's forward-most area which made me think of a dying cyclopean eye. The squeal of bearings caught my ears, then the grate of an air-brake . . .

Erwin uttered, "This is it."

The vehicle's forward lamp shined so faint it scarcely served a purpose, but finally there came another surge of gas into the closest street-lamp, and this is when I got my first full glimpse.

It was an older-style trolley, opened all around in a vestibuled fashion (in other words, lacking windows), and was of the antiquated twin-car, double-truck type, whereas all city trolleys that I'd seen were single-carred. Flaking yellow paint, quite a murky yellow, covered all of the decrepit vehicle's side panels.

"This is most definitely *not* a city trolley," I muttered to Erwin.

"No, Mr. Phillips. It's a *private* trolley. It's not from the city transit system at all."

A *private* trolley . . .

At the forward car's head, I spied the motorman's station, little more than a cubby; the capped motorman himself stood scarcely moving at the controller handle. In the drear, his face looked dead-pan, bereft of life; indeed, the darkness reduced his eyes and mouth to black slits amid a waxen pallor. Above the frame of his look-out, the car's identification number could be seen in black-stencil letters: *No. 1852.*

The vehicle squealed to a halt. Erwin, in an excitement that seemed touched by fear, grabbed my arm and urged, "The conductor'll size you up cos you're new, but don't worry. He'll let you on since you're with me."

"Size me up?" I had to question.

"They don't let ruffians on."

"Oh." But in a city *aswarm* with ruffians and every other manner of human flotsam, the policy was to be expected. "But who enforces order, should the conductor mistakenly allow some roysterers aboard?"

"The motorman," Erwin answered in a whisper tense with unpleasantness. "I seen it happen once. Hobos, all riled with liquor, jumped on and started a ruckus, but the ruckus didn't last long."

"The motorman's something of a tough customer, I take it."

Erwin looked troubled. "Let's just say that them hobos are probably *still* in the hospital."

Oh, my, I thought.

"Come on!"

The overhead cable sparked and crackled. I followed Erwin up the sheet-metal steps of the first car, and in doing so, I noticed other silent riders sitting among the wooden cross-seats; however, the wee hour's dimness reduced their faces to smears of shadow. The metal floor *tapped* at coming footfalls: the boots of the conductor, a short but sure-footed figure, who approached directly, eyed Erwin with a nod, and waved him aboard. "This here's my friend," Erwin softly informed. "Not a trouble-making bone in his body, I can vouch for it . . . "

The conductor, like the driver, wore a regulation cap and heavy brass-buttoned jacket as was the fashion. He stared at me, or seemed to, for the car's irksome darkness forbade any details of his face, much in the same manner as the motorman. My skin crawled, however, in what I can only describe as a most abrupt accession of dread; for whatever unhealthful reason, I imagined I was being evaluated by either a mask of the most pallid parchment or the face of a dead man . . .

The moment locked in stasis.

"How do you do?" I bid with a bit of a stammer.

TROLLEY NO. 1852

The conductor waved me aboard, then returned with lugubrious steps back to the vicinity of the motorman's station.

Sparks burst overhead in a brilliant blossom, and then the trolley lurched once and commenced down the nearly lightless street.

Erwin showed me the way down the aisle; carefully, we stepped over the heavy-iron coupling and passed into the rear car. "We've got to keep our voices down," came his incessant whisper. "That's why I brung us back here." I could hardly object; we both took seats at the car's rearmost section.

As I sat, I stared, astonished, into the grim, nighted city. The trolley clattered along the rusted rails to traverse unknown streets of ballast-cobble and past cramped lay-bys of various municipal departments that seemed long out of service. Was it my suspicious fancy, or did each successive street-lamp put out less and less illumination? Brick facades and lichen-encrusted stone walls pressed ever inward; at one point, we crossed what I believe was Amsterdam Avenue, but as we did so, the sinister car rose to a clamour as the motorman increased speed, almost as if to pass through the dimly peopled intersection with as much haste as the motor would allow. Along this dismal way, we stopped on several occasions along similarly unfamiliar and quite ruinous corners to pick up additional passengers. As each boarder stepped up, he was assayed by the conductor for what I could only guess were traits of "approval": the smell of liquor on one's breath, loose talk, and perhaps even a subjective air of rowdiness would, of course, be disqualifiers. But as each man was allowed to come aboard, I noted quite readily that all possessed likewise bodily characteristics. These were all men of brawn and muscle, wide-shouldered, pillar-legged men of a solid working caste, much like Erwin. The only oddity to be admitted thus far was myself; with shoulders stooped, frail-bodied, and but 146 pounds, I hardly bore any commonality with these strong, ox-necked young men. (As a child, my mother perpetually referred to me as her "little waxbean." How complimentary . . .) But it was then the notion insinuated itself—in a manner I cannot explain by any substance—that the conductor was indeed "sizing up" potential visitors to the mysterious 1852 Club in hopes of selecting the most virile, the most sexually *potent* candidates. I couldn't imagine what might cause me to make such a conjecture. Two or three times, however, thinner and less-fecund-looking chaps were turned away. So . . .

Why on earth would a spindly-form such as myself be let aboard? Evidently, the club held much stock in Mr. Erwin's credulity.

The car clattered onward for a time, then—

We were swallowed into darkness.

It was a musty, dripping tunnel we'd darted into, whose arched walls were eerily webbed by the faintest luminescent fungi. When I turned to look Erwin full in the face, I could make no trace of him. Ahead, in the forward car, did a passenger gasp in sudden startlement?

"I told ya, Mr. Phillips. There be a tunnel or two." He chuckled nervously. "Hope you're not one to be afraid of the dark."

"I daresay even a man of the stoutest heart might be timid in darkness this complete," said I, looking around but seeing essentially nothing save for the foxfire-like etchings. "This is a queer trek indeed."

"It's worth it, though." He tugged my sleeve just to give me a bearing. "Remember what I said—the women are *lookers*."

"Yes," I grated.

"Best-looking one of 'em all is the madam—Miss Aheb—though she don't, you know, turn a trick herself. I only seen her once but . . . her *body* . . . It's enough to make a man bay at the moon."

A cruel trust on my part but I couldn't help but rib my

"Christian" friend about his continuing hypocrisy. "By perfect, I'm certain you mean that all that God creates is perfect and therefore exists in a totality of beauty, eh, Erwin? You couldn't even remotely be founding your observation upon the venal sin of lust . . . "

Erwin said nothing in response until I assured him I was joking.

"Very funny, Mr. Phillips."

I chuckled over several rude bumps in the rail. "But, excuse me, Erwin, did you say the 'madam' of the club goes by the name of *Aheb*?"

"Yes, a furren name, I s'pose."

Furren? I pondered, then, *Ah, he means foreign.* "It's actually Egyptian and . . . " I paused in the clattering dark. "Almost sinister . . . "

I could sense him peering at me. "Sinister? You should *see* her, man. Ain't nothin' sinister about her. She's *beautiful.*"

"So you've said. It's simply the name," I related. "As you know, I was once a professor of history, but my most refined field of study was that of secret ancient mythologies. I'm referring to the mythological queen of a pre-dynastic Egyptian culture known as the Ahebites, whose cryptic ruler was a notorious witch-priestess called Isimah el-*Aheb*. We're talking circa 5000 B.C., Erwin, which pre-dates the first official hieroglyphs by over fifteen hundred years. The story of Aheb, though very obscure, was similar to the mythologies of ancient Greece—Homer's *Iliad,* for instance, or the legends of Zeus and Poseidon— only rather than portraying the conquest of good over evil, we find quite the opposite—*fictions,* I mean, written either to entertain or to fabulise the inception of humankind." I raised my finger in utter dark. "Ah, but there are always those who attest that certain fables aren't fables at all but *fact.*"

This, of course, I in no way believed, but the mythology at large was one that had long held my interest. Whose interest it was *not* holding, however, was that of Erwin, who merely replied to my dissertation with an unemphatic "Oh, uh, really?"

I needed to put the pedantry of my bygone university days behind me; after all, I was a man on his way to a whorehouse. Common working folk such as Erwin would not be roused in the least by such an arcane mythos. It was merely curious, though, the name of this "madam": Aheb. How could it *not* cause me to reflect upon those fascinating older-than-ancient myths which detailed the supernatural revel of the Ahebites and their sacrificial reverence to an immense commune of limbless gods hailed as the Pyramidiles? These hideous deities existed as but pallid hulks of flesh, never moving, only thinking, only *perceiving.* The Pyramidiles, yes. Their human agent upon the earth was the obscene sorceress Isimah el-Aheb, who had enspelled her people to bow down to these revolting cosmic abominations, paying homage to their nether-dimensional *bulk* by way of enfrenzied orgies and ravenous blood-baths, which in turn generated the psychical horror on which these gods so thrived; indeed, it was the carnally beauteous el-Aheb who orchestrated rampant earthly horror in veneration and to whom the Pyramidiles had blasphemously blessed with the gift of immortality via the sickish mold-green tincture that was but one of their wicked secrets. To her also they'd whispered their arcane manner of writing: a form of gematria, the substitution of numbers for letters. Once learned of all the Pyramidiles' harrowing secrets, el-Aheb ruled the ancient outlands, to slaughter, pillage, rape, and defile, all in the name of the Pyramidiles, who lived on realms not of this earth or even this solar system, but in the screaming upside-down crevices between space and time; indeed, the Pyramidiles, the Putrid-Flesh Gods, eyeless, brain-filled masses of otherworldly *organa,* each the size of a mountain and, suspiciously, the shape of a *pyramid* . . .

What an intriguing and ultimately macabre old legend!

TROLLEY NO. 1852

With more iron clatter and a swoosh, the previously unrelieved darkness broke—much to my commendation—as Trolley No. 1852 at last exited the deleterious tunnel and now roved down more dim, tenement-lined streets. Looking behind me, I noted that the overhead power-cables were no longer in evidence, and we seemed to be traveling along railways so long out of use that their heavy wooden ledgers had gone to rot. I could only assume that batteries now provided the trolley its propulsion, for how else could this be without the connexion of the overhead electricity cables?

"Almost there," Erwin whispered.

Through more stone archways the sullen car delved; archways in the most decrepit brick walls; block-rimmed *maws* agape and garlanded by sickly ivy. Next, we crept through a series of grotesque yet captivating courtyards of what could only be abandoned edifices, each bizarrely interconnected by narrower archways. This was the old city, no doubt, one of several urban nooks left to disrepair and rendered tenantless via the contagion of outside squalor and ruination; truly, we were traveling amid the very bowels of New York. Grainy wedges of moonlight cast a feeble pallor over all as broken statues watched the trolley from neglected sconces and rats scurried about fieldstone tiles and garbage-filled fountain basins. But it was in one of these eldritch inner-courtyards that the trolley suddenly slowed, jostled, then squealed to a stop . . .

I looked about, nearly at a loss for words. This courtyard stood in no less disintegration than the others: festooned by ivy, verminous with weeds. Rotten fabrics hung from the stone rails of second-, third-, and fourth-story verandas, while numerous once-fine marble statues stood armless, headless, and stained by lichens and bird-waste.

"What *is* this place, Erwin?" I whispered.

"This is it," he told me. "Don't be fooled by how it looks outside; I think they do it on purpose."

I could only imagine he meant a deliberate subterfuge was at hand, to throw off suspicions of the uninvited, for who would think that any desirous activity could possibly take place behind so unkempt and dismal a facade?

Erwin and I were the last in line as the passengers all stood up to file in utter silence off the car. When I happened a glance to my pocket-watch, I saw that it was 4:12 a.m. As the queue moved down the aisle, however, I took notice, first, of the trolley's position; it had stopped mid-yard, yet the rusted tracks continued forward to disappear beneath a great iron-beamed and rivet-studded door set solidly within yet another wide stone arch. Was it the shifting moonlight or my strained imagination that made me believe I saw traces of an oily, ill-coloured mist leaking through the door's seams? What I noticed next must've been still another trick of poor-light: my glimpse forward, past the slowly descending line of debarking passengers, threw my gaze onto the motionless form of the motorman, who remained in his piloting cubby, his broad back to us and his hand on the vehicle's controller handle—his *hand,* I say . . .

My stomach knotted.

His hand, though I only glimpsed it for a moment, appeared as no hand at all but a cluster of rather stout worms wrapped about the controller handle's end. Just as disturbing as the morphology of the hand was its *colour:* a bloodless white splotched with ill-toned green . . .

When a stiff chill passed, I realised it must either be dirtied utility gloves or some regrettable genetic malady.

The line dwindled; before I stepped off, my gaze felt preternaturally summoned to my left. There I spied the capped conductor staring right at me through the mask-like deadpan facial expression . . .

Gads!

I deboarded in haste and hurried up to Erwin, who was following the others in. A rotten wood-plank sign hung upon the transom of worm-eaten but iron-strapped door.

TROLLEY NO. 1852

The letters on the sign appeared branded in char: *1852 Club.*

Torches, not electric bulbs, lit an expansive and ornately decor'd atrium which borrowed much from the greater Georgian period; clearly, this place must once have been an exorbitant hotel. Swirling dark mosaic tile-work could be seen in the gaps between Old World throw rugs; a marble fountain gushed crystalline water through the mouth of a horned cherub. Pilastered walls surrounded all, while great winding staircases rose upward from each end, to the first of three splendidly railed stair-halls, which steeply overlooked the atrium below.

I allowed Erwin to take the lead; he and most of the others seemed nearly at home here, and all walked at once to a long, fringe-linened banquet table which sat heaped with fresh fruits and (much to *my* displeasure) ice-filled bins loaded with half-shelled oysters. It was to the latter that most of the men repaired, greedily slurping down the hideous, lumpen things one after another. As I most infrangibly *detested* all shellfish—most especially oysters, which made me think of grey phlegm—I made every attempt to appear at ease while sampling some tidbits of fruits and a glass of some superb vegetable juice. Eventually, to Erwin I whispered, "So . . . where are the, uh—"

"The girls? Before you know it," he promised with a guilty grin, "they'll be all about."

Only moments after he'd made this assurance, every face turned upward at the detection of svelte motion. Upon the fourth stair-hall my gaze held, on the stunning woman who'd just appeared: a raven-haired, Cleopatra-faced figure whose voluptuous curves and thrusting bosom were made even more pronounced by a diaphanous, black evening dress.

"That's her," Erwin sighed in awe. "Miss Aheb . . . "

Ensconced torches burned to either side as this shimmering *vision* of feminine beauty leaned over the carven rail and smiled. "Welcome, gentlemen, all of you," issued a lilting and vaguely accented voice. The words echoed. "Your presence is much appreciated, and as you will soon see, the very exclusive 1852 Club will do everything in its power to reward you for the privilege your esteemed presence . . . "

What an odd thing to announce . . . as denotations such as "esteemed" and "privileged" hardly described this lot of respectful yet otherwise brawny and likely not-well-educated working-classers. I struggled to identify the seductive woman's sweetly flowing accent; yet I'll admit that the mere sight of her compacted beauty filched my breath. There was something about her mien, her very *deportment.* Even at this precipitous distance, her physique's details seemed to gleam via some supernal clarity, as though an incorporeal magnifier hung invisibly before her: the poreless white valley of her bosom, the relief of the papillae of her magnificent breasts, the diamond-like sparkle of perfect teeth within the titillant smile—*all* of these traits seemed amalgamated into a single focus which left every man below speechless and irretrievably enraptured.

Erwin elbowed me. "What did I tell you, huh?"

"I'll confess," I said, still staring up, "that I dismissed your description earlier as the stuff of exaggeration, but now . . . I stand corrected."

Her voice swirled downward, a spiriferous aural wraith; and from the painfully seductrene lips, warm words flowed: "And now, my good and vital men, may you go forth in the natural pursuit of your pleasure, as is the gracious will of our benefactors . . . "

The room hushed in the lovely echo's wake . . . but I frowned. Even the clearly distracted Erwin seemed flummoxed by the words.

"What d'ya s'pose she means by that?" Erwin said in a wee voice.

Benefactors? I wondered. "You've got me. 'Natural

pursuit' notwithstanding, I sorely doubt that her reference to 'benefactors' can be a spiritual reference, nor a reference to the popular Judeo-Christian God, no, not in a whorehouse."

I paused to chuckle at my ever-guilt-ridden friend, but when I re-glanced upward?

Miss Aheb was gone.

A modest murmuring of approval rose in the room—at once—as a procession of over a dozen women moved soft-footedly down the curved, plushly carpeted staircase. I've already intimated that my own natural impulses with regard to sexual attraction must be relatively inactive compared to most men; yet, the registration of this drove of encroaching sprites (all without a stitch on, mind you) caused an undeniable stirring, shall we say, southwardly of the belt. The well-brawned patronage was already dispersing as this bevy of long-legged, high-bosomed, and pertly nippled women came off the stairs.

Erwin, a smile so long it contorted his face, made to approach them, but I clutched his sleeve in a sudden self-consciousness.

"Gads, Erwin! I've never been to a place like this before. What should I do?"

The question flabbergasted him. "Do? Come on! You pick a dish and go with her, man!" and then he walked briskly to the feminine congregation and its sea of wanton grins.

I remained, standing nervously and watching couples pair off. The girls seemed to swoop upon the men with a hearty enthusiasm; but, lo, none "swooped" toward me. Never much of a ladies' man, I expected as much; these younger and much more masculine specimens easily overshadowed my thin-limbed form. I would always tell myself that what manly attributes nature had left me lacking in was more than made up for in my superior intellectual capacity, but what a facile consolation that was now! In a whorehouse with no whore showing the least bit of interest in me! Erwin was latched on to and led summarily up the stairs by a doe-eyed, plushly curved girl with a head full of shining black tousles. *Good for you,* I thought with some bitterness. Within the merest of minutes, the men were arm in arm with each of these delectable women, whose bare bottoms I was left to peer forlornly at as they each in turn took their partners up the steps.

I felt akin to the perfect ass, but just as it seemed that all the denuded girls had found their match, my arm was snatched by a short, voracious thing with beaming green eyes and nary an ounce of excess fat on her splendid little body. "I've got you now!" she exclaimed and quickly hauled me toward the stairs. "My name's Ammi, but don't bother telling me yours. In a place like this?" and she laughed. The sight of her, and the feel of her hot hand about my wrist, left my tongue sufficiently tied. Instead, my eyes drunk up the vision of her gleaming white nudity; the compact buttocks flexing with each step up, the seductively trim waist and adorable bellybutton. Already my groin was tightening . . .

"Don't talk much, I see," she commented, and now we were on the first landing, where a statue of, I believe, Tycho Brahe, telescope in hand, seemed to cast an approving eye my way. "But we're not much about talk here at the club." Her hand slid up my arm. "We're all about *doing.*"

Finally, my powers of speech were re-afforded to me. "You're, uh, quite a delight, Ammi. I, um—"

Her hand brazenly cradled my rump as we stepped up to the second landing. "Oh, don't be so nervous. I'm going to show you a great time!"

Patrons ahead of us disappeared behind various doors. Ammi took me sprightly along the carpeted hall, almost *bounding* with each step. She approached a door and simultaneously slid her hand across my groin, whereupon I came close to lifting off my heels.

She paused at the door, turning to me with a scolding

grin. "Shame on you, sir. There's no reason to do *that,* you know. Not *here!*"

It was only then, receiving my first frontal look at her, that I became apprised of the extent of Ammi's *diversity.* To call her a "colourful" girl would be a howling understatement: her hair was a long, silken coppery red, while obsidian-black eyebrows adorned her forehead. The abundant hair of her pubic area, however, shined blond as sunlit wheat. Breasts the circumference of tangerines sat erect on her chest. Only after fathoming this full glance at her did I recollect her odd remark.

"Pardon me, but I don't know what you mean. There's no reason to do *what?*"

Her hand found my groin again and played there ever intently. "This *package,* sir, can't all be you," she giggled. "Oh, I know how men sometimes stuff socks and whatnot in their briefs to make themselves look bigger to the ladies but—really!—in a brothel, sir, the truth is always out once the breeches are down."

I stared in utter bewilderment. "*Socks,* did you say? Really, miss—I can't imagine what—"

"Come on!" she exclaimed, opened the door, and pulled me in.

The door itself was a marvel: nine panels, and hung within a stunning embrasured frame that I knew at a glance to be pure Federal Period. The bed-chamber impressed me even more, as I'd always been one to revel in the designs of the past rather than those of tasteless modernity. "A genuine William and Mary poster bed!" I gasped. The black-oak bedstead was a work of carven art. A Chippendale half-table sat beside the splendid bed, while opposite stood a grand armoire that could only be a genuine Hepplewhite.

My host's delightful breasts bobbed as she closed the door, then strode toward me. She grabbed my hand and pulled, and said as if to a naughty toddler, "You're a *bad boy,* sir. Ammi might have to punish you with a spanking for what you've done."

She grabbed an exquisite steamed-wood chair about and plopped right down in it, positioning me to stand before her.

"I say, you'd be advised to treat that chair with care, miss," I warned. "Unless I'm mistaken, it's a genuine Adam. The canework alone is without peer."

"Oh, shut *up,* you," she sputtered and at once fumbled with my belt. "We'll get to the bottom of *this.* If it's all you in here, I'll be a monkey's aunt . . . "

I remained mystified by her coy complaint. A sudden modesty overwhelmed me when she unfastened my trousers, then hastily slid them down along with my briefs.

Ammi stared with a dropped jaw, stared right at my bared groin. "You've *got* to be kidding me . . . "

"What?" I asked, but my feet shifted a bit from the cringing embarrassment of being so closely and privately examined. All I could think to utter was, "I, uh, I suppose it's not as large as you're used to," and I chuckled nervously "But there's little I can do about *that.*"

She gaped up with jade-green irises burning beneath the blacker-than-onyx eyebrows. "Not as *large?* This is the biggest prick I've ever *seen . . .* "

Her remark befogged me, for in her tone, I detected not a trace of prevarication. "You, uh, you mean to say that my . . . member is more sizable than the average you're accustomed to?"

She snapped in a course delight. "It's the biggest *cock* I've ever had hanging in my face, and I can tell you, there've been quite a few!" and with that, she began to stroke the drooping shaft of flesh with a lithe finger.

I chuckled. "You flatter me, Ammi, but I'm sure you're being over-lenient in your assessment of my privates."

She giggled another "Shut *up!*" and, without reservation, sucked the entirety of my flaccid penis into her mouth. The adroitness of her oral skill sent shivers through my being. (This, for me, was a pleasure long forgotten; my ex-wife had a knack for it, I will say, but her preference for penetration always won out. Many was the night I'd gaze at the ceiling contemplating Poe, Machen, and Blackwood whilst she hopped ludicrously up and down on me, enfrenzied akin to a mare in heat.) But as for this highly spirited and deliciously naked Ammi, erecting my manhood seemed to be her most steadfast desire. It didn't take long before its girth actually stretched her lips. She nearly gagged sliding it out. "Jesus *Christ*, mister! It's so big I can't even get it all in my mouth!"

"I-I . . . don't know what to say . . . "

She checked my hands, examining them, evidently, for traces of a wedding band. "So you're *not* married?"

"Oh, no, not anymore."

"Well, it's an awful shame that some happy woman isn't getting *this* stuck in her every night!"

I felt foolish presuming to converse whilst my nearly erect privates wobbled up and down, and that was not to mention the *preposterous* entails of our discourse. "I was married once, but I'm afraid the halls of academe proved far more my forte than the pastures of domesticity and wedlock."

She glared at me. "Shut *up!* " and then she yanked me to the bed and nearly threw me down on it. "Now . . . I've just *got* to know!"

I peered toward where she now rummaged through a drawer in the spectacular armoire. "Know what, if I may ask?"

"Just how *big* this monster is!" she replied, returning with a tin ruler. Her frenzied hand pumped the penile shaft in utter awe until full erection had been achieved, whereupon she aligned the rule to it . . .

"Holy *shit!*" she profaned.

My penis, now fully invigorated, slightly exceeded the rule's maximum length.

It was a twelve-inch rule.

Ammi went all in a frenzy now, retrieving something else from the armoire and then returning to the bed to boldly straddle me with her bare hips. "No more fooling around," she determined, opening a modest foil package. "For every minute that this gorgeous cock isn't buried in my bush, that's a minute of *horrible* waste!"

"What's that . . . you've got there?" I asked, my eyes asquint.

"Don't want to put a bun in little Ammi's oven, do you?"

The frail, flavescent object in her hands was a barrier prophylactic, one of the newer Latex versions by its look. I could hardly object to its non-prescriptive and hence *illegal* utility here, as prostitution was no *less* illegal.

Ammi's face turned flustered, and again, she profaned, "Shit, your cock's so big, I hope it doesn't *bust* the goddamn thing!"

My frown was all too quick. "Ammi, if I may? Profanity does your demeanour *precious little* justice."

She squinted at me. "The *fuck?*" and then she carefully rolled the prophylactic all the way down my penile shaft.

"*Now* we're talkin'," she gasped with a smile after essentially sitting on my erection and licensing it full entry into her womanly channel. "God—yeah, oh, *fuck* that's good . . . *All* the way in, yeah! *All* the way in!"

The sensations were admittedly quite pleasing, but I'm afraid Ammi's vandalism of the English language and her crude, splayed-legged pelvic locomotions left much to be desired. At one point, she reached behind herself and cosseted my scrotal sack, only to further profane, "For fuck's sake, mister. Even your *balls* are huge! They feel like something in the goddamned *hen house!*"

Indeed.

Her copulative motions accelerated, hands on knees as she continued to *pound* her loins upon my phallus. As she tended to the act, I, instead, surveyed more of the room's splendid features. The elaborate wainscoting was absolutely fabulous (more of the Georgian Period) while the wall-coverings couldn't have pleased me more:

herringbone patterns of gold and vermillion. When I craned my neck to examine a considerable oil landscape on the wall, I had to request, "Pardon me, Ammi, but would you know if that formidable painting there is an original Turner? It seems to be."

Her lust-pinkened face smoldered. "Shut *up!* We're doing *this* now! *This! Shit* on the goddamn painting!" Sweat beaded on her face and misted her bosom. "With my luck, you'll be one of these guys who gets off in a minute . . . "

Hmmm, I considered.

In not one but *twenty minutes'* time, Ammi was balloon-cheeked and shrieking in an undisputable ecstatic bliss. The purse of her womanhood spasmed desperately about the stiff meat of my sexual organ; I dare say, it seemed to squirm in time with her rising shrieks. When she'd had her protracted moment, her head wobbled on her neck, and she sidled over on the priceless bed, tongue hanging. Fast-breath'd, she grinned lazily. "That was the best fuck of my life . . . ," and after a few more moments of recapturing her wind, she manipulated herself around to look flabbergasted at my still-stiff-as-a-baker's-pin penis.

"Did you come?"

I elevated a brow. "If by that, you mean did I experience an ejaculatory release and sequent orgasm? No."

"Wait right there!" she exclaimed and abruptly roused. She stalked, if a bit painfully, toward the ornate door but stopped to point absurdly at my erected member. "And don't let *that* go away!"

Oh, for goodness sake! Where did she expect my penis to *go?* After she'd made her exit, I felt *ridiculous* lying there with my trousers down and a rubber-sheathed erection throbbing. Where could she be off to?

And I mustn't forget to show her Selina's photo . . .

Ammi's return brought four more women into the room: two svelte blondes, a lissome brunette, and a fox-eyed, coif-headed waif with raving auburn hair and a *monumental* mammarian endowment.

"Good *God!*" one croaked, eyeing me.

"She wasn't lying!" excited another.

The auburn-head seemed locked in a rigor. "Is that . . . *real?*"

It was one of the blondes that lunged before the others and asserted, "This guy may be able to out-fuck Ammi, but he ain't gonna out-fuck *me,* and that's just as sure as pigs can *shit!*"

The language absolutely *appalled* me.

It was a rather monotonous foray which ensued; four more giddy naked women clucking over my genitals like great-grandams over knickknacks. One by one, they punctured themselves on my stiffened-to-numbness erection, shrilly giggling in betwixt moans, gasps, and outright shrieks of lascivious liberation. Musky aromas swam about the chamber, accompanied by a rapid, wet *clicking;* sweating bellies sucked inward and out; eyes rolled up in sockets and tongues jutted; crystalline sweat dripped off tumid nipples. They rode me like some brute beast of sexual burden (which reminded me, quite regrettably, of my ex-wife). It was that second blonde, ostensibly the dominant of the five, who banged my penis to the proverbial hilt in a screaming, staccato madness fit for some carnal chasm in Dore's *Inferno,* and after achieving a head-whipping crisis, she leeringly lifted her pelvis off my member and, without abatement, then inserted said member into what I can only think to describe as a more *netherly* orifice.

"Right up my butt now, Mr. Big Dick," she guttered. "Just the way I *like* it!"

It unnerved me, needless to say, to know that I had been hoodwinked into performing the forbidden and historically blasphemous act so named for the ancient city of iniquity, Sodom. The sluttish woman's squat strained wider, affording me an all-too-precise view; and the ease with which she was able to admit the full depth and width of my member into this alternate and most uncomely cavity left me to conjecture that she was hardly a stranger to the act. She chuckled at my gape, then pressed two fingers to either side of her clitoral bulb, to isolate the mysterious nerve cluster. I visibly gulped, noting its size: nearly that of an avocado pit!

"Ammi likes to eat a box," she grated, "so she can get her little fuck-face over here and eat *this* one!" whereupon she grabbed the wickedly grinning Ammi by a crude fistful of coppery hair and shoved her face into the tensely splayed crotch. Ammi's mouth squandered no time whatever in ministering as directed. The activity begat a sound like an animal nursing.

"Fuck!" the blonde grunted. "This guy's tallywacker is so big it's punching my goddamn *stomach!*"

All the girls shrieked laughter at the remark.

Between the sensation of my organ buried in her bowel and that of Ammi's tending oration, the blonde soon became a veritable dervish of flesh as, once again, she clenched and shivered and then was wracked by another clearly thoroughgoing orgasmic salvo. And though I'll admit that the much more precise purchase of the act of sodomy rendered some pleasing sensations to myself, I was now quite lost in an unfathomable ennui. Women could be so *silly* sometimes, could they not? I forced my mind to focus on the task of letting nature, however contorted, take its course, and was grateful to then deliver the viscid proof of my own crisis into the prophylactic.

Finally!

"Fuck," the blonde moaned, only to sidle over as if narcolyzed. Ammi giggled, wiping her sheened mouth. "Mister," she said to me, "you just fucked five *whores* to kingdom come!"

The remark, which I supposed was a compliment, left me inwardly very weary. "Well, Ammi, ladies. That was, uh, quite nice, but I think I'll bid my adieu now and repair to the atrium." I frowned at the sullied condom on my now-slackening penis. "But I'd best get rid of this thing first . . . "

I prepared to remove the vulgar sheath, but then Ammi reached forward, strangely as if in alarm.

"No, no!" she shrilled. "I'll take care of that! After all, it's, uh . . . it's my job," and with *that* curious comment, she gingerly removed the soiled vulcanized barrier.

Then, even more curiously, she held the thing out, suspended from her fingertips, for all to see, and in an excited squeal, said, "Girls! Look at this!"

The four other docile women looked at the unrolled object in what seemed absolute astonishment.

"Can you *believe* all that *jism?*"

Indeed, my expended seed was quite milkily obvious as it depended at the prophylactic's tip, though I couldn't imagine what the fuss was about. *What else would these silly girls expect?* I wondered.

"That's a *lot* of nut!"

"Shit. Looks like enough cum for *half a dozen* guys . . . "

"Mr. Big Dick is a walking creamery!"

Ammi chuckled her way out of the room, carrying with her the ridiculous sheath of latex. But in all this ballyhoo, and in spite of the undeniable attractiveness of my coarse-mouthed companions, I'd simply had enough. Ah, but I couldn't leave just yet, could I?

"Ladies, if I may impose upon you a moment?" I requested and showed them the photograph of my only sibling. "This is my sister, Selina Phillips, and I'm most dire to locate her. Might any of you have seen her about anywhere?"

The question set my heart to racing!

The naked and quite exhausted quattro all squinted at the photo, registered blank expressions, then shook their heads no.

Drat! All that tomfoolery for nothing!

I mumbled specious niceties in my departure, and bound for the door . . .

"'Bye, Mr. Big Dick!"

"Yeah! 'Bye!"

"There goes the cream-wagon!"

"Come back again, please!"

I didn't waste my breath in informing them that such a prospect presented a very *low* order of probability . . .

Whew! I thought once back on the stair-hall and finally away from the dizzy cluster of trollops. More trollops (and likely just as dizzy) would have to be sought out and questioned about Selina; for the moment, though, I desperately needed a breather.

Past the stair-hall rail I noticed a spectacular hanging candelabrum; from there, I looked down and saw several male patrons loitering about the banquet table, most seeming to slurp down more of the loathsome oysters. These men had obviously finished their first sexual assignations and were affording themselves a break before pursuing another. There was no sign, however, of my associate Mr. Erwin.

A shrill rabble of feminine bombast resounded at the hall's end, where I spied Ammi's bare form proudly displaying the depending condom to another nude sprite— a pointy-breasted brunette. "Holy *cow!*" exclaimed the latter one, eyeing the semen-filled reservoir. "*Look* at it all!"

"I know," gushed Ammi. "Can you believe it? And the guy fucked the daylights out of all of us!"

"Holy *cow!*"

Great Pegana, I thought dismally. Could I help it that my seminal deposits were evidently much more voluminous than the average?

"And you should've seen his goddamn prong! Big as a baby's leg, I swear—he fucked me so hard I'll be walking like a cowboy for a *week!*"

I hid behind a somewhat Doric display pedestal, so not to be seen; what I needed less than anything just then was this pointy-breasted one wanting to sample my wares too.

"I better get this upstairs," Ammi said, more quietly, of the ludicrous condom. "You already take yours?"

"Yeah, two so far . . . "

I felt my brow furrow at the arcane discourse. *They're clearly talking about . . . spent prophylactics. How eccentric . . .*

The elfin pair separated, Ammi moving up the stairs to the fourth story—or I'd be more accurate to say *limping.*

At that same moment, a door farther down clicked open and out stepped another brazenly unattired prostitute—this one with nipples sticking out like persimmons—only to turn up the stairs and proceed behind Ammi. But this woman, too, had a spent prophylactic dangling from her fingers!

And a moment later?

A third woman did the same . . .

My astonishment was plain. *What cryptic onus could POSSIBLY charge these petite strumpets with the task of carrying away used prophylactics UPSTAIRS?* Surely, the nearest waste basket would do . . .

The hall remained clear, but when I emerged from my hiding, my eyes inadvertently fixed on the previously unnoticed object sitting atop the display pedestal: a crude beige cylindrical clay-shape roughly the size of a common pail; when recognition alighted, I muttered beneath my breath a shopworn, "Oh my God!" for I knew all too well what the unlikely object was:

A *cuneiform* cylinder.

As any archaeologist and, indeed, professor of ancient histories would know, these objects provided humankind with its very first "books," the most famous example being the Cyrus Cylinder, which, in intricate cuneiform, detailed the conquest of Babylon by the Persian warrior Cyrus the Great and verified the prophet Isaiah's prediction in Old Testament papyri scrolls of the same two centuries previous. *This* cylinder, however (as, I add, without meaning to brag, that I am well-versed in many variations of cuneiform), did not bear the typical assortments of logograms, pictoglyphs, and polyphonous sequences of wedges and slants that the early writing system is known for. Instead, the clay cylinder before me was covered entirely with the exclusive stylus marks used to denote *numbers.*

The entire cylinder, I reiterate, had been so inscribed.

Oh, if I only had a month's time to decipher this cylinder, I lamented.

I let my considerations stew, along with my adjacent perplexity regarding the mysterious redeposition of expended condoms to some paradoxical upward recess of the building. I knew I must not make myself obvious; therefore, I strolled about the stair-hall, half-pretending to examine various statues, paintings, and other pedestalled *objets-d'art.* Periodically, however, I took hasty opportunities to put my ear to each invaluable nine-paneled door I passed . . .

"Ooo-ooo-ahh-ahh . . . oh, YES!"

"Churn me like butter, honey!"

"Good, good! That's a *good* boy!"

All of the shrill exclamations were in feminine tones and clearly indicative of some manner of fornication.

The hall quieted, then, in seeming increments; alternately, the doors I'd just quitted opened to release, first, a brawny man with a sated smile on his face, and then his corresponding fornicatress.

Each naked woman, as I might've suspected by now, dispatched at once from the room to the stairs, and *up.* And from the fingertips of each suspended a spent prophylactic.

The bizarreness of my observations was by now getting the best of me. Clearly, more rooms existed upstairs on the fourth floor, yet not one prostitute had taken a man thither; which left me to deliberate: *The only person I know for fact to be up there is the club's madam . . . Miss Aheb . . .*

Could it be to Miss Aheb *that these shapely, bouncing-breasted "slatternettes" were delivering the epigrammatic soiled condoms?*

And if so . . .

Why?

I hadn't a notion. Eventually, I repaired back to the exorbitant atrium, where I found my friend Erwin (looking a bit dogged) helping himself to some refreshment. His grin greeted my arrival. "This place is something, huh, Mr. Phillips?"

"Something . . . yes," I uttered.

"The girl I got was pure dynamite, and she was none-too-disappointed with my performance, if ya don't mind me sayin' so."

"Not at all," I told him distractedly.

"Which girl did you get?"

I nearly moaned. *If you mean which FIVE GIRLS did I GET, I couldn't begin to tell you.* I simplified the response by merely saying, "A more-than-satisfactory little hussy by the name of Ammi, quite uniquely possessed of various hair colours."

"Don't know what mine's name was, but I can tell you, she's quite good at putting more than food in her mouth."

"A laudable endorsement indeed," I chuckled. I leaned over to keep my whisper more discrete. "But allow me to ask, and I apologize for the crudity, but . . . did your partner, um, make off with the soiled condom once the business was done?"

"Matter'a fact she did, Mr. Phillips, and now that'cha mention it? They always do."

"Doesn't that strike you as singularly peculiar?"

He stroked his stubble-blued chin. "Yeah, it does. Ya'd think they'd just drop it in the room's waste can, but maybe they dispose of 'em all in the same place, as a safety precaution."

I squinted at his conclusion. "I'm afraid I'm not comprehending you, Mr. Erwin."

"Well, any red house is always leery of a raid. If the coppers broke in and found used skins in every room, it'd be a snap to get a prosecution, wouldn't ya think?"

"Why, I hadn't thought of that," I confessed, and I admitted, too, that in the remotest sense, it did make some juris-prudential sense. But . . .

Somehow, however abstractedly, I couldn't quite fathom the notion to any sufficient degree of acceptability.

"I'll be going back for seconds, Mr. Phillips. You?"

"Oh, indeed," I transfigured the truth. More sexual frolic was most definitely *not* my preference, but I thought it best to obfuscate the truth to maintain more the air of a "team player." I did very much need to screen more of the working girls, to show them Selina's photograph.

Erwin seemed suddenly frustrated. "That is if there're any girls left I could grab seconds with. You heard the rumor, Mr. Phillips?"

"Rumor? Why, no."

"Heard two girls yacking about it a minute ago. Apparently, one of the men was with us on the trolley is *quite* the stud. They say he took care'a *five girls* in one go-round and wore 'em completely out. They won't be hob-knobbin' with no one the rest'a the night. They also said the fella had something 'tween his legs that should'a been hangin' in the smokehouse." He elbowed me with a wink and a smile. "That fella wouldn't be *you,* now would it, Mr. Phillips?"

I let out a strapping laugh. "Only in my most delusory dreams!"

"Well—" He theatrically dusted off his hands. "I'm ready as I'll ever be . . . and may God forgive me."

I rolled my eyes and laughed.

"You coming up too?"

"I'll be along presently," was my erroneous response.

Erwin embarked for the stairs, in his search for "seconds."

The other refractors, as I'd come to think of them, had also returned upwards in the same search, leaving me the atrium to myself. At once, I contemplated my next tactic; any women who might recognise Selina's photo would be upstairs as well, on the second or third story. However . . .

An echoic click came to my ears that elevated my gaze.

The conductor, I thought.

For there he was, the regulation cap perched atop the macabrely immobile white face. In the fashion of an automaton, he took slow steps up the winding stairs—to the *fourth* story . . .

Though my tactic remained undelineated, it was my sheer curiosity that overrode any action of greater utility.

You see, I *had* to know exactly *what* was taking place on the ominous *fourth* story.

I gave the conductor only enough lead-time to conceal my movements; then, with stealth, speed, and deliberation, I traced his identical steps. Upon the fourth-floor landing, I hid behind another Doric display pedestal; this one providing the base for an ancient basalt idol whom I believed to be the notorious demon Baalzephon so actively worshiped by luciferic sects of the Middle Ages. Eye lined up along the pedestal's edge, I watched the conductor propel himself to the center of the grandiose stair-hall, pause, and then enter a door.

Now's my chance, I realised.

No one else occupied the hall, so I made haste across the plush carpeting. But my dilemma was plain; for although more than half a dozen doors lined the wall-side of the hall, I could not be certain exactly *which* door the blanch-faced man had entered.

Somewhere near the center, was all I could deduce. Each door I silently passed stood identical to the previous, until (somewhere in proximity to the hall's mid-point) I stopped to stare at the tiniest brass emblem mounted upon the door I currently faced. Inscribed upon this plaque were, I'm utterly certain, the cuneiformic markings that denoted the following numerals: 1852.

I checked both ways down the hall, was satisfied I was not being surveilled, then stooped to one knee, and to the ornately plated keyhole, I then put my wide-open eye . . .

It troubles me that I cannot in any accuracy convey to

you the details I now beheld. It was a spectacular bed-chamber displayed to my clandestine view: sumptuous carpet and wall-coverings, lovely antique furniture and, in addition, a veiled four-poster bed whose gorgeously carved post and headboard appeared adorned in gold leaf; oil portraits and statuary that were no doubt high-mark collector's items. These facts, however, rendered the chamber *nondescript* when compared to the room's (and I'm not sure I can even summon an adequate term) *sensorial bearing* . . .

There seemed to be a light that was not light but some peculiar cast unlike any I'd observed. This *counter-luminescence* (somehow foggy yet clarity-sharpening) made the room and its contents fairly shimmer as if through mist and seemed preternaturally magnified via some phantasmal *lens-obscura;* and to that, I must not fail to add . . .

Two rod-like objects stood upright at either side of the grand bed. These objects were likely simple wooden dowels (nothing peculiar there), but what covered the top half of each was a mass of some unidentifiable substance that seemed to be partly translucent and rather ill-hued. The only simile I can summon is to say that these poles looked like bunches of wizened white grapes on a stick.

"There you are," issued the unmistakable and faintly accented voice of Madam Aheb. She immediately stepped into view from the rightward side of the key-way, and it was the paste-faced conductor to whom she spoke. The madam's black hair as well as the diaphanous, low-cut gown iridesce'd in the bizarre accentuation of the room's light.

Her voice turned scolding: "And it certainly *took* you long enough to get here. You know how I can't abide to have this awful *stuff* on me for a minute longer that it need be."

I could only see the conductor's back from this voyeuristic vantage point, yet the capped, heavy-jacketed man appeared to bow his head at Miss Aheb's remark of disapproval.

"But of course, I'm aware you and the Thogg were preparing the trolley for the next ingression . . . "

My head turned atilt. *Thogg?* What was *that?* And what did she mean by *ingression?* And what was this "awful stuff" she'd referred to? What I'd seen thus far assured me there was nothing at all awful about how she appeared.

"I'm ready now," Madam Aheb said and sat eloquently in a spectacular spoke-backed Revolution-era chair.

My view of her was blocked when the conductor stood in front of the madam and, with a linen towel, appeared to be wiping off her arms, shoulders, and graceful legs. "Good, good," she half-moaned. The conductor's hands kept busy in their task but remained a frustrating visual blockage to exactly *what* was being done. Nevertheless, he continued to wipe the exposed skin of his mastress.

What in the name of Pegana is he wiping off? I pondered.

Still blocked by the bulk shape, Miss Aheb stood up from the chair, and it was the movements of the conductor that led me to believe he was now removing the madam's gown.

"Ah, there. That's better. I just so much prefer to be naked . . . "

When the silent conductor stepped away, Miss Aheb stood in full view to my prying eye—

The image forced me to press my hand across my lips; otherwise, the horrific image of what I now saw would've surely caused me to scream quite blood-curdlingly . . .

I was looking at a dichotomy of unspeakable magnitude: a collision of *obscene and utter opposites* stripped bare; indeed, the *force majeure* of physical beauty and physical horror. I say, Miss Aheb now stood naked, and in her nakedness came the accentuation of the sum of all her parts: flawless contours and perfect feminine lines, the sweep of impeccable legs, a sleekness that was robust and healthily slender simultaneously, and high-riding, distendedly nippled breasts that existed without flaw.

The *horror* was in her *complexion.*

Any impeccability of Miss Aheb's physique was howlingly counter-weighed by what I could only conceive of as some ghastly epidermal defect or pitiable disease. Every square inch of her exposed skin was made appalling by a condition far worse than the pallor, say, of the conductor's face but instead by a *skin tone* that was absolutely revolting. It was not the strange *un-light* that held dominion in the room: of this, I was sure. It was a physical fact of the woman's heredity.

Her skin looked like the unpleasant white of a bullfrog's belly marbled by swaths of a mucoid green.

The image nearly overpowered me; I nearly voided my stomach's contents. It occurred to me now that what the servile conductor had been wiping off was no doubt some mode of cosmetic make-up to conceal the madam's true appearance to this evening's guests; what's more (and I don't know how I knew this), I felt all-too-certain that this aberrancy of Miss Aheb's skin was her natural condition!

Between her protuberant yet malignantly toned breasts hung a modest pendant whose elongated stone reminded me of a common stalactite of chalcedony, nearly colorless and rather lackluster. Yet from the thin, two-inch-long stone, after I stared a moment, I took note of the pendant's only *un*common characteristic . . .

It seemed to, however irreducibly, generate some aspect of the room's overall *anti-light.* And as this registered, my eyes slowly roved upward to the most macabre chandelier I've ever beheld. Uneven elongated crystals hung from each setting in the same stalactite fashion (*hundreds* of them, each quite similar to the pendant), inexplicably giving off the light that was not light.

Miss Aheb grinned to her servant in an almost

vulturine way. "I simply adore you so much," came a wanton whisper and, with it, her gracile hand to the conductor's crotch. "Kiss me now . . ."

The conductor's gloved hand came to his chin—

"No, no," the appalling-skinned madam interjected. "Keep the mask on—"

So I was right! I thought. It *was* a mask the conductor wore!

"—I want you *hideous* at first," she continued. "I want you *repulsive!* It makes my juices flow all the more hotly . . . "

I forced my thoughts to still, and merely watched—

—as the conductor's waxen face lowered to Miss Aheb's and their mouths joined.

Minutes passed; the oral contact roused Miss Aheb noticeably. She stood in a slowly rising craze as the mouth-hole of the conductor's abhorrent mask ranged from her lips and down the slope of her scum-hued throat, then lower to suck into its lurid parchment aperture each gorged nipple.

"Yes, yes," panted the raven-haired madam. "Harder . . . That's just . . . so . . . lovely . . . "

The conductor continued his ministration until a veritable *gloss* of excitement effused from Miss Aheb's vulval groove and shined down the insides of her thighs. Eventually, rapid-breath'd, she pushed her servant's counterfeit mouth away and ordered, "Get the thogg. I'm ready now . . . "

There's that strange word again, I mused. *Thogg . . .*

While the conductor parted, Madam Aheb lay back on the high, plush bed and crudely brought her knees to her face, whereupon her mal-coloured hand began to titillate the furred pubis. Again, I was in paresis from the dichotomy of her unflawed curves made monstrous by the mysterious skin disease.

When the conductor returned, he brought with him the equally masked motorman . . .

No words were spoken then as the demented

procedure began. My stomach quivered, for when the bulky motorman displayed his hand, I recalled my impressions when I'd glimpsed it getting off the trolley, dismissing a trick of moonlight as the cause for my initial alarm.

I now saw the *fact* of the matter.

It was no real hand that existed at the end of the motorman's arm but instead a hideous facsimile: a cluster of elongations of boneless, jointless flesh. Just as harrowing, though, was the *hue* of the boneless flesh: the same grub-white spotted by pond-scum green.

First, these fingers, if one could call them that, extended, then wriggled; and then they curled inward to form a parody of a fist which then incredibly swelled in size, then shrank, swelled, then shrank, as if throbbing with some unearthly pulse. Miss Aheb seemed delighted by the demonstration, her splayed legs tensing and buttocks writhing at the sight. Next, her fingers parted the shining lips of her vulva within the nest of hair—a lewd invitation.

Without abatement, the motorman contorted the boneless digits forward and inserted his "hand" into the teeming, pink purse of Miss Aheb's vaginal vault . . .

In and out, then, the monstrous hand delved, begetting a regular slick, wet sound that reminded me of one trudging through mud, the digits obscenely undulating and obviously heightening the pleasure of his (or I should say *its*) mastress. Soon the derrick-like penetrations probed deeper, to the extent that Miss Aheb's reproductive orifice had swallowed the motorman's hand nearly to the point of *mid-forearm* . . .

"Now," the abyssally-skinned woman panted. Her pleasures mounted to tighten every muscle and tendon in her body.

It was to the stoic conductor that the order was directed, for first he removed his gloves, then woolen regulation-blue jacket, then the white shirt beneath . . .

Expression *gaping,* I now beheld the length of this

evil ruse: when the conductor's clothes were tossed aside, his nudity revealed him to be no "he" at all but a woman, and one with a physique nearly as comely as Madam Aheb's.

My shock racked me at my peeper's post.

But the conductor (or I should say now the conduc*tress*), even in her stunning beauty, shared some of the same hideous dichotomy as the madam and this "thogg": that nauseous sickly white skin-tone blended with the mucous-green splotches.

The carnal aberration I bore witness to now was surely a scene forged in hell . . .

Butternut hair fell when the regulation cap was undonned, and then the conductress removed the parchment mask . . .

Simultaneously, I felt on the precipice of cardiac failure and a fit of madhouse screaming. How I was able to stave off both, I know not. But this was the *coup de grace* of all I'd visually attested to thus far: the revelation of the conductress's face, which I suspect the perseverant reader has already deduced.

It was my sister *Selina's face* that had been until now secreted beneath the gruesome mask.

What has that hideous BITCH done to my sister! my thoughts railed. Dangling between Selina's ample yet similarly discolored breasts was a pendant like that of Miss Aheb; this, I could glimpse as my either brainwashed or subjugated sibling turned for a moment, knelt up on the bed, and then lowered her mouth to her superior's clitoral nub. All the while, the motorman's unearthly hand plungered wickedly in and out . . .

"Yes, yes," issued the accented hiss. "Lick it faster, dear, faster." Dung-brown nipples erected to inflamed teepees as the order was complied with. Meanwhile, as if by psychic cue, the dead-faced motorman finally withdrew the marauding forearm while the madam's bare foot caressed the thing's trousered crotch. A lump hardened there, and with the attendant stimulation, this less-than-human being lowered said trousers—

I nearly fell into a swoon!

—to reveal genitals as monstrous as its facsimile for a hand.

Indeed, less-than-human was no exaggeration; I could only thank Selina and Erwin's God that it retained the parchment mask, for by now, I could not, would not contemplate what its true face must be.

"What a beautiful cock," the madam profaned, eyes enkindled by the throbbing sight.

From the wax-white and utterly hairless groinal region, an identically waxen *prong* of queer white flesh stuck out. I estimated the erect pudenda's length at roughly eight inches, with perhaps two inches' girth at the base. It seemed to lack the sheathing skin as one would typically expect, and tapered queerly to a fleshy point rather than sporting an also-expected dome of glans; I could only think absurdly of a paste-white carrot. Blue traceries of veins ghosted beneath its dread whiteness as it throbbed; likewise, it shined as if effusing its own preludial lubrication. The only aspect that made this vision more hideous was the curious absence of scrotum and hence testes.

Selina's next instruction didn't have to be voiced; she held back her madam's legs to more effectively part the groove of the shapely buttocks.

"Now, now," Miss Aheb seethed—

—and it was into her nethermost aperture that the motorman—this *thogg*—inserted the macabre phallus and began to pelvically thrust; all the while, Selina re-tended her superior's swollen clitoral *metus*. The sought-after effect took little time; soon Miss Aheb's hideously skinned yet voluptuously curved body began to buck madly on the bed as the obvious crisis of her climax was at hand. She shrieked, then whinnied as the spasms of release began to pulse—a sound barely human—while in concurrence, the motorman's frame stiffened, then began to quiver.

"I can feel it!" Miss Aheb lewdly rejoiced. "Pouring into me! *Filling* me!"

The denouement wound down; then the motorman withdrew its carrot-like "cock" from the woman's bowel. My sister turned away, appalled.

"That was lovely, dear," Miss Aheb commended. She lay slit-eyed and grinning, the quaking orgasms leaving her limp on the plush bed. "But now that I've had my moment . . . You know what to do . . . "

The thogg stepped away, stuffing his sullied organ back into his trousers; yet my sister, in motions that were clearly gruelling, came round to kneel at the edge of the bed between the madam's upthrust thighs.

"I just can't abide the idea of the thogg's jism being in me for long," Miss Aheb remarked as Selina pressed her lips to the plumbed sphincter and began to suck.

"There, good, good, dear. Suck it all out . . . "

Numbed to stupefaction, all I could do was watch as poor Selina engaged in the revolting process of evacuating Miss Aheb's rectal vault of the thogg's semen. When her face came away from the cleft, she wobbled on her knees.

"Swallow now, dear," the madam dictated, "and then you'd both best be on your way."

Selina stared in the chandelier's sinister *unlight,* lips pursed as her mouth obviously remained full of the creature's spermatic void. She steeled herself, went tense, then audibly swallowed.

I watched then as my sister rose to listlessly redress herself and re-don the grim parchment mask.

Miss Aheb indicated the strange poles standing to either side of the bed. "The carriers are full, as you can see. Take them now—the back stairs as usual, and be on your way through the ingression brink."

At this incomprehensible command, Selina lifted up one of the poles while the motorman hoisted up the other. These poles or rods or whatever they were continued to mystify me. What exactly was the mass of shriveled, semi-lucent things adhered to them? Again, I thought of wizened grapes . . .

Miss Aheb stood up, her nude body stunning in its curvatures yet appalling in its discolour. "Go in glory," she oddly bid my sister, "and sing praise to our benefactors."

Here was the only occasion for a vocal utterance on Selina's part. "Yes, Madam Aheb."

"And have the trolley back by bell-time. Soon, our very generous guests will have had their fill of the evening's delights." She grinned wickedly in the shimmering light that was not light. "As we so have our fill of *them* . . . "

Selina and the motorman departed through an adjoining door and disappeared. I was able to detect the sound of descending footfalls . . .

They're going down a set of ancillary stairs, I realized, *to the trolley.*

My own footfalls took me in haste, down the sweeping main stairs to the atrium; I realized the import of moving faster than my sister and the cumbersome motorman and was confident of this goal's achievability. From each stair-hall, I detected the sounds of sexual traffic (moans, murmurs, squeals of lascivious release) and was relieved to find the atrium devoid of prostitutes and male suitors alike. At once, I passed through the large outer door to the decrepit courtyard, and in the moon's bedimmed light, I boarded the vacant trolley and piloted myself to the rearmost seats of the second car to hide myself.

Before I'd stowed my person behind the wood-slat seat, however, I paused to take further note of that great archway of lichen-stained blocks embrasuring the mammoth door of rusted iron beams studded with rivets. Again, I was perplexed by the almost mirage-like image: a sickly colored *mist* that seemed impossibly oily, sifting beneath the great door's gap, and, with it, evidence of some weird half-light that I was now able to correspond to the indefinable shimmer of Miss Aheb's bed-chamber.

What could possibly be behind the door that would

possess such strange traits? This was New York City, for goodness sake . . .

I ducked back down, as the footsteps I knew would come had arrived. I heard my sister and her monstrous companion clatter aboard the trolley. Exposing myself to an obvious risk, I dared to steal a split-second peek above the seat-back's edge . . .

Selina and the motorman—that thing—had planted the pair of mass-cloaked rods in mounts of some sort or other, where they now stood upright as they had upstairs. Selina tended to some flicking of switches on a control board, but it was the motorman who dismounted and plodded toward the massive arched door.

A loud metallic *clang!* reverberated as a bolt was thrown, then came the keening grind of old hinges as the thing secreted beneath the garb of a transit motorman pulled open the doors.

With half an eye over the seat-back, I stared in utter befuddlement . . .

More stone blocks filled the archway, rendering passage impossible! *What on earth?* I thought. Yet the negating blocks were not of normal stone as were those of the arch and the courtyard's walls . . .

They were of the same cryptic material that comprised the stalactitical crystals of Miss Aheb's chandelier, and her and Selina's pendants!

The trolley jerked; metal abraded as the vehicle's wheels squealed over the ancient rails, and it was then . . .

Impossible!

Trolley No. 1852 rumbled forward toward the *solid wall* within the arch and—

Ineptly, I covered my head with my arms, awaiting what . . . I could never estimate.

The trolley, without so much as a hitch, *passed through* the wall of outerworldly blocks.

There came a noisome *sucking* sound, then one of soft grinding; I myself felt as though I were being pulled through a range of sand, yet no physical substance was observed; barely visible mist, however, *was* observed, akin to the seeming mist I'd thought I noticed in the madam's chamber. I received the notion that the mist (warm and somehow oily) existed in some direct or indirect relativity to that inexplicable counter-luminescence, for that same trait now—that light which was *not* light—held dominion over the queer space in which the trolley now ranged.

And a queer space it was, indeed.

I sensed *barrenness* even before I opened my eyes, and felt inordinate pressure as well as a peculiar absence of air temperature; it was neither hot nor cold, just simply *nothing.* I thought of vacuities and voids, of inhuman realms and lost worlds. It was then that I actually looked out of the trolley-car's vestibule . . .

Should this manuscript ever be found, I suspect that by this point, the reader will have no choice but to dismiss me as one fit for some refuge for the deranged. Translating what I then witnessed into communicable lexicon would overbound the skill of even the most preeminent writer. Sufficient words, you see, simply do not exist. I will endeavor, though, toward a feeble attempt . . .

I saw a sky hazy with the anti-light, whose source could not be perceived, as there was no object of provenance, such as a sun or a moon. Yet beyond the spectral shimmer, the nature of this phenomenon I can only think of as a sky existed in layers, or *stratum,* the darkest being the most elevated, the lightest being in the closest proximal relation to the land, if indeed it could be called as such. Yet each strata bore colours defying category; instead, they seemed gradient shades of tone, bereft of what we're taught to be primary and/or secondary colouring which, when amalgamated, result in the visual character of what our eyes perceive. Forgive my convolutedness, and I apologize for any ensuant frustration. Alas, this is the only description my anaemic grey-matter can generate.

Even more spectral, though, than this "sky" was the

terrain itself over which the clattering trolley now traversed. The physical realm I now beheld (what I mean is the solid ground) existed not as earth nor desert, not as hillock nor woodland. It was merely flat, barren *space*, flat to exactitude and extending as far as the eye could register retinal images. I knew then that I must be on another planet, or (recalling the forbidden mythologies of the ancient Ahebites) within some other dimensional plane that existed in contestation with the three aspects of dimensionality we are comfortable with, for the Ahebites, led by the dread witch-priestess Isimah el-Aheb, were worshipers and human physical agents for the drab, featureless beings known as the Pyramidiles, who did indeed inhabit a realm that was not planetary and thereby could only be para-dimensional.

This, I knew, was but grim fable; or at least I'd always *thought* it to be . . .

How, though, could I deny it *now?*

More surveillance was necessary for me to make a proper assessment of this *phantasmata* I was now sitting in the middle of. I required a forward view, which would no doubt expose me to the greatest risk yet. Nevertheless, I took my chance, realising no other subsidiary manoeuvre.

I stood upright at the back of the trolley.

What faced me were the backs of my sister and the aberrant motorman; nothing could be more imperative, I knew, than to prevent them from seeing me. Yet *I* was the one who needed to see. And *see* I did . . .

To my unabating horror.

Past the shoulders of Selina and the *thogg*, there stretched a vista so strange, so unutterably alien, that the very glimpsing of it fleeced the breath from my lungs and instigated a slugging of my heart. It was a horizon of sorts, extending to sheer endlessness, a screaming, demented infinity that transcended all manner of measure. Sounds like wicked wind blended with some *human* aspect seemed to shriek from all directions, and dust (though dust that glittered) flitted through the ultra-terrestrial haze, filtering a purview of impossibility. The only apparent "natural" objects in view were the two track-rails extending in perfect linearity for incalculable miles ahead. *Who could possibly have lain them?* I wondered in fascinated terror. *And just how long do they extend?*

These and myriad more questions overflowed in my struggling and shock-wearied mind. This land and sky of undefected planes, I knew, could not exist via any known laws of nature or relativity, nor could the trolley's very passage—a vehicle with no perceptible mode of power. But my unblinking eyes bloomed then, when the flat, vacuous void ahead at last relinquished some of its unfathomable homogeneousness, the blistering panorama's monotony finally breaking to reveal the tiniest eruptions of some facet of *feature.*

Pyramids! I realised through a headache-inducing squint.

Yes, miles or hundreds of miles distant, their ranks rose as the trolley approached: a morass of pyramid-shaped objects whose angles all existed in perfect uniformity. Some spired higher than others, but beyond that, they were all of the same, and I knew now what they could only be . . .

The Pyramidiles.

That hideous race of faceless, immobile *anti-beings* so decadently and blood-thirstily revered by the Ahebites of pre-dynastic Egypt.

It's true! It's all true! my palpitating thoughts screamed.

The myth of the Pyramidiles was no myth, so then neither could be their principal servitor on Earth, the witch-priestess Isimah el-Aheb, now known as Madam Aheb of the 1852 Club . . .

And it was into the midst of these appalling parasites of undying turmoil that the trolley ventured. God only knew what would happen once we arrived.

Whether it was hours which lapsed or days, the prospect was beyond my mental potency to estimate. Neither Selina nor the noxious motorman moved from their forward posts, but eventually, the range of minuscule pyramidic eruptions grew larger as more distance was gained; then, hours or days later . . . they *loomed,* and in their looming, I stood utterly paralyzed. The smallest of them stood hundreds of feet high, yet the tallest easily spired thousands of feet into the obscure, unilinear stratum above; each Pyramid was indeed a colossus, and being cognizant that each of these things were alive made the observation all the more horrific. That incessant living wind-like screaming rose in pitch as the trolley clattered directly into the thick of the things. I could see them and their mammoth flesh-walls, could *see* the most horrific trait of all: whatever it was that covered their living pyramidal bodies (presumably some foreign laminae that served as skin) was of a wet, sickly white, like that of a bullfrog's belly, tessellated with an even more sickly green.

Just like the skin of Miss Aheb and Selina . . .

It was an uncontemplatable labyrinth that existed between the bases of these horrid, titan creatures; and through that labyrinth, the trolley now wended. I thought of a lone skiff coursing betwixt glaciers, or the most meager train locomoting between the most enormous mountains. The Pyramidiles' "skin" made me physically ill to behold, yet now, given their size when compared to our proximity, it was all I could see to either side. The slimy dermis shivered as we passed, showing revolting dilating pores that shuddered as if via some mode of respiration. Great hose-like lines swerved in every direction, pulsing—and I knew that these could only be the things' veins. But in veins flowed *blood,* circulated by *hearts,* and it was the nature of such that I would've preferred to kill myself than to speculate or, worse, bear witness to. Just as frightening queries, however, did race mad through my mind; for one:

How much space did these appalling hulks of flesh occupy? Dozens of square miles? Thousands? *More?*

The trolley stopped.

I ducked to re-conceal myself behind the seat just as my horribly masked sister turned. Two sets of footsteps on metal told me that she and the motorman had debarked . . .

Now was my chance, risky as it may have been, to make a closer examination of the two poles covered with the inexplicable masses, but I knew I must be very careful and very quick.

A peek over the side showed me Selina and her grim attendant walking down a queer lane formed between two of the monstrous pyramids of flesh. On hands and knees, then, I traversed the entirety of the rear car's aisle, hopped across the coupling, and continued as such to the trolley's forward area, and slid into the footwell of a seat nearest the debarkation steps. Small oval holes had been cut out at the bottom of the vehicle's sideboards (likely for drainage during rain), so with my cheek to the floor, I again looked out. There was no sign of my sister or the motorman . . .

Next, my hands and knees took me to the simple mounts into which the bizarre dowels had been erected.

What in the name of . . .

This close, I was easily able to discern the strange substance which composed the "wizened masses" that the poles were designed to carry. Easy to discern, quite, but easy to cogitate?

By no means.

These masses that could be likened to bunches of shriveled grapes were actually multiple hundreds of unrolled prophylactic sheaths. Each had been fixed to dozens of outward pointing metal rods spouting from the dowel; and onto each, more than several of the barrier sheaths had been fixed via tiny clips. Each dangled limply, weighted at its end by the portion of human sperm that had been jettisoned into it. *Rows and rows of soiled condoms, two veritable TREES of them,* came my outrageous yet clearly incontestable observation. It was to these outlandish "trees" that the club's harlots had been clipping the spent, vulcanised barriers all along; and no doubt for a considerable time—many days, I would reckon, or, more than likely, many weeks . . .

I ducked back, to hide myself again several seats rearward, not knowing what to do or what even to think. Moments later, the footsteps re-boarded, and a peek around the side showed my masked sister lifting one of the dowels from its mount and the grub-handed motorman lifting the other. Again, then, they debarked, carrying with them the sperm-laden dowels . . .

When I peered through the current drainage port, I gasped; for now, standing before the trolley were a dozen hideous, naked *creatures* beyond the stuff of nightmare. Their hands and openly displayed penises existed identically to that which I'd seen of the motorman during his service to Miss Aheb. However, unlike said motorman, these wore nothing and had no parchment masks—which was surely the worst part, for their faces . . . Their faces . . .

The pallid things sported faces that were but drooping cones of the alien flesh, each cone tapering to single scarlet-tipped tentacle. I shuddered where I lay. The things (*thoggs,* I could only presume, the same devilish, outerworldly species as the motorman) stood bereft of eyes, nostrils, ears, and mouths. What is more, though they stood upright on two mucilaginous legs, there seemed no evidence of any joints where elbows, knees, and ankles should be. Boneless, in other words, utterly lacking in ossification. Their penises dangled obscenely at the joists of their legs. And save for their bellies and genital regions, which were an exclusive pasty-white, the rest of their skin shimmered in identical hue to that of Miss Aheb and Selina: that awful white covered by greenish swirls and splotches . . .

Two of the horrendous beasts took the poles and disappeared with them, while the others appeared to be in some sort of non-verbal concert with Selina, though how this could be, I could scarcely ideate. *What are they doing?* my thoughts ground like old hinges, for upon sensing some instruction from the most paramount thogg, my sister's head drooped as if disheartened.

Then she began to disrobe.

I could only presume that these naked monstrosities served as common laborers (proles) to tend to various duties that the mammoth Pyramidiles required—such as the aforementioned: the collection and redeposition of human reproductive discharge. Evidently, however, their toil was on occasion rewarded, as it was clear that my poor sister had been ordered to sexually avail herself to these ghastly things as some mode of recreational release . . .

Once stripped naked and unmasked, my sister turned, posing her beautifully formed yet hideously discolored body for the sensorial pleasure of these things. It was as though, even without eyes, they could somehow *see* her physique's enticing attributes, the positive reaction of which was more than apparent. The thoggs' penises, tapered like waxen carrots, erected with promptitude, while the overall image remained somehow more revolting by their absence of scrotums and sequent testicles.

Selina lowered herself to the strange polychromatic soil and parted her legs . . .

The first of the nauseating things diminished no time in mounting her and burying its inhuman pudenda into her sex. The pallid rump rapidly cycled up and down (all quite perfunctorily) until its climax was achieved and the thing was slaked. Then the next one mounted her, and the next, and the next after that. As each of the creatures neared the point of orgasmic crisis, the suckerless tentacle dangling from its face turned a deeper scarlet, as if to denote excitement. Then more came, and more . . .

Though Selina had not been physically forced to submit to the abhorrent beasts, this sufficed for rape *en masse* nonetheless. I cried as morbidity forced me to watch further. My first impulse, of course, had been to take the thoggs by surprise and give fight, but this, I knew, was useless as it was futile. Surely, I'd be overpowered and killed with relative simplicity and hence never be able to rescue Selina from this wretched supernatural plight. What dejected me all the more was the angle at which Selina had arranged herself for the monstrous submission: her parted thighs and splayed buttocks directed precisely toward the port from which I observed, which only afforded me a depressingly accurate view of the actual coitus. I was forced to watch as each unearthly phallus divided my sister's sexual folium and slid all of its tumescent length into her. It was from these monstrous loins that their seed was thereby transferred into the loins of my poor sister; and it was quite an abundant transfer, indeed, for upon satisfaction, the current creature withdrew to make way for the next, but not before a *flood* of their sexual fluids issued out like so much effluence, leaving a great and widening tarn of the stuff between Selina's pried-wide legs. It was that strange *anti*-light, I knew, that lent blade-sharp clarity and preternatural magnification to this bitter effusion; for even as my distance from the scene exceeded twenty feet, I saw details as though they were just inches away, which served to only heighten my disconsolation, and even more regrettably, this visual enhancement detailed to me the very *inhumanness* of the thoggs' discharge. I could only surmise that even in the thoggs' lack of visible testes, they were obviously possessed of *ample* seminal vesicles and prostates of the stoutest kind, and as for the semen itself?

It was like no man's semen at all but thicker, more opaque, akin to semi-curdled buttermilk but laced with threads of resolute black, like squid ink.

My outrage began to roil from within: these abyssal things were utilising the cavity of my poor sister's womanhood as a *receptacle* of brute lust, and there was nothing I could do about it. I was left with no recourse but to cringe and silently sob.

TROLLEY NO. 1852

It was the ninth or tenth thogg who forewent intercourse and opted instead to audaciously straddle Selina about her belly. Into her mammarian valley its waxen penis was lain, whereupon it *cocooned* said penis by pressing both breasts inward, forming a seat for false-coital purchase. The splotched buttocks then rocked back and forth, drawing the dread phallus in and out of the compressed vale, and when the sought-after moment arrived—

Selina groaned.

—my sister grimly inclined her head in time to allow repeated spurts of the monster's seed to be jettisoned into her opened mouth via the thogg's aboriginal replication of the sin of Onan: masturbation. The alarming voluminousness of its seminal product did, upon completion of the unnatural act, in all truth fill my sister's oral cavity right up to the brim of her lips. Even without a face, the thogg glared down as if in some scolding expectancy, and that is when my most unfortunate sibling swallowed the entire mouthful. The sight had a nearly emetic effect on my own stomach, knowing that all that evil sperm had been swallowed into hers, yet I wished I could swoon or even die when I next watched *two more* thoggs fill Selina's mouth similarly, producing, if anything, *more* ejaculant than the previous contributor.

All of it was swallowed.

A final creature finished the foray by copulating with and spending itself into Selina's bowel.

My GOD, my thoughts quaked when it was over.

Some sensibilities returned when I knew that this heinous victimisation was (for now, at least) at a terminus. But one point had eloped from my mind whilst witnessing the gruesome proceeding:

The motorman, I realised.

He had not joined in the festivities with his diabolic brethren, unless he'd somehow gotten shed of the mask and regulation uniform without my seeing. *Perhaps he went unseen to tend to some encumbrance or other for the Pyramidiles,* I considered. *Or perhaps—*

From where I crouched in hiding, I felt a tap upon my shoulder; and in horrific slowness, I turned my head and looked up . . .

The motorman loomed above me, still clothed but unmasked now and somehow glowering, however facelessly. The tentacle sprouting from the drooping splotch-fleshed cone where its face *should've* been jiggled hideously, the tip reddened as if dipped in blood.

God save me, I prayed for the first time in my life.

The motorman shot its boneless hands downward, latched onto my shoulders, and dragged me up; and as if I weighed no more than a grasp of straw, I was flung over the vestibule to land with a shuddering thud upon the dead, lackluster soil of this deranged place. At once, I was surrounded by the troop of naked, flaccid-penised thoggs.

Selina raised herself to elbows, the pain of this surprise plain on her face. "Oh, Morgan, you shouldn't have done this. Coming to the club was bad enough, but now? Stowing away on the trolley? You've no idea what peril you've put yourself in . . . "

Winded, I staggered to my feet. "I've been searching for you for years, Selina," I nearly wept. "And now that I've found you, I know I must do everything in my power to rescue you from this, this *evil.*"

"There can be no rescuing, Morgan—it's impossible. Miss Aheb will never let me go, and these thoggs are undefeatable. This is my plight now, and it will never change unless Miss Aheb grows weary of me."

"Weary? Selina, I don't understand."

"When it started out, I was just one of the working girls at the club. Free food and shelter, in *this* economy? We were starving on the street, Morgan. The club provided us with an arrangement none of us could refuse," she explained. "But Miss Aheb soon took a *personal* fancy to me, and I would no longer service the johns, only her, plus other duties . . . like *this*.”

What an atrocious subjugation, I thought, but even as a hundred questions occurred to me, I was prevented from giving voice to a single one, for the most brutish of the naked thoggs shoved me roughly and pointed with a jointless finger down to where my sister lay.

“The thoggs are ultimately vicious,” Selina told me with a tear in her eye, “and ultimately perverse.”

The thing shoved me again but for a reason that alluded me.

“It wants you . . . to fuck me, Morgan,” came my sister’s groaning voice. “They want to watch.”

I stood aghast. “I could never in a million y—”

“Morgan, sick as it is, you *must*.”

“But that’s incest!” I outraged. “The most irredeemable of nature’s aberrations!”

She sobbed openly now. “If you don’t . . . they’ll kill you. But you can be guaranteed that it will be a very slow death. The thoggs are bred for torture, Morgan. They *exist* to inflict pain, and they’re very good at it.”

I turned to the most salient of them. “Then so be it! You’ll not coerce me to defile my sister, you pestiferous, para-dimensional degenerate! Go ahead and kill me!”

Two of the things grabbed my arms, but it was not toward me that the commandant embarked. It was toward Selina.

It fell on her at once, and when she screamed, it was into her opened mouth that the ghastly beast inserted its boneless hand. Meanwhile, one of the others did the same to her sex, until they were both *reaching into her* from either direction. I sensed all too clearly that they intended to eviscerate Selina, trans-orally and trans-vaginally.

“Stop!” I bellowed so loud I feared my eyes would leap from their sockets. “I consent to your demand!”

Had the things been able to grin, I’m certain they’d have been doing so now. They removed their offending hands from Selina's body, while some psychic command urged her to position herself on hands and knees. Now it was *I* who sobbed openly; to my own knees I then fell, and unfastened my trousers.

The pallid monsters clustered closer around, their eyeless faces intent on the scenario. I concentrated on the plushness of Selina's rump while forcing myself not to perceive the grotesque skin-tone. My member, however, hung limp, useless.

I croaked. "Selina, I can't possibly grow sufficiently aroused under *these* circumstances! You're my *sister!*"

"You have to try," she panted, and shot a pleading glance over her shoulder. "They'll kill us both . . . "

Humiliated, I stroked my flaccid flesh, all to no effect. More inhibiting was the notion that I was being spectated by not only the revolting thoggs but by the immense Pyramidiles who towered all about. All the while, my member remained very grimly *un*erect; and while Ammi and her slatternly sorority back at the club had marveled over its ostensibly greater-than-average size when inflamed, this situation's horror left it anything but. I stroked on in futility while I knew that, however voicelessly, the thoggs were laughing at its pitiable size.

"Let me help," my sister whispered, and up betwixt her own legs came her hand to gently manipulate my penis. *I MUST perform to their satisfaction.* I focused on the thought and its severity. *Otherwise, both of our lives could end in this wretched place . . .*

"Just relax, relax," she whispered further, fingers first tending my slack testicles, then the even more slack shaft, and then—

Perhaps the decadent French writers were correct in their esoteric allusions to a link between death and sexuality (their *La Petite Morte*), for the more I focused on the possibility that impotence would result in our destruction . . .

My member *swelled.*

If anything, the sudden erection sprouted even longer than before—longer than *ever*—until it thumped, bobbing up and down. I knew that the thoggs had been, in their own non-verbal manner, laughing at me before, but—

They're not laughing now, I thought, assured. They could all detect that the dimensions of *my* genital shaft easily exceeded that of even the largest of them. When Selina's hand measured its entire length, she gasped, "Good *gracious,* Morgan. I had no idea you were so . . . "

She needn't finish; instead, it may have even been with some secret eagerness that her deft fingers brought my purpled glans to her folds.

"Now!" she panted.

I nudged it in, then grasped her hips and commenced to stroking. The familiar wet slapping resounded as I increased tempo, sliding my erection (each and every of its proven twelve inches) all the way in and all the way out. Simultaneously, my left hand slipped round and under to gently agitate her surprisingly excited clitoris, and with that, Selina began to moan with vigor. I stepped up my pelvic rhythm then, pursuing a crescendo, whereupon my sister quite waveringly squealed. Her back arched like that of a cat, every tendon in her body tensing, and then her climax spasmed and broke most obviously. She writhed and bucked, even shrieked to the capacity of her lungs, to the extent that the blissful vociferation echoed within the vast valleys between the mammoth Pyramidiles. I cursed myself for acknowledging my own incestuous pleasure, for as her orgasm drew on quite lengthily, Selina's interior vagina constricted to an unfathomable tautness, which brought me past the margin of my own return. This next seminal ration *gusted* from my loins in innumerous spurts, and with the release, I experienced my own ecstatic culmination, the potency of which I would've never believed possible . . .

When both of our spasms abated, Selina collapsed. "For goodness *sake,* Morgan. Never in my life have I had such a wonderful f—"

"You needn't say it, Selina," I severed her profanity. "As you've directed, we had no choice but to sully ourselves for the whims of these things." But when I looked around, I sensed disappointment about the mien of the thoggs, or rather even displeasure. My forced performance for their mere sport seemed to have left them in agitation rather than satisfaction.

Selina sensed it too, obviously attuned to them either by indoctrination or some totemic function of her queer pendant. She even giggled. "They're *jealous*, Morgan."

I refastened my trousers. "Jealous?" I questioned, but suddenly the notion made sense. Not only was I possessed of more substantial genitals (the utmost symbol of masculinity) but I had also demonstrated a further degree of sexual superiority over them: my efforts alone had brought Selina to a devastating climax, whereas theirs had not.

"Will they let us go, now that we've done as they ordered?"

Selina knelt as she faced me; her shoulders slumped. "Not . . . just . . . yet . . . "

It was the clothed motorman who approached, then slapped me across the head.

"What?" I blathered. "What is this?"

"They're furious that you out-performed them, Morgan," came my sister's disconsolate reply. "They won't let us go back until you've sufficiently debased yourself. It's their way of getting back at you for proving that you're more masculine than all of them."

I couldn't imagine what she might be implying, but then imagination was hardly necessary a moment later when the motorman lowered his trousers and extracted the harrowing genitals.

"You have to take him in your mouth," came Selina's regretful words.

"In the name of all things decent and pure!" I caterwauled.

"And you'll have to swallow it all. Only then will they be satisfied . . . That way, they get their last laugh, in spite of your manly prowess . . . by turning you into their bitch, so to speak."

Despair couldn't have lengthened my face further. Since the motorman's release with Miss Aheb, enough time had passed to permit full sexual revivification; the thing was ready again, in other words, and to that state of readiness I could all-too-awfully attest. The grotesque organ had already become engorged by the thing's mere thought of what impended.

"Just do it, Morgan," my sister pleaded. "You don't want to *know* how many times I've had to . . . "

To this end I resigned myself; I'd be doing it not only to spare my own life but Selina's as well. So I steeled myself with every mental fortitude . . . and took the appalling thing into my mouth.

Having had no experience in such things, however, I hadn't a clue as to what I was doing. I harnessed initiative only via the deduction that I must do my best to *imagine* the proper technique . . .

In only seconds, that dreadful "carrot" hardened to full size in my quivering mouth.

Inept as I was sure my oral subventions were, the motorman seemed overly pleased by the effort. Each time I drew my lips rearward, along the organ's tapering form, I increased the suction, which caused the beast's hips to fidget.

"Faster now," Selina instructed. "And . . . get ready . . . "

I forced the implication from conscious thought, proceeding as instructed. Then . . .

The motorman's "jism" *poured* into my mouth.

The effect was worse than any conjecture. My face seemed to turn to stone after my first gulp. To assign simile to the *taste* of the evil slew defied possibility. Gout after gout, it issued, each mouth-filling allotment seeming thicker than the previous, and more lumpen.

"Keep swallowing, Morgan!" my sister implored. "Don't spit up!"

Easier communicated than achieved. Numbed to my brain, I forced myself to mechanically pause, then swallow, pause, then swallow. The stuff was hot, and I could swear I actually felt spermatozoic constituents *moving around on my tongue* each time my oral cavity was re-filled. I could only imagine that the forced consumption of carrion or even excreta would be more agreeable than this . . .

I reeled on my knees after the abatement of the motorman's final spurt, that last deposit being thick as gelatin. My stomach threatened to heave and properly eject the violation, but I gathered all my forbearance, fisted my hands, and, shuddering, swallowed the whole gelatinous mass.

"You did it!" Selina congratulated.

When the hideous lump at last sunk to the pit of my squirming gut, I collapsed posthaste into a dead faint.

(II)

SOME INESTIMABLE TIME LATER, my senses seemed to rise, akin to putrefactive gases voiding from a lime-pit. It was upon the pristine floor of Miss Aheb's lavish yet eldritchly lit bed-chamber that my consciousness re-found me; in fact, my first sight was that of the corrupt chandelier suspended overhead, shimmering in its queer anti-light.

Of the dimension-transcending trolley-ride back, I remembered nary a detail. I was alone, however, and as I roused myself, I checked my pocket-watch to see, to my dismay, that the time was but four-thirteen in the morn . . .

Only *one minute* later than when I'd checked so long ago!

The watch continued to tick, though, the second-hand revolving . . .

Just like Erwin mentioned. This place, and that horrendous domain I've just returned from, must exist in some Daedalic contravention of time . . .

A strange tapping cut into my ruminations, tapping which I recognized eventually as footsteps. It was my sister, maskless but dressed once more in her conductor's garb, who crossed the mosaic flooring. The chamber's bizarre acoustics lent to her voice an uncanny echo. "Oh, Morgan, I'm so sorry about what they made you do."

"It was of my own free volition that I came here in the first place, and of my own free volition that I smuggled myself aboard Trolley 1852," I recited. "All in the interest in finding you."

"You're such a gallant man, Morgan. I can only imagine your disgust with me."

"Disgust?" I asked, irked. "You're my only sibling, and I love you with my whole heart. Please know that."

"But to learn that your only sibling could stoop so low as to submit to prostitution . . . "

"My dearest sister, what you must also know is that I fully understand the travails that force women to resort to such alternatives. In these times of economic cataclysm, women even more than men suffer from the throes of subjugation." Groggily, I sat up. "This, believe me, I comprehend, and I love you no less."

Selina seemed relieved to hear this, relieved enough even to sob. But what I simply could *not* reckon was the hideousness of her maligned complexion, the once-beauteous countenance made appalling by the swirls of phlegmatic-green mixed with fish-belly white. "I had no choice but to consign myself to the life of a common street-whore, but even then, I was homeless and barely able to eat . . . "

"I *understand* that," I reiterated. "But . . . what I *don't* understand is . . . "

"The change," she finished for me, and touched her face with loath. "Eventually, some girls corralled me into the club, but as I briefly explained earlier, I did not service johns for long after my arrival. It turned out, Miss Aheb fell in love with me, so . . . she *changed* me . . . "

"Your skin," I knew. "She effected a metamorphosis, to make your skin like hers"—I gulped—"and like the skin of Pyramidiles and the thoggs."

"With this, yes," she explicated, fingering the pendant. "The change allows me to live forever, but this is what I'll have to do . . . *forever*. She wants me all to herself; and when I'm not servicing her, I conduct the trolley and, every week or so, see to the transport of our . . . collection across the ingression threshold."

Collection, I thought numbly. *The constant collection*

of human semen to be used for God knows what by the Pyramidiles . . .

"The legend is true," I droned. "The club's matron, Miss Aheb, and the witch-priestess Isimah el-Aheb of thousands of years bygone are one in the same!"

Did the chandelier's counter-light suddenly climb in intensity? It was Miss Aheb herself who next strode into the chamber, adorned in the diaphanous black gown which highlighted her preeminent physique. Yet the sleek arms and legs, the plunging decolletage, and her face remained abhorrent by her skin's similarity to that of the mountainous Pyramidiles. I knew now that the leviathanic monsters had, through some occult mode, shared their hideous skin with Miss Aheb and Selina. What other traits beyond appearance might this dermal metamorphosis have instigated?

"Why, immortality, Mr. Phillips," the lithe madam answered via some manner of psychic surveillance. Her coy smile beamed down on me as her accent buoyed her words. "You know much of what very few know at all."

"The legend of the Pyramidiles and their utmost servitor is obscure to be sure," I asserted, "but some trace of their history has remained. Cuneiform cylinders analogous to the cylinder in your own possession, for instance. It is a legend that *pre-dates* legendry . . . "

"And therefore?"

My words abraded like stones grinding. "The *oldest* legend in human history."

"Very good," she congratulated and sashayed about Selina. Her grotesque-coloured hand caressed my sister's bosom as she did so; whereupon, she proceeded to a great armchair nestled in the room's corner: a *throne,* for all intents, composed of adhered jewel-like crystals of the same composition as the pendants. It was here that she sat, elevated and grinning cunningly, as some sluttish, monstrous version of Cleopatra, some iniquitous *queen* of the Halls of Eblis. "And now? Whatever shall we do with you?"

"Answer my questions," I dared. "What harm can there be in that, given that my chances of surviving the night are in all likelihood non-existent."

Her expression turned wanton as she considered my request; likewise, her hands lifted her plenteous breasts out of the accouchement of her gown, where she then titillated herself before me. "Your desire to know is like the lust of a beast in rut, Mr. Phillips. Do you believe that you will be better fortified by such knowledge when I have your life snuffed out?"

"I quite indubitably do."

Her fingertips twirled the papillae of each distended nipple, generating a sensation which caused her to seethe. "Very well . . . "

"In exactitude, just what *are* these mountain-sized creatures known as the Pyramidiles?"

Some psychic directive compelled Selina to approach the throne and, with immediacy, bring her lips to Miss Aheb's bosom. "They are so much more than *creatures,* Mr. Phillips, and even so much more than *gods.* I'm surprised a man of your erudite distinction has failed to make that deduction. They are not millions of years old, nor even *billions,* but so much older that their existence transcends time as we know it. They are *ageless.*" She paused to concentrate on the pleasures lent to her via my sister's lips. "Creatures? No. They are poly-sentient bio-machines, self-perpetuating organic industries, Mr. Phillips. They create vast technologies via their immeasurable intellect and then *produce* their own laborers to make those technologies transitive."

"The thoggs," I uttered.

"Oh, yes. But the thoggs you've beheld are but one variety of a multitude. The Pyramidiles breed them, you see, specifically for implementation on *this* planet. There are hundreds more incarnations, for hundreds of other worlds, and when I say 'worlds,' I mean not only other planets in this and other solar systems but also planes of alternate existence in other dimensions and other terrestrial realms the likes of which even an advanced mind such as yours could never cogitate."

"So that awful abode of theirs is not a planet of itself?"

"No, nor is it a dimensional firmament, Mr. Phillips. It is an esoteric terrascape of their *own creation,* just as the thoggs and all their multiple variations are the Pyramidiles' very creation as well."

I felt enslimed by the sheer *evil* of the implication. "And through these vast technologies and with these thoggs, you travel from world to world!" I outraged, "from dimension to dimension and from realm to realm, to unleash *horror* upon the populace of those places!"

"Exactly," she cooed and moved Selina's lips from the current, well-tended nipple to the next. "The thoggs you saw were the bipedal hybrid propagated for *this* world."

"An invasion is what you're talking about!" I shouted.

"Quite right. But this invasion, whenever it might come to pass, will not be initiated for the purpose of conquest."

I knew all too well of the legend's most atrocious entails. "It is instead for the blatant molestation and torture of the human race, the psychic horror of which the Pyramidiles *subsist* upon!"

"It is their food, which they derive from countless worlds and innumerable domains—yes. We've just come from one such domain, a quasi-terrestrial sphere that existed in another phase-shift. It had a population of a trillion, Mr. Phillips, and the slow, systematic torture, mutilation, and protracted murder of its pacifistic inhabitants fed the Pyramidiles full to bursting. It was *glorious.*"

And eventually, they'll do the same here, I realised.

Miss Aheb broadened her sluttish smile. "Yes. They will."

The rest, now, remained fairly elementary. "Depositions of human sperm," I croaked. "This is the purpose of your inviting the most virile of men to this 'free' bordello, and hence the ruse. It's no real bordello at all but a *collection outpost!* You pilfer the semen from all these men, night after night, then deliver it all to the Pyramidiles, whose bio-mechanical capabilities isolate the *human* characteristics that are specifically desired and then immix those characteristics with that of their own!"

"Custom-made thoggs, Mr. Phillips," she went on. "Genetic constituents from human semen are amalgamated with certain constituents belonging to the Pyramidiles. The result: creatures of servitude and utility that are ideally suited to Earth's environment." The ardour imparted to her sensitive nipples via Selina's mouth was all-too-ostensible; the noxious woman's chest rose and fell more rapidly, her infernal skin beginning to sheen with perspiration. Still, though, she continued to explain as though this revelation of diabolism was of itself libidinally stimulating. "The average human ejaculation contains hundreds of millions of spermatozoa, Mr. Phillips, yet only several hundred are chosen for propagation: the choicest, most motile, and highest quality per batch. That is why it's taken several millennia to produce a serviceable number of thoggs. But since time *per say* is of no significance, what does it matter?"

"It matters quite a bit with regard to your actual mass-dispersal of the heinous creatures upon the earth!" I yelled. "When exactly is this 'invasion' of yours to take place?"

"Only when we've manufactured exactly *two billion* thoggs, Mr. Phillips."

My indignation spilled over. "But that's the human population of the world today!"

"Precisely."

"At least give my race a fighting chance!"

"Really now, Mr. Phillips. Fairness is not on our agenda. Only the efficacious slow-destruction of mankind. I know that the Pyramidiles will enjoy a veritable *feast* on the pain and horror generated at the hands of the thoggs."

By this point, my infuriation left me utterly stupefied . . .

Miss Aheb urged my sister's mouth from the well-sucked nipple. "That felt delicious, dear." Her svelte hands directed Selina to the foot of the throne. "Do here now, my darling," and then she raised the hem of the gown. "You know how I simply adore your mouth on me."

Selina knelt before the madam's parted thighs, then lowered her face . . .

More, more outrage. "Release her! You've demeaned her enough for tonight!"

The atrocious woman's brow rose on the tainted face. "Oh, but not just her, Mr. Phillips. You too, yes?"

"Indeed," I growled.

"Tell me. How did the motorman's jism taste? Was it delectable? Ambrosial? Hmm? I've a mind to send you back there, where you'll be forced to suckle their cocks for time immemorial." She chuckled rather fatly, closing her eyes against the pleasures now being administered. "I can arrange it so that the wares of their lusty loins will be all you ever eat—*ever*—for a million years."

"Give my sister her freedom, and I will consent to that!" I spat.

"Consent? Oh, Mr. Phillips. Your chivalry is quite laughable. I hardly require your *consent* to do with you as my fancies direct." She pressed the back of my sister's head, to affect keener purchase, then looked at me again and laughed.

Being forced to watch this further exploitation insinuated a feeling of utter uselessness on my part. Whatever excess of intellect I may have been possessed of seemed just as useless, for my faculties delivered nothing in so much as a plan of action. Primordially, at least, I might try to give direct fight to Miss Aheb, but being apprised of her powers—for instance, of psychic thought-decryption—I could only imagine that far greater proclivities were at her disposal; while I also suspected that the motorman must be lurking about in some reasonable proximity. I tried to dim the tenor of my conscious thoughts, therefore (to keep them out of her telepathic grasp), and pray that some *sub*conscious resolution might spring to mind.

Her hips writhed in response to Selina's oral tendings, and not long thenceforth came the patented spasms that signaled orgasm, Miss Aheb's monstrously skinned yet comely body flexing and clenching in the midst of the sought-after release. Once sated, she nudged Selina off with a flick of hand. "That was wonderful, my love."

"You've changed her just as you yourself have changed," I blurted loudly, "in the atrocious tainting of your skin. It allows you to share some aspect of the Pyramidiles."

"It does far more than that!" she scolded. "It's their blessing to us, Mr. Phillips. Just as your earthly babies are 'christened' with holy water to receive the anointment of your so-called God, so, too, are Selina and I anointed, as the Pyramidiles give us grace by bestowing the cosmic beauty of their skin to our paltry human bodies." She held out her arms to give accentuation to her breasts' "anointment," the flawless orbs made revolting by the swirls of discolour. "But in their anointing us, we receive not only an aspect of their beauty but also the blessing of their immortality, along with other wondrous traits."

"That obscene pendant," I hastened. "Like the crystals of the chandelier, it generates a similarity to the Pyramidiles' atmosphere, correct? This grotesque light that is *not* light but somehow illuminating nonetheless."

"You're correct, indeed. It's not mere light, it's the *Abhorrescence,* whose nether-rays halt aging to all those in the midst of them. Even you, Mr. Phillips. For the time you've spent in this room as well as your time on the terrascape, you have not aged a single minute."

This, too, seemed to explain the cessation of time during the soul-searing journey to that wretched domain.

The witch-priestess was giving answer to my questions, yes, but a question even more paramount remained . . .

When?

"Exactly how many thoggs have been birthed thus far?" I asked.

Her grin couldn't have broadened any more wickedly. "Of that . . . I'll leave you to guess," and then, as if summoned by a bell-toll, the motorman made its entrance, clothed but maskless, the most salient feature of its face—that grotesque, scarlet-tipped tentacle—writhing.

"I presume it is telepathy that enables you to communicate even to a monster with no ears," I said.

"The thogg's proboscis is the nerve cluster which allows it to see and hear. But it is to the beast's *brain* that my thoughts are delivered," Miss Aheb said. "However, if you *must* know, these mental commands are reflected in the actual language of the Pyramidiles. Not words, but numerals."

"Gematria," I uttered. "The substitution of letters with their corresponding numbers. The little written record there is indicates that theirs is a language of *mathematics.*"

"I'm *impressed,* Mr. Phillips," she seemed to genuinely enthuse. "Your studies of my gods are quite extensive. I don't think in words to the motorman, for instance. I think in numbers. Were you a little brighter yourself, you might have deduced the meaning of the trolley before you even got here."

My expression clearly showed I did not understand.

"1, 8, 5, 2," she said. "One, denoting the first letter of the alphabet, Mr. Phillips."

"The letter A."

"And 8?"

"The letter H."

Her smile beamed as the rest of the truth dropped to my gut.

"5 is E, and 2 is B," I quailed. "1,8,5,2 equals AHEB." How could I not have seen that before?

"Very good," the woman mocked. "And were I to think the numbers, 11, 9, 12, and 12, and then make an indicative gesture toward your beloved sister?"

11, 9, 12, 12, I thought desperately, then calculated each number's letter-equivalent: *"K, I, L, L . . . "*

"Yes, Mr. Phillips! Kill. The thogg would then, by my mental command, *kill* Selina. Or, how about, say, 6, 21, 3, 11?"

I quickly made the translation, and gulped. *"Fuck."*

"Um-hmm. How would you like that?" she continued to mock. "How would you like to watch the motorman *fuck* your sister?"

The thought sickened me to unto death. "I *beg* you, Miss Aheb. Don't do that. I just watched a dozen of his kind do the same."

"Indeed, or perhaps I could order the motorman to fuck *you,* Mr. Phillips." She chuckled shrilly, in a manner that actually caused the chandelier's myriad crystals to clink musically together. "The sight might very well amuse me."

"Let my sister have her freedom, and I'll consent to that," I directed.

"Ah, there you go with your chivalry again." The bright eyes within the maligned face narrowed on me. "Tell me, is that what you want more than anything? Selina's release?"

"Indisputably, yes!" Was the obscene woman toying with me, or did I stand some unfractionable chance of getting my sister out of here? I stepped boldly forward. "Let's bargain. Quid pro quo."

"So you'd like one thing exchanged for some other, hmm?" she tittered inhumanly. "You regard your sister with the utmost importance, Mr. Phillips, but surely, you understand that I do as well."

"Then what could be more challenging than a wager?" I argued. "It's easy to be courageous when one has the powers of telepathy and immortality, not to mention"—I jabbed a finger toward the motorman—"the services of a thing like *that* at your beck and call. Hear me, Miss Aheb. To whatever degree this evil *Abhorrescence* has imbued you with a likeness to the Pyramidiles, you're still *human,* are you not? Humans are known to be intuitive, subjective, and often even *sporting.* You can't deny the appeal of a good wager, can you? So let's do that, Miss Aheb. Accept my challenge."

A finger dawdled over a well-sucked areola as she deliberated over my "challenge." "Win or lose, I see nothing to be gained on my part. How fair is that?"

My mind clicked like an ancient abacus, desperate for a resolving quotient. "If I win the wager, then Selina goes free, yet I stay in her stead."

Selina objected, "Oh, Morgan, I could never let you!"

"Silence!" I raised my voice to her, then returned my proposition to the grotesque madam. "I will replace her as the trolley's conductor as well as the deliverer of your necessary seminal rations via the periodic ingressions."

"Is that *all?*" she complained.

Never one given to crudity, I opened my trousers without hesitation and displayed my genitalia, which, I now had on unimpeachable authority, was larger and more enduring than that of most men. "Being a woman so carnally inclined, I would think you might find some gratifying utility . . . for *this.*"

Miss Aheb's sinister eyes went wide at the vulgarian display, just as I suspected they might.

"My," she uttered. "The rumours are no exaggeration! It was reported to me quite early, Mr. Phillips, that you are quite the sexual exemplar."

Some attendant braggadocio on my part seemed in order. "My prowess in the act of fornication reduced five of your highly experienced prostitutes to *putty* earlier in the evening."

"So I've heard, while I've also heard that the *quantity* of your dispenses of seed are most excessive." She rested her chin on her fingertips. "That would prove useful around here as well."

"And whenever you're feeling a thirst for pleasures of

the *lesbian* variety, this thirst can easily be quenched by any number of lascivious harlots residing here at the club."

"You make a most interesting point . . . "

"Then it's settled," came my declaration. "*I* shall replace Selina and her duties as a servitor of the Pyramidiles."

The ill-skinned woman shrilled in amusement. "Not so fast! As you've said, Mr. Phillips. One thing in exchange of another. But I must insist that you earn the privilege of the exchange. You've neglected to propose an actual wager."

"A physical fight," I said and re-trousered my member. I looked at her in close to a glare. "You're more than just a woman, madam. You have *superhuman* powers which would seem to level the playing field. *That* is my wager. I'll bet that I defeat you."

She guffawed. "How quickly the chivalrous gentleman turns to a cad. So you want to fight a *woman?*"

"But you're a *monstrous* woman, Miss Aheb. The odds are clearly in your favor."

"So if it's a fight you want, it's a fight you'll get," she intoned. "A fight to the death. Is that *sporting* enough for you? The way I see it, this can be the only way your mettle will be proven sufficiently enough to *earn* the exchange."

Great Pegana! I thought. *She's going to allow it!* "Yes! I want it very much!"

"But it won't be a fight against *me,* Mr. Phillips. I simply *must* insist that you fight my *motorman.*"

My spirits couldn't have plummeted any lower. "The thing is an alien monstrosity! That's hardly a fair fight!"

She coyly shrugged and *har-umphed.* "Take it or leave it; and mind you, if you leave it, I'll have you consigned to the terrascape"—she purred akin to a cat—"where the service thoggs will greatly appreciate your skills in the act of fellatio"—and now she laughed outright—"as I'm told those skills are rather *expert.*"

This seemed about as fair as the Treaty of Versailles; nevertheless, I rendered the only available reply. "I accept the challenge," and then, hoping for the element of surprise, unleashed every reflexive action within my human capability and launched myself at the very *in*human motorman.

With all the strength and viciousness that could be tapped of my 146-pound frame, I struck blow after blow to the creature's face and mid-section, exerted choke-holds and threw finger-gouges to the hideous faceless face, and when I noted the futility of all this effort, I then stooped so low as to kick the thing repeatedly and as hard as I could in the groin . . .

All to no effect.

"Fight, damn you!" I cried, now foolishly trying to lift its bodily bulk off the floor and slam it down, but, lo, the sheer *density* of its flesh gave it an unfathomable weight. More kicks and gouges, then, the impacts of which were like striking sandbags. At one point, I even took the appalling frontal tentacle between my teeth, yet even as it was fleshy and pliable, I only succeeded in cracking two of my incisors, for this proboscis was resilient as metal. During the entirety of my assault, the uniformed thing only stood there, unmoving; and I received the impression that it was amused.

"Oh, Morgan, please!" Selina sobbed aside. "Beg Miss Aheb's pardon! I told you, the thoggs are virtually *undefeatable*."

This, I was finding out the hard way, indeed. As for begging the madam's "pardon," I realised that would prove as useless as the fight I was now giving the monstrosity. "I'm dead either way!" came my harried shout. "But at least, I won't die on my knees!"

Meanwhile, Miss Aheb chortled from her arrogant throne. Now I had taken to breaking furniture over the thing's head; I jabbed it with a shard of broken porcelain, even tried to impale it with a snapped table leg (from an absolutely splendid Thomas Sheraton library table, by the way, circa 1790). The only result of this act was the splintering of the leg's sharpened end. Lastly, I spied on a wall-mount a sword (an authentic Toledo saber, I believe), yet when I took it down and attempted to cleave the motorman's head down the middle, the razor-sharp and exquisitely folded blade only bounced off . . .

"Oh, Mr. Phillips, you really are quite comical," the horrid woman chuckled. "The reason the thogg hasn't killed you already is simply because I haven't yet directed it to."

"Then be done with it!" I spat. "I'm ready to die!"

"Very well . . . "

No words, of course, issued from Miss Aheb's lips to trigger the motorman's violence; it was instead the merest numerical *thought,* and in the time it takes lightning to fulgurate, the boneless arms of the beast were wrapped around me, python-like, and I was dragged helplessly to the floor. Any resistance I made to push off the thing's bulk went *utterly without effect.*

It mauled me; the terrifying "hand" sliding into my mouth felt like the admission of a live octopus. Even worse, though, was the action of its other hand: it began to unbuckle its trousers . . .

Gagging, I now felt the morbid, carrotlike pudenda growing to full hardness against my belly.

Miss Aheb amusedly explained, "What you must know, Mr. Phillips, it that thoggs kill what they fight . . . and *fuck* what they kill . . . "

This charming exposition was scarcely perceived. I felt the hand fully in my mouth now, and even slither a length down my throat, whereupon it swelled so in size that breathing became impossible. I sensed quite clearly that the monster meant to effect my total loss of consciousness, after which it would surely commence to the task of *sodomizing me to death . . .*

As the flow of oxygen decreased, the frantic activities of my brain began to darken. It was not with any conscious regard that I must have considered something akin to this:

If Miss Aheb had launched the motorman's attack merely by *thinking* the proper numerical sequence, what might happen if I did the same, remembering that their language exists as a form of substituting numbers for letters?

Fading away as I was, a thought abstractly directed toward my marauder crossed my mind; the thought was this: *4, 9, 5 . . .*

The motorman suddenly bucked, seizing up with an inexplicable rigor. Then . . .

The wretched, bone-bereft hand oozed out of my mouth as the motorman rolled off me, dead.

I struggled to regain breath and collect my thoughts after being so close to death. An errant glance upward showed, first, my sister standing tensely, hands clasped as if in prayer. Her face was flushed with relief. A scan to the right, however, showed Miss Aheb sneering from her throne, none-too-pleased.

"I must credit your industriousness, Mr. Phillips, particularly under such conditions." Her eyes smoldered. "4, 9, 5 . . . D, I, E . . . "

I rose, however shakily, looking down at the dead thogg. "Surely, I anticipated that the thing's mind was weaker than yours. You may have read my thoughts, but I'm happy to see that you could not occlude them. You've lost the wager, Miss Aheb."

"So I have," her accent trailed off to meagerness.

I rubbed my hands together. "So what now? You asked me to prove my mettle, and I have indeed done that. Now's your chance to prove yours, yes?"

Here was the moment that this entire evening of horror had built up to: I had overbound all odds, but now, would this evil matron *honour* her end of the bargain?

I wasn't sure, but it seemed that the anti-light—this *Abhorrescence*—had noticeably dimmed as if it somehow paralleled her spirit's pulse . . .

"You were correct in your appeal, Mr. Phillips. All humans enjoy the sport of a wager. I suppose, in a sense, it's not all that different from the purpose of the Pyramidiles, who live off the psychic horror very much derived from the *sport* of torture, rape, and prolonged murder on a massive scale." She sat slumped in her grandiose seat, unenlivened and quite defeated. "It's true that I'm the ultimate traitor to the human race, as—for the last seven thousand years—I live to serve the Pyramidiles; and I will one day orchestrate the slow extermination of mankind, all for the sustenance and pleasure of my gods." Her lips drew up into a thin smile. "However, I will keep my word. You've earned your exchange; your precious sister shall go free, unharmed, and you shall take her place . . . "

Was this to be believed? I sensed yes, in spite of the desolate consequences in store for myself.

I turned to my sister. "You must leave now, Selina, and forget me."

She stood frantic. "But I can't, Morgan! I can't allow you to trade your freedom for mine!"

"You can and will. I've lived my life; now go live yours." I handed her my billfold and keys. "Here is the address for my room and the keys to the door. The rent is paid for several months, and you'll find a small sum of money hidden behind my bookshelf. It should be enough to get you on your feet."

"I can't!" she sobbed.

"Go!" I yelled back.

A macabre fugue-state seemed to overwhelm the chamber, but I knew it could only genuinely be amid my mind. In what appeared to be retarded motion, Miss Aheb came down off her chair, whereupon she took Selina by the shoulders and kissed her once. Then—

She removed my sister's pendant.

With instantaneousness, the revolting, pond-scum skin that so molested Selina's physical beauty . . . *reversed!* In only seconds, her face beamed in a creamy and quite normal hue.

Miss Aheb turned Selina about and gently nudged her toward the door.

TROLLEY NO. 1852

"Goodbye, my beloved sister," I bid, and suddenly what occurred to me was something more than simple relief but the resplendent positivity that so enraptured my friend Mr. Erwin. "Every day is a celebration. Never forget that. *Revel* in that celebration, Selina, while I, here in my own way, shall share in your joy . . . "

She walked shakily to the ornate door, opened it, but halted, to turn her tear-streaked face to me a final time.

I smiled as I hadn't in decades. "Go."

And she was gone.

Miss Aheb traipsed slowly about the grand chamber, as if mulling penetrative thoughts. "You seem a sincere man, Mr. Phillips, in a world were men are anything but. Your thoughts remain surprisingly clear, and I'm impressed by that. But should you ever harbour hope of escape, don't bother. Perhaps you'll one day entertain the notion that your sister will report the existence of the 1852 Club to the authorities and they'll storm through the door and wrest back your freedom. But what you must know is that no one ever finds the club save for those I *allow* to find it."

"I'm not surprised by the intricacies of your powers, madam; rest assured, I shall never challenge them. After all . . . A deal's a deal."

She turned, then, to slowly approach me.

She snapped her fingers, and in moments, I stood in the midst of the brothel's ladies of pleasure, all of whom remained naked and raving in their slatternly appeal. One by one, they undressed me of all my garb, then commenced to *re*-dress me . . .

. . . in the trousers, tunic, boots, and regulation cap of a trolley-car conductor.

That bizarre fugue, impossible as it was, rose to a steady, lamenting dirge in my head, and it was then that Miss Aheb placed the pendant about *my* neck.

"Consider yourself blessed," her lithe accent hissed. "You are the *new* conductor for the trolley."

"So be it," I croaked.

It was the delightful and very spirited tart named Ammi who, with a lascivious grin, held the mirror before my face.

The silver veins shined back . . .

Into the features of my nondescript visage the brand of the Pyramidiles had now been imbued: that nauseating swirl of swamp-foam green with corpse-white.

"From here on, you exist to serve the Pyramidiles," Miss Aheb's hellish voice echoed so very softly, and then over my face, she placed the parchment mask . . .

"Go now, Conductor Phillips. The trolley is ready to depart."

(III)

HENCE, THE SUM of all my destiny's parts. I conduct the trolley now, in my ghastly mask of death, during the blackest and most silent hours of eventime. A new motorman was easily procured, identical in function—and in atrociousness—to the first. When not transporting appropriately virile guests to and from the club, or making the periodic "ingressions" to that howling terrorscape upon which the execrable Pyramidiles live to suck up like wine the horrors of countless worlds, I serve these abyssal mountains of flesh and their blasphemous, aeons-old acolyte, Isimah el-Aheb. I serve the latter quite carnally and in ways too lewd to iterate; and I serve the former quite traitorously via the inter-worldly deliveries of sperm so abundantly pilfered from the club's unsuspecting suitors. Much of that consignment, to my eternal shame, is my own, and when on one bleak day in the future two billion thoggs are unleashed upon my planet, I shudder to think how *many* of them will have been sired by me . . .

And as for the question of how long the earth shall last, I cannot estimate. Another day, perhaps, or another thousand years. Whichever the case may be, my new grotesque immortality will ensure that I am here to witness it all. As for my beloved sister, I never saw her again, and I can only, however thinly, pray to Erwin's God that she is safe, unexploited, and, above all, alive.

And in times when I am in farthest proximity from my wretched mastress (and hence farthest from her prying grey matter) I dare to entertain the hope that I may eventually condition my mind to veil its thoughts soundly enough from her psychically-clutching powers and then devise some manner by which I may destroy her and close forever this horrid ingressional rive. But until that day may dawn . . .

My name is Morgan Phillips, and I am the conductor of Trolley No. 1852.

THE END

***

When the sudden and rather annoying series of raps sounded from the downstairs foyer, Howard frowned up from his current work-in-progress which, upon conclusion, he believed he would entitle "The Shadow Out of Time." But, oh, how he deplored interruptions! What's more, he hoped the intrusion didn't disturb his aunt, who was still feebly recuperating from a broken hip.

"Howard!" came her shrill voice. "There's someone at the—"

In the name of He Who Is Not To Be Named! "My perfectly serviceable auditory functions have left me so apprised, Auntie," he raised his voice in response. "We can at least rest assured that it's *not* the landlord, since I've paid the next six months' rent."

"What a fine, gifted boy you are, Howard . . . "

I'm forty-four and she still calls me a boy . . . He shot down the stairs, hoping to circumvent more rapping, but upon opening the door, he was taken startlingly aback by the physical presence of the visitor. Poised opposite within the doorway was a significantly handsome woman with shining, shoulder-length tresses of hair the colour of sunlight, and penetrating noon-blue eyes. Even in the long, autumn-leaf overcoat, her sonsy bosom and copious curvations were so evident, the writer's power of speech stalled outright.

"Do I have the pleasure of standing before the renowned H.P. Lovecraft?" she asked in a silken wisp of a voice.

"I . . . er, uh . . . " Not one to ordinarily be struck dumb by the vision of a notably attractive woman, the writer could only gulp ludicrously in repeated attempts to make an affirmative response. The woman's cleavage *blared* at him from the V beneath her smart collar.

"Oh, I'm so sorry, sir. Perhaps I have the wrong address . . . "

"I'm Howard Lovecraft, yes," he finally erupted, "but-but-but I'd hardly refer to myself as renowned."

"You're too humble, sir!" she exclaimed, and then a smile that could've been painted by Rubens illuminated her flawlessly angled face. "Do pardon the interruption, Mr. Lovecraft. I'm Francine Wilcox, the publisher of *Erotesque.*"

Howard nearly fell into a faint and could do little more than stammer syllabic fragments. "I—but. The directory said. Um. *Franklin* Wilcox. I could never. Imag—"

A casual laugh as she tossed her head, piloting luscious scents off her shining hair. "Oh, no, sir, that's my brother. I only share the flat with him." She hunched her shoulders, compressing the already-awesome mammarian cleft. "It's quite chilly out, Mr. Lovecraft. If I could just impose on a smidgen more of your good nature?"

Howard felt as though he'd somehow just kicked *himself* in the back of the head. "Oh, *do* forgive me, Miss Wilcox," and with a shaking hand brought her into the foyer.

She turned to him as he closed the door. "I'm sure you're quite busy with your writing, so I won't tarry . . . "

"Oh, tarry, please, tarry all you like," his words jerked. "I'm actually taking a breather from my current bit of work."

Did those radiant blue eyes steal a glimpse to his groin? *Don't be outlandish!* he thought.

"At any rate, your wonderful submission, 'Trolley No. 1852' brought such accolades from myself and my entire editorial staff that I simply *had* to visit you in person in order to notify you of its immediate acceptance."

Howard felt petrified in jubilation, to the extent that his heart skipped a few beats. An acceptance meant . . . *Another cheque!* "Why, that's-that's-that's—"

Did the subtle accentuation of her grin indicate some cryptic signal of the lascivious? "Oh, yes, sir! Your story caused quite a row!" Like a card player's sleight of hand, she at once offered a bank cheque. "So without further delay, I'd like to give you this, with my greatest thanks."

Howard's heart skipped a few *more* beats when his eyes found the words *Pay to the order of H.P. Lovecraft the sum of $500.* So not only had the second cheque arrived, it had been, of all things, *hand-delivered!*

"I-I-I," he mumbled.

"The story will appear in next month's issue, and, well . . . " She paused as if uncomfortable. "I couldn't impose by asking . . . "

Howard finally rid himself of the proverbial frogs that had found their way to his throat. "Ask, um, what?"

"We know that authors in such popular demand as yourself have so little time for alternate demonstrations of their talent, as I'm sure you're far too busy with your *important* work to ever entertain the prospect of, say, writing for us on a regular basis—"

Howard nearly fell back against the wall.

"Say, four times a year? And for no less payment, naturally."

The frogs returned in multiplicity, and after coming close to choking on them, he croaked, "I accept . . . "

She looked beyond belief, batting her long-lashed eyes. "Thank you very much, sir," and then she opened her hand over her heart. "It's been a true honour meeting you."

Howard looked at her, agog. "You're-you're not leaving already?"

"Oh, but I couldn't impose further. I know you're terribly busy—"

"I'm *not* busy!" he came very close to shouting. *Think, you lackwit! Think!* "Um, well . . . oh! Please adjourn with me to my . . . writing chamber. I have coffee!"

Francine seemed to fully blush, and she replied in a hot gush, "I was *so* hoping you'd ask, sir."

Only when Howard had climbed half the flight's steps was he stricken by a propulsive sense of dread. *My room . . . it's-it's . . .* It stood in such unkemptness and disrepair that he didn't *dare* let her see it. There were empty bean cans all about, and myriad ginger snap crumbs, not to mention mouse droppings galore.

He cleared his throat. "But I'm afraid we'll have to take our coffee in the hall—"

"*What?*"

"You see, I wasn't expecting a guest and-and-and . . . "

"Oh, Mr. Lovecraft, please! All great artists are messy. They're too busy crafting their great art to piddle valuable time with mundane chores such as housekeeping. It's said that Michelangelo never once cleaned his floor, and in fact only cleaned *himself* a few times per year. Samuel Coleridge wrote 'Rime' in what he described as his 'happy hovel.'"

Howard turned, encouraged. "You don't say? Coleridge?"

The comely face nodded behind him. "Really, sir, don't be self-conscious over your room's appearance. In all honesty, I'd be disappointed to find it tidy. However, clean or dirty, I'd be honoured to stand in the very room where the great H.P. Lovecraft has written so many ground-breaking tales."

"Well . . . since you put it *that* way."

He brought her to the landing; whereupon, his aunt's voice sailed from the next room. "Howard! Who's that you're talking to?"

For the love of Pegana! Howard let his face stiffen to sternness. "Auntie, *please!* I'm in the midst of a consultation of import with a very noteworthy editor from New York."

"How wonderful, Howard . . . "

Next, he took a deep breath, thought, *My room probably smells more foul than the cellar of the Shunned House,* and opened his door. "Rrrrr-right this way, Miss Wilcox."

"Oh, please. Call me Francine . . . "

He stepped aside and let her pass.

Instead of gagging or rolling her eyes, her long, shapely legs took her in haste to his writing-table. She smoothed her hands, as if in adoration, over the cluttered desktop, let her fingers trace across the keys of his decades-old typing-machine, then picked up his fountain pen and held it as if it were an icon. "This is so exciting," she whispered and even appeared to have a tear in her eye. "To touch the same desk upon which so many masterpieces of horror have been composed . . . and to have in my own hands . . . the *same pen.*"

Howard didn't know what to say. *I stole the pen from the library, and the desk came from a neighbour's rubbish heap.*

"You must tell me, sir—"

"*Howard,* please."

Her cheeks turned rosy. "How did you devise such an imaginative tale as 'Trolley No. 1852?'"

Here in the light from the window, Howard took greater note of her body's voluptuous secrets beneath the smart, belted overcoat. Certainly, she wore a brassiere and blouse as well, yet he could swear that the distinct out-dents of formidable areolae were evident. "Oh," he sloughed off, "it was more creative self-cannibalism than any feat of elaborate imagination. I merely took several samplings from my *Yog-Sothian* pantheon, stripped them to the bone, and added new flesh. Old wine into new bottles? The nefarious ancient hag, Keziah Mason, was metamorphosed to the lusty-physiqued but corrupt-skinned witch-priestess Isimah el-Aheb; the planet Yuggoth became the paradimensional terrascape; my sho*ggoths* became *thoggs;* the shimmering violet flux of 'Dreams in the Witch-House' became the *Abhorrescence;* and my 'daemon-sultan' Azathoth, who lives lifelessly at the pith of Chaos, became the Pyramidiles." Howard's stooped shoulders shrugged. "It was quite simple, actually."

"You're too lenient in your appraisal of your talent, Howard." She took a breath, then grinned and blushed once more. "And the *sex scenes!* I won't even *ask* how you conceived of those!"

Howard fidgeted. Delighted as he was by her charming presence and flattering air, face-to-face discourse entailing matters of licentiousness with a member of the opposite sex made him *uncomfortable.* Instead, he uttered, "Oh, they just came to me and I wrote them."

Perhaps she sensed his discomfiture, for next, she abruptly turned her back to him and gazed through the window in the space between the swags. (Regular folk had "curtains" over their windows; poor writers had "swags": any sundry fabric that had outlived its original purpose, such as old bedsheets or holey shirts, tacked over the panes. One writer, in the distant future, would have showercurtain liners and dollar-store beach towels over his windows, a note mentioned here only in passing.) However, Francine seemed awed. "So this is the view that the master of modern horror sees every day when he writes . . . "

"Why, yes, and it's a view near and dear to me," Howard said, but just as the comely woman seemed awed by the sight of west Providence, Howard remained equally awed by the sight of her jutting rump as she leaned over his writing-table. His eyes inched downward, scouring first the derriere's exquisite curves, then the legs, which could only be described as absolutely and inarguably *bereft of defect.* Momentarily, her heels rose out of her shoes as she stood on tiptoes, and Howard actually cringed like a fetishist, for the action caused her gorgeously toned calves to flex . . .

"The epicenter of what you're looking at is called Federal Hill," he remarked after a gulp. "Oh, pardon me! I forgot the coffee!" and then he embarked for the alcove where the pot percolated.

When he was out of Francine's view, Howard did something he *never* did . . .

He gave his crotch a squeeze.

Oh . . . my . . .

He heard her voice as he tended to the cups.

"But, Howard, why are your swags half-closed? You'd have a much better view if you opened them more."

Howard's hands shook minutely as he poured the brew, yet as he did so, a mouse popped its head out of a toppled soda-cracker box. *Wonderful,* he thought with a frown. But he *hated* spending money on traps! To her query, however, he responded, "Oh, I suppose you're right, but I never bother, in fear that the swags might fall and, hence, inundate me in dust."

She laughed. "You're so silly, Howard! But you really must let me improve this view for you . . . "

What an odd choice of words, he mused and then took the twin aromatic cups back to his writing chamber.

He stopped cold.

The view, indeed, had been improved, as he found it impossible not to take immediate notice of two paramount changes.

One, Francine hadn't opened the swags at all but instead had closed them! She'd also turned on the shadeless incandescent lamp he used at night . . .

Two, she sat up now upon the writing-table after having shed completely her handsome overcoat, to reveal that all along, she'd been utterly nude beneath . . .

"Have I improved the view for you, Howard?" her whisper flowed like some warm, ambrosian fluid.

"I . . . should say so." The mere vision of the woman's flawless nudity left Howard feeling as though he were staring down from a precipice of insurmountable height.

"Oh, Howard. Please come closer to me . . . "

In gingerly steps, he did so, making every effort not to allow his shaking hands to spill the coffee. Even knowing, as he did, the extreme degree by which he now violated every gentleman's law, he stared unblinking at, first, the dizzyingly full breasts, whose tea-rose-pink nipples stood so gorged they even seemed to minutely *beat* with the pace of her heart; the poreless skin, smooth as the finest white chocolate; then—in the most shameful departure from urbanity—the glorious mound of pubic thatch shiny as new-spun gold and the tantalizing, half-seen secret of its precious folds which clearly glimmered in anticipatory excitement.

Her face looked dreamy yet burning up in wanton intent. "Make my dream come true, Howard . . . "

Howard stammered, "But-but . . . the coffee!"

"Oh, *bugger* the coffee!" Francine whined, and so excited was she that those secret folds tucked beneath the blond private hair had leaked her equally private nectar onto the very pages of his holograph of "The Shadow Out of Time."

"I need to have the *dickens* fucked out of me," she pleaded now, "by the great H. P. Lovecraft . . . "

So upon the universal edict that the true gentleman *never* fails to oblige a lady, Howard, after setting aside the two cups of Postum, lowered his trousers and engaged himself as requested. The details of this engagement need not be elaborated upon; however, *attentive* readers will very much want to be educated as to whether or not the real Howard was possessed of a masculine endowment commensurate with that of his courageous protagonist, Mr. Morgan Phillips.

The answer to this query would be, regrettably, no, for Howard's member, when fully aroused, measured only *eleven and a half inches,* not twelve.

ABOUT THE AUTHOR

Edward Lee is the author of over 50 horror, fantasy, and sci-fi books, and dozens of short stories. He has also had comic scripts published by DC Comics, Verotik Inc., and Cemetery Dance. A great number of his novels have been reprinted in Germany, Poland, Italy, Romania, Japan, and other countries. He is a Bram Stoker Award Nominee; his Lovecraftian novel *Innswich Horror* won the 2010 Vincent Price Award for Best Foreign Book (Austria), his novel *White Trash Gothic* won the 2018 Splatterpunk Award for Best Extreme Horror Novel, and in 2020 Lee won the Splatterpunk Lifetime Achievement Award. In 2009, the movie version of his novella *Header* was released by Synapse Films. He lives in Seminole, Florida